A BULLET FOR LINCOLN

A BULLET FOR
LINCOLN

By BENJAMIN KING
A Novel

PELICAN PUBLISHING COMPANY
Gretna 1993

Library of Congress Cataloging-in-Publication Data

King, Benjamin, 1944-
   A bullet for Lincoln : a novel / by Benjamin King.
   p.   cm.
   ISBN 0-88289-927-9
   1. United States—History—Civil War, 1861-1865—Fiction.
   2. Lincoln, Abraham, 1809-1865—Assassination—Fiction. 3. Booth,
   John Wilkes, 1838-1865—Fiction. I. Title.
   PS3561.I473B84   1993
   813'.54—dc20   92-40408
                                                      CIP

Manufactured in the United States of America
Published by Pelican Publishing Company, Inc.
1101 Monroe Street, Gretna, Louisiana 70053

To my wife,
Loretta

Acknowledgments

THE AUTHOR WOULD LIKE to thank the following: Mr. Richard Silocka and Mr. A. DiConsati for opening their collections to the author; Mr. Timothy Fulton for his expertise on firearms of the period; Mr. Joe Fortner for assistance with the manuscript; Ms. Renee Escoffery Johnson for information on black culture during the Civil War; Ms. Marion Knihnicki, chief librarian of the Transportation School library, and her staff, Ms. Valerie Fashion, Ms. Diane Forbes, and Ms. Nancy Reinfeld, for their assistance in obtaining hard to find reference material.

A BULLET FOR LINCOLN

CHAPTER 1

New York City
Monday, August 8, 1864

THE WORLD WAS CHANGING and everyone knew it. After three years of terrible war, the rich knew it, the poor knew it, the smart knew it, and the slow knew it. Everyone from high-born to low knew it and it was all because of this strange war that involved three nations. One of the nations was dead, one of them was dying, and one was undergoing a painful, violent birth.

The dead nation was the old United States. The United States was killed with the first shot fired at Fort Sumter on April 12, 1861. The dying nation was the Confederate States of America. It was born in a blaze of glory on April 12, 1861, with the same shot that killed the old United States. The dying nation defied the Northern states with cavalier gallantry, not realizing that it arrived on the scene half a century too late. After three years of bloodshed, all but the most deluded Rebels knew their cause was in jeopardy. What had begun as a glorious adventure had turned into a nightmare. Feather plumes and flowing capes had been replaced by plain, mass-produced uniforms. Heroism and reckless gallantry were giving way before cold intellect and superior numbers. Maneuver and skillful thrusts had been supplanted by attrition. The Confederate army in the field was no longer just fighting an opposing army. It was battling a nation at war.

In that sultry summer of 1864, few realized that the final act had already begun and that the end was little more than nine months away. Nor could they imagine how violent the end would be. Lee was attempting to hold Petersburg, for without Petersburg Richmond could not be held. Without Richmond the Confederacy would have no capital. And without a capital, there would be no central rallying point. Laying siege to Petersburg was Lee's most dangerous opponent, the tenacious and relentless Ulysses S. Grant. Grant, conscious of his tremendous resources, hammered the Army of Northern Virginia mercilessly. Neither the skill of Lee's generalship nor the heroism of his ragged soldiers mattered any longer. One by one, Grant was cutting the roads and railroads that were the lifelines of the Confederacy. By August 22, 1864, Grant's troops had already cut the Weldon Railroad and the Jerusalem Road. Lee counterattacked at every opportunity and even gained some victories, but even a success meant that the South bled a little more.

If Grant were not enough, there was Sherman. On the same day that Grant cut the Weldon Railroad, this irascible genius was already south of Atlanta. Nine days later, the transportation hub of the heartland of the Confederacy would be in his hands. After occupying the city for nearly two months, Sherman would wreck and burn Atlanta, then march south. By December he would be in Savannah after cutting a swath through Georgia sixty miles wide and three hundred miles long, but this was only a foretaste of what "Uncle Billy" and his "bummers" would do to South Carolina. The day of total war had arrived, and the Confederate States of America was the first to experience it in all its fury.

The nation being born was the United States of America. Although it had the same name as the dead nation, it was a new creature. It was young, self-confident, prosperous, and thoroughly self-indulgent with a sense of its own destiny. In less than a century its culture would dominate the entire planet, but in the middle of 1864 only a few prescient men could foresee the possibilities. One of these men was Abraham Lincoln.

Abraham Lincoln was the sixteenth and last president of the old United States. He was tall, ungainly, and homely. His features were coarse and his face was easily caricatured by the cartoonists of his day. By far, most cartoons were unflattering. Lincoln was called a gorilla by many Northern newspapers who preferred to see someone more handsome and charismatic (and, by their lights, more efficient) in the White House. Every decision he made was criticized and, in most cases, his critics were proved wrong. He steered the Northern states through two years of military disaster that brought the South close to recognition as a nation by the European Powers. Patiently, he sifted through one incompetent general after another to find the gold among the dross. After, McClellan, Pope, Burnside, and Hooker, he found Grant and Sherman.

Politically, his job was even more difficult. Not only was he facing the rebellious states of the South, but he was forced to cope with Northern politicians who were more than willing to let the nation dissolve rather than lose votes. There were also businessmen who speculated in gold and gloated as each Confederate victory sent the price of the precious metal soaring. Then there was slavery. At first Lincoln was content to let the "peculiar institution" remain untouched if the country would stay united, but the ambitious and arrogant men of the South were determined to have it all their own way and the monkey Lincoln was hardly the man to stop them. Unfortunately for the South and the nation, they miscalculated. The ungainly man who was so easily caricatured was not a buffoon. He was a political genius of the first order and saw as his primary duty the preservation of the Union. For this task, he used every weapon and trick he could.

He maneuvered the South into firing the first shot of the war, which infuriated the people of the North and made many in the South feel uncomfortable. When an unbroken string of Southern victories seemed to promise recognition of the Confederacy from Europe, he used McClellan's bungled victory at Antietam to publish the Emancipation Proclamation. The proclamation is probably one of the most cynical documents in the history of the United States, because it only freed the slaves in the rebellious states. Nevertheless it worked. From that time on, the Confederate States of America was branded as pro-slavery and no European power would recognize it as an independent state.

Behind his genius and cynicism Lincoln had a vision of a peaceful, united nation in which all of its citizens would share the benefits of freedom and the opportunity to prosper by their own toil.

It was a plan that required the careful reconstruction of the South. It would take a long time and lots of money, but it would heal the nation's wounds, and Lincoln had the determination and the energy to see it done. It was a vision worthy of a great man.

There were three other men who were as intelligent and as prescient as Lincoln, but they shared a vision far different from that of the president. It was a dark, avaricious vision of unlimited wealth and power. One of these men sat in a horse car of the Third Avenue Railroad in New York City. He was considered handsome even though his nose was a bit large and his skin was mottled by a puzzling condition. Some might find it odd that a healthy, twenty-seven-year-old man was not in uniform. In later years admirers would say that he was unable to serve in the army because of fainting spells. The truth was that he had hired a substitute, because he could ill afford to waste a minute on non-essential activities such as military service. As a result he was investing wisely and was making a name on Wall Street. He was John Pierpont Morgan. Morgan came from a very good Connecticut family. He received his basic education at some of the better institutions in the United States and then attended the University of Goettingen in Germany. He had a gift for mathematics and, upon graduation, Morgan's professor asked him to give up his plans for business and devote himself to mathematics and teaching. Morgan politely declined. He was a young man with goals and ambition.

Morgan stared out the window of the horse car, but saw nothing of the amazing activity that was New York. Hundreds of thousands of people walked purposefully on their daily business. Prosperous shops lined the street and, on the sidewalks, and in the street itself, hawkers and placard bearers informed the populace of the best places to buy goods of every description. It was a city of contrasts. In the center of town the city boasted wealth and prosperity, but from Fortieth Street to Harlem it was a city of shacks and slums. In the winter New York was cold and in the summer it was hot and humid. In summer there was also the odor of the horse manure that was daily packed onto the streets by the city's primary means of conveyance. It was difficult to imagine that six hundred miles away two of the largest and most efficient armies the world had ever seen were locked in a deadly climax to a titanic struggle.

Morgan's mind was neither on the present nor the past. For him they didn't exist. His concern was for the future, which was why he was on his way to an important meeting. He was traveling in a public horse car, instead of his own carriage, because of his desire for anonymity and secrecy. Despite his later fame and large family, Morgan was intensely secretive. A doting son, he wrote his father in England at least twice a week. His father bound the letters and locked them up in binders. Morgan kept the letters after his father died in 1890, but in 1911, two years before his own death, Morgan would burn every letter except two that were not in the binders. Yet, Morgan had not always been this way. Until the death of his wife of four months in 1861, Morgan was just another ambitious young man of good family with an aptitude for mathematics. The death of his first love had scarred his soul and beneath the surface lay a man obsessed with wealth and power. He had the objective and the desire. He lacked only the method.

It was almost dark by the time Morgan descended from the car. There was little chance that he would be recognized by anyone because he was not yet famous, but he wanted to take no chances. Morgan was a careful man. It was this attention to detail and care along with a streak of utter ruthlessness that would eventually make him one of the richest and most powerful men on the planet. Morgan had already taken his first steps toward acquiring that wealth. In 1862, he loaned Simon Stevens twenty thousand dollars so Stevens could purchase five thousand condemned Hall carbines from the War Department for $3.50 each and sell them to Gen. John C. Frémont, the commander in Missouri, for twenty-two dollars each. Although the deal was investigated, and condemned by Congress, Morgan still made fifty-four hundred dollars in clear profit and emerged from the investigation untainted because he had loaned Stevens the money in "good faith."

In 1863 he made the considerable sum of eighty thousand dollars by speculating in gold with Edward Ketcham, who would later swindle thousands when his gold empire collapsed after the war. Speculating in gold was considered by many to be unpatriotic because the price went up when the Confederates won and down when Union forces were victorious. Morgan and Ketcham bought gold surreptitiously and amassed a sizable quantity of the precious metal. When the time was ripe they conspicuously shipped half of their hoard overseas driving the price higher still. In 1863, many would have considered eighty thousand dollars a good basis for living a very comfortable life. To Morgan it was a merely a paving stone on his road to a massive fortune.

Morgan walked the few short blocks to his destination. The Fifth Avenue Hotel was a preferred watering hole for the denizens of Wall Street. It was a large hotel with luxurious appointments that was used to catering to a clientele with money. Inside, the walls were paneled with dark hardwood paneling waxed to a deep luster. The floors were covered with the finest Persian carpets in rich reds and blues. The floor of the bar was gleaming checkerboard black-and-white ceramic tile. The huge crystal chandeliers were illuminated by gas and lit the place brightly. The doorman gave Morgan a slight bow because he was a patron. In later years the doorman would grovel. Morgan did not announce himself at the desk. He went straight through the lobby and up the stairs to a room on the third floor and knocked on the door. It was answered promptly by a large man with a pleasant round face graced by a modest mustache. His hair was combed with a lightly perfumed tonic. He wore an elegant navy blue worsted suit with a silk shirt and cravat. There was a heavy gold watch chain across his vest and a diamond stick pin in the cravat.

"Ah, Mr. Morgan," the man said, smiling expansively and offering his hand. "So good of you to come."

"Thank you, Mr. Fisk," Morgan said shaking the hand of Jim Fisk. Fisk stood aside as Morgan entered.

The room was part of a suite and it was richly appointed with half paneling and floral pattern wallpaper. The curtains were damask and the carpet was crushed velvet. It was a grand room that fit the style of Jim Fisk, who was considered a minor success on Wall Street. The large man had recently suffered several sharp setbacks at the hands of gleeful competitors and rumor had it that he had sworn revenge on all of Wall Street. Most took such threats lightly, but Morgan did not, especially when he considered that at the height of the war Fisk was buying Southern cotton for Jordan & Marsh and making enormous profits. Jim Fisk was obviously not a man with whom one trifled.

"You know Mr. Gould, do you not?" Fisk asked gesturing to a medium-sized man in a brown suit. Jay Gould was a young man only two years older than Morgan himself, but his hairline was already receding and he had a full beard. These two features made Gould seem much older than either of the other two men.

"Nice to see you again, Mr. Gould," Morgan told him as they shook hands.

Gould was well known on Wall Street and was already a power to be reckoned with. His speculations had won him widespread condemnation since he made many of them without the knowledge of his partners. During the panic of 1857 some of his speculations proved worthless and Charles Leupp, his partner in the tanning business, shot himself in despair. Gould then calmly offered to buy out Leupp's heirs. A misunderstanding led the Leupps to try and occupy the tannery in question whereupon Gould hired a bunch of toughs to seize it, which they did.

"May I offer you some refreshment?" Fisk asked.

Fisk motioned to a table in the center of the room. It was covered with oysters and other delicacies and on one end was a bottle of champagne in a silver bucket of ice. Fisk could always be relied upon to be flamboyant. Morgan accepted a glass of champagne from Fisk and ate three of the oysters. Gould drank his champagne with a smile. He was enjoying himself. Gould and Morgan accepted cigars from Fisk and the three men took their time lighting them. When it was evident that all were drawing freely, Fisk motioned to upholstered armchairs.

"Shall we get down to business, gentlemen?" he asked.

The chairs were arranged so that each could talk comfortably to the other two. They sat in no prearranged order. Fisk sat on Morgan's left and Gould on his right. Fisk began the meeting.

"Since this meeting came about as a result of discussions which we both have had with Mr. Morgan, I feel it only fair that he should begin," Fisk said.

"Gentlemen," Morgan began. "The war is drawing rapidly to a close. It will be over in a matter of months."

"That's being very optimistic, isn't it?" Gould asked. "Lee's army is still intact and Hood still holds Atlanta."

Gould's tone was not one of criticism. The three men were there for a frank exchange of ideas and it was important that no aspect of the problem be left unaddressed.

Morgan drew on his cigar and used the moment to think. He wanted to present his plan as concisely as possible.

"While it is true that the Confederates are still maintaining two armies in the field, their resources are dwindling rapidly. Since Mobile Bay was taken the other day, Wilmington, North Carolina, remains the Rebels' only port. Even if Wilmington were allowed to operate freely it could not supply the South with the material it needs. Their railroads are in a sad state. The damage from each raid on them takes longer and longer to repair. They have no resources and no capital.

"It's a matter of resources, " Morgan continued. "The Federal government has a nearly inexhaustible supply while the South has none. I do not pretend to be a military man, but it should be evident to the most casual observer that while the South may have had a chance in the first two years of the war, it has none now. Some may fool themselves into thinking that the South can obtain a negotiated peace, but with Lincoln in the White House they haven't a chance. Lincoln has outwitted them at every turn."

"And what about cotton?" Gould asked. Gould had slipped into the role of devil's advocate and he was making the others think. This time Fisk answered.

"Cotton is a dead issue," he said getting up to pour himself another glass of champagne. "First of all, there's a lot of it in the South that remains unsold. In '63 I was buying it for one-tenth the pre-war value for hard currency. I can honestly say that in obtaining it I paid more for bribes than I did for the cotton.

"Even after the war there will be no great upsurge in demand. The warehouses in the North and in Europe are full. In addition to that, the English have learned to comb Egyptian cotton. King Cotton has been deposed, I assure you."

"Gold?" was the next question.

All three men smiled. They knew the price of gold would plummet as soon as the war was over.

"What about Lincoln?" was Gould's next query.

"We have only to remember," Morgan continued, "that before becoming president, Mr. Lincoln was the highest paid attorney in the country. Might I also add that Mr. Lincoln was making that money writing briefs for other lawyers? He himself cultivates the bumpkin image, but I assure you he is anything but. He has prosecuted this war with great skill. Despite the fact that the Union's early generals were inept, Lincoln managed to keep France and England from recognizing the South. As we speak, Grant and Sherman are strangling the life out of the Confederacy. The noose grows tighter every passing day. What we must do now is look to the future."

Morgan stopped and looked at the others.

"Please proceed, Mr. Morgan," Gould said after a short silence.

"Whereas Mr. Lincoln is very astute politically, he is, unfortunately, very naive when it comes to matters of finance. This is more than evident when he talks about the post-war era."

"How so?" Fisk asked.

"Consider, please, his statements about his plans for the future. He refers to the rebellious states as 'erring sisters' and longs to welcome them back into the fold. He is willing to forgive and forget and let bygones be bygones. Gentlemen, the South is utterly ruined financially. Its facilities are right now near to ruin. No one can possibly foresee what further damage can be done but it will hardly be insignificant. Virginia is rapidly becoming a desert and I dare say Sherman's army will do no less to Georgia. It will take tens of millions of dollars and dozens of years to repair the damage. On top of that, Mr. Lincoln wants to free the Negro and educate him so he can live as a citizen of these United States."

"Damn," Fisk muttered. "Damn. Now I see. Morgan, are you suggesting what I think you are?"

Gould smiled. "Yes, he is. If the South is to be rebuilt then most of the available capital will go to the South. It will go to already established businesses and it will be controlled by the government. The market will stagnate."

"After the war the market may stagnate for a while anyway."

"I don't think it will if the South is left to recover with only its own resources," Morgan told them.

"If it does not get a great infusion of capital it will lay prostrate for years," Fisk said. He was smiling.

"That is just the point," Morgan continued. "What will happen to the nation if the South is left to its own devices?"

Gould and Fisk were beginning to grin. Their faces were aglow with the same vision.

"Instead of sinking money in the South, they will go west," Fisk said. His voice was an excited whisper. "And in order to move west they will need railroads and the telegraph."

"And who will build those railroads?" Morgan asked.

"Never mind who will build them," Gould declared. "Who will finance them?" He almost laughed as he beheld the future according to John Pierpont Morgan.

"The problem remains Lincoln," Morgan remarked softly, bringing them all back to earth.

"What about McClellan and the Democrats in the upcoming election?" Gould asked.

"They haven't a chance of winning in November," Morgan said flatly. "The entire Union is sensing victory. They are like a pack of wolves that senses its prey weak and vulnerable. Lincoln has led them to this. They won't vote him out of office. He will be re-inaugurated on March 4 of next year. You can count on that."

"So," Fisk said picking up the thought. "He will lead the country to victory and at that point he will outlive his usefulness."

"Precisely," Morgan asserted with a self-satisfied smile. At this point he rose from his chair and walked over to the table to pour himself another glass of champagne.

Fisk rose from his chair and set his cigar in an ashtray. He went over to the table and picked up an oyster. He squeezed lemon juice on it and ate it. He then refilled his own champagne glass.

"That still doesn't address the solution to our problem," Gould said joining Fisk and Morgan at the table.

"Suppose Lincoln were not in the picture at the moment of victory?" Morgan asked.

"The public would be irate," Gould answered. "If he were laid low by the hand of a Southerner, it would go poorly for the South indeed."

"Yes," said Fisk. "There probably wouldn't be much trouble getting a Southerner to do the deed, but if he were caught he might tell all. That would leave us in a rather sticky situation."

"Leave that to me," Morgan said flatly. "What I need right now is capital in order to finance the scheme."

"That isn't a problem, providing the cost isn't too high," Gould said. "How much are we talking about?"

"I don't know." Morgan said seriously. "I imagine the price will have to be negotiated as with any other transaction. I will make whatever arrangements necessary and then inform you of them. From this moment on we must follow Benjamin Franklin's advice."

"And that is?" Gould asked.

"'We must all hang together or we will all hang separately,'" Fisk quoted.

"Then by all means begin your inquiries, Mr. Morgan," Gould suggested raising his glass. "May I propose a toast to a most prosperous future?"

The three champagne glasses met with a light clink.

New York City
August 11, 1864

The euphoria of the meeting with Fisk and Gould quickly evaporated. Morgan now had willing partners who would help finance his venture, but schemes were one thing; reality quite something else. The man Morgan needed would have to be much more than a common thug. He would have to be an artist to do the things Morgan planned and succeed. But who would that man be? Morgan had no idea but the man would have to be someone extraordinary. Morgan thought for a moment. He might as well start with Stuyvesant. Morgan called for a messenger and while he was waiting he penned a quick note and sealed it in an envelope. He gave the boy a fifty-cent bill, or "shin plaster" as they were now called, and the note. Morgan told him the address, admonished him to be quick, and the first part of his plan was finally underway.

Piet Stuyvesant was a descendent of the original settlers of New Amsterdam who had lost his ancestors' penchant for thrift, industry, and cleanliness. He was a large man with thick forearms, a full head of flaxen hair, a narrow mouth, and small eyes that were lacking in mirth even when he smiled. His beard was sparse and scraggly and he looked like a tradesman. If anyone asked Stuyvesant his occupation, the answer might vary from tinker to carpenter, but he had no shop or even a pushcart. His place of business was a small tavern on Front Street near the Fulton Market. Stuyvesant was a man of many talents and many employers. He had been employed by Gould in the Leupp Tannery affair. Morgan used

Stuyvesant very seldom. Usually it was to persuade small creditors, whose debts did not justify legal action, to honor their obligations with more alacrity. The tradesman Stuyvesant had a reputation of being very persuasive with an ax handle or a pair of brass knuckles.

He was sitting in the back of the tavern drinking whiskey when Morgan's messenger walked in the door and asked for Mr. Stuyvesant. Before the bar keeper could point Stuyvesant out, the large man gruffly called, "Here, kid." The messenger walked over to the darkened corner where the voice came from, handed Stuyvesant the envelope, and left. Stuyvesant opened the note. It said to meet Mr. Morgan at the New York and New Haven Railroad Depot in the passenger waiting area between Twenty-Sixth and Twenty-Seventh Streets at ten o'clock the following morning.

The New York and New Haven RR Depot
August 12, 1864

The New York and New Haven Railroad Depot was a busy place. On one side, there was a steady stream of passengers crowding on to the platforms or streaming from arriving trains. On the other side, crates, boxes, and sacks were being loaded and unloaded. Outside the station, cabs and wagons created a traffic snarl that seemed to get worse every day. It was a place where upper-class individuals like Morgan could mingle with tradesmen without arousing suspicion. Stuyvesant, wearing a black-brimmed hat, dirty brown overalls, and a red-striped cotton shirt, was sitting on one of the benches reading a copy of the *New York Herald*. When he saw Morgan he rose.

"Good morning, Mr. Morgan," Stuyvesant said politely, tipping his hat with a smile.

"Good morning, Mr. Stuyvesant." Despite the fact that Stuyvesant was a tradesman Morgan also tipped his hat. After all, this was a business venture and one had to be polite to one's colleagues.

Stuyvesant turned the front page of the paper toward Morgan. "Not much longer, now, and Sherman will be in Atlanta."

"May I?" Morgan asked. Stuyvesant handed him the paper and Morgan perused the article about Atlanta. It would not be much longer before the city fell. The capture of Atlanta would almost guarantee Lincoln's reelection. It also meant that the war would probably end in six to eight months if Morgan's estimates were correct. That meant a plan had to be put into effect immediately. Was there enough time? Morgan felt a twinge of anxiety.

"I want you to find someone for me, Stuyvesant," he said, handing the man back his newspaper.

"Somebody need convincing, Mr. Morgan?"

"No, I'm looking for a man to do a job for me. It's a very special job."

"I'm always at your service, Mr. Morgan."

"I sincerely appreciate your offer, Stuyvesant, and you won't go unrewarded. It's just that I need someone very prominent removed from the scene, if you catch my drift?"

Stuyvesant looked at him blankly for a moment and then his lips stretched in a cruel, understanding smile. "Ah, yes," he said. Then he scratched his beard. "Prominent, huh? That is a bit out of my line," he said honestly. Stuyvesant was one of those people whose success depended upon his staying in the background. "I'll have to ask around." Noting the concern on Morgan's face he added, "discreetly, of course."

Morgan looked around and when he saw no one was looking he removed an envelope from his inside coat pocket and handed it to Stuyvesant. The tradesman nodded and left the railroad depot. It would take him nearly two weeks to report back. They met again at the New York and New Haven Depot on August 25.

"I am afraid that the kind of man you are looking for does not work here in New York," Stuyvesant said. His tone was one of disappointment as if somehow his civic pride was hurt by not finding a hometown assassin. "There is supposed to be such a man in Washington City."

"Supposed to be?" Morgan felt his anger rising. He didn't need "maybes," he needed facts.

Stuyvesant held up his hand before his employer became angry. "This man exists," the tradesman declared, his voice unsteady. He looked around nervously. "But he is extremely secretive. It is dangerous merely to inquire as to his existence unless you are acting for a prospective client."

Morgan noticed something in Stuyvesant's voice that he had never heard before—fear. "From here you will have to deal with him directly, sir. You can reach the man you're seeking through Mr. Joseph Fitch who may be found most evenings in the Chain and Anchor Tavern near the Washington Navy Yard. It is a rough place, Mr. Morgan, so be careful." Hesitatingly, Stuyvesant said, "I can honestly do no more."

Morgan was impressed. A man who could frighten a tough like Stuyvesant must indeed be formidable. Morgan nodded. Stuyvesant was right. At this point it was best to contact the man himself.

"Thank you, Mr. Stuyvesant. I appreciate what you've done, and as usual may I rely on you to forget either of our meetings?" He handed Stuyvesant another envelope for his work.

"What's this for?" asked Stuyvesant with a crooked grin.

Morgan returned the grin and left the depot.

Washington City
September 2, 1864

Morgan arrived at the Baltimore and Ohio Station at 6:05 in the evening. He wanted to go directly to the hotel but a boy hawking papers caught his attention by calling the name "Atlanta." Morgan walked over and bought a paper. Sherman had taken the city. Time was now critical. He hired a cab to take him to the Kirkwood Hotel where he had reservations. The hotel was a square four-story building with an ornate iron balcony on the second story. It was located on the corner of Pennsylvania Avenue (just "The Avenue" to Washington residents) and Twelfth Street. Morgan would have preferred Willard's, but that was one of Fisk's favorite places and he and Fisk had many mutual acquaintances. The National was another excellent hotel, but Morgan decided to be careful by choosing a place that was adequate without being too ostentatious. He checked in under the name of Wolfgang Mueller and spoke with a German accent. If anyone should accost him in that language he could easily carry on a conversation thanks to his German education. Morgan was tempted to find the Chain and Anchor that same evening, but he was unfamiliar with the seedy parts of Washington and decided to find out where it was in daylight, then go there the following evening. Right now he needed rest and time to think, so after an excellent supper, Morgan took care of some business paperwork he had brought with him and wrote a few lines to his father. He went to bed early; the morrow would be busy.

On the morning of September 3, Morgan hired a horse. Ordinarily he would have hired a carriage and a driver, but he wanted speed and maneuverability in case he needed to get away from trouble in a hurry. It took him a while to find the tavern even though he stopped several times for directions. When he did stop, people would give him a strange look as Morgan explained in broken English that he was in the beer business. After passing by the tavern several times, Morgan finally found the Chain and Anchor and almost wish he hadn't. Even in daytime its environs were disagreeable in the extreme. It was a sailor's tavern near the waterfront a short distance from the Washington Navy Yard. It was located at the end of a dark alley that stank of urine and vomit. Prostitutes who were long past their prime stood at the entrance to the alley, even in the afternoon. Morgan was glad he hired a horse and decided that when he returned that evening he would bring a pocket pistol and a knife.

Morgan left the hotel for the Chain and Anchor at dusk. As he approached it he felt the knife and pistol in his pocket, but they didn't make him feel very safe.

He was dressed as a tradesman and kept reminding himself to use a German accent. The Chain and Anchor was crowded. The clientele were just the kinds of people one would expect in a waterfront dive. They were a rough lot, most of them sailors. Morgan gave himself odds that more than a few of them were toughs. The few women in the place were coarse and loud and Morgan wondered if any of them were not ladies of the evening. As soon as he entered, the bartender and the patrons sized him up. He looked out of place, scared, and not particularly strong. More than one of the out-of-work sailors at the bar looked upon him as easy prey. Two went so far as to position themselves near the door in order to follow him quickly when he left. Morgan stepped to the bar and ordered a mug of beer.

"I'm look for Mr. Fitch," he said stumbling over his English.

The greasy fat man behind the bar pointed to a man sitting at a table in one of the darker corners of the room. Frowning at the poor illumination, Morgan picked up his mug of beer and walked toward the man. He didn't notice that the other patrons in the bar suddenly began minding their own business. If this man knew Fitch, he probably had business with Fitch's employer and that made him untouchable by anyone who valued his life. The man at the table was a small man with a slight build. He wore a shabby overcoat and a worn top hat. He was not wearing a beard, but had at least two days of growth on his cheeks and chin. The glass of whiskey in his hand was smudged from his dirty fingers. This could not possibly be the man I'm looking for, Morgan thought. The man looked up. His eyes were sharp and intelligent.

"Mr. Fitch?" he asked.

Fitch nodded and motioned to a chair. Morgan sat extending his hand. "Mr. Fitch, I'm . . ."

"Shh," Fitch said putting his finger to his lips. He did not take Morgan's hand. "There may come a day when you don't want to know me and I don't want to know you, so no names. That's rule one. Are you the reason the Dutchman was here?"

"Stuyvesant, *ja*," Morgan replied.

"Rule two is ten dollars—gold," Fitch told him.

Morgan handed over the ten-dollar gold piece without comment. This was obviously the price of doing business. Fitch smiled and bit into the coin, an act which revealed rotten, stained teeth. Fitch sized up Morgan and decided he was all right to do business with. He wasn't wearing fancy clothes and he paid without question. He looked like an ordinary shopkeeper but Morgan's hands gave him away. They were clean and uncalloused like a woman's and there were ink stains on the right forefinger. Fitch figured he was a banker.

"I'm looking for . . ."

"This ain't the place," Fitch told him. "I'll meet you in two days. Where do you live?"

"I'll meet you," Morgan said. He didn't want the likes of Fitch knowing where he stayed.

"Two nights from tonight in front of Brown's hotel on Sixth Street. Do you know it?"

Morgan nodded.

"Leave and don't look back. No one from here will follow you."

Morgan did as he was told. Once outside, he mounted his horse and left the area quickly. He was in too much of a hurry to notice the bearded man mount a horse and trot after him. Morgan could not hear the shoes of the horse behind him because the horse's hooves were covered with leather to lessen the noise on the paving stones. It was a dangerous thing to do, but the rider of the leather shod horse didn't care if the horse slipped. He only cared about not being noticed.

The man following Morgan was the man Morgan was seeking. His name was Anderson and he was one of those whose reputation is passed by whisper. He was known as the best man to do away with a troublesome spouse or a business partner. His work was expensive but guaranteed, because his work never looked like murder. Just who actually committed suicide or had a genuine accident or was one of Anderson's "commissions," as he referred to them, no one really knew. The rough-and-tumble milieu of the Washington underworld were in awe of him. Joseph Fitch was his helper. Any further knowledge of either man was unhealthy.

Morgan made no attempt to cover his trail and he made straight for the Kirkwood. Anderson watched as Morgan handed the horse to one of the colored boys who waited at the front of every hotel to make money by running errands. Morgan handed the boy a sum and said something to him and the boy led the horse away. Anderson's quarry disappeared into the hotel. Anderson tethered his horse, removed a newspaper from his saddlebag, then walked across the street to the Kirkwood. He entered the hotel and loitered around the desk with the paper under his arm. A few moments later the colored boy returned with the receipt from the livery stable where Morgan had hired the horse.

"This is for Mr. Mueller," the boy said.

The clerk handed the boy a coin then placed the receipt in the box numbered 319. Anderson smiled and left the hotel.

Early the next morning, Anderson sat in the lobby of the Kirkwood reading a copy of the *Daily National Intelligencer*, waiting patiently for "Mr. Mueller" to have breakfast and leave. When Mueller walked out of the lobby, Anderson followed to insure that his quarry was, indeed, leaving. He watched Morgan get into a cab, then went back inside. He moved quickly upstairs to 319. The hotel lock was no challenge. On a small table near the bed was a nearly finished letter to Junius Spencer Morgan in England that began "Dear Father." In the valise in the wardrobe were several letters addressed to John Pierpont Morgan at "Dabney, Morgan and Company" and to his home address. One letter was in a neat feminine hand. It was signed by Miss Frances Tracy. Anderson read the letters quickly committing the facts he needed to memory. He then put everything back precisely the way he found it. Anderson left the hotel and walked to the telegraph office in the National Hotel on the corner of The Avenue and Sixth Street. Since he worked from time to time for the Pinkerton Detective Agency, Anderson had access to all the agency's services, so he sent a telegram to the Pinkerton Office in New York requesting the description of one John Pierpont Morgan, giving Morgan's address. After receiving the reply to his query the following morning, Anderson was ready to meet Mr. Morgan personally.

Morgan arrived in front of Brown's Hotel twelve minutes early because of the difference in time between New York and Washington. He had known of the time difference but in the excitement of the moment had forgotten to reset his watch. The entire time, he paced near the entrance of the hotel, afraid of missing Fitch. The shabby little man was punctual. He stopped in front of Morgan with his hand in his pocket. Morgan supposed he was waiting for money so he gave him a five-dollar gold piece. Fitch looked at the coin and looked back at Morgan with an expression of disappointment that was so tragic that Morgan nearly laughed. Morgan held out his hand and Fitch handed him a note. It was addressed to "Mr. W. Mueller, Kirkwood Hotel." Morgan stared at the envelope stunned. How could Fitch or his employer possibly have known? He had not even told Fisk or Gould where he was going or what name he was going to use.

"How . . ." he said looking up at Fitch, but Fitch was nowhere to be seen.

Puzzled, and a little apprehensive, Morgan thrust the envelope into his pocket and returned to his room. He was not about to read the note in public as it no doubt contained the name of a secret rendezvous. Once the door was locked, Morgan opened the envelope and received another shock. There was no secret rendezvous; no dangerous place like the Chain and Anchor. The note merely read:

September 6, 1864

Dear Mr. Mueller,

I would be happy to meet you at Willard's Hotel tomorrow at 9:00 P.M. Please come alone so that we may discuss our business in private. I am looking forward to making your acquaintance.

Your obedient servant,
ANDERSON

Morgan read the note twice and wondered if Anderson were a lunatic. Willard's? It was as public as one could get. Morgan then tried to get a clue to the man's personality from the script. It was neat and flawless as if it had come from a school primer. Morgan was tempted not to go, but he had come this far and his disguise was intact. Willard's? So be it!

Morgan arrived at Willard's Hotel at eight forty-five in the evening. The dining salon was not very crowded and he got a table immediately. His nerves had killed his appetite so he ordered soup and baked trout. Since he needed a clear head, he ordered coffee instead of wine or beer. At precisely 9:00 P.M. a man approached his table. He looked so ordinary that Morgan at once thought he must be a member of the hotel staff on some errand. The man stopped at his table and bowed slightly.

"Do I have the honor of addressing Herr Wolfgang Mueller?" he asked.

Morgan, taken aback for a moment said "*Ja*. Please sit down," in a heavy German accent.

"I am Anderson. Mr. Fitch told me that you wish to commission me to do some work for you."

"*Ja*, that is so," Morgan said.

The man smiled pleasantly. "There is no need to continue your charade if it is uncomfortable, Mr. Morgan."

The statement was made so blandly that, at first Morgan was not sure he understood what had been said. When he realized the full implication of the statement, Morgan blinked and looked closely at the man across the table from him for the first time. He was of medium height with a medium build. He had brown hair and wore a mustache. His hands were smooth and untanned. Morgan's first observation was confirmed. Anderson looked like any clerk in any government office. Morgan was disappointed. Anderson was hardly the robust character that Morgan imagined would be required to carry out something as daring as an assassination. He was wholly unremarkable except for his eyes. Anderson's eyes were gray and when Anderson fixed his gaze on him, Morgan felt as if Anderson could see his brain and viscera as well as his clothes, face, and skin. Anderson's gaze was so unnerving that Morgan avoided looking directly into the man's eyes. All of this took no more than a second or two, but to Morgan it seemed an eternity. During this eternity, Anderson continued looking at him without saying a word. This Morgan understood. They were negotiating a business contract and Anderson had demonstrated an advantage. Nevertheless, Morgan refused to be outmaneuvered. It was not in his nature.

"*Bitte*," he said continuing in character. "*Meine Name ist Mueller, Wolfgang Mueller.*"

"Sir," Anderson said politely. "I meant no offense, and I fully understand the need for discretion, but your name is, in fact, John Pierpont Morgan. You reside at 249 East Thirty-eighth Street in New York City with Mr. Peabody. You are a partner in Dabney, Peabody and Company, which is at 53 Exchange Place near Wall Street. Your father is in London and is in the employ of Peabody and Company. Since much of this is public knowledge, may I also add, and please don't take offense, that your sweetheart is one Miss Frances Tracy."

Morgan stared, speechless. He had never set eyes on this man until this very moment and Anderson seemed to know some of the most intimate details of his life. Anderson continued, his tone matter-of-fact and polite as if he were discussing the weather.

"I have brought up these facts for two reasons. The first is, I deal with my clients on a face-to-face basis, and that includes their real names. Second, you need to understand that I investigate any subject thoroughly and that my work is guaranteed."

With that, the waiter arrived with Morgan's meal and took Anderson's order. Anderson explained that he had already eaten but ordered a glass of sherry.

"Please eat, Mr. Morgan. I'm sure you already know that the cuisine here is excellent."

Morgan didn't feel like eating but he took a spoonful of the soup. The mechanical act of eating meant that he did not have to look at Anderson's penetrating eyes. That would help to slow down the maelstrom of confusion in which he found himself. As Morgan ate, Anderson made no attempt to observe the amenities and be pleasant or to carry on a conversation. After several spoonfuls of the soup, Morgan wiped his mouth with a napkin and looked back at Anderson. The waiter returned with Anderson's sherry and left.

"Whom are we discussing?" Anderson asked politely.

Morgan looked around. The dining room was full but not crowded.

"No one will be suspicious, Mr. Morgan. We are just two men in a public place discussing business. Too many these days have a need for melodrama. Were two gentlemen to meet in a place like the Chain and Anchor we should quickly attract attention and arouse suspicion. Now, whom are we discussing?"

"Lincoln," Morgan said feeling more in control of himself.

"The president?"

"Yes."

Morgan expected a reaction from Anderson. He expected Anderson to be astonished, or frightened. He would not have been surprised if Anderson had suggested he was crazy and stormed out. But, there was no emotional reaction. Morgan then explained the reasons behind the need for Lincoln to die.

"There is another matter," Morgan said after a moment's hesitation.

"A second party?" Anderson inquired.

"No. All of this is a matter of timing. It must occur at the end of the war or as soon thereafter as possible."

"How am I to judge the end of the war? It covers the breadth of this country."

Anderson had a point. Morgan was not a military man, nor did he follow the war except to watch the events that were affecting the stock market. He thought for a moment.

"Consider the destruction of Lee's army or its surrender the end of the war."

Anderson nodded and sipped his sherry.

"There is one final thing," Morgan added at the last minute.

"And what is that?"

"It must be done so that the blame falls on those with Southern sympathies. It must be done so that there is no question of the offending party. In other words, Mister Anderson, this Caesar must have a Brutus, a Brutus so evident that no one will be tempted to look elsewhere once the deed is done."

Morgan wasn't sure, but he thought he saw Anderson's lips move in a slight smile.

"The cost for the commission is $125,000," Anderson said calmly. He saw Morgan's eyes go wide but pretended not to notice. "I do not expect you to pay the full amount in advance, of course. For operating expenses, I will need $10,000, half in gold and half in greenbacks or paper from a reliable bank. This sum is not part of the actual commission. The full amount for these expenses is to be delivered to Mr. Fitch when he calls for it in two days. That should be sufficient time for you to raise the money. The payment for the full amount will be forwarded as soon as the commission is complete. Fitch will give you the address. The payment will be $50,000 in gold, $25,000 in paper, and $50,000 in a reliable railroad stock of your choosing. Since the object of this commission is a public man, you will know almost immediately when the commission is complete. If the task is not performed within two weeks of the time specified, you will assume that I am dead and need not forward the money.

"This is the last time you and I will meet face-to-face, Mr. Morgan. Should we happen to meet accidentally you will pretend you don't know me. Should we be introduced at some function you will treat me as a stranger and accept whatever name is given for me. Fitch will always use his real name and if the need arises I will contact you through him. As soon as I leave this dining room our contract begins. I do not boast when I tell you that I have never failed in a commission. My service is expensive, but it is guaranteed." Anderson fixed his gaze on Morgan, "Since there is nothing between us in writing, I pride myself on selecting clients of good character such as yourself, Mr. Morgan. Unfortunately, sometimes even honest and honorable men are tempted to do things which are, shall we say, foolish in the extreme. Perhaps it is the times. The point is, Mr. Morgan, that betraying me in any way would be most hazardous to your person."

Anderson communicated the threat without malice. He was so casual that he might have been discussing a minor fluctuation in the market. "If you have no further questions, Mr. Morgan, I will take my leave."

Morgan could think of no questions. He nodded and Anderson rose.

"Good night, Mr. Morgan. It has been a genuine pleasure."

Morgan watched Anderson go. When he was alone, Morgan felt a great wave of relief wash over him. He felt giddy and could barely suppress a giggle. Without knowing precisely why, he knew he had hired the right man for the job. Anderson's motivation for doing what he did was not Morgan's concern. He sold a commodity and charged what the market would bear. Those were terms that Morgan could understand. Anderson had also taught Morgan something very important and that was to know everything possible about those with whom he dealt in business, and he took the lesson to heart. From then on Morgan would conduct business with his associates precisely the way Anderson had with him. He would always deal from a position of complete knowledge and strength. Morgan felt very good. He called the waiter and ordered a whiskey.

Anderson didn't need to hire a cab. The weather was pleasant and his boarding house was only a few blocks away on The Avenue itself. The evening was warm but not oppressively so for Washington City in the summer. The streets, as usual, were not very crowded at this time of evening. In a little while the only people on the streets would be soldiers and prostitutes. The main thing on his mind was this new commission. Anderson normally dealt with people who were not constantly in the public eye. In those cases an "accident" or "suicide" usually did quite nicely. Lincoln was quite a different matter. He was the most public man in the country and he was always well attended if not well guarded. That didn't mean that some maniac couldn't kill the president, but he probably wouldn't live to enjoy his own success. Anderson's business was to dispose of his client's problems and live to enjoy his fee. This is what made each commission an interesting challenge. In fact, Anderson lived for his commissions. They were the only things that had saved him from a life of ennui. In this instance, killing a public person was much more exciting than killing a private citizen. Then there was the stipulation that the act be committed so that the blame fell on someone else. This was a new twist and it amused Anderson. He had always let events take care of the blame as he did when he killed the Confederate general Stonewall Jackson. That was the way he did everything. Blaming it entirely on someone else was going to take all his skill.

Anderson resided at Mrs. Wellman's boarding house which was located on the north side of The Avenue between Second and Third Streets. It was nestled among other boarding houses, shops, and small unpretentious hotels. The neighborhood was becoming run down but it was still quite respectable compared to neighborhoods like "Murder Bay" a few blocks south between Thirteenth and Fifteenth Streets. Mrs. Wellman, the owner of the boarding house, was a stout, hard-working woman typical of many in the city. She had a special pride in the way she kept her boarding house respectable by allowing no Irish, actors, or salesmen in her establishment. Her boarders consisted mostly of military men and clerks from government offices. The rent was a reasonable twenty-five dollars per month due promptly on the first. The table was ample. To the other boarders, Anderson was an officious, fussy busybody whom they avoided like the plague. The role and the attitudes of his fellow boarders suited Anderson well.

· The only people awake when Anderson arrived were three army officers. Two were playing cards and sharing their nightly bottle of whiskey. The other was dozing on the sofa. The man on the sofa was recuperating from a wound and had recently left the hospital. That was why he spent much of his time sleeping. A wounded man required rest as Anderson well knew. He had been wounded rather badly in the commission to kill Jackson and it had taken him months to recover. The major who wounded him must have assumed that Anderson was dead, because when Anderson regained consciousness after being shot he was on an undertaker's table, next in line to be embalmed. The experience of regaining consciousness in such circumstances would have unhinged most men, but Anderson remembered that he was posing as an English journalist. The undertaker was an old man and was upset by the thought he had nearly embalmed a living human being. Anderson was taken to a doctor where his wounds were bound. How he found the strength to dress and ride away from the doctor's house he never knew. When he arrived at Mrs. Wellman's, badly injured, he told her he had been shot and robbed by ruffians. Mrs. Wellman fussed over him and offered to take him to the E Street Infirmary, but he refused. His own doctor would come and treat him. There was no question of the Metropolitan Police coming to a "respectable" boarding house. Fitch hired a good physician, but it took six months before Anderson was up and around. Even now, his shoulder bothered him, but Anderson refused to let a minor inconvenience interfere with his profession.

CHAPTER 2

The Kirkwood Hotel
Washington City
September 7, 1864

JOSEPH FITCH PARKED IN FRONT of the Kirkwood Hotel and stepped inside. The clerk behind the registration desk gave Fitch the look that hotel clerks and head waiters reserve for people whom they feel don't belong in their establishments. Fitch ignored the man. To him clerks were one of the lowest forms of life next to policemen.

"Please tell Mr. Mueller his carriage is here," Fitch told the clerk.

Still regarding Fitch as if he were one of P. T. Barnum's exhibits, the clerk rang the bell for a boy to carry a message to Mr. Mueller. A few minutes later, Morgan and the boy came down carrying two valises. One was heavier than the other and Fitch smiled.

"Good morning, Mr. Mueller," Fitch said, tipping his hat.

Morgan nodded and replied, "*Guten Morgen, Herr Fitch*," in perfect German.

Morgan paid his bill and tipped the boy, while Fitch put both bags in the buggy. The morning was already warm and it promised to get more uncomfortable as the day wore on. Morgan climbed into the buggy, happy to be going back to New York where Septembers were cool.

Neither man said a word as Fitch drove to the Baltimore and Ohio Station. Fitch stopped in front of the main entrance.

"Good bye, Mr. Fitch," Morgan said in unbroken English.

"Have a pleasant trip, sir," Fitch said with genuine civility.

Morgan picked up the light valise and walked into the depot. He left the heavy valise on the floor of the buggy next to Fitch who manfully resisted the temptation to look at the money, before he flicked the reins across the horse's back and steered the buggy south on North Capitol toward The Avenue.

For the first time in his career, Anderson was in a quandary. Killing Lincoln was not the problem. Lincoln was a very public man. He could be seen on the streets and in the theaters. There was hardly any place he didn't go. Seldom was there an escort of cavalry or any precautions for his personal safety. Lincoln had two bodyguards appointed by the Metropolitan Police. The daytime guard was Joseph Sheldon, a slim, dark-haired young man who took his duties seriously. The night guard was John F. Parker. Parker was short and sandy haired. About the nicest thing anyone could say about Parker was that as a policeman, a bodyguard, a husband, and a father he was worthless. Since Anderson worked from time to time as a Pinkerton detective, he knew of most of these men and had met many personally. They were all, as a rule, bad, and Parker was one of the worst. Nevertheless, Parker could not be ignored. He might just do his duty by accident and ruin everything.

There were many ways Lincoln could be killed. One alternative was to shoot him at long range. There were now rifles with telescopic sights capable of hitting a man at a distance of half a mile or more. The firer would be betrayed by a cloud of smoke issuing from the discharge, but that was not the problem. At a great distance many things might happen such as a carriage crossing the line of fire at the wrong time. Anderson threw out the idea of using a long-range rifle immediately. A long-range shot was too anonymous and would not fulfill his commission. The act had to be done in such a manner that no one had any doubt as to the perpetrator or his reasons. Having a group of men rush the president might also be effective for killing him, but again it would be too anonymous and a number would be killed. A fanatic, on the other hand, could easily rush up to the president and shoot him at point blank range. That would be the end of Lincoln and there would be no doubt as to the perpetrator or to his motives. Unfortunately, it would also mean the end of the fanatic. If the assassin were not killed outright, he would, no doubt, be tried and hanged. During the interrogation process he would surely give away the person or persons who put him up to it. There did not appear to be a satisfactory solution, but Anderson was undaunted. This was a challenge and he enjoyed it.

Anderson eliminated the first two options as impractical. The third offered precisely what was needed, but how could he get a fanatic to do exactly as he wished? The obvious solution would be to convince or perhaps mesmerize someone into accomplishing the act, then make sure that the someone did not live to tell the authorities. Anderson smiled. He didn't believe in mesmerism. It was all right in music hall performances when the mesmerist made a member of the audience act like a chicken, but it would hardly do for a killing. Killing was an art and Anderson never trusted anyone to do the job except himself.

Anderson decided that his first task was to search for a man who wanted to kill Lincoln. It had to be someone who was not just a crank but who would do it if given the chance. The hard part was that the someone had to be a person that, if not famous, was reasonably well known in the community and had expressed hostile opinions about the president. That included most newspaper men but Anderson discounted them as being of little importance. Where would he find such a man? Did one exist? Anderson did not like having questions with no answers. Until this commission he had always been able to study his prey without the victim becoming aware of his presence. With Lincoln he could do just that. There were so many men around the president that another would not be noticed. In the past, Anderson had many times used unwitting and unwilling accomplices, but there had never been a situation like this. It would be a long search.

Washington City
September 22, 1864

In 1864, Washington City was unlike any other city in the United States or the Confederacy. At first glance it was obvious that it was the seat of power of a nation at war. In that fall of the third year of the Civil War, it was undoubtedly the best fortified city in the world. It was surrounded by dozens of earthworks mounting more than a thousand guns, manned by more than thirty thousand men. This was a lavish scale of protection that the South could ill afford for its capital in Richmond, but Washington City needed it. More than anything else, Washington City was the cornerstone, symbol, and shield of the Union. It contained stables, harness shops, foundries, and manufacturers of everything from gun carriages to locomotives, as well as the seat of government. Should the city fall, the consequences would be dire. That was why in the preceding three years Union field commanders in the East had the double mission of defeating the Army of Northern Virginia and keeping Washington covered. It was an impossible task, which was why Grant had merely paid lip service to guarding the city and went after Lee and his army. There was no doubt that Grant's strategy was the right one, but it had nearly been overturned by Jubal Early's raid on Washington in July. The entire city had been thrown into panic and Grant had to dispatch troops to cope with the threat. On August 7, a disgusted Grant appointed Gen. Philip Sheridan to command the Army of the Shenandoah. In a few short weeks the dapper little general would destroy Early's army and the threat to Washington once and for all. Like Sherman, Sheridan would devastate the ground he covered.

Despite the fact that it was the capital of a modern nation at war, Washington as a city had severe problems. When the war began in 1861 it was nothing more than a sleepy little Southern town built on a malarial swamp. Slaves were bought and sold within sight of the Capitol. In fact, the slave business was so brisk that the St. Charles Hotel had special slave pens built in the basement and offered to reimburse a client should the client's slave escape. The city came awake only when Congress was in session. During the session lavish parties costing thousands of dollars were the rule and they were in stark contrast to the way most Washingtonians lived.

The war changed Washington forever. Before the echoes of the first shots from Fort Sumter died away, thousands were flocking to the capital. There were soldiers, politicians, office seekers, and power brokers on the official end. On the unofficial end were salesmen, contractors, and engineers. Last but not least were the saloon keepers, the brothel madams, the prostitutes, and the criminals. Washington had become a boom town in which the commodities were power and wealth.

In stark contrast to the wealth and power were sections like "Murder Bay," which was the notorious slum south of The Avenue between Thirteenth and Fifteenth Streets, an area that lived up to its name nightly. There was also the shanty town of Swampoodle through which ran the open sewer of Tiber Creek. It was an area of illicit trade in every sort of commodity from young women to stolen government quinine. It was the home of the aristocracy of the Washington underworld which flaunted its power in the face of authority. However, even those with the bravado to openly defy the law spoke Anderson's name in whispers. No one really knew what he looked like and none wanted to find out. What was known was enough. Anderson was paid to do away with those that the rich and powerful wanted out of the way. This he did silently and efficiently. He worked alone and used Joseph Fitch for errands. Fitch was closed-mouthed about Anderson for two reasons. The first was that Anderson paid extremely well. The second was that two previous partners who made trouble for Anderson were at the bottom of the Potomac feeding the turtles. Whatever Anderson wanted and needed, he paid for and paid well. The alternatives were clear. Do what Anderson asks and you will be paid well. Ask too many questions and you will be dead. Only one man other than Fitch knew what Anderson looked like. He was a very talented forger who lived near the Chain and Anchor. Anderson used him because he was a more talented forger than Anderson himself. An ordinary man might find it odd that Anderson had no pride or ego when it came to his skill, but Anderson was no ordinary man. His only reason for being were his commissions. Nothing else in life mattered. The money was important only as a measure of what people were willing to pay for his services.

As soon as Morgan left Washington, Anderson began to circulate. One night he would attend a party given for senators and government officials. The next he would be found in an illicit gambling house in Swampoodle and the third night he would be in a middle-class tavern off H Street. He spoke with policemen and detectives, tavern keepers and teamsters, and housewives and tradesmen. There were numerous threats against Lincoln's life, many of them in writing. Most were anonymous but some were not. In 1860 one Pete Muggins wrote from Fillmore, Louisiana, threatening Lincoln and "goddamning" him over two dozen times in a twelve-line letter. One note which claimed that a group of one hundred young men were ready to kill the president was signed "Joe Bradley, Joe Points, Mike O'Brien." Anderson could find no trace of Bradley, Points, O'Brien or their ninety-seven compatriots. One name, however, did emerge. The person in question obviously hated the president, and he had forcefully stated his views on numerous occasions in public. But since he was an actor he was considered harmless. His name was John Wilkes Booth.

Booth! Here was an individual who obviously hated Lincoln and had stated the fact publicly on more than one occasion. Booth was not only a public figure, he was famous! Were he to do it in sight of witnesses, no one would doubt that it was the actor John Wilkes Booth. Nothing was guaranteed, of course, but it was a beginning. On October 12, 1864, Anderson disguised as a would-be theater impresario from Philadelphia called on Mr. Booth at the National Hotel.

"I'm sorry, sir," the clerk said. "Mr. Booth isn't here. I believe he's gone to Canada."

"When will he return?" Anderson asked.

"Who knows?" the clerk said. "He comes and goes. What can you expect from an actor?"

Anderson didn't reply. He put on his hat and left the National. He tried Grover's National Theatre, but no one there knew when Booth would return either. His next stop was Ford's Theatre where the answer was the same. Frustrated, Anderson went to Taltavul's Tavern a few doors down from Ford's. It was a gathering place for actors who often knew when a fellow thespian was due to return for an engagement. Anderson bought a drink and stood at the bar. No longer an impresario, he was just someone whom Booth had helped out when he was down, and now that he was flush he wanted to repay him. The question went around the bar as such things do but Anderson saw nothing but beard-scratching and head-shaking. Anderson finished his drink and set his glass down.

"Well," he said with a smile. "Guess I get to keep the money that much longer."

Peter Taltavul, behind the bar, smiled as he always did at paying customers and nodded. Anderson was leaving when a clear feminine voice behind him said, "Excuse me, sir."

Anderson turned. The woman had bright red hair. She was petite with a pretty face and fine features. There was a hardness around the eyes and she was in the tavern alone. A prostitute, perhaps, Anderson thought. Nevertheless, he removed his hat. "Yes, ma'am?" he said politely.

"Forgive me," the woman continued. "But I couldn't help overhearing you mention Wilkes Booth. He is a friend of mine and I wondered if I might be of service?"

"The truth is Miss . . ."

"Turner," she said. "Ella Turner."

"The truth is, Miss Turner, that Mr. Booth helped me out a while back and I just want to repay him."

"Wilkes is a very generous man," she said.

Anderson thought he saw a faint blush. Could it be that Miss Turner was in love with Booth? This was an opportunity he could scarcely afford to miss.

"Miss Turner, I'm a stranger here in the city and I'd like to sort of look around, but I'm afraid of going somewhere I shouldn't. With someone like yourself who is from here as a guide I could avoid those places. Could I impose upon you to show me the city? Dinner, of course, is included in the invitation."

"Why Mr. . . ."

"Miller, ma'am. Joe Miller."

"I'd be delighted, Mr. Miller."

Anderson called for Miss Turner at her sister's home on Ohio, only two blocks from the White House. It was a plain-fronted house with heavily curtained windows a few doors from the corner of D Street. Smiling as he approached the door, Anderson recognized the address as one of the more popular pleasure houses in the area. A Negro servant met him at the door, but he had only stepped into the foyer when Miss Turner came down the steps. She was dressed in a plainly trimmed, attractive, emerald-green dress. Her hair was pulled back from her face, and her lips and cheeks were rouged tastefully. She was, on the whole, a very attractive woman.

"Good evening, Miss Turner," he said, bowing slightly.

"Good evening, Mr. Miller," she said as the Negro doorman helped her with her shawl.

"I met a gentleman at my hotel who recommended we go to Harvey's Oyster Saloon for a light snack and then to the Varieties Theatre for entertainment before supper. Is Harvey's a decent place?" he asked innocently.

Ella Turner smiled pleasantly. "Oh, yes. You've certainly planned a wonderful evening. I'm sure it will be enjoyable."

If you loved oysters (and who didn't?), Harvey's was the place to be. Located between Tenth and Eleventh Streets on C Street, it was unlike any restaurant anywhere. It was always packed with soldiers and civilians consuming oysters by the hundreds of gallons. Harvey's guaranteed them fresh every day and this was not without some risk. The boats had to pass under the Confederate batteries along the Potomac, so, Harvey's oyster boats were really blockade runners. Fortunately, during the course of the war only one of the boats was sunk. In addition to enjoying oysters on the premises, customers could also get them to go, and it was not unusual to see soldiers leaving with forty or fifty gallons of oysters for an entire regiment.

Anderson and Ella each had a dozen oysters and a glass of beer. Ella was obviously enjoying herself and that was good. Anderson genuinely liked women. In fact, women were his only weakness and he was now painfully aware of that fact, since his infatuation for a woman had nearly gotten him killed during his commission to murder Stonewall Jackson. It was a debt to be repaid, but not now. Their next stop, the Varieties Theater on Ninth Street, was a music hall. Grover's and Ford's theaters were for serious theatrical productions. Outside the Varieties a wheel of colored lights rotated above the entrance. Through the double doors was a huge open auditorium with roughly plastered walls and bare rafters. The music hall was filled with soldiers since drinks were only ten cents. The performers were scantily clad ladies, Negro comedians, acrobats, jugglers, and singers. The air was thick with smoke and from the back it was sometimes difficult to see the stage clearly. It was also difficult to hear since the soldiers in the audience were constantly screaming catcalls and spitting. Nevertheless, Ella laughed at all the jokes and applauded the jugglers who, Anderson had to admit, were very talented. One of them kept eight objects in the air at once. At the end of the performance was the obligatory patriotic tableau. This night it was "Washington Crossing the Delaware." Anderson found it amusing that all of the people in the boat were wearing modern army overcoats. After the tableau came the equally obligatory patriotic song. Someone who was not a friend of Lincoln began singing "Marching Along" and if anyone doubted the loyalties of the audience, all they had to do was listen as the audience began singing along with the chorus.

> *Marching along, we are marching along.*
>   *Gird on the armor and be marching along.*
> *McClellan's our leader,*
>   *He's gallant and strong.*
> *For God and our country*
>   *We are marching along.*

Ella sang along lustily and was smiling as they left for a quiet supper at Brown's hotel. She was happy.

"It must exciting being the friend of a famous actor like Mr. Booth," Anderson said.

Ella Turner's eyes brightened and they lost some of their hardness. "He's really marvelous," she sighed. Anderson watched her. Perhaps she was in love with Booth.

"Have you ever seen him on stage?" she asked.

"Why no, ma'am. You see my folks don't approve of the theater. My momma says it's immoral."

"Nonsense. It's just like reading a book and have it come to life. You really should see Wilkes act," she continued. "Most actors just stand and recite their lines. Wilkes is different. He moves and puts his whole soul into a part. That's why he's so popular."

When the waiter came to take their order, Anderson chose flounder with vegetables and Ella ordered roast pork and boiled potatoes. Both drank beer. Ella reminisced about the show at the Varieties, giggling when she remembered a few of the jokes. Most of them were off-color. Anderson steered the conversation back to Booth.

"I never thought I'd hear a song about McClellan in this town," he said. "I guess he'll beat Lincoln in the election."

Ella was well mannered and wouldn't dream of speaking with her mouth full. She shrugged as she chewed a mouthful of pork.

"I don't see where it matters. They're all politicians. If you don't bribe them, they arrest you. Who cares whether it's Lincoln or Mc-Clellan? You're just like Wilkes. The way he goes on."

"I don't suppose he cares much for the president."

"What Lincoln is doing to the nation upsets Wilkes very much, because Wilkes really loves the South. He'd as soon shoot that gorilla as look at him—if he were capable of doing such a thing, but he's not. Wilkes wouldn't hurt a fly. That's why he never enlisted. That, and he promised his mother he wouldn't go to war. Wilkes is really a wonderful man," Ella said a little dreamily. "He makes you feel like a lady and yet he can sweep you away." Suddenly she stopped, looked at Anderson, and giggled.

"What's so funny, ma'am?"

"He obviously wouldn't treat *you* like a lady and sweep *you* away." Ella giggled again and it was obvious she had too much to drink.

"When is Mr. Booth due back?"

She leaned toward him conspiratorially and whispered. "I'm not supposed to tell anyone, but he's due back on the ninth of next month."

"Why aren't you supposed to tell anyone? He's an actor. Certainly he would want people to know when he was in town."

Ella shrugged. "I don't know, that's just the way he is. Besides, why are we talking about Wilkes anyway?" she said. She looked dreamily at Anderson and reached across the table to touch his hand. "You know, you have very nice eyes," she said.

Anderson was tempted but, this was a commission and he had learned not to mix business and pleasure. He withdrew his hand. "Uuuh, Miss Turner, we hardly know one another," he said, looking around in embarrassment."

"Why don't you call me Ella, Joe?"

"Uh, I'd like that, Miss Ella."

"No, not Miss Ella. Just Ella."

Anderson maneuvered Ella Turner out of Brown's Hotel and back to her sister's establishment. She tried to lure Anderson to her room, but he declined.

"Oh, I almost forgot. I have to leave tomorrow. Would you give the twenty-five dollars to Mr. Booth?"

Ella's eyes smiled at the greenbacks and Anderson wondered if Booth would ever see the money. He returned to the cab and on the way back to Mrs. Wellman's, he removed his false whiskers and the small amount of make-up. When he entered, one of the officers called to him and asked him if he'd been with a woman.

"Sir, please!" Anderson said taking offense. "This is a respectable establishment."

"I'll bet the last woman he was with was his mother," another officer said sarcastically and the other officers laughed. Walking up the stairs Anderson could not suppress a smile.

In his room Anderson undressed, washed, and stretched out on the bed. The old injury to his shoulder hurt. He had learned a great deal this evening, but was it of any value? He had found a prominent person who hated Lincoln and had said so publicly, but there were many people who hated Lincoln and said so publicly. How Booth would be more useful than any of the others he didn't know. Booth would not return until the ninth of November. That meant a month in which to find someone else, if necessary. Assuming that Booth were the right person, what would he do with the actor? There was no way to kill Lincoln on stage. Pondering a solution to the puzzle, Anderson fell asleep.

St. Albans, Vermont
October 19, 1864

A bullet splintered the window frame near George Ingalls' face. He didn't have to worry about flying glass. That had been shot out moments before. He couldn't tell if anyone was shooting at him personally, but he wasn't taking any chances. He could see figures gathered in Taylor Square, the town green, but it was impossible to tell who they were. Ingalls was furious. All this could have been prevented, but no one in authority wanted to look like a fool by taking precautions against something that "couldn't possibly happen." Well, it had happened.

A large group of Confederate sympathizers who were based in Canada decided to "do something" for their cause. The "something" consisted of three plans for raids on Northern towns and cities. The raids, concocted by Lt. Bennett Young, were sanctioned by James Seddon, Jefferson Davis' Secretary of War. The first was the raid here at St. Albans, Vermont. Although it was common knowledge that the group was about to try some sort of raid, the Canadian authorities did nothing. They were mostly Confederate sympathizers themselves, and preferred to turn a blind eye to the proceedings even if it meant allowing Canada to be used as a base for armed raids into a neighboring country. In 1863, Gov. J. Gregory Smith of Vermont requested five thousand muskets and the authority to raise troops to guard the border, but they were refused when Lord Russell, the British Foreign Secretary, protested that this was an unfriendly act. Ingalls, a National Detective working for Col. Lafayette Baker, had been sent to Canada to try and discover the Confederates' plans. That was the easy part. The hard part was getting the state and local authorities in Vermont to do anything about it. They didn't. On the afternoon of October 18, Young's raiders began arriving in small groups. There were twenty of them and, at three in the afternoon, they appeared in the town square. Each man was armed with two pistols. The plan called for them to wear Confederate uniforms but only Young had one. They rounded up as many citizens as they could in the town square and then proceeded to rob the town's three banks before trying to set fire to the place.

Suddenly the gunfire in the town died down. Ingalls was positive the raiders were getting ready to leave. He knew they were supposed to burn the town but there were only a few small fires here and there. Fortunately, for the citizens of St. Albans, the incendiary mixture Young's raiders had obtained was defective. In addition, resistance in the town had stiffened. Two of the townspeople had been wounded, but he didn't know if any of the raiders had been shot. From his window, Ingalls watched the raiders form up in sections of four and gallop north on the muddy track of Main Street. The militia was on its way and the townspeople were aroused so he didn't doubt that Young and his group were happy to get away with nearly two hundred thousand dollars in loot.

Ingalls let the militia chase Young and his band. He had other work to do. He brushed the splinters and the shattered glass from his tweed coat and returned to his room at the St. Albans House on Lake Street. He retrieved his overcoat and valise and checked out. Then he walked across the street to the Vermont Central RR Station. He was returning to Montreal where he was known as George Branscombe, a businessman representing Fordham & Sons, a dry goods company which was a transparent ruse for speculating in cotton. Branscombe was loud and a bit stupid, so it was a good disguise. Ingalls would have preferred to be more surreptitious about his movements, but that was impossible. The twenty-six-year-old detective was a shade over six feet in height and had broad shoulders. No one that big could be inconspicuous. If he tried to be then he would arouse suspicion. As a physically big man he was less conspicuous if he was not too bright. For some reason people feel less uncomfortable if a large person is stupid.

Ingalls was anything but stupid. He had grown up on a small farm in Western Pennsylvania. His father was hardworking and prosperous by the standards of the area. His mother, while not a beautiful woman, was one of those industrious, thrifty people who also knew when to have a good time. All six children (four boys and two girls) were taught to read and do sums. George was the second oldest after his sister Esther. It was a happy family but somewhere young George had picked up a case of itchy feet. His first real job had been as a prizefighter. At the age of eighteen he knocked out the prizefighter in a carnival that had come to town. His prize was twenty-five dollars and a job as the new prizefighter. He tried it for a while, but found he didn't like hurting people for sport, so he quit. It was a prosperous time and a strong young man had no trouble finding a job as he made his way east. As he went from job to job, George began to discover surprising things about himself. First was that he was an individual instead of Darryl Ingalls' oldest son. Along with his individuality he discerned that he was making his way on his own and he liked that. Second was the realization that he had principles. George's mother would not have been surprised but George was honest and decent and he hated injustice, lawlessness, and slavery. He had never seen a slave until he visited Washington City at the age of twenty. There he saw human beings being bought and sold and the entire process filled him with an anger that he could barely suppress. Until then slavery was just a word. It had never occurred to him, since he was free, that others were not. Ingalls was to learn through the coming years that few, if any, are really free. At the age of twenty-two Ingalls became a policeman in Philadelphia and just before the war, he signed on as a detective for the Pinkerton Agency.

Despite his years in a cynical world, Ingalls still retained a touch of his boyish enthusiasm and looks. He had dark brown hair and a handsome face, unmarked by his profession unless someone looked closely, then he could see the faint scar across Ingalls' nose where it had been broken by a tough in Philadelphia. That was just before Officer Ingalls had broken the man's collarbone with a nightstick. There were other scars but they were not evident when he was dressed. He was a friendly man, not easy to anger. On bad days he walked with a slight limp that was the result of an encounter with a Rebel spy on a train traveling from Relay to Harpers Ferry. In the fight the spy, who was a lot tougher than Ingalls imagined, managed to shoot the detective in the buttock then throw him off the train. The result was a fractured arm, three cracked ribs, and a broken ankle. Ingalls managed to limp to a Baltimore and Ohio RR maintenance crew who helped him get to a doctor. It took the detective nearly a year to recover. Now he was back doing what he did best.

St. Lawrence Hall
Montreal, Canada
October 25, 1864

The Confederates were openly active in Canada since both the Canadian government and the people actively supported the Southern cause. The headquarters of Confederate activity was located in St. Lawrence Hall in Montreal. It consisted of a group led primarily by Jacob Thompson and Clement C. Clay. Thompson was a young man with black hair and beard without mustache. With straight lips and piercing eyes, this former U.S. Secretary of the Interior was now Chief Confederate Commissioner in Canada. Clay, an older man with drooping eyelids, a receding hairline, gray hair, and full beard, was the head of the Confederate Secret Service in Montreal. Their associates were George Sanders, Beverly Tucker, a professor named Holcomb, and a messenger named James Thompson. Thompson regularly traveled to and from Richmond with messages. Thompson's real name was Richard Montgomery and he was actually a Union spy. The group was financed through letters of credit deposited in the Ontario Bank. Collectively this group was known by both sides as the "Canadian Cabinet."

St. Lawrence Hall was a five-story hotel that was located on the corner of St. Francis Xavier and St. James Streets in Montreal. It was an excellent hotel, very staid and elegantly appointed. It was a favorite of wealthy Europeans and had played host to members of the Royal Family. It was also the headquarters of the Canadian Cabinet. It was perhaps a trifle too good for a cotton speculator but no one questioned Ingalls' choice of hotel. The advantages of staying at the St. Lawrence were obvious since it allowed Ingalls to be there at all hours of the day. He could sit in the lobby and read a newspaper or stand at the bar and eavesdrop on conversations without arousing more than casual interest. He appeared to the suspicious and class-conscious Confederates to be a man trying, unsuccessfully, to rise above his station, which made them despise Ingalls. Still, they were not fools. When he first arrived they had him followed. Ingalls' tail was so amateurish that it was laughable. Ingalls discovered the man almost immediately. First he strolled around the city taking in the sights. The man who was assigned to follow him was much shorter than the detective and it was an obvious effort for him to keep up with Ingalls' long strides. After tiring his companion with a long walk, Ingalls visited several shops in rapid succession and nearly lost the man. Finally, Ingalls decided they both needed a rest so he stopped to have supper at a decent restaurant. The man didn't follow the detective inside. His instructions were to be as unobtrusive as possible. Ingalls read the evening paper and had a leisurely meal. Ingalls had preferred to go home, but the short man was still shadowing him so Ingalls ended the evening by going to a house of ill repute to stay the entire night. He found his tail the next morning still waiting across the street, tired, unkempt, and in need of a shave. Ingalls left the house and strode across the street toward the man. The tail looked up, eyes wide. Ingalls reached into his pocket. The movement made the man quiver with fear. He was convinced that he had been discovered and Ingalls was drawing a gun to kill him. Ingalls produced a cigar.

"Excuse me, friend. Would you happen to have a light?"

The tail exhaled a deep sigh of relief and lit Ingalls' cigar. "Thanks," Ingalls said. Then looking at the sky added, "Nice day," and walked down the street looking for a cab. After that the Canadian Cabinet no longer considered him a threat and merely tried to avoid him. After more than a week at the St. Lawrence,

Ingalls decided he had done what he could. He was ready to send a coded telegram to Baker's headquarters advising them of his decision. He was sitting in the lobby of the St. Lawrence reading the Montreal *Telegraph* when someone familiar walked into the hotel and asked the desk clerk for Mr. Clay.

"Oh, yes, Mr. Booth," the desk clerk said. "Mr. Clay is expecting you."

Booth? Ingalls thought. Where had he heard the name? Then it occurred to him that it was the actor Edwin Booth. No, Edwin Booth was older and more dignified. It was the youngest Booth— John Wilkes. He was reported to be a rebel sympathizer, but there had never been any evidence to connect him with anything like this. For a moment Ingalls was stunned. What could he do now? He almost smiled at the solution. When in doubt, act stupid.

Booth was surrounded by the Confederates at the bar and they were speaking in low tones. Ingalls walked right up.

"Say, aren't you Booth, the actor?"

Clay, Thompson, and the others turned disapproving looks at Ingalls, but Booth, always pleased to speak with fans, smiled. "Yes, I am," he said.

"I've seen you a couple of times," Ingalls said truthfully. He stuck out his hand to shake Booth's. The actor had a firm grip. "You were great as Macbeth and when you did Pescara in *The Apostate*, you were about the most evil man I could imagine."

Booth bowed gracefully. "Thank you, sir. You're most kind."

"There's one thing, and I hope you won't take offense, Mr. Booth." Booth tensed as Ingalls continued. "I think you're a better actor than either of your brothers."

Booth's face broke into a wide grin. "No offense, Mr. . . . . er."

"Branscombe, sir. I represent Fordham & Sons, Dry Goods."

"Well, Mr. Branscombe, I appreciate a man who speaks his mind. Why don't you join us for a drink?"

Clay and his associates looked pained, but Ingalls said. "Why, thank you, Mr. Booth. That's very kind of you. Wait 'til I get back home and tell folks I had a drink with John Wilkes Booth."

For the time being, Ingalls had prevented the group from discussing business. He had no time to find a way to eavesdrop inconspicuously. That was going to be a problem and it was a problem Ingalls never solved. All he could do was catch bits and pieces of conversations. The most frequent was Lincoln, which was not surprising with the election drawing near. Both North and South were intensely interested in the outcome of the election. Seldom in politics was an issue so clear cut. The Democrats and the Copperheads were trying to cloud the issues but they had failed. If McClellan won the election, there would be some kind of accommodation. The South was hoping that accommodation meant that it would be allowed to go its own way. If Lincoln won the election, it meant the merciless continuation of the war and the extinction of the Confederacy in a few months. Nevertheless, it made Ingalls suspicious, because he knew it was more than just election talk. Perhaps it was just a hunch but it was there. He didn't want to think about the word or the concept but it seemed unavoidable. It was a word he had heard as a Pinkerton, but now Ingalls perceived it in all its terrible consequences. The word was *assassination*. My God, he thought, Booth is going to kill the president! A sweat broke across Ingalls' forehead. He had just had a premonition. It was a precognition from the ancient classics or a prophecy from the Old Testament. For a brief moment, Ingalls peered into the future and, like others who have experienced the phenomenon, he was terrified. What frightened him most was that without a shred of evidence or proof he knew with absolute certainty that the assassination would take place unless he could prevent it. What also horrified him was that, like Cassandra, no one would believe him. Booth was a popular, talented actor with Rebel sympathies, who appeared totally harmless. Who better for the job than someone who could be discounted as a harmless crank? Ingalls followed Booth for the next few days, but there was nothing unusual in his actions until he stopped in the Ontario Bank. Inside he overheard Booth's transaction as he was attended by Mr. Campbell, the first teller.

"Let me see," Campbell said adjusting his pince nez spectacles on his nose. "You wish to deposit $455 to your own credit in the Ontario Bank, and you wish to purchase a bill of exchanges for sixty-one pounds, four shillings, and ten pence."

"That's right," Booth said. "I'm going to run the blockade. If I'm captured, can my captors make use of the bill?"

"Only if you sign the bill, since it is made payable to your order."

From behind, Ingalls watched Booth nod in assent. "Then let me also have a bill for three hundred dollars in United States gold."

"Very well, Mr. Booth. Will there be anything else?"

"No thank you, Mr. Campbell."

When Booth turned he saw Ingalls and smiled. "Mr. Branscombe, is it not?"

"I'm flattered you remember, Mr. Booth."

"How are you, Mr. Branscombe?"

"As well as to be expected. Haven't been able to find any cotton and I have no taste for the whiskey up here. I shall be going home soon."

Booth smiled pleasantly. "I never drink whiskey myself. I prefer brandy. '*Chacun a son goût*,' eh, Mr. Branscombe?"

"I beg your pardon?"

"To each his own—it's French."

"Oh, sure," Ingalls said, pretending he really wasn't sure. Then he asked. "Where are you playing next, Mr. Booth?"

"I may have an engagement in Washington City in a week or so," Booth said. "I would be happy to get you complimentary tickets. Come 'round to Grover's Theatre."

"That's most kind of you, sir, but I am returning to St. Louis in the next few days."

"Pity," Booth said. "Nevertheless, if I am playing in a city where you happen to be, please call on me."

"I'll be sure to do that, Mr. Booth."

Booth tipped his hat and bid Ingalls good day. Ingalls waited a few minutes and then left. There was something here that didn't make sense. Why did Booth say he was going to run the blockade when he was actually going to Washington? Was it to throw off suspicion? Ingalls at least had a coup. He knew where Booth would be in a few days. It was time to remove himself and leave Canada before he was compromised.

CHAPTER 3

Secret Service Headquarters
Washington City
November 3, 1864

INGALLS LEFT HIS VALISE and sample case at the B&O station, with instructions to have them delivered to his rooms, and hired a cab. He was tired and dirty, but there would be time to clean up later. When he gave the cabby the address, the man looked at him queerly and appeared to be about to say something, but decided better of it. The building at 217 Pennsylvania Avenue was a place most Washingtonians feared and loathed. It was the headquarters of Col. Lafayette C. Baker, head of the War Department Secret Service. Ingalls rode to his destination in silence. He entered the two- story brick building and stopped at the desk of Baker's receptionist, Judge Lawrence. Lawrence was an older man with small, pleasant eyes and a perpetual smile. As usual he was wearing a white vest. Lawrence checked a ledger to confirm that Ingalls had an appointment with Colonel Baker, and then he gave Ingalls a broader grin than ever when he saw how begrimed the detective was.

"Hello, Mr. Ingalls, have a pleasant trip?"

Ingalls smiled at the friendly sarcasm. The colonel's door was closed so Ingalls sat down in an upholstered chair. "It shouldn't be too long," Lawrence explained. "Major Eckert has just brought the latest news from Virginia."

Maj. Thomas Eckert was the War Department's chief telegraphist. His office in the War Department Building on the corner of The Avenue and Seventeenth Street joined that of Edwin Stanton, the Secretary of War. Before Ingalls could get comfortable, the door opened and Eckert, carrying a black leather dispatch case, emerged from Baker's office. He nodded to both Lawrence and Ingalls as he left. Lawrence rose and stepped to the door.

"Mr. Ingalls is here to see you, sir."

"Send him in."

Lawrence motioned to Ingalls and the detective entered the office of the most hated man in Washington. The office was nothing you would imagine that a dictator would have. The room was decorated like the average sitting room, which it probably was. There was a square India pattern on the carpet and striped paper on the walls. The colors were primarily blue and burgundy, which were very popular. The paper on the ceiling was also striped but the color had faded to an indistinct beige or gray. In the corner was a heating stove built into the fireplace. Beneath an ornate gas chandelier in the center of the room was a plain oak desk with no roll top or drawers. It was littered with papers.

Col. Lafayette Baker was standing at the desk smiling as Ingalls entered the room. Baker was a tall, robust man with a florid, handsome face. His dark hair was cut short and he wore a full beard that showed no trace of gray. His eyes always looked at a subject intently. He wore a dark blue coat with brass staff buttons and a staff colonel's rank insignia. His attire was complemented with a bow tie and a heavy gold watch chain draped across his vest. Baker was not a military man. He had begun his career before the war as a vigilante in California. With the perfect vigilante mentality, Baker believed in swift and merciless justice. Although never rising above the rank of private, he was efficient and popular. So popular, in fact, that the merchants of San Francisco gave him a cane with a top encrusted with gold nuggets as a going away present.

Baker's first service for the Union was under Gen. Winfield Scott, who sent Baker south to Richmond as a spy. Baker was apprehended, but through a combination of guile and strength, his hallmarks, he was able to escape. His various employers included Secretary of State Seward, Postmaster General Montgomery Blair, and finally Secretary of War Edwin Stanton. It was Stanton who recognized Baker's vigorous and efficient ruthlessness. It was Stanton who told Baker:

"Your job is going to be the dirtiest of this war, Mr. Baker. You will be hated as no man has ever been hated, but you will perform a service for this nation that no one has been called upon to perform. Furthermore, you will never be allowed to disclose the authority for your actions."

Baker's reply was simple. "Mr. Secretary, I am here for your orders."

Stanton knew he had found the right man. Baker was not just some half-baked military man ready to flood Washington City and the rest of the country with troops. He knew there was a difference between a scout and a true detective. Baker's idol was the infamous French detective Vidocq who, during his life, was the most admired, feared, and hated man in France. Vidocq was dismissed and eventually staged a brilliant robbery which only he could solve to get his job back. He was found out and died penniless in 1857, but he had set a new standard for detectives and later plainclothes policemen. Baker was Vidocq's disciple and relied more on subtlety, observation, and disguise rather than brute force to achieve his ends. He interviewed his detectives personally and hired women and colored men as operatives. Baker's operatives, male and female, wore a special badge. Baker wore one different from the rest. It was larger and made of solid silver. On it was engraved "Death to Traitors."

Baker's methods were a mixed blessing. His vigorous prosecution of any hint of espionage destroyed most of the major Confederate spy rings and reduced the others to impotence. Baker smashed the Conrad Ring, Belle Boyd's ring, and had even reduced the effectiveness of the legendary Frank Stringfellow, J. E. B. Stuart's best agent. Unfortunately, there were no limits to Baker's use of his power. Many men and women in Washington were arrested and held in the Old Capitol Prison without benefit of counsel. He was also known to use forged evidence to detain his suspects. It was decidedly unconstitutional and it made Ingalls uncomfortable. But, Baker did what the legendary Alan Pinkerton could not, and Ingalls found the lure of Baker's organization with its new vision of detective work too appealing to resist. When he recovered from his wounds, Ingalls applied to Baker personally and was accepted.

"Well, Ingalls, nice to have you back. You did a good job in Vermont. Too bad the local authorities didn't act with more dispatch. We could have had Young and his entire band of spies to string up," Baker said extending his hand.

Ingalls shook Baker's hand. "Thank you, sir," he said.

"What did you learn in Montreal that requires my immediate attention?"

Ingalls hesitated for a moment. Baker was one of those men who was ready to put his own ideas into action without much thought, but was always ready to find fault with other people's ideas no matter how well thought out they might be. Ingalls had to choose his words carefully and perhaps pander to Baker's vanity.

"It's something that I came across at the St. Lawrence Hotel and I am at a loss to handle. This is why I feel you need to know the unvarnished facts," Ingalls began. Baker looked at him with interest and sat down.

"I am more than aware that there are many cranks about who say that they are going to kill the president when they're liquored up, but I have a feeling the Canadian Cabinet is hatching such a plot."

Baker put his finger tips together and placed them under his lower lip. "What makes you think this is different from anything else they've tried?"

"For one thing, the St. Albans raid. They have done a lot of talking but now they seem desperate enough to try action. The other thing is that I saw John Wilkes Booth up there."

It took Baker a moment of thought before he replied. "Until now I have always considered Booth a nuisance more than anything else, but this is the first time he has actually been seen with Rebel agents. Have you a current assignment?"

"No, sir."

"Is Booth in the city right now?

"No, sir. He said he would return in the first part of November."

"Go home, get cleaned up, and take some rest. When Booth returns, watch him for a while and see if he does anything suspicious."

"Yes, sir."

"Mind you, I still think Booth is a crank, but now that he's been seen with that group in Canada he may have become a dangerous crank. We shall see."

"Thank you, sir."

Baker nodded. Ingalls was dismissed. He left 217 Pennsylvania Avenue feeling as if he'd won a small victory. Baker did not humor his operatives. He either accepted what they said or told them no. Nevertheless, Ingalls didn't feel as if it were enough. His hunches were seldom wrong and he knew that the affair with Booth might quickly get beyond the limits of what one man could handle.

Election Day
Tuesday, November 8, 1864

As prescribed by the Constitution, Election Day was held on the first Tuesday after the first Monday in November. Tuesday, November the eighth, dawned cloudy and rainy over most of the nation. In Washington City, and in Maryland where John Wilkes Booth voted, it was also cold. It was, by any definition, a dirty campaign in which the Democrats pulled out all the stops to the point of claiming that Lincoln would be having black men marrying white women. The slurs and innuendoes backfired. Wilkes Booth cast his ballot and walked away convinced that Lincoln would lose. The following morning he was sadly disillusioned. Lincoln and his running mate, Andrew Johnson of Tennessee, won handily. They garnered over half a million more popular votes than McClellan and took every state except Delaware. The final count in the Electoral College was 212 for Lincoln and 12 for McClellan. Even the Copperheads' appeal to the troops in the field did no good. Over 116,000 soldiers cast their votes, but less than 30 percent voted for their former idol McClellan. From the Army of the Potomac before Petersburg to the Union forces in Nashville and those under Sherman in Atlanta, the troops in the field sensed victory and so did the people at home. The people of the North had sent a message. They were willing to see the war through to the bitter end. The election of 1864 had been the South's last ray of hope and it had slipped away. Only Jefferson Davis refused to see it.

Washington City
The B&O RR Station
November 9, 1864

John Wilkes Booth stepped down from the train at a few minutes past 6:00 P.M. He had just come from visiting his sister and mother in Maryland. To Ingalls, watching him from behind a copy of the *Daily National Intelligencer*, Booth looked disoriented as if he were a little drunk. On further scrutiny he decided that Booth looked more stunned than drunk, and Ingalls was correct. Booth was stunned. He still could not believe Lincoln had been reelected. He found a porter and paid him to see that his luggage went to the National Hotel. Ingalls followed Booth to the National and waited outside near the corner.

Inside the hotel Booth stepped up to the registration desk. George Bunker, the desk clerk, smiled when he saw Booth and turned to get a key.

"Good evening, Mr. Booth," Bunker said pleasantly. He turned the ledger toward Booth so the actor could sign it. "Number twenty, sir."

"Thank you, George," Booth said politely. "It's nice to be back."

The clerk leaned closer to Booth and whispered. "There's a lady waiting for you. The redhead. If I've made an error I'll send a boy up."

"No, George. It's quite all right."

Bunker smiled in relief. He picked up a small bell and rang for a boy to carry Booth's luggage.

An older man sporting chin whiskers didn't look up from his paper as he listened carefully. Anderson was disappointed. He needed to get close to Booth but he knew the actor would be occupied by Miss Turner for the rest of the evening. As Booth went up the stairs, Anderson folded his paper and put it under his arm. He might as well get some rest himself. He went out into the night air which had suddenly turned brisk. His instincts were suddenly aroused by the tall man across the street. The man was standing by the lamppost in front of Brown's Hotel smoking a cigar. Anderson dismissed the man because he wasn't trying to conceal himself. Still, one could not be too careful. Anderson resisted the temptation to cross the street and get a good look at the man's face. It was too early in the commission to do anything that might reveal his interest in Booth. When he went back inside, George Ingalls also decided it was time to go home and get some rest. He put out his cigar and left his place in front of Brown's Hotel.

Room 20 in the National Hotel was a suite which had a bedroom, a sitting room, and a washing area. Booth tipped the boy at the door, and the young luggage bearer bowed respectfully. The National was a big hotel and the soul of discretion when it came to its clients. Booth unlocked the door, pushed it open, and entered the room.

"Hello, Wilkes," Ella Turner said seductively as Booth entered the room. She was sitting on the sofa wearing an oriental green silk dressing gown.

Booth put down his bags and stepped toward her. She rose from the sofa, threw her arms around his neck and gave him a long passionate kiss.

"I've missed you so much," she told him.

"I've missed you, too, Ella," he said.

"Why don't you close the door and show me how much," she said huskily.

Booth went to the door, closed it, and turned the key. When he turned around, the dressing gown was sliding from Ella's shoulders. For the moment he forgot the national election.

Later Booth had a light supper sent up to the room. Ella ate but he had no appetite.

"What's the matter, Wilkes? You're not eating. Are you ill?"

"It's the election."

"Why bother about the election? You're an actor, not a politician."

"I don't like tyranny," Booth said.

"Whose tyranny?"

"Lincoln's tyranny against the South."

Ella didn't reply. She had heard most of this before and she couldn't understand why it bothered him so much, but she loved Wilkes dearly so she listened politely.

"The people of the South are the true descendants of the English aristocrats who settled this country. They are the noblest race on the continent. They have grace and refinement unlike the shopkeepers and factory workers of the North, and that madman Lincoln is trying to destroy them. No one could possibly believe

Lincoln's cause is just. All you have to do is look at the facts. This was no election, no exercise of the will of the people. If it were, then all of mankind would have let the South go with a shout of joy. The election was rigged by Lincoln's agents. That dictator won't be inaugurated next March, he will be crowned king by Stanton and all his toadies. Something must be done before the South suffers a terrible fate."

"But what about all this slavery business. Isn't Lincoln going to free them?"

"Free them? That's a joke. It is well known that the black man is inferior to the white. It is only through his subservience to the white man and his exposure to white culture—the greatest ever seen on earth—that he can rise above his semi-animal state. No, my dear, the Negro race needs slavery to ennoble itself. The South is the only civilization on earth which has chosen to tread that divine path and yet Lincoln has not only freed them, but he has put muskets in their hands so they can kill their white masters and rape white women. He is a monster and must be stopped!"

Ella was taken aback at the vehemence of Booth's speech. He was looking at her with burning eyes and it frightened her a little because he didn't seem to be talking to her. It was as if he were making a case before some elusive ethereal jury.

For a moment Booth stood silent, his hand in the air in a dramatic gesture. He seemed embarrassed for a moment then sat next to Ella on the sofa. She put her arm around his shoulder.

"You shouldn't upset yourself like that, Wilkes," she said softly. "It's not healthy."

"I wish I could go fight like the others," he said. "It would be so easy, but I promised Momma that I wouldn't go fight. Besides," he said looking at her with a soft smile. "What if I were hit in the face? It wouldn't do to have an actor hit in the face. I'd like to be like John Brown."

"John Brown?" Ella couldn't help exclaiming. "He was a damned abolitionist."

"I know, but he was very brave. You know I watched him hang?"

"You did?"

"I was in the Richmond Grays and we guarded the gallows when they hanged him. He was so brave. It probably broke his heart when he found himself deserted. I felt sorry for him."

Ella ran her fingers through his dark curls. "You should really get some rest," she said.

He looked squarely into her eyes. "Ella, what am I going to do? The South is dying and I'm powerless to save her." It was a *crise de coeur*.

She cradled his head on her bosom. "Get some rest, my love."

The National Hotel
November 10, 1864

Anderson waited patiently in the lobby for Booth to appear. He had followed Booth around the city, making sure that no one else was following the actor. Anderson was relieved to discover that no one, other than himself, had an abiding interest in John Wilkes Booth. Booth went to Grover's National Theatre then to Ford's Theatre where he picked up his mail. When Booth returned to the National shortly after lunch, Anderson sat in the lobby and waited. He chose a seat by the window so that if Booth left by another exit, he could see him. Ella Turner had left in the morning and not returned. That meant Booth was alone. Wherever Booth was going to have supper, Anderson was going to be there with him. Patience was one of Anderson's greatest virtues. He would wait for hours in the most uncomfortable circumstances just to get one bit of information that would help him complete a commission. It was this patience and attention to detail that made him the most sought-after assassin in Washington City, and perhaps, the country.

Booth descended the stairs a little past seven and went into the National's dining room. It was more public and well lighted than Anderson would have liked but his disguise had been well chosen and he followed Booth into the dining room. The maitre d' stopped him at the entrance.

"Do you have a reservation, sir."

"Yes," Anderson said. "The name is Demming, Alan Demming."

The waiter checked his list. "Ah yes, Mr. Demming. We have the table you requested."

Anderson had paid the man five dollars to place him next to Booth. Booth was his favorite actor and he wanted to meet him. For five dollars the maitre d' would have placed Mr. Demming next to the Almighty. A mere actor was not a problem.

Booth was obviously distracted because he didn't notice Anderson sit down at the table next to his. Anderson took his copy of the Washington *Daily Star* and threw it down, so that it touched Booth on the leg on its way to the floor. Booth jumped back.

"Oh, sir," Anderson said apologetically. "I am terribly sorry. Please forgive me. This entire business of this election has me so upset. How anyone could say that tyrant won in a fair election is beyond me. You know there must be something wrong when they say that the soldiers voted for him."

Booth looked blankly at Anderson. What he saw was an older man with chin whiskers. "I beg your pardon, sir."

"That gorilla getting reelected."

Booth's eyes narrowed. "A travesty," he said.

"You see. There you are. You and I are perfect strangers and yet we agree that this man must be stopped. There are thousands like us, yet tyranny keeps him in office. It is not right."

"Excuse me, sir," Booth asked. "Do we know each other?"

"I don't believe so," Anderson said extending his hand. "I am Alan Demming. Tanning is my business."

"I am Wilkes Booth," Booth told him as he shook Anderson's hand."

"John Wilkes Booth, the actor?"

"The same."

"Ho, ho. This my lucky night. I honestly thought you were older. I mean no disrespect but the quality of your Richard III bespoke a much more mature man."

"You must be thinking of my brother Edwin, then," Booth said a bit warily.

"No sir, it was you. Your brother speaks an elegant part, but you, sir, bring your characters to life. You have no idea how much your sword play on stage excites me. Am I to understand that you were injured in such work?"

"Twice and only slightly. Would you care to join me, Mr. Demming. I would like to hear your views on our president."

"If it would not be an indisposition, I would be happy to."

"Then, please, join me."

Anderson moved to Booth's table. The waiter came and looked confused until he realized that the two men were now at a single table. Booth ordered a brandy and water and Anderson had whiskey. They both ordered oysters for appetizers. Anderson ordered the roast chicken with greens and Booth ordered beef with potatoes. They agreed to share a bottle of wine.

Anderson barely sipped his whiskey. Booth took a long drink of his brandy.

"I cannot imagine how a man like Lincoln could have been re-elected when you consider what he has done to this country and especially the South. The man is undoubtedly a tyrant with delusions of becoming emperor of this continent. I think he is mad and right-thinking men must do something before he destroys us all."

Booth gazed at Anderson as if hypnotized, then taking a sip of his drink anxiously asked, "Do you really think he is mad?"

"He has made war on God-fearing white Christian people by putting guns in the hands of niggers whose real place is working for their masters. Tell me, sir, am I wrong?"

"No, sir. You are not wrong. I have felt this way for a long time. At times I thought I was the only one."

"There are many of us, Mr. Booth, many. There are hundreds of thousands of honest white people who are determined to right Lincoln's wrongs. They are merely looking for a man of action to show them the way."

"You sound like you're the man, Mr. Demming," Booth said suspiciously.

"You mock me, sir."

"Mock you? How?"

Anderson took his walking stick and struck his leg. There was a hollow wooden sound from the wooden casing strapped to his leg. It sounded as if he were wearing an artificial limb. Booth's mouth drooped open for a second before he blushed and shut it.

"I am sorry, Mr. Demming. I honestly didn't know. Did you lose your leg in the war?"

Booth's entire attitude changed from suspicion to sympathy as Anderson knew it must. Pretending to have an artificial leg not only gained the sympathy of his listener, it also removed him from the requirement to play any physical part in the scheme he had for Booth.

"Fate denied me even that. I lost it in a railroad accident in '58," Anderson said with a touch of pathos. Then he added. "Forgive me, you couldn't have known. It's just that I feel so helpless when something ought to be done. I sometimes wish I could find the right man. Money is certainly not a problem."

Booth looked at him strangely and was about to make a comment when their oysters came. Anderson realized he had lost the moment and was about to turn the conversation back to Lincoln when Booth said, "I'm going to play *Caesar* with my brothers at the end of this month."

"It should be the performance of the century," Anderson said happily. He was wondering if Booth were deliberately changing the subject or if his mind were wandering.

"Yes," Booth said staring off into nowhere. "It must."

Suddenly the actor was back in the present. "Mr. Demming, I unfortunately have business in the city which will occupy my time the next few days and then I must leave, but I will be back on the fourteenth and perhaps we could continue our discussion about the tyrant."

"I'd like that, Mr. Booth."

"My friends call me Wilkes. Alan, isn't it?" Booth said offering his hand.

"Yes, Wilkes," Anderson replied with genuine pleasure as they shook hands.

"Good. I'll see you when I return."

Alan Demming was delighted and so was Anderson. He had planted a seed that had not been rejected. He was to have another meeting with Booth. Anderson also decided that it was time to get a room at the National. Booth normally stayed there, and residence at the National would allow him to keep an eye on the actor without having to justify his presence. There was another reason he needed the room. Alan Demming was just one of many disguises he would need and he couldn't very well tramp through Mrs. Wellman's boarding house at all hours of the night wearing make-up. Even the whiskey-soaked officers in the parlor would eventually notice that. He notified Mrs. Wellman that he had taken a new position with a firm in Baltimore that would require a lot of traveling. Mrs. Wellman's eyes grew wide.

"No, ma'am," he assured her in his most sincere voice. "I have not become a salesman. I am helping them establish an office in Baltimore and I won't be home regularly. I would appreciate it if you would accept my rent two months in advance and hold my room so that I may use it at any time."

At first he thought his stout landlady was going to kiss him when he produced the greenbacks. For her, two months of rent without a person to feed regularly was a windfall. Anderson's base was secured.

The National Hotel
November 10, 1864

On Thursday evening Anderson noticed Booth escorting a lady to his room. She was dark-haired and a little plump, but nonetheless attractive. She carried herself with grace and was obviously no prostitute or actress. He wondered who she was or if she was significant. Ingalls, waiting outside the National, knew exactly who she was and wondered if her presence would overly complicate things. She was Bessie Hale, the daughter of Sen. John P. Hale of New Hampshire. Hale was a Democrat but he was also a friend of Lincoln, and he and his daughter lived at the National. It was a complication the detective could have done without.

On the morning of Friday, November 11, George Ingalls watched John Wilkes Booth get on the morning train to Baltimore. In the three days he had shadowed Booth, the actor did nothing suspicious. He went to Ford's Theatre and collected his mail, then he had a drink at Taltavul's with his theater cronies. The actor contacted no one suspicious. His success with women, Ingalls found, was nothing short of phenomenal, but not suspicious. The only stranger Booth had spoken to was an older businessman with a wooden leg who was also staying at the National. The fact that the man had bribed the maitre d' to get a seat next to the actor was nothing unusual. Booth was a very popular actor. Ingalls, himself, had seen him perform and always enjoyed watching the vigorous young actor. Booth moved around the stage and gave energy to his characters when too many actors just stood in one place and talked. Audiences loved the way Booth animated his characters. Ingalls thought that there were a great many women who would give a lot more than a couple of greenbacks to get a seat next to Booth. The detective watched the train pull out, then left the station. He still had a hunch that Booth was his man. All he could do now was wait.

The National Hotel
Washington City
November 16, 1864

When Booth returned to Washington on Monday, the fourteenth, he went directly to the National to pick up the key to Room 20. Anderson didn't discover that Booth was back until that evening. The first evening was reserved for Ella Turner and the second for Miss Hale. Undoubtedly, Ella knew about Bessie Hale, but said nothing. Bessie, a starry-eyed young woman infatuated with the famous actor, had marriage on the mind. Her father was less than understanding and was doing his best to prevent Bessie from seeing her beloved Wilkes.

Ingalls found out about Booth's return by accident. He was on an errand on Sixth Avenue and saw Ella Turner in a cab heading for the National. He found himself suddenly frustrated by the situation. He would usually have bribed a couple of the colored porters to look out for Booth's arrival except that there was always the chance that they would tell someone that they had been paid. This was not the time to let the actor know he was being watched. At the same time Ingalls didn't know if Booth had any accomplices. He needed to ask Colonel Baker for some assistance. After staying up for nearly thirty-six hours, he decided to ask for help. He went to 217 Pennsylvania Avenue as quickly as possible. It was dark by the time he arrived. Baker, as usual, was working late. Several telegrams were piled on his desk.

"Good evening," he said as Ingalls entered the room.

"Good evening, sir," he said bluntly. "I have a favor to ask."

"What's that?"

"I need two men to help me with the Booth case." This was the first time he had used the word "case" in regard to the actor.

Baker rubbed his eyes tiredly. Then he looked at Ingalls and said sincerely. "I can't give them to you, Ingalls. We do not have enough agents. Many of our people are in Chicago where the Rebels in Canada are planning to free the prisoners in Camp

Douglas and lay waste to the city. At the same time they intend to burn New York City. If that weren't enough, that damned Garfield wants to investigate me, and Chase has asked me to investigate the Treasury.

"Mr. Ingalls, I am not doubting your instincts. I would like to find out myself whether Booth is a menace to the president or a harmless crank, but we just don't have the men. I'm sorry. Perhaps later. Right now I want you to go to bed and get some rest. I may need you to go to New York."

"Thank you, sir." Frustrated, Ingalls left Lafayette Baker's office. For a moment the cold evening air revived him and he thought about going back to the National. He hailed a cab but as soon as he sat in it, the fatigue of the last two days overcame him. Exhausted, he went home to bed.

Anderson was having better luck. Without a superior, who was coordinating the security of the entire nation, Anderson could concentrate on Booth. He was still not sure the actor was the person he was looking for, but he knew he would have to find out soon. That evening Booth honored his promise to see Alan Demming again and came looking for him. Booth knocked on Anderson's door a little after 8:00 P.M.

"I hope I'm not disturbing you, Alan."

"Not at all, Wilkes. Please come in. I took the liberty of getting a bottle of brandy. Would you join me?"

"Yes, thank you."

Anderson poured two glasses of brandy and added water from a pitcher. Booth accepted his and took a drink without any ceremony. He glanced over at the corner where a sample case full of pieces of tanned leather lay open. On the desk were order forms and invoices. Anderson believed in detail. It helped to create and maintain the illusion. The guise of leather merchant was one he had used before and he could talk intelligently about tanning processes and quality of the product. He smiled as Booth's eye caught on the sample case.

"We have some excellent leather," Anderson said.

"Alan," Booth said his name and hesitated. "Alan, I have been thinking about what you said about doing something about Lincoln. You're right."

Anderson feigned mild surprise. "What do you propose we do?" he asked.

Booth smiled. "We're going to capture Lincoln."

"I beg your pardon." This time Anderson did not have to act surprised. He *was* surprised. He was prepared to listen to the plans for an assassination plot, not for a kidnapping.

"I have thought it out completely," Booth said, sounding a bit excited. "I haven't worked out all the details, but we can capture him at the theater when he is in his box. One of us can turn off all the lights which are centrally controlled from a single gas valve. Then, in the dark, we can whisk him away."

Anderson looked at him as if he were hanging on Booth's every word. In fact, he thought kidnapping the president in a theater full of people was one of the most incredibly stupid ideas he had ever heard. He was hardly prepared for the rest.

"Once he is in our hands," Booth continued. "We will take him to Richmond and hold him for the ransom of all the Confederate prisoners in Yankee hands. That will give the South the men it needs to fight Grant at Petersburg."

It was only Anderson's innate ability to sense what other people were thinking and feeling that prevented him from asking Booth if the whole thing were some sort of joke. It obviously wasn't.

"There's one thing more," the actor said.

Anderson wondered what else there could be. Booth had done everything so amateurishly so far that Anderson was out of his depth. As a professional spy and assassin with a mania for secrecy he really could not imagine anything else the actor could do wrong. Booth produced a thick envelope and handed it to Anderson.

"I want history to understand why we are doing this," Booth told him, dramatically.

Anderson read the letter carefully. It was a long missive full of rambling thoughts and trite phrases like "I love peace more than life" and "how I have loved the old flag." It explained Booth's attitudes to the war and slavery and ended, "A Confederate doing his duty on his own responsibility." After reading it Anderson considered Booth a genuine lunatic, but a useful lunatic. Now Anderson knew he had the right man. He reached over and affectionately clasped Booth's forearm.

"You are the man to lead us," he said, his voice hoarse with emotion.

Booth smiled. "I must go. I will be leaving in the morning and will not return until next month. I will send you a telegram before I return."

"God be with you, Wilkes."

"I will give this to my sister for safekeeping," Booth told him.

Neither said a word after that. Booth somewhat embarrassed finished his drink and left. Anderson sat on the sofa and tried to think the matter out. Could Booth be jesting with him? No, he thought not. The actor was serious. But that still led to a great many questions.

—Was Booth capable of organizing and executing such a plot?

—Was Booth in his right mind?

—Could Booth be controlled?

Only time would tell, and Anderson was beginning to wonder just how much time he had. Rumor was that Sherman and his army were moving south from Atlanta.

Washington City
November 19, 1864

Booth left the city on the seventeenth and Ingalls was suddenly without an assignment. Colonel Baker was in New York investigating the Rebel plot to burn the city and there was no one at headquarters to give him any instructions. Tired, confused, and a little angry at being left out of things, Ingalls went home to his rooms on quiet Nineteenth Street north of The Avenue. Ingalls did not live in a boarding house. He did not like them and it would have been ridiculous to pay for meals when he was never there. Instead, he found rooms in the home of Mrs. Evelyn Harriman, a handsome fifty-six-year-old widow whose children were grown and married and who now lived in different parts of the country. Ingalls' rooms were on the second floor and he had a key to the front door so he could come and go at any time. The bedroom and sitting room were comfortable with heavy furniture, Turkish carpets, and floral wallpaper. The rent was only fifteen dollars a month and Ingalls speculated that Mrs. Harriman rented it just to have someone around, because she would occasionally bake cookies for him or invite him to supper. Ingalls never told her what he did, except that he worked in the War Department. He doubted that she would approve if she knew he was one of Baker's men.

Whatever he planned to do was quickly forgotten, because as soon as he arrived home, he stretched out on the bed and fell sound asleep. Ingalls slept well into the next morning and awoke angry with himself for sleeping so late. Fortunately, the rest had done wonders and he was better than he had in days. His mind was clear and he was ready for anything. He took a hot bath and went for a hearty late breakfast before going for a walk. For the first time in months, he could walk freely through a city without pretending to be someone else. He walked the seven blocks to the observatory, enjoying the stroll past well-kept houses and shops. The day was chilly and slightly overcast, but it made no difference. The fact there were armies locked in deadly combat little more than a hundred miles away also made no difference. For the first time in months, George Ingalls felt good. He arrived at the observatory in time to watch the black ball perched high on a flagstaff above the dome take its daily plunge to the bottom of the pole signaling noon. Like everyone else, Ingalls checked his watch. It was a minute fast.

At the moment the ball plunged, George Ingalls, former policeman and former Pinkerton detective, made a momentous decision. It was the kind of decision that makes the world a far better place. It was the sort of decision that many men should make and all too few do. It was a decision that was usually foreign to George Ingalls' nature.

"I'm going to indulge myself," he said out loud. The observatory grounds were nearly deserted and there was no one nearby to hear him and perhaps think him mad.

Ingalls spent the rest of the day strolling about the city. He visited several shops and purchased a new traveling grooming set with comb, hair brush, shaving brush, and razor in a handsome leather case that fastened with two small straps. He bought a new cake of shaving soap, but eschewed the men's cologne. Although Ingalls had spent nearly all his adult life in cities, the farm boy from Pennsylvania still could not understand how men could wear perfume. Along with the grooming set, Ingalls bought a new shirt and two collars. He thought about getting a new suit but wasn't sure he wanted to be that extravagant. He did make it a point to stop at Willard's Hotel for a glass of beer and a late afternoon snack of oysters.

By the time he left Willard's it was after 5:00 P.M. and getting dark. While walking along not watching where he was going, Ingalls bumped into the back of two young women walking in front of him. The shorter, dark-haired one dropped her packages and so did Ingalls. She turned, obviously angry.

"Sir, you should watch where you are going."

Ingalls stooped to pick up the young woman's packages. He was very embarrassed. He handed over her packages and tipped his hat.

"I am very sorry, Miss," he said apologetically. "I wasn't watching where I was going."

He stood to his full height and noticed the women for the first time. They were about twenty. The older of the two was blond and slim. The dark-haired one was about an inch or two shorter than her companion which made her nearly a head shorter than Ingalls. She had nice features and was wearing no rouge or makeup. He could not tell the color of her eyes in the lamplight but they were nicely shaped and looked at him with anything but hostility.

"Accidents do happen," she said in a much softer tone than the first. Her eyes moved away from his reluctantly. "Thank you for retrieving my parcels," she said.

"My pleasure," he said tipping his hat again.

The two of them turned and began walking away. The dark-haired one looked over her shoulder, stopped, and turned. She smiled and said with a touch of a laugh in her voice. "Sir, you forgot your package."

Ingalls looked at his feet. He had forgotten to pick up his grooming set and his shirts. As he picked them up, the dark-haired woman and her friend disappeared in the crowd. On impulse he went after them. He walked quickly in the direction they were going but failed to find them. They probably turned down a street or took a horse car, he thought. He knew one thing, though. He wanted to see the dark-haired one again.

Ingalls took the horse car to Nineteenth Street and walked straight back to his rooms without having supper. He went upstairs and sat in his room. Ingalls was a man of action and had never allowed time for introspection. He applied his intelligence toward the problems of others and rarely gave a thought to his own comfort or feelings. His life had not lacked excitement. He loved the discovery and the chase and the satisfaction of bringing a miscreant to justice. Of course, there had been women. Ingalls liked the fair sex, and he smiled as he thought of those he had known, but they had all occupied a distinctly separate place in his life. The reaction he felt to the dark-haired stranger was something totally different from the momentary distractions other women provided him. It reminded him of his father and mother and the life they spent together raising Ingalls and his brothers and sisters. There was a warmth and tenderness between them that Ingalls, in his adult life, had never known. The feelings these thoughts brought to the surface were not all pleasant. Ingalls found the thought of being responsible for a wife and (why not?) children, scary. Smiling, he thought about her eyes. For once, he was going to use his skills as a detective for his own ends. He was going to find her.

Ingalls searched for two days without finding her, but he had patience and was confident that he could pick up her trail. He felt a bit embarrassed at the term "pick up her trail." She wasn't a criminal but he couldn't think of any other term. He first checked to see if she worked in any of the government offices. He checked lunch places and stood outside the treasury at 6:00 P.M., waiting to see her face in the throng of Treasury Girls at quitting time. He did this two nights in a row without any luck. On the morning of the twenty-second his search was interrupted by a messenger knocking at his door. He tipped the boy and opened the telegram.

November 21, 1863

St. Nicholas Hotel, N.Y. Need you here 10:00 A.M. November 23rd.

BAKER

For the first time in his life Ingalls was reluctant to go on an assignment, but he packed his valise and was soon on his way to the B&O Station. The long train ride home would get him there on the twenty-third.

The St. Nicholas Hotel
New York City
November 23, 1864

It was cold and overcast in New York when Ingalls arrived. Shivering, he was glad he wore his heavy wool coat. He carried his own valise and hired a cab to take him to the hotel. The St. Nicholas, located on Broadway between Broome and Spring Streets, was one of the most luxurious hotels that Ingalls had ever seen. In addition to that, it was a huge place six stories tall, with a thousand beds. Was Colonel Baker finally giving up his rough-and-tumble life to enjoy some of the finer things? Baker was waiting for him in the lobby. There was no hello and there were no pleasantries.

"I have arranged for you to have a room, here, Ingalls. This is one of the hotels the Rebels plan to burn. Our agent, Stidger, has thoroughly infiltrated their organization and gained their confidence. They were going to try to burn the hotels on election day but the Copperheads told them it would ruin McClellan's chances. Now they want to do as much damage as they can. They will strike at 6:00 P.M. on the twenty-fifth, so I want you in the hotel all day on Friday. The safety of the hotel is your first consideration. Capturing the arsonists is the second. We know who all of them are, so they can't get very far. We must be on guard. I will contact you with more instructions if there are any changes. Until then, look around and keep your eyes open.

"Yes, sir."

Ingalls had one of the cheaper rooms on the fourth floor. "Cheap" was a relative term. The room rivaled anything in Willard's Hotel in Washington. The furnishings in the room and the hotel were nothing short of lavish. Every table top and chimney piece was marble, and every carpet was velvet pile. Even the mirrors were in carved frames covered in gold leaf. It was, Ingalls thought, a very comfortable place.

Ingalls ate in a restaurant near the St. Nicholas then went for a stroll. This served to stretch his legs after trying to fit his large frame into a cramped seat on the long train ride. It also helped him become familiar with the neighborhood in case he had to chase a suspect. The activity on Broadway was frenetic. Never had he seen so many hawkers, placard bearers, and street vendors.

Next to this chaos Washington was subdued. He passed a group of gentlemen and he was several steps past when he realized that one of them was Booth. He stopped in front of a store window then gradually made his way closer to the knot of men. They all appeared to be theater people. Ingalls recognized one man other than Booth, Samuel Knapp Chester, a character actor who worked regularly with Booth. Most of the men in the group were laughing good-naturedly.

"Wilkes is going to make us all look pretty silly if his oil investments do make him rich," one of the men said.

"I don't see how it can be worth that much," quipped another. "All it's good for is lamp oil."

"We shall see who will have the last laugh, gentlemen," Booth told them good-naturedly.

At that point the little group broke up, leaving Booth and Chester alone. Booth's affability suddenly ceased.

"I have a better speculation than oil on hand and it will wipe the smiles from their faces," he said menacingly.

"What do you mean, Wilkes?" Chester asked.

"Nothing," Booth said. "I'll tell you later. Let's go. I need a drink."

Ingalls followed the two men as far as he dared, but learned nothing new. He wanted to keep following them, but his orders were explicit and he reluctantly watched Booth and Chester disappear into the crowd. The remarks he just overheard made Ingalls more positive than ever that Booth was planning to kill President Lincoln.

The incident in the St. Nicholas hotel on the night of the twenty-fifth was an anti-climax. A young man in a brown suit and hat walked nervously into the lobby. Ingalls followed him to the back stairs, but was unable to prevent him from removing a small bottle of incendiary mixture from his coat and smashing it on the steps. There were a few reluctant flames which Ingalls smothered with some draperies while the man got away. The rest of the Confederate plot to burn the hotels in New York turned out similarly. It was the same defective incendiary mixture that they used in St. Albans, Vermont, so no fires occurred. The following morning, Baker's men rounded up the arsonists and Ingalls took the train back to Washington City.

CHAPTER 4

Bryantown, Charles County, Maryland
December 1, 1864

WHEN BOOTH LEFT NEW YORK on November 27, he did not return directly to Washington. He took the train to Baltimore, then hired a horse and headed south. The journey took him through Surrattsville to Bryantown in Charles County, Maryland, to reconnoiter the route by which he would take the captured president to Richmond. This was a roundabout route, but it was the safest. The direct road south from Washington to Richmond was heavily patrolled by Union soldiers. The route through Maryland was populated with Southern sympathizers and was used as a highway for Confederate couriers. The actor had used this before to run the blockade with quinine, but he had always been a single man on horseback. He was not sure he would be able to use it for a carriage with a bound prisoner.

Booth had with him a letter of introduction from Patrick Martin in Montreal to Dr. William Queen in Charles County. He was posing as a wealthy man looking for property so he would not be seen as a stranger with no purpose in the area. Booth had not been through the area in over a year and he found to his chagrin that things had changed. Although Confederate couriers still used the route successfully, they were neither as boastful nor as pretentious about their work as they had been. Secessionist opinions and attitudes were not expressed openly, especially to strangers. Lafayette Baker's raids into the area frightened many of the people as his detectives arrested and imprisoned a number of pro-secessionist citizens, many of whom languished in the Old Capitol Prison without trial. Postmasters of questionable loyalty were replaced. Daring Confederate agents, who seemed to lead charmed lives, like the legendary Walt Bowie, were hunted down and killed. In addition to the fear instilled by Baker and his men, there was also the undeniable fact that the South was losing the war and no one wanted to be caught on the losing side.

On the way south Booth stopped off at the tavern in Surrattsville. Even this had changed. It was no longer run by the handsome and pleasant widow Surratt. The proprietor was now John Lloyd. Lloyd was no older than thirty-five or forty, Booth thought, but his face and nose were red from drinking too much and he had bad posture, a combination which made him look much older. His eyes reminded Booth of those of a dog looking for an opening to bite someone when the victim wasn't looking. There were only three others in the tavern and they were all farmers. Nevertheless, he wanted to test the lay of the land without revealing his contacts. There was a way to be a stranger without raising suspicion.

"What can I do for you, mister?" Lloyd asked.

"Some brandy and water and a little information."

"No brandy, and the other depends on what kind of information you're looking for." Lloyd now looked as if he were thinking of running away. He glanced over at the three others in the tavern.

"Whiskey and water, then. My name's Booth, and I'm looking to buy a farm in these parts. I was wondering if you might know of someone offering a nice place for sale."

Lloyd poured a glass about a third full of whiskey and the rest with water. He handed it to Booth and the actor took a small sip. It was cheap whiskey. Lloyd's expression softened.

"Dr. Mudd, I think, is offering his farm for sale. Don't know what he's asking, but he's not far from here. 'Bout twelve, fourteen miles as the crow flies. It's a white house right off the road. You can't miss it."

"Thanks, friend, you've been most kind." Booth paid for his drink and left. He now had a reason for being in the area. He mounted his horse and headed south.

It was late in the afternoon when Booth arrived at the Mudd home. It was a small white house just off the road as Lloyd had described. After his days of farming as a youth, the actor had no desire to be a farmer again, but his experience would be invaluable in convincing people that he had an interest in agriculture. When he knocked, Dr. Mudd answered the door in person. Dr. Samuel Mudd was tall with a pale oval face. His eyes bespoke a person of intelligence. Though not an old man, his head was bald and he wore the type of beard known as an imperial, which added years to his appearance.

"Dr. Mudd, I presume," Booth said, tipping his hat and bowing slightly. "Allow me to introduce myself. I am Wilkes Booth and I am looking for land and horses to purchase in this area. I have a letter of introduction to Dr. Queen of Charles County from Mr. Martin of Montreal. On my way here I was informed that you might also have property for sale."

"That's true, sir. Would you care to come in?"

"I have no wish to disturb you, Doctor. Right now I am just becoming familiar with the area and finding out which gentlemen are interested in selling property. I would like to ask if there is an inn nearby. It's been a long ride."

The doctor smiled pleasantly. "There's an inn in Bryantown run by a man named Harbin about three miles from here. I think you'll find it a decent place."

"Thank you, Doctor." Booth tipped his hat again. "I look forward to calling on you again."

"Thank you, Mr. Booth. It's been a pleasure meeting you."

Booth knew the inn that Mudd spoke of and he knew Harbin, though not well. The Bryantown Inn, like the one in Surrattsville, was a relay station for Confederate couriers, blockade runners, and other smugglers. Booth was pleased. He headed directly for the inn.

Harbin was one of those tavern owners who never forgot anyone. He was a portly man with dark curly hair, a full beard, and a red face. His eyes were blue and pleasant. Harbin always looked as if he'd just heard a good joke. He was a man of strong Southern sympathies and was disturbed by the course of the war. There were several customers in the bar. He smiled when he saw Booth.

"What'll it be, sir?"

"Brandy and water, please," Booth said pleasantly.

Harbin poured a generous helping of brandy into a glass and handed Booth the glass and a small pitcher of water.

"There you are, sir. That will be ten cents," he said out loud for the benefit of the other patrons. "Running quinine?" he asked quietly.

Booth laid ten cents on the bar. "Do you have a room for the night?" Then he added softly, "I have bigger fish to fry. I must speak with you."

Harbin nodded. "Of course." He took a key from a hook behind the bar and handed it to Booth.

The room was small, homely, and uncomfortable compared to the National, but Booth didn't mind. He washed up at the sink then stretched out for a few minutes on the straw-filled mattress. He woke refreshed nearly two hours later and went downstairs for a supper of local beef and sweet potatoes. By the time Booth finished, it was nearly closing time. There were no other customers so Harbin closed the bar and locked the door. The tavern owner poured himself a large whiskey and sat opposite Booth.

"If it isn't quinine, what kind of goods are you running, guns?"

"In a few weeks I will be bringing one man through the lines. He will be the most important goods ever to run the blockade."

"A man?"

Booth hesitated, enhancing the moment of drama. "We are going to capture Lincoln and take him to Richmond and hold him for ransom."

Harbin froze with his glass nearly to his lips. He put it down without taking a sip.

"Lincoln? The Yankee president?"

"The same."

Harbin let out a low whistle and took a large drink of his whiskey. "How do you . . ."

"You don't want to know," Booth said, enjoying the drama of the situation. He continued. "There are enough of us and we are well equipped," Booth told him. "We may have to stop here. May we depend on you?"

"Of course. Anything you want."

"There is one other thing. I need someone who can get us across the river with no questions."

"There's a man in Port Tobacco who is odd, but very dependable. His name is Atzerodt. Mention my name. He will help. When do you plan to do this?"

"I don't know exactly. Right now I'm reconnoitering the area. I'm posing as a man looking for property and horses. I've already met Dr. Mudd and I have a letter of introduction to Dr. Queen. Is there anyone else who has land for sale?"

"Mr. Bowman, I think. I'll show you how to get there."

Booth had a pleasant stay in the area, learning a great deal about the countryside and its inhabitants. Four men wanted to sell him land and horses. These were Mudd, Bowman, Queen, and Queen's son-in-law, Thompson. All these men were Southern in their sympathies, but were very careful about outwardly expressing their pro-Southern opinions. Lafayette Baker had done his job well. Booth spoke with them and had supper several times with Dr. Queen. He even went to church with the Queen family. He was careful not to commit himself to a price in any of his conversations. Early on the tenth of December he left for Baltimore.

Washington City
December 2, 1864

The demise of the conspiracy to destroy New York and Chicago did not mean that Lafayette Baker's secret detectives could look forward to a rest. If the Rebels were finally being brought to bay, there were domestic threats that were nearly as critical. One was the continuing problem at the Treasury and the other was a cotton speculation scandal that involved senators and high-ranking military officers. There was another threat, and that was a threat to Baker personally. He had made many enemies but few friends and now the enemies were mustering their strength. Regardless, Baker pursued his duties as he saw them and was spending a great deal of time away from the capital. Since he trusted Ingalls, he left the detective in Washington to look after things. It did not occur to Baker to establish a chain of command for his organization in order to make it run more smoothly. He was a man of action who did everything himself, never dreaming that, one day, he might become overextended.

With Baker gone there was little for Ingalls to do except routine paperwork. He began, a bit guiltily, to search for the dark-haired woman he had met before he left. The trail was cold but he was determined to pick it up. He had seen her and the blonde heading east on The Avenue near Thirteenth Street. They disappeared quickly from view so they must have taken a horse car. That eliminated anything within the next, say, five streets, he reasoned. So they had to live somewhere east of Eighth Street. That still left a lot of city and he couldn't possibly cover it alone. Even if he could, the odds of his running into her were astronomical. He tried another tack. He had seen her in the late afternoon on a Saturday. Perhaps she and her friend always went to that area on Saturday. It had quite a few shops, so why not? Tomorrow was Saturday and unless there was an emergency, George Ingalls was going to look for the young woman with the pretty eyes and the nice smile.

Saturday, December 3, 1864, was clear and cold. Ingalls left his rooms in the afternoon and went to Willard's. He then began his search from Willard's to Eighth Street and back. After the walk on the way back he was cold and discouraged but decided to try one more time. That was when he saw them. They were getting on a horse car going east. Ingalls bolted for the car and reached it out of breath. The car was so crowded that he couldn't get near the woman without attracting a lot of attention and his resolve failed him. He stayed on the car until they got off on Sixth Street. Now that he had caught his breath his resolve returned.

"Miss," he called from a few feet behind them.

They both turned with looks of uncertainty.

Ingalls tipped his hat and approached them. "Please forgive me," he said. "I'm not sure you remember me. I knocked some parcels out of your hand on The Avenue two weeks ago. I was wondering if you might let me call on you."

The dark-haired girl looked at him in astonishment. "Sir, this is very irregular."

"I know," he said, feeling utterly helpless. "And if there were any other way I would take it. If you would give me your father's name and let me introduce myself, perhaps that would be a way."

"My father's away," she said.

"Oh." Ingalls was crestfallen.

"She lives with my mother and me," the blonde said with a mischievous smile. "Our name is Surratt and we live at 541 H Street. You can ask my mother."

"Anna!" the dark-haired one said.

"Nora, don't be such a ninny," Anna Surratt said.

Ingalls tipped his hat again. "I'm happy to meet you, Nora," he said sincerely. "My name is George Ingalls."

"My name is Honora," she said looking at him. In the dim light he thought her eyes were smiling.

"Honora Fitzpatrick," Anna concluded.

"Will you tell your mother I will call tomorrow evening at 7:30, if its convenient?"

"I'll be sure to tell her."

"Then good evening to you both," he said, tipping his hat the third time with a slight bow.

George Ingalls, detective extraordinaire, walked back up the Avenue. He felt like skipping or jumping high enough to catch a star. He could hardly wait for tomorrow evening. "Nora," he sighed. "What a pretty name."

The two young women continued on their way.

"I don't know that it was such a good idea to tell him who we are, Anna," Nora said.

"Rubbish," Anna said. "If he wanted to do us any harm, why would he have waited two weeks to find you and then ask where you lived?"

"I guess you're right."

"Nora Fitzpatrick, did you or did you not tell me he was handsome?"

Nora sighed. "That I did, Anna. Do you think he'll come?" she added with genuine concern.

Anna laughed good-naturedly at her friend. "I would bet on it."

"I hope you're right. Oh, Anna I've never had a beau. Do you think he's too old?"

Ingalls was not exactly inexperienced where women were concerned. He was a healthy man who enjoyed the company of the opposite sex. Unfortunately his career kept him moving and he was never around long enough to enter any of the social circles in Washington. As a result many of his female companions were not ladies of genteel family, so trying to meet a woman under polite circumstances with parents or family present was not something he was used to. Although excited over the prospect of seeing Nora, he was also concerned about the way she and Mrs. Surratt would react to the fact that he was a secret detective. Ingalls frowned. They probably wouldn't like it. Lafayette Baker was easily the most unpopular man in Washington and his detectives were next on the list. No, he wouldn't tell them the truth — at least not right away, so he decided to tell them he worked in the War Department. That would be enough. Thousands worked in the War Department. If they asked for additional details, he would tell them that he was a clerk in the Telegraph Office. He knew most of the clerks there so it would be a good cover. He felt guilty about not telling Nora the whole truth, but it would have to do.

The Surratt House
541 H Street, Washington City
December 3, 1865

George Ingalls appeared very different as he stood before the Surratt House. He looked splendid in his best suit of dark brown wool with a top hat. To complete the ensemble, he was wearing his new white shirt and collar with a silk cravat. He was quite presentable. His right hand held two bunches of fresh flowers which were very expensive at this time of year, but at this point money was not an object.

The Surratt house was a brick house with an addition. The main and older part had three stories and the addition which was built on the left had only two. A flight of wooden steps led to the front door from the left. Ingalls took a deep breath. When he exhaled his warm breath formed a mist in the cold air. He walked up the steps and knocked at the door. Expecting Anna, Nora, or Anna's mother to answer the door, he was surprised when it was opened by a round-faced young man with a pale complexion and a sparse mustache.

"May I help you?" the young man asked politely.

"I'm," at this point Ingall's voice almost failed him. "My name is George Ingalls. I'm here to call on Mrs. Surratt and Miss Fitzpatrick."

"Oh, please come in," the man said, opening the door wider.

Ingalls removed the top hat and stepped into the house.

The young man looked up at Ingalls, suddenly realizing how tall he was. "I'll get Mrs. Surratt," he said.

When Mrs. Surratt's name was mentioned, Ingalls was seized with panic. Would Mrs. Surratt approve? What would he do if she didn't? He didn't have time to dwell on it as the young man arrived with Nora and an older woman who was about fifty and handsome. Her hair was pulled back from her face and she wore no rouge. Her dress was gray with a plain collar and when she drew near, he noticed that she was nearly a head shorter than he.

"Mr. Ingalls?" she inquired.

"Do I have the pleasure of addressing Mrs. Surratt?" he asked.

"You do, sir." Her tone was neutral, but betrayed her curiosity.

"Thank you for having me in your home, Mrs. Surratt." He handed her one bunch of flowers.

Mary Surratt smiled in surprise. "Thank you, Mr. Ingalls." Then motioning to the young man. "Have you met Mr. Weichmann?" she asked.

"Briefly," Ingalls said. "How do you do, Mr. Weichmann?"

"Happy to make your acquaintance, Mr. Ingalls." Lewis Weichmann's handshake was as bland as his personality.

"Mr. Weichmann is one of our boarders," Mary Surratt explained. "Lewis, will you help the gentleman with his coat?"

The young man stepped up and helped Ingalls with his coat, then hung the detective's hat and coat on an ornate hall tree. During this entire time, Nora stood without saying a word.

"Why don't we sit in the parlor?" Mrs. Surratt said.

Ingalls turned to Nora and handed her the other bunch of flowers. "Miss Fitzpatrick."

"Thank you, Mr. Ingalls."

Weichmann volunteered to put the flowers in water while Mrs. Surratt, Nora, and Ingalls sat in the parlor. Nora and Mrs. Surratt sat on the sofa and Ingalls was offered a chair.

"I don't mind telling you, Mr. Ingalls, that this is highly irregular, but I suppose it's the times."

Mary Surratt tried to sound serious but there was a faint smile which Ingalls, in his attempt to maintain proper decorum, failed to notice. Mary Surratt thought Ingalls' pursuit of Nora very romantic and was pleased to find that Ingalls was, indeed, tall, handsome, and well mannered. It also amused and pleased her that he was ill at ease. She felt his intentions were good and he would be an appropriate escort for Nora.

"I agree, Mrs. Surratt, but this seemed the only way to meet Miss Fitzpatrick." He looked at Nora who looked back and smiled directly at him. His heart sang. He then related the incident with the packages to Mrs. Surratt.

Nora, until this moment, had been left out of the conversation. When there was a brief pause, she leaped into the breech.

"Would you care for a cup of tea, Mr. Ingalls?"

Ingalls hated tea. "Yes, Miss Fitzpatrick, that sounds delightful."

Her eyes shone as she rose to put the kettle on. George Ingalls began to relax. The first hurdle had been overcome and he felt as though a great burden had been lifted from him. For the first time that evening, his smile wasn't forced. Mary Surratt thought it was a nice smile.

Ford's Theatre
December 10, 1864

Nora took Ingalls' arm as they left the theater. "That was wonderful, George," she said. Her voice was light and clear, like a crystal bell.

Nora was wearing a dark blue dress with a white collar. There was a cameo brooch pinned to the collar. Her auburn hair was pulled back with a few ringlets around her ears. The only jewelry she wore were her earrings, which had small garnets in them. Nora had applied lip rouge which made her appear more worldly and even more attractive. Ingalls, used to maneuvering in a throng of people, skillfully wormed his way through the crowd with Nora on his arm. Hailing a cab, he directed it to the National where he had reserved a table. Ingalls would have liked to take Nora to Willard's but he knew it would be crowded and noisy. This evening he wanted a quiet spot to talk, since this was the first time they had together alone.

"Have you lived in Washington City long, Nora?"

"Only a few weeks," she said. "My father is a bank collector and gone a good deal of the time. We were lucky Mrs. Surratt opened her boarding house in October. It's nearly impossible to find decent rooms at a reasonable price."

"I'm glad you did. Are you having a good time?"

"It's truly grand," she said, betraying a touch of an Irish brogue. "You're very nice, George. I still find it hard to believe that you ran after us that way, but I'm happy you did."

The waiter arrived and they ordered fish and potatoes with beer to drink with the meal. Everything was thoroughly pleasant and Ingalls, loving the sound of Nora's voice, let her talk. Her conversation was chatty and revolved around the household she now called home. He smiled at her the entire time, enraptured with her looks and her intelligence. Although much of what she said was small talk, it was the kind of dull information that detectives used daily and he couldn't stop being a detective. But what Nora Fitzpatrick had to say about the Surratts was hardly dull. Mary Surratt's late husband had run a large plantation with slaves as well as a tavern in Surrattsville where he was the postmaster. The plantation was ruined because it fell within the defenses of Washington and could not be worked. Then the slaves ran away and the authorities would not return them. There was a little money, but Mrs. Surratt's husband had drunk it up before he died. Mary Surratt could have made the tavern pay, but her son was a Southern courier and she wanted him out of that line of work so she moved to Washington City and rented the tavern to a man named Lloyd. Like so many widows of limited means, Mary Surratt made a living renting rooms. She ran a respectable place and her son seemed to be staying out of trouble so far.

The evening passed all too quickly and Ingalls found himself next to Nora in a cab on the way home. When they arrived he accompanied her up the steps and she turned to look at him.

"I had a wonderful time, George," she said.

"I did, too. May I call on you again?"

"Yes, I'd be disappointed if you didn't."

He picked up her gloved hand and kissed it.

"George!" She wanted to sound shocked but she laughed softly.

"Next Saturday?"

"Only if you behave."

"I promise."

"Next Saturday, then." She disappeared inside.

Anna Surratt was sitting in the parlor waiting for Nora.

"Did you have a nice time?"

Nora removed her cloak, spinning around as she did so. "He kissed my hand, Anna."

"Be careful, or you'll get swept away."

"Oh, Anna, I hope so."

The National Hotel
Washington City
December 12, 1864

On Monday afternoon Booth returned to Washington and checked into Room 84 of the National Hotel. He had taken the opportunity to visit his sister Asia who was married to the comedian John Clarke. Asia was the one person who loved Booth and whom he loved without question. Clarke did not approve of Booth's secessionist sympathies and refused to talk to him, but the comedian was seldom at home and Booth could see his sister nearly any time he wished. These were precious times for both of them, but even the loving Asia was beginning to worry about her brother's mental well-being.

Ingalls was torn by Booth's return. He was disappointed because the actor's presence would interfere with his courtship of Nora, but he was glad that Booth was back in Washington where he could watch him since he was convinced that Booth had been assigned to assassinate President Lincoln.

Anderson was a patient man, but he didn't like people he couldn't control, so he was relieved when Booth returned to Washington. He wanted to reassure himself that the actor hadn't had a change of heart, after an absence of nearly four weeks, but he found it difficult getting to Booth privately. The actor spent his days wandering around Washington visiting his cronies and his evenings with either Ella Turner or Bessie Hale. Turner didn't worry Anderson as much as Hale. Ella Turner might love Booth but she was probably content with his affections. The senator's daughter was another matter entirely. She could easily interfere with Anderson's plans.

Bessie Hale sat beside Wilkes Booth and ran her fingers through his curly hair. To say that she was smitten by him would be a gross understatement. For a young woman to find a celebrity like Booth fascinating and desirable was not unusual. It was also not unusual for that kind of attraction to lead to a physical relationship. Wilkes Booth had literally fulfilled her most private dreams and the thought of being torn from him worried her even when they were together. Wilkes had always had melancholic moods but he was brooding now more than ever.

"Wilkes, what are you thinking?" she asked girlishly.

The actor turned and smiled at her. "Nothing, really. It's this stupid war. I can't think of anything else. I can't even think about acting. Sometimes I wonder if I'm not going mad the way my father did. They say all the Booths are crazy, you know."

"Why don't we go away, then? We could go to England and forget about the wretched war. You could act there and we could return after it was all over. If it bothers you that much, we should get away." Bessie moved closer and pressed herself against Booth's arm. Just the feel of him close to her was enough to excite her. She wanted to use her body to take his mind off whatever was troubling him. For a moment she thought she had succeeded when he disengaged himself from her and stood up. He walked over to the table and poured a glass half full of brandy, then filled the rest of it with water.

"I have to do something, don't you see?"

"Do something about what?" she asked exasperated. "About the war?" For her, life had two simple alternatives, an exciting existence with her lover Wilkes or a dull one without him. Wars had no place in the scheme of things. "Thousands of men are being killed every day trying to do something about the war. You've already done what you can by running the blockade with quinine. Why do you think you can change things any more than anyone else? No one notices anything about them other than their names on the casualty lists. It's different with you, Wilkes. You're a great talent. The world needs you."

Booth took another swallow of brandy and water. He looked in the glass and watched the alcohol swirl about.

"When I was a boy, an old Gypsy read my palm. She said it was full of trouble and sorrow. Yet, at the same time I would be rich and many would love me, though I would break many hearts. She also told me that I was born under an unlucky star and that I would live a fast and glorious life and come to a bad end. She advised me to become a missionary or a priest to overcome my fate."

Bessie said nothing. She hated talk of war and fate and wanted Wilkes to take her in his arms again.

"Do you know what she told me when I paid her?" He didn't wait for Bessie to answer. "She told me that she was glad she was not a young girl, because she would follow me through the world for my handsome face."

"Superstitious rubbish," Bessie muttered, but Booth didn't hear her.

"I don't know what I would do if Richmond fell," he said. "That thought alone is enough to drive me mad."

The National Hotel
Washington City
December 16, 1864

Booth sat at the bar of the National Hotel. He was in a foul mood as were most Southern sympathizers on that cold, gray Friday evening. Until this evening, the news pouring in from the west had been hopeful. On November 30, Hood and his Army of the Tennessee defeated the Yankees at Franklin then marched north and besieged the Federals in Nashville. It appeared that the gallant Hood of Texas had done the impossible by invading Tennessee, making it seem impossible for Sherman to succeed in Georgia. The siege of Nashville also raised Southern hopes that Grant might be forced to send troops from Petersburg to help Gen. George Thomas who commanded in Nashville. That would relieve the pressure on Lee at Petersburg. There were even rumors that Grant was going to relieve Thomas for his lack of action. For the first time in months there was a bright spot in the newspapers for those with Southern sympathies. On the evening of December 16, those who held out hope for the South suddenly found their hopes mercilessly crushed by the news from Tennessee. On December 15, Thomas came out of his fortifications and attacked Hood's army in overwhelming force. By the evening of the sixteenth Hood's Army of the Tennessee had ceased to exist.

Now nothing remained of the Confederacy except some minor forces across the Mississippi and Lee's Army of Northern Virginia.

Anderson laid a kind hand on Booth's shoulder. The actor looked around and managed a brief smile. "Ah, Alan," he said. He turned to shake the hand of the man he knew as Alan Demming.

"It's good to see you, Wilkes. I fear that Satan has dealt us a terrible blow. This is not a time for the righteous."

Booth made a fist and pounded it on the bar in frustration. "There must be something we can do," he said. "There has to be." He looked directly into Anderson's eyes pleading for an answer. "Isn't there anything that can be done?"

"There is only one man who can alter events now."

"Who? Tell me."

"You already know. The would-be emperor who will anoint himself and place the crown upon his own head the way Napoleon did."

"Lincoln, always Lincoln. How I hate him. It's not because he's an abolitionist. John Brown was an abolitionist, but he was a hero, a real hero. I was in the Richmond Blues when they hanged the poor old man. It must have been terrible for him when he found he had been deserted by those abolitionists in the North." His voice softened in pity for John Brown, but it hardened again. "Lincoln is a tyrant who is choking freedom from these shores. The South needs more troops to fight. If we capture Lincoln then we can exchange him for all the Southern troops now in Northern prisons. With all those men, the South could gain its independence even now." He grasped Anderson's forearm and tightened his grip.

Anderson looked at Booth sympathetically, but he was positive that Booth must be at least partially mad. If it were true that the entire Booth family was touched by melancholia and madness, John Wilkes was undoubtedly suffering from it now. Anderson did not like unstable people. If he had his way he would let the actor stew in his own self-doubt and plan the execution of the president himself, but the contract stated that the assassination of Lincoln had to be blamed on someone whom everyone would accept without question. Unfortunately, Booth was his best possibility. As such, the actor was a double liability. The first was that Anderson had to cajole Booth into performing the act. The second was being around to prevent the actor from doing something stupid and rash before the time to dispose of Lincoln drew nigh. Since Anderson did not believe in either chance or fate, he knew he had to have an alternate plan should the actor not cooperate, but he had to admit that he could not really think of one. It was a problem he would have to solve later.

"Of course, you're right," Anderson said softly. "But it would take the right kind of men. You know, good loyal Southern men. And," he added for emphasis, "considerable cash."

"I can get exactly the kind of men we need," Booth told him. "But why would we need much cash?" He was obviously puzzled.

"You said it yourself," Anderson said, pandering to the actor's ego. "In order to take him we will need a carriage and horses. We will also need provisions and weapons. Then we will have to provide our men with the means to live while we hold them in readiness. Since they must be ready at a moment's notice we surely can't expect them to work as day laborers in order to feed and house themselves. Who knows where they might be at the moment we need them?"

It took a moment for Anderson's words to sink in, then the actor smiled. "Yes, yes, I see." Quickly the smile faded. "I'm afraid I don't have that kind of money, Alan. I haven't acted in a while and my savings are nearly gone. Recently, I found my oil stocks to be worthless. What am I going to do?"

"Please, Wilkes," Anderson said. "I know I am a cripple and cannot be with you to do the deed, but I have considerable means. Allow me to place them at your disposal."

"I couldn't ask you to do that, Alan."

"You didn't ask, I offered. Would you deny a friend the chance to contribute to a deed that will illuminate the corridors of time by its daring?" Anderson removed a thousand dollars from his coat pocket. Booth's eyes opened when he saw the wad of bills thrust toward him. "Take it, please, Wilkes. Don't spurn me."

Booth smiled. "You're right, Alan. It would be a deed that would illuminate history. I would be famous for eternity if I captured that tyrant and restored the South's fortunes. It would not even matter if I died in the attempt. I would be famous."

"You would be one of the world's heroes, Wilkes."

The actor reached tentatively for the money. "I'll pay back every cent," he said sincerely.

"I have no doubt of that, Wilkes," Anderson told him. There was no irony in his voice.

"I will begin assembling the men tomorrow, Alan." Booth's voice was full of determination.

"If they are all like you then I'm sure we do not have to worry about the fate of the South."

Booth left the National on Saturday morning and he headed south again, masquerading as a wealthy man wanting to buy land. He stopped and spoke briefly with Dr. Mudd and the others, then continued his journey south. This time he was determined to set his plan to capture the president in motion. By the time he arrived in Port Tobacco, he decided that this was the route he would use. A light barouche would not be too heavy for the roads.

Booth's plan was simple and he knew it would work. He would have someone turn out the lights in Ford's Theatre when Lincoln was in attendance. Booth and several men would rush into the president's box and manacle him. They would then lower him to the stage and carry him to the back alley where they would put him in the barouche and leave the city via the Navy Yard Bridge. Southern men like Harbin would help along the way. The next problem to solve was in getting across the Potomac. He easily found the man Harbin recommended.

George Atzerodt was in a ramshackle shed practicing his trade of carriage painting. The vehicle was a small phaeton with a dark red body which was up on blocks. The ocher wheels were laid across saw horses. Atzerodt looked up as Booth entered the shed. He was a small man dressed in dirty brown workman's clothes. He had a weasel-like face with small eyes. His expression was devoid of any cunning and he appeared to be a man of limited intelligence. He wore a mustache and chin whiskers.

"Yeah?" he said.

"Mr. Atzerodt?" Booth asked.

"That's me," Atzerodt said, continuing to paint the body of the phaeton. Drops of red paint covered the dirt floor of the shed.

"My name is Booth. Mr. Harbin of Bryantown told me you could do a job for me."

Atzerodt stopped his painting and looked at Booth. "You want to go across, five dollars. With a horse, ten dollars. We go on nights with no moon."

Booth couldn't tell if the man were speaking with an accent, whether he just spoke bad English, or both. Regardless, Atzerodt seriously underestimated his services. Some of the cargoes crossing the Potomac in small boats were worth thousands.

"I don't need to cross immediately, but I must be sure that the boat is ready when I am. Also it must be large enough to carry a barouche. It's very important."

"Carry barouche, no. Boat not big enough."

"How much to get a larger boat? A hundred dollars?" Booth removed five twenty-dollar greenbacks from his wallet. Atzerodt's eyes widened when he saw the money.

"Hundred dollars is plenty," he said, stepping closer.

"I must depend on you, Mr. Atzerodt. You must have this boat ready. I will send word ahead a few days before I need it. You must be ready immediately." The actor thrust the money toward the carriage painter.

Atzerodt took the money and looked at Booth with awe. It was the first time he had ever seen that much money in one place at one time.

"Perhaps we could have a drink to settle our bargain. Besides, I am in need of someone I can count on, Mr. Atzerodt. It would pay well."

"I could use a drink. I work hard," Atzerodt said. "You can count on me." The carriage painter was very conscious of the greenbacks he held tightly in his fist. If this Mr. Booth had this kind of money, he could be very dependable.

On Saturday evening, Ingalls paid a call on Nora again. The night had grown cold and bitter so they stayed at the Surratt house, drank hot cider, and ate cookies. On this evening he saw Lewis Weichmann again and had to watch his tongue. He didn't like the man, but Nora and Anna seemed rather fond of him. Perhaps they consider Lewis "one of the girls," Ingalls thought nastily. The other boarders in the house were the tombstone cutter John Holohan, Olivia Jenkins, and John Surratt. Holohan, his wife Eliza, and their fourteen-year-old daughter lived on the third floor in the front of the house. Olivia was a cousin of Anna's and roomed with her. The boarder Ingalls hardly expected to see was Mary Surratt's son John, the Rebel courier, who was home that evening. Ingalls saw him going up the stairs. John Surratt was slim with dark hair, a moustache, and wispy chin whiskers. They were not introduced. The detective wondered if Surratt had given up his job as a courier in deference to his mother's wishes, and decided he probably hadn't. Nora smiled at Ingalls and passed him the plate of cookies. He smiled back and forgot about John Surratt. With her around it was easy to forget about business.

Savannah, Georgia
December 21, 1865

On Wednesday morning, Gen. William Tecumseh Sherman's army marched into the city. Savannah had defied the Union Navy for three years, but Sherman's men stormed Fort MacCallister, Savannah's only landward defense, and took it in a single rush. The city was taken from behind. Sherman and his jubilant army now looked menacingly north to the Carolinas. Booth knew he had to do something and do it quickly.

Washington City
December 22, 1865

John Wilkes Booth returned to Washington and checked into Room 84 at the National Hotel. Ingalls followed him as closely as he could without becoming obvious. On December 23 Booth entertained a group of men in his hotel. His guests were John Surratt, Lewis Weichmann, and a Dr. Mudd who lived near Surrattsville. Ingalls wished he could get inside the room, but there was no way he could without revealing who he was. After Surratt and the others left, Booth went to see if his friend Alan Demming was in his room. He knocked on Anderson's door.

"Who is it?"

"It's Wilkes, Alan. I have some exciting news."

"Just a moment." Anderson put on his phony wooden leg and limped to the door. "What is it, Wilkes?" he asked, letting the actor into his room.

"I have reconnoitered the route and decided on a plan," he said excitedly.

Booth then went on to relate what he had done. Anderson listened with great enthusiasm as Booth detailed his harebrained scheme. After Booth's glowing account of his plans they sent for drinks. Anderson wondered how he was going to encourage Booth's machinations on one hand and subtly thwart them on the other. There would soon be others that he needed to watch and he and Fitch could not watch them all, which meant they would need helpers. Anderson didn't like helpers. They were, as a rule, unreliable. In spite of the problems, Anderson smiled. This was a most interesting commission.

CHAPTER 5

**National Detective Headquarters
January 2, 1865**

INGALLS NODDED AT JUDGE LAWRENCE as he entered the door of 217 Pennsylvania Avenue. It was bitterly cold outside and it felt good to get into the warm building.

"He's expecting you," Lawrence said. Ingalls was tempted to ask the old man why he always wore a white vest but decided he didn't have time just now. Baker was back in Washington for only a short time and Ingalls needed assistance.

"Ah, Ingalls. Good to see you. The capital seems to have remained quiet in my absence."

"Quiet, yes, restful, no. I'm even more concerned about Booth. He appears to have made a few acquaintances since you went to New York. One of them is a man named Surratt."

"John Surratt?"

"Yes, sir. The very man."

"H-m-m." Baker leaned back in his chair and stroked his beard. "John Surratt, huh? Now there's a puzzle. He's a wily devil. I never learned who he worked for, or even if he's still in the business of crossing the lines. I never arrested him because I wanted to find out who controlled him. His mother is another one I'd like to get something on. While she was running that tavern, that virago harbored every Rebel courier traveling the route. Maybe this time we'll get both of them." He mused with a smile. "All right, I know just the man who can help you in this. Come back tomorrow and meet him."

Ingalls left Baker's office feeling much better about having a partner. With an additional detective, they could easily follow Booth and Surratt and find out what they were up to. The information about Mary Surratt made him uncomfortable. She had invited him into her home and been nice to him. He hoped she no longer had anything to do with Rebel couriers.

The National Hotel

Booth was in an expansive mood. Now that he had decided to capture the man he considered the most evil being in the world, he was busy with his plans. "Busy with his plans" meant boasting of them to Anderson and visiting Ella Turner and an occasional tryst with Bessie Hale. The fact that Booth had accomplices complicated things. At this point there were only Booth and John Surratt. Anderson could watch Booth, and Fitch could watch Surratt. If Booth hired anyone else, Anderson would have to hire additional help, even though he tried his best to avoid it. In the meantime he had to find an alternate plan.

Lafayette Baker's Headquarters
January 3, 1865

Ingalls hurried into the house on 217 Pennsylvania Avenue. He was hoping his new partner was an experienced detective. He didn't feel like breaking in a new man on the job. He said hello to Judge Lawrence and nodded to the colored man sitting outside Colonel Baker's office.

"I need to see Colonel Baker," Ingalls said to Lawrence.

"He's not here. He went back to New York."

"He said he'd get me a new partner."

"He did," Lawrence said, pointing behind Ingalls. "George Ingalls, Clarence Everett."

Ingalls turned around and the colored man stood up and offered his hand. Ingalls took the hand out of habit and his jaw dropped. The man shaking his hand was in his mid-twenties. His hair was cut short and he sported a goatee and mustache. His smile revealed a gold left canine tooth. He was well dressed and was obviously bemused by Ingall's discomfiture.

"I'm pleased to make your acquaintance, Mr. Ingalls," Everett said.

"I . . . er . . . that is . . . uh." Ingalls could not think of a thing to say.

"You didn't expect a colored partner, right?"

Ingalls shook his head not trusting himself to speak.

"I hope there are no objections," Everett said.

Ingalls shook his head again and managed a "no."

"Why don't we get a beer and you can fill me in on the case," Everett suggested.

"Sure," Ingalls agreed.

They left the headquarters and walked down the street to a small tavern. It gave Ingalls time to gather his thoughts. He had been caught totally off guard and he was embarrassed. Everett seemed a nice enough man with considerable presence and a good sense of humor. The fact that he was one of Lafayette Baker's detectives spoke volumes.

At the tavern neither detective ordered alcohol. Ingalls ordered coffee and Everett ordered cider.

"I apologize for my reaction," Ingalls said. "It's just that . . ."

Everett held up his hand. "No offense taken, Mr. Ingalls. You were a lot more polite than some, and downright gracious compared to others." He was smiling warmly as he said it.

"Well, since we're going to be partners, you'd better call me George," Ingalls said with a sincere smile. He offered his hand again.

"Clarence," Everett said as they shook hands.

"Where are you from, Clarence?"

"Baltimore," Everett said. "And although it may be unglamorous these days, I am not a runaway slave. My family has been freemen since before the Revolution. My father owns a grocery in Baltimore. My mother died when I was eight. I have two sisters, both of whom are married. One to a minister and one to a lawyer. My brother helps my father in the grocery business. If you will forgive the pun, I am the black sheep of the family. When they found I wanted to be a policeman, they threw up their hands in horror. Colored people have little use for police, as you can well imagine, but we need colored police just as much as we need colored ministers and lawyers. I went north and was hired in Pittsburgh. When the war started, I heard about Pinkerton and Colonel Baker and decided I wanted to be a detective. Baker hired me on the spot. I've been working for him since '63. How about you?"

"Pennsylvania farm boy," Ingalls said. He gave Everett a quick sketch of his background. "Now let me catch you up on this case."

Ingalls told Everett all he knew so far. The colored man's face lost its grin and he looked at Ingalls with interest. By the time Ingalls finished he was frowning.

"Those stupid bastards," he said. "If they kill Lincoln, they'll kill the only friend they have left. He's the only one I know of that wants to show the South any mercy. If they kill him, they deserve what they get."

"It's going to be tough with just the two of us," Ingalls continued. "Right now it's only Booth and Surratt that I know of, so one can follow Booth and the other Surratt. I would like to have gotten in the hotel, but it's difficult to be unobtrusive when you're my size. It's going to be even more difficult if they get any more men."

"You say Booth usually stays at the National, George?" Everett asked.

"That's right."

"This is one time being colored may be an advantage," he said, a devious grin spreading across his face.

"How so?"

"Most of the waiters and bellboys are colored. If we could get someone to 'hire' me, I could wait on Booth and his friends."

Ingalls looked at him as if he were not sure that the idea was a good one.

"Yas suh, sho' is a nice day, Massa Booth. Would you an' t'otha gennelmen have anotha drink?" Everett said in a genuine serving man's patois.

Ingalls could not suppress his smile. He shook his head. "It's very dangerous, Clarence. If they learn you're a detective, they would probably kill you."

Everett shrugged. "That's what we both get paid for, George."

"Well," Ingalls commented smiling, "I don't think I'm ready for that kind of dedication, so let's not rush it. However, the idea of getting into the National is a good one which we may have to use eventually, but I think it's a little soon for that. Right now we need to see where these two go and with whom they meet. You start with Surratt and I'll start tracking Booth. I'll track him even if he leaves the city. I want you to stay in the city even if Surratt leaves. There are only two of us so one of us has to stay here."

"Where can we meet?"

"Leave any messages with Judge Lawrence at headquarters. I'll do the same. Where do you live?"

Everett gave Ingalls his *carte de visite* with his photograph on the front and his address penciled on the back. It was a rooming house on K Street two blocks from South Capitol. Ingalls gave Everett his card with his address on Nineteenth Street.

The National Hotel
January 4, 1865

Booth paced back and forth in the room while he outlined his plan once again to Anderson.

"I have two men in Baltimore," he said. "Their names are Arnold and O'Laughlin. Both are loyal Confederate veterans and both are skilled in the use of firearms. In Washington City there are David Herold and John Surratt who both know the route. I also have a reliable man in Port Tobacco who knows boats. He will have everything ready to ferry us to Virginia.

"Lincoln will be at Ford's Theatre on the eighteenth of the month to see *Jack Cade*. We will drive to the theater in the carriage and park it in the alley behind the building. Just before the end of the first act, Herold will turn the valve which will shut off all the gas in the theater. O'Laughlin and Arnold will manacle the president and hand him down to me. We will carry him out the back to the carriage and drive south via the Navy Yard Bridge. Herold will arrange for relay horses along the way the weekend before. Once we have Lincoln we can use Harbin's inn at Bryantown to refresh ourselves. After that we will be hailed as heroes for all time."

Once again Anderson shook his head. "I am in awe of your attention to detail in your plans, Wilkes. You have thought of everything. Is there anything I can do?"

Actually Anderson could think of at least a dozen things wrong with the actor's plans. One question he wanted to ask was why Booth's "loyal Confederate veterans" were living in Baltimore instead of fighting with the Confederate army. They sounded like two men who had a belly full of war and had deserted their noble cause. As to the others he would have to see who they were.

"There are a few things I need, Alan. I will need four carbines, four pistols, four knives, and at least one set of manacles for the president. I would like to have them before I return to Baltimore on the tenth of the month. Do you think you can get these things by then?"

"I will try my best, Wilkes. I'm new at this. I hope it can be arranged."

"I'm sure it can, Alan." Booth gave Anderson a condescending smile. Anderson was gratified. Booth was treating him as just another helper. He had been accepted.

"I'll be in contact with you as soon as I procure these items. Good day, Wilkes," he said, limping toward the door.

"Good day, Alan."

Anderson, leaving nothing to chance, limped back to his own room. When he arrived in his room his shoulder was hurting so he rang for a boy to bring him a whiskey while he penciled a quick note for Fitch to come see him immediately. Fitch had taken a room in a small boarding house at 502 Pennsylvania Avenue. It was not a wholesome place since it was between Tiber Creek and the equally polluted City Canal. Yet it was reasonable, and no one questioned an occupant like Fitch.

Fitch, as usual, was prompt. Anderson was pleased when he could smell no liquor on the little man. During a commission he was supposed to stay sober.

"How are your new surroundings, Joseph?" Anderson asked. The question was not merely a sociable one.

Fitch shrugged. "Not bad. You could probably keep someone there a couple of days. Most of the people mind their own business except for one. His name is Whitman and he works as a nurse in the Armory Square Hospital."

"Walt Whitman?"

"I think so."

"He is a poet of some note, I believe, Joseph."

"He may be a poet but he's nosy and I think he's funny."

Fitch wrinkled his nose as if the thought of Whitman reminded him of a bad odor.

"I don't think Mr. Whitman is a problem," Anderson said. Then abruptly changing tack, "I need some guns, knives, and manacles. Make sure they are Army and make sure they are obviously stolen. I need them for our friend, Mr. Booth. Here is the list," he said, giving Fitch a piece of paper.

Fitch looked at the list. "Do you want this all at once?"

"Yes, in a single crate."

Fitch nodded. "When?"

"In a few days. Sunday will be fine. Don't haggle over the price. Booth wants to take these items to Baltimore on Tuesday."

"What are we now, his errand boys?" Fitch asked testily.

"Precisely, Joseph. We are now his trusted confederates, all puns intended."

Fitch snorted, then smiled.

"How much money do you need?" Anderson asked.

"About five hundred dollars should be enough."

Anderson removed five hundred dollars in greenbacks from his wallet and handed it to Fitch. He knew that Fitch would not return all the unused money, but Anderson didn't mind. Fitch was, after all, a thief, and what little he took was worth his services. Fitch raised the list to the brim of his dirty brown hat in salute and left. He knew precisely where to go for the items on the list. It was in Swampoodle.

The shop was in an alley off G Street between North Capital and Delaware. It was run by a fat, bald man in his forties. The man, who had a full beard and wore wire-rimmed spectacles, was known merely as Jake and the faded sign outside said "Jake's Gen'l Merchandise." Jake was a fence, a pawnbroker, and a procurer who drove such hard bargains that he was known to the less charitable members of Swampoodle society as "the Jew" even though it was doubtful that any of Jake's ancestors had ever been Jewish. Jake was one of the elite of the Swampoodle underworld and he could obtain or get rid of anything in the right amount of time for the right price. No one would ever know how many public officials from metropolitan policemen to government clerks supplemented their incomes from Jake's coffers. He was well protected and it was doubtful if anyone who crossed him was still alive. There were only two men whom Jake considered more ruthless than himself. Consequently, they were the only men he feared. One was Lafayette Baker and the other was Anderson.

Jake's store was unlike any stores anywhere. There was no rhyme or reason to the layout of "Jake's Gen'l Merchandise." The store consisted of rows of tables that contained merchandise piled on top of merchandise. On each table were goods as varied as worn shoes and clothes next to boxes of Army lanterns still in unopened boxes. Hanging from the walls and ceiling were harness, horse collars, saws, and other tools. On the end of the shop farthest from the door were several large glass cases filled with watches, rings, and other jewelry that Jake had acquired.

To help him run the store, Jake had the O'Malley brothers. Bob O'Malley, better known as Slim, was the oldest and meanest. At twenty-six, he had already served five years in the penitentiary for bludgeoning a man to death. He was about five feet, six inches tall with a strong frame and broad shoulders. He had black hair, a low forehead with bushy eyebrows over deceptively soft brown eyes. His nose was round and red and his lips were thin. His skin was mottled from too much whisky. His younger brother John favored him except that John had fair skin and was better looking. Both men had beards but no mustaches and they dressed in overalls and cotton shirts. Slim preferred settling disputes with knives except with customers who owed Jake. In those cases pick handles were preferred. John followed his older brother's lead. In addition to their financial duties they also swept up the shop, kept the back room straight, and procured unused military equipment that Jake's customers might require.

Fitch thought little of his surroundings as he walked up the garbage-littered, rutted dirt alley to Jake's establishment. It was barely wide enough for a freight wagon and certainly no better or worse than his own haunts near the Chain and Anchor. Jake smiled as he walked in the door. Jake knew Fitch very well since the grubby little man did a lot of business with him. Like the rest of Swampoodle he knew that Fitch was Anderson's man.

"Good afternoon, Mr. Fitch," Jake's greeting was businesslike and pleasant.

"Hi, Jake. I need some merchandise." He handed Jake the list.

Jake reached for the list, his stubby fingers showing black-rimmed fingernails. He looked at the list through grimy spectacles and frowned. Fitch said nothing. Jake always frowned. It made the customer think things were more difficult than they really were.

"It's for Anderson," Fitch said to remind Jake whom he worked for. Jake forced a smile. He hadn't forgotten.

"When?" Jake asked.

"I'll pick them up Saturday," Fitch told him. "Put it all in a single crate."

Jake nervously wiped his hands on his dirty linen shirt. "Two hundred dollars," he said.

Fitch looked at him and after a moment of dramatic hesitation gave the storekeeper two hundred dollars in greenbacks. Jake didn't count it. He took the money and stuffed it in his pants pocket.

"Saturday," Fitch said as he left.

Washington City
January 7, 1865

Ingalls took Nora to supper at Willard's. She had never been there and she was impressed.

"I don't think I've ever seen a place so grand, George," she said. "Thank you for bringing me."

"Someone as pretty as you should be seen regularly in a place this nice, Nora," he said sincerely. After their first two meetings, Ingalls wondered if his infatuation with her was just a passing fancy, but it wasn't. He found every moment with her precious and all too fleeting.

"How is Mrs. Surratt?" he asked. His concern was genuine, because of her kindness to him. He found it difficult to believe that she was the hard-bitten Confederate sympathizer that Baker said she was.

"Angry as a wet hen at her son, John, I'll tell you," she said tasting the soup.

"Why, what's he done?"

"Well, I suppose I shouldn't say this, but half of Washington must know it by now. One of the reasons Mrs. Surratt moved here was to keep John out of trouble. A couple of weeks ago he got a job at the Adams Express Company starting at ten dollars a week. His mother couldn't have been more pleased. Then, after only a few days, he quits."

"But why?"

"He's back to his old habits, I think. Plus he's been seen in the company of Mr. Booth, the actor. He's a great actor, to be sure, but an actor is not the sort a respectable woman wants her son carousing with. What bothers her most is the way he flashes around his money."

Ingalls froze. This was a priceless piece of information, but it didn't come from an informant. It came from the woman he cared for and she was living in the same house as a man of known Southern sympathies and who was keeping company with a man Ingalls suspected was an assassin. Should he warn her? Professionally, he knew he couldn't. Nora had brought two firsts into his life. She was the first woman he really loved, and this was the first time his professional and private lives had clashed.

"George, are you all right?" she asked, then repeated.

He heard her the second time. "What?"

"You looked as if you were in a trance. Is anything wrong, then?"

"No, I'm sorry. I just remembered something I forgot to do at work." He felt himself blush with the lie.

"Then it's a poor companion I am if I can't keep your mind off the telegraph."

"No," he said reaching across the table for her hand. "It isn't you, and I apologize. You are a most wonderful woman, Nora."

She didn't pull her hand away. It seemed so small and soft in his. Their eyes met and she smiled warmly.

"George," she said, finally withdrawing her hand.

They continued their supper in silence letting their eyes do the talking. When Ingalls drove her home he parked in front of the house. He stepped down and walked to her side of the carriage and held her hand as she stepped down. She seemed to melt into his arms and his lips found hers. They were soft and slightly parted. He held her against him, feeling her body soft and yielding against his. Her arms went around his neck and they kissed for a long time. When she pushed against him, he reluctantly released her.

"I had a wonderful time, George." Her voice was soft and husky. "I'd better go in."

"When can I see you again?"

She stood on her tiptoes and kissed him lightly on the lips. "Whenever you wish." She went quickly up the steps and into the house. He watched her, a big smile on his face. It was everything he could do to keep from shouting.

Ingalls left a note for Everett at headquarters the following morning. On Monday they met at a small tavern on D Street known for its hearty breakfasts. It was a small place with tables crowded in every corner. If the sawdust-covered floor had ever seen a touch of varnish, there was no evidence of it now. The walls were bare plaster covered with white paint that had faded to a dingy tan from kitchen grease and tobacco smoke. The only decoration in the place were prints of racehorses and fighting cocks. There were several photographs of actors, one of whom was Booth. Not far away on the same wall was a bunting-framed picture of Lincoln. Ingalls and Everett arrived after 8:00 A.M. and the morning work crowd had thinned.

"What have you found out, Clarence?" Ingalls inquired over their coffee.

Everett smiled briefly. "Not much. Surratt's a hard man to track. He's in and out of the city constantly. I'll say one thing. For a man out of work, he certainly has plenty of cash for eating in restaurants and renting horses."

"I have some pretty reliable information that Surratt is working for Booth," Ingalls said circumspectly. He was careful not to mention Nora, even though he felt guilty about withholding information from a partner. The less anyone knew about Nora and him, the better.

"That must be why he quit his job at the Adams Express Company," Everett remarked, "He's getting all the money he wants from Booth."

"That's my guess too," Ingalls agreed, "but where is Booth getting it?"

"He's a famous actor. He probably has thousands in the bank," Everett suggested.

"I'm not so sure. I was in Montreal in October. That was when I saw him with the Canadian Cabinet. He didn't seem to have a lot of money then. When I happened upon him in New York he was talking about oil stocks and speculations, but I don't think his investments are that large."

"How much money would it really take?" Everett asked sipping his coffee. "There's only Booth and Surratt. Booth pays his hotel bills and Surratt lives at home. Certainly that isn't much. How much money would it take, a hundred dollars a week?"

"Even if it's only a hundred a week, you have to consider that Booth hasn't worked in months except for the one benefit he did in November of last year. It's needless to speculate. We'll have to make some discreet inquiries at the local banks. Maybe they can tell us what Booth's financial situation is. At the same time we have to keep following Booth and Surratt until we can figure out what they're up to."

The two detectives went their separate ways after breakfast. Ingalls wished he knew a better way to keep tabs on Booth.

The B&0 Railroad Station
Washington City
January 10, 1865

Ingalls listened to Booth tell the ticket agent that he wanted a round-trip ticket to Baltimore. The detective scribbled a note for Everett telling his partner where he was going. He folded it up with a fifty-cent shin plaster, and gave it to one of the boys in the station.

"Take this to 217 Pennsylvania Avenue and tell the man there that this is for Mr. Everett."

"Yes, sir," the young man said with a smile and started on his errand.

Ingalls had just enough time to buy a ticket and get on the train to follow Booth, which was seldom difficult, because the actor never seemed concerned that he might be shadowed. Regardless, Ingalls was careful to look over his own shoulder. If Booth were working for someone else, that someone else might be watching Booth's back. Ingalls got on the car behind Booth's and watched the platform for anyone interested in the actor's movements. The train pulled out and he could see no one.

There wasn't anyone. Anderson left the station before Booth went to the platform, because he had to be circumspect. Most people would not have associated the man leaving the station with Alan Demming, but Booth was not most people. He was used to seeing people in make-up and could usually tell who his compatriots were behind their disguises. Within Booth's sight, Anderson could ill afford to be anyone other than Alan Demming.

Baltimore
January 10, 1865

At the B&O station Booth took a cab to Barnum's Hotel. Ingalls followed, then waited until the actor had time to check in and go to his room. Carefully, the detective entered the hotel and made sure Booth was not in the lobby before he approached the desk.

"Do you have a room free?" he asked.

"We have one on the third floor, sir," the clerk answered pleasantly.

"I'll take it."

"Very well, sir," the clerk said pushing the registration ledger toward him. He indicated the line on which Ingalls was to sign. Above it was the signature "J. W. Booth, rm 104."

Ingalls signed his own name for Room 312, and realized that the clerk was eyeing him with suspicion because he had no luggage.

"Could you please tell me where I might get some toilet articles and a shirt," he said. "The fools in Washington mislaid my bags. I just hope they weren't stolen."

That seemed to mollify the clerk. He nodded sympathetically. "Not surprising in that place," he said. "I have a razor, soap, and brush you can use, Mr. . . . ." he glanced at the register. "Ingalls. There's a haberdasher a few doors down to the right, reasonable prices." He reached under the desk and handed Ingalls the articles.

"Thank you so much." Ingalls tipped the clerk amply, and rushed up the stairs to deposit his toilet articles on the bed. Then he hastened back downstairs. Booth's key was still missing from its hook behind the desk, which meant he was still in his room. Ingalls took a newspaper from the rack and sat in a chair so he could see the desk. He really wanted something to eat, but he couldn't let Booth slip past him. Forty minutes later, John Wilkes Booth came downstairs, handed his key to the desk clerk, and strode out of the Barnum Hotel with a sense of purpose. Ingalls waited a few seconds and followed. He arrived just in time to see Booth leave in a cab, so he hailed a cab himself and told the driver to follow the cab transporting Booth. The actor led Ingalls to one of the less affluent neighborhoods in the city. The buildings were a mixture of brick and wood, and all were dilapidated. The streets were narrow and piled with trash and manure. The cab stopped in front of a boarding house and Booth descended. He paid the driver and the cab drove away. Booth stood in front of the boarding house at 57 North Exeter Street and looked up at it. If ever there were a man who looked out of place, it was John Wilkes Booth. He was elegantly dressed in a dark suit and a black overcoat with a fur collar. The top hat, silver-tipped walking stick, and the gray kid gloves completed the picture of sartorial elegance in this Baltimore slum. Unaware of any inconsistency, Booth strode up the steps and knocked on the door.

The woman who answered the door was gray-haired and painfully thin and her burgundy dress and shawl were threadbare. She had sallow skin and few teeth and her eyes reflected neither curiosity nor hostility, only the dullness of a life of ennui and despair.

Booth, the gentleman, removed his hat. "I am looking for Messrs. Arnold and O'Laughlin," he said.

"Upstairs, second door on the right," the woman said, stepping aside.

Booth was moving quickly up the steps before she closed the door. He knocked loudly on the door the woman had indicated. "Arnold, O'Laughlin," he called.

The door opened slightly and Michael O'Laughlin peered out. O'Laughlin was a small man with black curly hair. He had fine features and was always kidded about his youthful appearance. He was dressed in a clean white shirt, dark tweed trousers, and a striped brown vest.

"Hi, Wilkes," he said with easy familiarity as one would expect of a boyhood friend.

"Is Sam here?" Booth asked.

"Sure," O'Laughlin replied, stepping back from the door. "Come on in."

The room was small and neat. There was one bed, a table with two chairs, and an armoire, all of heavy dark wood. In the corner was a dry sink with a pitcher and basin decorated with a green and pink floral design. Sam Arnold sat in one of the chairs. He was a man of medium height with straight brown hair, a straight forehead, and a nose that was slightly flat. He smiled when Booth walked into the room and rose to greet him.

"Well, how are you boys doing?" Booth asked.

"Real fine, Wilkes," O'Laughlin said.

"I suppose you both have jobs?"

"As a matter of fact we do, Wilkes," Arnold told him. It was the truth.

"I need you both," Booth said. "This is very important."

"Wilkes, is this about kidnapping the president?"

Booth smiled disarmingly. "Look, why don't we go to a tavern and discuss this?" he suggested. He knew that his boyhood friends were more tractable after a few drinks.

Ingalls watched as they left the boarding house and walked down the street to a tavern. Ingalls paid his cab driver to wait and followed once Booth and his companions had gone inside. It was nearly lunchtime and Ingalls was determined to have a meal. The tavern consisted of a bar with no stools and a few tables in the back. Booth and the other two men sat at a corner table with their heads together. Ingalls sat a few tables away and ordered stew with a cup of coffee. He could barely catch bits of their conversation.

"Wilkes," Arnold said. "We can't just get up and leave. You're talking about the eighteenth. That's a little more than a week away."

"Damn it," Booth said. "Don't you understand? The Confederacy needs us. The most noble nation on earth, a nation of genuine chivalry. What would history say if we let her down?"

Arnold and O'Laughlin looked at each other but said nothing. To Wilkes the Confederacy was a utopian ideal. For them it represented three years of bloody war and they wished to distance themselves from it. Nonetheless, Wilkes was an old friend and they owed him something.

"Wilkes, we'd really like to do it, but we can't at such short notice."

"I can't believe you'd let your country down," the actor said with a tinge of anger in his voice. He rose to leave.

"Next time, Wilkes," Arnold said. "Honest."

"There won't be a next time," he said and stalked out.

Ingalls didn't react. These two men didn't want to join Booth and that was interesting, but it didn't tell him much. The stew was greasy, but it was good and Ingalls quickly finished it and the bread that came with it. After a final sip of the bitter coffee, he left thirty-five cents on the table and departed. The cabby was still waiting.

"Did you see a well-dressed man leave the tavern?" Ingalls asked the driver.

"Sure, he caught a cab and went east."

"Follow him."

Booth returned to the hotel and stayed in his room for the rest of the afternoon, depressed at his failure to recruit his friends. That evening he ate in the hotel and stepped outside to get a breath of fresh air and smoke a cigar. To hell with them, he thought. He would capture Lincoln without them and would not have to share the glory with them. He returned to Washington City on the twelfth.

The National Hotel
Washington City
January 17, 1865

Anderson paced his room looking at the clock, needing a solution. Tomorrow evening, Booth and his band of ne'er-do-wells were going to try and kidnap Lincoln at Ford's Theatre during the performance of *Jack Cade*. It was a stupid venture and Anderson smiled when he thought about it. Too bad this was part of his commission. It would be better than a comedy watching them try to abduct the president. Returning to the problem at hand he decided that the indirect approach would be best. He left the hotel as himself and returned to his rooms at Mrs. Wellman's. There, he retrieved his Pinkerton credentials from their secret hiding place in the armoire and penned a note.

January 17, 1865

Col. W. H. Lamon
Dear Sir:

The president is in grave danger if he goes to the theater tomorrow.

A FRIEND.

Anderson sealed the note in an envelope and addressed it to "Col. W. H. Lamon, Provost Marshal, personal and urgent."

Ward Hill Lamon, the city provost marshal, was a good friend of the president and a man deeply concerned for the president's safety. He could be counted on to overreact to any situation. If an anonymous note delivered to the desk sergeant by a Pinkerton didn't work, then Anderson would have to thwart Booth himself even if it meant stopping the kidnapping personally.

Ford's Theatre
January 18, 1865

Ingalls and Everett watched with baited breath as Booth and the others gathered at the Cleaver Stables. There was no sign of guns or other weapons and Ingalls was puzzled.

"I don't like this. Watch them," he told Everett. "But don't do anything unless they get near the president. I'm going for help."

"Don't be too long, George. This is suspicious as hell."

Ingalls mounted his horse and hurried the ten blocks to Ward Lamon's office in the city jail. The building was known to all as the "Blue Jug" because of the faded blue paint in its shabby interior. Lamon, as usual, was working late. A stocky, square-chested man with brown hair and beard, he nodded as Ingalls entered his office. The two men knew each other, but not well. Lamon was a good friend of the president and he was a fanatic about his safety. He often counseled Lincoln to think and act with caution, but the president usually chose to ignore his advice.

"Well, Mr. Ingalls," he said politely. "What sort of trouble brings you here tonight?"

"The president must not go to the theater tonight. He's in grave danger."

"He's not going to the theater tonight," Lamon said.

"What?"

"He's not going," Lamon repeated. "I received an anonymous note yesterday and convinced the president not to go, but it wasn't easy. He only agreed after I told him the note was delivered by a Pinkerton."

"A Pinkerton? Who?" Ingalls knew a great many Pinkertons from his time with the agency.

"Damned if I know," Ward told him. "The note was addressed to me but it wasn't signed. The man who delivered it to the desk sergeant didn't give his name, but he did show him a Pinkerton badge. And you say there is a plot?"

"Yes, if you send some men you can arrest them."

"For what? Being at Ford's Theatre?"

Ingalls said nothing; he just shook his head. "I see your point. Thanks." He left the Blue Jug very confused. An anonymous note? Something didn't wash.

At 7:00 P.M., Booth and his men rode into the F Street alley behind the theater. David Herold drove the hired carriage which would carry the shackled president. Behind the seat was the crate containing the carbines, pistols, knives, and manacles. Surratt, Atzerodt, and Booth rode hired horses. Booth told them all to be quiet, then he and Herold went inside to check the president's box. It was to the upper right of the stage. The partition was removed, making a double box for the president. His rocking chair was there and the bunting was there, but the president was not. They waited through the first act and the president still didn't come.

"They know about us," Herold whispered. He was on the verge of panic. "We have to escape."

Booth looked at him for a moment, then his eyes grew wide. "You're right. We've been discovered. Let's go."

Even in the darkened alley, without being able to see Booth's or Herold's faces, the others sensed something was wrong. Panic seized them. Each hurried to go his own way, leaving Herold to return the horses and carriage. Without inquiring about any of the others, Booth hurried back to the National. Anderson was waiting in the lobby and he didn't like the expression on the actor's face as he rushed in and asked for his key. Booth was pale and he was perspiring. He was so distraught that he raced up the stairs without seeing Anderson or anything else in the lobby. Anderson followed, moving slowly as would any man with an artificial leg. He knocked on the door.

"Wilkes," he called. "It's Alan."

The door opened only a few inches as Booth peered out.

"Alan," he said with undisguised relief and let Anderson into the room. "We've been betrayed. Lincoln wasn't there. I have to leave."

"Betrayed?" Anderson asked, wondering if he himself had been discovered. "Are you sure? Tell me what happened."

"I . . ."

It was then that Anderson realized that the actor was so terror-stricken that he was near mental collapse.

"This has been a terrible blow, dear friend," he said soothingly. He put his arm around Booth and the actor looked him in the eyes seeking some comfort. "Sit down. I'll get you a drink."

Anderson went to the wardrobe where Booth kept his brandy and poured him a generous serving without water. Booth took the glass and gulped it down. For a moment Anderson wondered if it would do any good. Booth sat in the chair, glass in hand, staring at the floor. Neither man said a word. Finally, Booth looked up.

"Thank you, Alan. You're a good friend."

"I hope so, Wilkes. What you need tonight is a good rest. Perhaps what happened this evening was just one of those coincidences, a twist of fate. Remember, Caesar almost didn't go to the senate on his fateful day. We must have resolve and determination not to be dissuaded by a single mishap. You are the only leader we have, Wilkes. It is you who must guide us in this great venture."

Booth seemed to be regaining his composure. He said, "You're right, of course, Alan," but he didn't sound convinced.

Anderson took his glass and refilled it. "Drink this," he said.

Booth drank the brandy straight down.

Anderson took a gamble. "Maybe if you left for a few days, just to be sure that things are quiet. I could watch here for you and let you know."

"Yes, I think I will," Booth mumbled, sitting wearily on the bed. His speech was slightly slurred. The alcohol was taking effect. Booth leaned back on the bed and closed his eyes. Anderson picked up Booth's feet and put them on the bed so he would be more comfortable.

"You must not desert us, Wilkes, you're our only hope," he said out loud.

The actor lay on the bed with his eyes closed. He was sound asleep. Anderson watched him with some satisfaction. He had given Booth enough brandy to knock out a horse to keep the actor from bolting. From this venture, Anderson had learned much about the man he had chosen to take the blame for Lincoln's death. Booth was immature, a bad planner, and he panicked easily. Anderson wondered if the actor were also a coward, but only time would tell that. Anderson took one last look at the sleeping actor. If he judged Booth correctly, money, if nothing else, would bring him back. Nevertheless, Anderson needed an alternate plan and he needed it quickly. He closed the door and left.

When Ingalls returned to Ford's Theatre, Everett was waiting for him.

"What happened?" he asked.

"I don't know," Everett said. "One minute they were here and the next minute they were running like hell. I followed them to Cleaver's stable. They turned in the carriage and horses and split up. I followed Surratt and he went right home. I expect the others did, too. Damnedest bunch of assassins I ever saw. Where's the cavalry?"

"They're not coming because the president is not coming. It seems that yesterday Ward Lamon received an anonymous note that the president was in danger and appealed to Lincoln not to go to the theater tonight. It was delivered by a Pinkerton." His tone was a mixture of frustration and fatigue.

"A Pinkerton? Who was he?"

"Lamon doesn't know, it was delivered to the desk sergeant."

"Are we smelling a rat?" Everett asked.

Ingalls looked at Everett strangely. "What did you say?"

"I asked if we were smelling a rat?"

"That's a curious turn of phrase. What are you thinking, Clarence?"

"Probably the same thing you are, George. For one thing this supposed attempt at assassination looked more like a kidnapping and it bordered on the absurd. Next, we find that last night there was an anonymous note delivered by a Pinkerton, of all people, to the one man who would do something about an anonymous note claiming the president was in danger. This is crazy."

"You're right," Ingalls agreed. "Let's get a beer."

"What about Booth and the others?"

"I guess they panicked when they figured Lincoln wasn't coming. We can't arrest them for being in an alley without any proof. Besides, I'd rather not tip our hand now. Let's give it a rest. Maybe we need to rethink this."

"How?"

"Come on."

"Lead the way."

They mounted their horses and Ingalls led Everett to Thompson's Saloon downstairs from Matthew Brady's Gallery. They tied their horses in front and went in. Thompson's, typical of Washington saloons, had a long bar of highly polished dark wood with a brass rail. Behind the bar was a huge mirror and stacks of glasses between rows of bottles and the floor was tiled. The bar was serviced by three bartenders and a cleaning boy was picking up the spittoons. Even though it was not crowded, the air was filled with smoke. Ingalls and Everett selected a table in the back and ordered two schooners of beer.

"So we both agree something stinks," Everett said. "But what?"

"That's the problem," Ingalls said, taking a sip of the foam at the top of the glass.

"What do we have?"

"Not much. I saw Booth in Montreal. Since then he hasn't done any acting except for one night in New York. He has been going back and forth to New York and Baltimore. He even went south a couple of times according to some loyal men who saw him in Maryland. He obviously controls a number of men and tonight they park a carriage behind Ford's Theatre. Then, without reason, they flee. None of it makes sense."

Everett looked at him. "You're right. None of it makes sense."

They discussed the affair further, but they found they were going in circles. They finished their beers and went home to rest.

The following morning Booth left Washington for a few days. Herold stayed at home with his mother and sisters. John Surratt went to Baltimore on the twenty-first but was back in Washington on the twenty-fifth.

On Saturday, January 28, Ingalls took Nora to the matinee at the Canterbury Theatre. Matinees were not as rowdy or as lewd as the night shows so they were respectable. Nora enjoyed herself and they had an early supper at Willard's. They returned to Mrs. Surratt's boarding house a little after 6:00 P.M., then sat in the parlor and talked while Mrs. Surratt made cookies. A little after seven Louis Weichmann entered the boarding house and came over to where Ingalls and Nora were sitting. He put out his hand.

"Nice to see you again, Mr. Ingalls."

Ingalls shook the pudgy hand. "Nice to see you, too, Mr. Weichmann," he said as pleasantly as possible. He had the sinking feeling that Weichmann wanted to join them.

"I'll be right back," Weichmann said pleasantly.

Nora smiled and shrugged then she leaned closer to Ingalls and whispered in his ear. "Come with me."

She took his hand and they went to the back of the kitchen to a store room with shelves of boxes and hams hanging from the ceiling. Before he realized what was happening her arms were around his neck and they were kissing. Their first kiss lasted a long time. When it was over he felt warm and she was trembling.

"I've missed you so much, George, dear."

"I've missed you, too, Nora."

He kissed her again.

CHAPTER 6

Barnum's Hotel, Baltimore, Maryland
February 6, 1865

ALTHOUGH JOHN WILKES BOOTH knew the only place that he would be safe from swift retribution by Lafayette Baker and his men was Richmond, he did not go there. He went to New York to see friends, then to Philadelphia to see his sister, and finally to Baltimore. It had been three weeks since the fiasco at Ford's Theatre, and no one had followed him or tried to arrest him. He read every newspaper he could get his hands on and he could find no mention of his attempt to capture Lincoln. Most men would have breathed a sigh of relief and forgotten the entire affair, but John Wilkes Booth was no ordinary man. He had dared the impossible and come within an ace of restoring the fortunes of the Confederacy. Now he was angry. It was not that he had failed in a worthwhile undertaking. Sometimes fate ruled against even the greatest of men and they failed in their most daring adventures. What John Wilkes Booth could not abide was that no one had noticed!

The actor paced like a lion in a cage. By not capturing the Yankee president, he had failed to achieve the two most important goals in his life: the salvation of the Confederacy and the immortalization of his name as the architect of the bold and daring act that did the deed. After a few minutes of soul searching, the panic of January 18 was completely forgotten, and Booth was now, more that ever, determined to try again. This time he would leave nothing to chance. He needed men who were more reliable than his current band, and more of them. They would be well armed and drilled to perfection in the necessary tasks required before the next attempt to capture the enemy president.

With renewed dedication to his cause Booth felt much better and decided to go to the bar for a drink. He picked up his wallet to put it in his coat and opened it. He had less than $150 of the money Alan Demming had given him. That was close to everything he had in the world. He wondered if Demming could be relied upon again. Why not? The old cripple seemed to have plenty of money and he was dedicated to the cause. That was the one thing that made Booth feel guilty about taking Demming's money. If the leather merchant had been just another Northern moneybags, Booth would have taken the money and spent it without a thought, but Demming was a true Southerner and it would be wrong to take his money under false pretenses. Booth decided to wire Demming the next morning and went downstairs to have a brandy.

After his brandy, Booth left the hotel to get a breath of air. He was standing on the steps when he saw the man. He was tall and young and powerfully built, but he was bent low in a pitiable attitude. Perhaps it was the sheer size of the man, but Booth recognized him instantly even though they had only met briefly in Richmond nearly four years before.

"Payne, Lewis Payne," he called.

The man looked up in amazement. "Mr. Booth?"

Booth descended the steps and took Payne by the arm. "My dear fellow, what on earth has happened to you?"

Payne, unshaved and in a battered hat and shabby gray overcoat, looked at Booth with a worshipful expression. It was the same expression Booth had seen the first time he met Payne. Payne came from a good Floridian family and had enlisted early in the Confederate army. Just before the outbreak of hostilities, his regiment was sent to Virginia. In Richmond the young and impressionable Payne saw his first play. The star was John Wilkes Booth. Payne was astounded by the performance and afterwards made his way backstage to meet the actor who had so delighted him. Booth was charmed by the large young man's naivete and spoke with him at length in his dressing room. The simple soldier was impressed by the actor's polished manners and elegant dress. The actor was impressed by the soldier's sheer physical size and strength.

Payne briefly recounted his experiences since he and Booth had last met. He had been both an infantryman and one of Mosby's Rangers, but after three years of war, he was tired and suffering from melancholia. He made his way north, took a new name, and signed the oath of allegiance.

"Now I am known as Lewis Powell," he said. "To tell the truth, Mr. Booth," he added pathetically, "I need bread. I'm starving."

"Look, Payne, or rather Powell, I need a man such as yourself to help me in a great undertaking." Booth reached into his wallet and pulled out fifty dollars in greenbacks. "Take this money, get yourself something to eat and some new clothes. Come see me in a few days. I am here at Barnum's."

Payne gratefully accepted the money. His worshipful expression now included sincere gratitude. When Booth called his name he had hoped perhaps for a small handout. Instead the actor whom he admired had become his benefactor. He agreed to see Booth as soon as he got cleaned up. Booth watched Payne hurry down the street toward the nearest eating establishment and the actor smiled. The meeting with Payne was a good omen. Booth, convinced he had another follower—and one who would not question his orders or motives— pulled out a cigar, put it to his lips, and struck a match. He rolled the cigar in the flame until it was glowing evenly and took a satisfying draw of the smoke. Yes, things would go differently this time.

The National Hotel
Washington City
February 7, 1865

Anderson returned to the National shortly after six in the evening. He had not heard from Booth in nearly three weeks and he was beginning to worry. Had all his cajoling gone for naught? As soon as the clerk at the desk handed him the telegram, he opened it.

Barnum's Hotel
February 7, 1865

I have begun again and once more need your able assistance.

J. W. BOOTH

Anderson smiled when he read the wire. Booth was broke and needed more of Alan Demming's money. Anderson had judged Booth well. George Bunker, the clerk at the desk, was taken with Anderson's smile. He had never seen Demming this pleased.

"Good news, Mr. Demming?" Bunker asked.

"Yes, Mr. Bunker, thank you," Anderson replied. "I need to send a wire."

"Of course, Mr. Demming," Bunker said handing Anderson a pencil and a form.

Your news wonderful. Will meet you tomorrow afternoon at Barnum's.

A. DEMMING

Anderson gave the form to Bunker who looked at it.

"Are you leaving, Mr. Demming?"

"Only for a day or two," Anderson replied. "Please hold my room, and I need a boy to go for a train ticket."

"Certainly, sir," Bunker said with a slight bow. He picked up a bell on the desk and rang it twice. A boy of about ten or twelve dressed in the hotel livery came up and looked at Bunker. The clerk nodded at Anderson.

Anderson pulled a ten-dollar greenback from his wallet. "I want a round-trip ticket to Baltimore for tomorrow morning."

The boy took the money and left. Anderson knew the errand would be done swiftly. He had the reputation of tipping well if something were done to his satisfaction.

Baltimore
February 8, 1865

Anderson was more than pleased with Booth's attitude when he saw him at Barnum's. Booth was intent on repeating the same sort of stupid scheme that had gone awry in January, and that was fine.

He needed Booth and as long as the actor was involved in his harebrained plots he seemed happy.

"You don't know how happy I was to get your wire, Wilkes," Anderson said seriously. "I must apologize."

"Apologize, Alan, why?"

"Forgive me, my friend, but when you left Washington in January I thought you had . . . well . . . I thought you had deserted the cause. I'm sorry."

Booth smiled warmly and put his arm around Anderson's shoulders. "No need to apologize, dear friend. I must admit I was faint of heart, but I have learned my lesson. I was too amateurish in the last attempt, so it is I who must apologize. This time I will have more men. Not only that but they will be more determined than those of faint heart I had last time, and they will also be better equipped. This time we will not fail."

"If anyone can do what needs to be done, it is you, Wilkes." Anderson reached inside his coat and withdrew an envelope. "Do not hesitate to ask for anything you need," he said, handing the envelope to Booth.

Booth took the envelope and looked inside. He flipped through the notes and discovered it contained two thousand dollars in greenbacks. He smiled. "Have no fear, Alan, this will be put to good use."

Anderson and Booth had supper together and the actor told him about the fortuitous meeting with Payne, then Anderson excused himself. He pleaded fatigue and the need to return to Washington as soon as possible in the morning. When Booth went for breakfast the following morning, he found that Alan Demming had already left. Had Booth been a suspicious man, he would have inquired as to precisely when Demming left and where he had gone. Had he so inquired, he would have found that Demming had left the hotel at 7:30 A.M. and that he had taken a cab to the station. There the ticket agent would have confirmed that a man of Demming's description had waited in the station and had gone to the platform when the train for Washington arrived from Philadelphia. From these facts one would deduce that Demming had taken the morning train to Washington. He had not. Anderson had, in fact, gone to the station and waited, but instead of going to the platform he went outside and hailed a cab.

He took the cab to a hotel that was less pretentious than Barnum's where he removed his make-up and false wooden leg and changed his clothes. At a nearby stable Anderson hired a horse and was waiting a few doors down the street from Barnum's when Booth emerged. This time he was going to learn as much about Mr. Booth's business as he possibly could.

Booth had no idea he was being followed as he rode a cab to N. Exeter Street to see Arnold and O'Laughlin. The same thin woman answered the door and nodded when he asked for O'Laughlin. He went upstairs and knocked on the door. His friend was surprised to see him.

"Wilkes, what are you doing here?"

"I have a job for you and Sam to do," Booth said walking into the room.

"Wilkes, I told you I already have a job."

"Then why don't you work for me? I'll pay you twenty dollars a week plus your room and board. What do you say?"

O'Laughlin looked at Booth apprehensively, wondering if the actor were going crazy like his father did. Nevertheless he smiled. Twenty dollars a week with room and board was certainly a lot more than he was making right now, and he doubted Booth's scheme would amount to much anyway.

"All right, Wilkes. When do we start?"

"Right away. I want you to come with me and help me buy a carriage, horses, and harness. Then I want you and Sam to drive it to Washington where I'll make arrangements for you to stay. There you must remain in readiness to execute the plan any time I call, and that means staying sober, understand?"

"Of course, Wilkes, whatever you say."

"Oh," Booth said, reaching for his wallet. "Here's something to help you get started." He handed O'Laughlin fifty dollars. "Let's go."

Anderson watched as Booth emerged from the shabby boarding house with a small man with dark curly hair. This must be either O'Laughlin or Arnold, the men Booth told him about, Anderson thought. He followed them to a house on High Street where they met another man who obviously knew both the actor and the other man. This had to be the second of the pair. The three men then went to a carriage maker, purchased a barouche, and then procured harness and a pair of horses. When they split up Anderson followed Booth. The actor returned to Barnum's where he met a young man who was tall and powerfully built. This was undoubtedly Payne.

Washington City
February 15, 1865

It was a cold afternoon but neither Ingalls nor Nora noticed. They hired a carriage and drove east on Maryland Avenue past Flynn and the Olivet Cemetery. Ingalls' brain was in turmoil wondering where Booth was and what the actor might try next. Ingalls suspected that the actor had returned to Canada for more money since investigation showed that Booth's oil investments were worthless and his bank accounts amounted to a few hundred dollars. The Canadian Cabinet was the only place Booth could get any money when he wasn't acting, but Montgomery could find no evidence of money going to Booth. Clarence Everett was busy following John Surratt who was at home doing nothing suspicious. Whatever happened, the detective had a strange foreboding that he would have to face the crisis alone. Baker was back in New York investigating the enlistment brokers who were bilking the government for millions by charging for false and double enlistments. Sometimes, they would have a man collect the bounty for several different regiments and collect a percentage for covering the man's tracks. Sometimes they used men they knew could not pass a physical, but collected the bounty anyway. With bounties as high as three hundred dollars, a man could make a tidy sum in a short period of time. As with the cotton scandal, many in high office were being paid to look the other way. Baker would not.

Past Flynn the vista turned abruptly from city to pasture and farmland. The countryside was open rolling terrain with white farm houses and rail fences. The fields were brown instead of green and the trees were bare but the air was clean and quiet, a far cry from the great city they had just left. Ingalls' mind gradually left the problems of the capital and in a short time the only thing that mattered was the lovely young woman beside him holding his arm.

"Are you cold, Nora?" he asked.

"Not here with you, George," she said. She smiled at him and leaned her head against his shoulder. "I am perfectly content."

They said little, looking at each other often and smiling, happy just to be in each other's company. A short way beyond the cemetery, Ingalls pulled the carriage off the road and stopped.

"Where are you going, George?" Nora asked.

"Just giving the horse a rest," he said, turning to her.

"George Ingalls," Nora said with a smile. "You are a devil. I don't believe a girl is safe with you."

At first he wondered if she weren't half serious, but her lips were already parted when his mouth covered hers. She was no longer content just to be kissed. Her fingers ran through Ingall's hair and she sought his mouth with hers. The road was deserted and they stayed there lost in each other until Nora, flushed and breathless, asked him to take her back.

The setting sun painted a buttermilk sky that turned to red and violet as they drove back. It was a perfect view for lovers, and Ingalls wondered if it were the right time to tell her what he really did. He was sure he wanted to marry her and he wanted her to know everything about him before he asked her. He smiled to himself as she dozed against his shoulder. He had faced dangerous men armed with knives and guns, but he was afraid to tell the woman he loved that he was a detective.

Columbia, South Carolina
February 17, 1865

The citizens of Columbia stared out from behind their drawn curtains. A brisk wind was whirling the smoke from thousands of smoldering bales of cotton that Wade Hampton's retreating troops had tried to torch as they withdrew that morning. Gen. John A. "Black Jack" Logan's blue-coated soldiers marched jauntily in formation up the main street. These were Sherman's men. These were the men who had supposedly been defeated before Atlanta. These were the men who were predicted to perish when they were cut off without hope in Georgia. These were the men whom the papers from Atlanta to Richmond had reported killed on a daily basis—and they were here in Columbia. It was not a pretty army, their uniforms were worn and patched, and they were lean with marching. Their beards were long, their faces were tanned and leathery, and their eyes were clear. There was a jauntiness in their step that Confederate soldiers had lost months before. They were an army that had left the parade field to fight the enemy in his own country and they were, to a man, happy to be there.

The eyes behind the curtains filled with tears. Many had believed the reports about Sherman's destruction and now they realized that they had been lied to. Others knew that this was the antichrist come to punish them for their sins, for surely if Yankees were in the capital of South Carolina, the world must be coming to an end. Some citizens, not content to sit idly by, tried to mollify the Yankees by bringing out buckets of whiskey and dippers. Too many soldiers drank too much and discipline broke down. A drunken frenzy of looting broke out and by 8:00 P.M. large fires whipped by a strong wind swept through the city. Neither the looters nor the fires could be stopped. Thousands of Union troops risked their lives to stop the fire while dozens of looters were shot down by their comrades. In the morning the center of the city lay in smoldering ruins and thousands were left homeless. Unmoved by the destruction, the conqueror ordered his army to move north. What was one more senseless tragedy in the midst of an even greater senseless tragedy? There were more to come.

Washington City
February 23, 1865

Booth was back in Washington and while Anderson was pleased, it meant that he had to keep the actor in the city if he possibly could. Wilmington, North Carolina, the Confederacy's last viable port, fell on the twenty-second and the war was drawing rapidly to a close. The only major forces left to that benighted nation were the Army of Northern Virginia and a few troops trying to stop Sherman in the Carolinas. Anderson now had to prepare Booth to kill Lincoln, though he doubted the actor would have the stomach for it. If he were crazy like his father, it was a brooding melancholia rather than a dangerous fanaticism. To add to his troubles, Booth now had several men which had to be watched.

Anderson had to hire men to shadow them. It was a good job for Fitch.

"Joseph, we are going to have to hire some talent to watch Booth's men while they are in the city. I want reliable men who look like they belong on The Avenue, not in Swampoodle. We will need four. And tell them to keep their hands out of other people's pockets while they're working for me."

Fitch nodded in understanding.

"One will have to watch O'Laughlin and Arnold; one will have to watch Surratt; one will have to watch Payne; and one will have to watch Atzerodt. I want you to concentrate on Herold. He seems to be Booth's most dedicated henchman. I originally thought it was Surratt, but I don't think Surratt is really taking this very seriously. I will, of course, watch Booth since he considers me his friend. Now hurry up."

"Yes, Mr. Anderson," Fitch said with a slight smile. He enjoyed the preparation and the watching prior to the act. "I'll need some money."

"Use the money left over from Jake's," Anderson told him and the smile left Fitch's face. "I don't forget details, Joseph. You must remember that."

Fitch nodded in resignation and left. His destination was a tavern four blocks north of Jake's in Swampoodle. The tavern was known as Pointer's. Although Mr. Pointer was dead, it was run by his widow, a stout woman in her fifties who hid the gray in her hair with henna. She had a passion for red and purple dresses, feather bonnets, and strong young men. Pointer's did not cater to soldiers, or citizens of the city who were looking for the delights that Swampoodle offered to visitors. Pointer's clientele were the elite of Washington's criminal class. As with lawful society, the Washington underworld had its gradations. There were many taverns similar to the Chain and Anchor which catered to toughs. Some catered to burglars and some to murderers. Human beings, regardless of their profession, always seek those with similar interests. Pointer's was the watering hole of pickpockets and confidence men and women, since crime has never barred ladies from demonstrating their skill in separating a sucker from his money. While nowhere as luxurious as Willard's, it was not the kind of shanty usually found in Swampoodle. It had originally been a house that was painted bright red. The color had faded to a dull, dirt-streaked brown. Outside it had a porch. Inside it had wooden floors and paneling halfway up the walls, which were painted a light blue and covered with mirrors and framed prints. The downstairs was dominated by a long bar with tables scattered in front of it. To the left of the bar were the stairs to the upper stories where Pointer's patrons could satisfy their various appetites. The ladies and gentlemen in the bar would not have been out of place in Willard's or the National. They were all well dressed and genteel. Many had been in some of the most famous ballrooms and drawing rooms in the city. All of them looked up when Fitch entered the room and stopped talking. The small shabby man was out of place in Pointer's and had he not been Anderson's subordinate, he would have been asked to leave. The specialties of the denizens of Pointer's were slight of hand and persuasion. They preferred to avoid violence, but none of them dared to say no to Anderson. Fitch walked up to the bar and ordered a glass of beer. Clem, the bartender, was a thin old man with a bald head and a full beard. His eyes never betrayed any emotion and he had a reputation for silence. He poured Fitch a mug of beer and passed it across the scratched surface of the bar without saying a word.

"I'm looking for Eddy the Sneak," Fitch said sipping the frothy brew.

"He's upstairs," Clem nodded in the direction of the stairs.

"With the nigger whore?" Fitch asked. Eddy was fond of a mulatto prostitute named Jasmine. The bartender said nothing.

Fitch drained the glass, set it on the bar, and walked up the worn oak staircase. Jasmine's room was the first door on the third floor. Fitch politely knocked.

"Who's there?" asked a man's voice.

"It's Fitch."

After a pause, Eddy opened the door about four inches and looked out. "I'll meet you downstairs in about five minutes. Have a beer on me."

Fitch smiled and tipped his hat. "I am yours to command," he said in a genuine attempt at humor.

Charles Wooding, alias Eddy the Sneak, was one of the most artful pickpockets that Swampoodle had ever produced. Always elegantly dressed, he was a man of good looks and exquisite manners. With his dark wavy hair and blue eyes, ladies found him irresistible, which made them easy victims. His area of work was The Avenue, and it was said that Eddy could steal from a woman's purse while tipping his hat to her. One of his favorite places was the Treasury on payday. What made Eddy a successful pickpocket was that he had a sixth sense about his victims and never over-worked an area. He came downstairs wearing his trousers, shirt, and vest, crossed with a heavy gold watch chain. The chain be-longed to a large railroad man's watch which he had "acquired" and decided to keep. He wore no cravat and on his feet were car-pet slippers. He walked over to Fitch's table and sat down looking decidedly unhappy.

"How are you, Eddy?" Fitch asked.

"What's this about, Fitch?"

"Is that the way to talk to an old friend, Eddy?"

"We were partners once, Fitch, but then you got a new partner and you know what I think about him."

"That's not very kind, Eddy. Mr. Anderson would be disturbed to find that you disapprove of him."

"Hah," Eddy said contemptuously. "Anderson doesn't care what I think. He only kills people others pay him to kill so don't try to frighten me with Anderson. What does he want this time?"

"He wants four people followed. I assume you can get the men," Fitch paused. "Or the women to do the job."

"Yes. The price?"

"The usual, $500 a month for you and $250 for the people you hire, and the usual stipulation. No picking pockets or doing 'sells' while you work for Mr. Anderson."

"As if I had a choice," Eddy said.

"You don't," Fitch said candidly. "Besides, you couldn't make that kind of money putting the touch on government girls anyway. Now, how about a drink for old times' sake? You haven't been the same since you met up with that nigger whore."

Eddy looked him with contempt and dropped ten cents on the table. "Buy your own damned drink," Eddy said. He got up and walked back to the stairs.

Fitch thought Eddy's attitude was very funny and laughed. With the ten cents, he bought a beer.

The National Hotel
Washington City
February 28, 1865

Clarence Everett stood on the southeast corner of The Avenue and Sixth Street in front of Brown's Hotel across from the National. He looked like any one of dozens of people going about their business on a damp, overcast Washington morning. With a copy of the *National Daily Intelligencer* rolled up and held under his arm while he lighted a cigar, he could have been waiting for a horse car. But, like so many adept detectives, he was watching the two men who stood between the two double columns at the front of the National Hotel. One was John Wilkes Booth. The other was John Surratt. Both were talking animatedly and Everett wished he could get close enough to hear what they were saying. Ingalls was inside the hotel in the lobby also trying to be inconspicuous. Everett considered walking across the street and going into the National, and weighed the pros and cons. With Booth's attitude toward colored people, he couldn't conceive that one might be a detective. Everett decided it was worth it and stepped into the muddy street, but before he could take a second step, Booth and Surratt ended their conversation. Booth handed Surratt an envelope, then the younger man nodded and left, walking north on Sixth. So, Surratt had been paid and Everett had a pretty good idea where he was going and that was up the street to Gardiner's Stable to pay for the horses that Booth boarded there. After two weeks, Everett knew Surratt's every move and decided the man was either very stupid or didn't care about being followed because he never tried to cover his trail. The detective was making his way across the street, avoiding the mudholes like every other pedestrian, when he noticed the well-dressed man by the lamppost on the corner glance at Surratt. He had dark wavy hair and was easily a dandy. The gold chain across his vest was conspicuous. What made this dandy so interesting was that he was unobtrusively interested in Surratt. Everett froze in the middle of the street. Was he imagining things? Was someone else following Surratt? Surratt passed the dandy and he didn't move. For a split second Everett thought he was wrong, then the dandy turned and began following John Surratt at a discreet distance. Everett began following the dandy, wondering why he was following Surratt.

The dandy followed Surratt to the stable where the young man paid Gardiner. Then began a long, uneventful day as the dandy followed Surratt around the city as the young man did a few errands and stopped for an early lunch. After lunch, Surratt made a visit to the telegraph office on Newspaper Row on Fourteenth Street. The dandy was obviously accustomed to following people. He maintained a discreet distance from Booth's subordinate and Surratt never realized he was being followed. Unfortunately, the dandy made one mistake. He was so intent on being inconspicuous around Surratt, he never checked to see if he, himself, were being followed. Everett always checked. The dandy followed Surratt home and waited for the lights to go out, then he left. Everett followed him to Pointer's in Swampoodle, but stayed outside. The detective didn't know what kind of place Pointer's was, but it was suspicious. There was no crowd outside as there was outside the other bars and pleasure houses in the area. Therefore, he surmised, a strange colored man would be too conspicuous and most unwelcome, so he returned to his boarding house. He would have to get up very early and be at the Surratt house to see if the Dandy would show up—and Everett would bet he would.

Dressed in light-green cotton pajamas and a black quilted smoking jacket, Anderson relaxed in his room in the National. He sat in an upholstered chair and allowed himself a glass of whiskey. He lit a cigar and mentally reviewed the events of the past few weeks. In all, the commission was proceeding well. Booth was back in Washington, planning another stupid venture. The men working for the actor were unknowns, but that was to be expected. Anderson was pondering the variables when a knock on the door interrupted his thoughts.

"Who is it?" he called.

"It's Wilkes, Alan," the voice called. "I have wonderful news."

"Just a moment, Wilkes," he said. Anderson put his false artificial leg back on and limped to the door.

"Wilkes, what a nice surprise. It's good to see you." The two men shook hands as Booth made his entrance. "What's the good news?"

The actor smiled and, with a flourish, reached into his coat and pulled out several slips of paper. Anderson thought he looked like a magician pulling a rabbit out of a hat.

"*Voilà!*" the actor said.

It took only a glance and Anderson knew that they were tickets to the Lincoln's second inauguration on Saturday. He would bet that he got them from Bessie Hale.

"What's that you have, Wilkes?"

Booth brought them closer and when Anderson looked at them closely, he eyes widened in feigned amazement.

"Wilkes, these are tickets to the inauguration, how did you . . . I mean . . ." Flustered, Anderson sat in his chair.

"I told you we had men everywhere, Alan," Booth declared smugly.

"Wilkes, you're not going to try and capture Lincoln at the inauguration, are you?" The concern in Anderson's voice was genuine. The actor was just crazy enough to try something stupid with all those people around. He didn't like it.

Booth smiled and hinted boastfully, "It's a possibility."

The tone Booth used was that of a little boy who has a nicer toy than any of his companions and is lording it over them. Anderson relaxed. At least for now, Booth had no intention of trying anything at the inauguration. The actor handed him a single ticket.

"This one's for you, Alan."

"For me?"

"You will be able to tell your grandchildren," Booth said dramatically, "that you once stood on the same platform as the greatest tyrant in the history of mankind and the man who liberated the nation from his yoke."

Anderson smiled warmly and placed his hand affectionately on the actor's shoulder. "Wilkes, you have no idea what our association means to me. I can not imagine any circumstance that would deny you your rightful place in history."

Booth was pleased with Anderson's remarks and blushed slightly. "I owe much to you, Alan. You have provided me with the means to carry out my plans and supported me when I was faint of heart. I don't know how I will ever repay you."

"Repay?" Anderson asserted waving his hand in dismissal. "I need no repayment. Just being part of this great venture is enough. As you said, I shall boast of this to my grandchildren. If I were not a cripple, I would join you in a minute." Anderson paused for a moment. The floor in the hallway creaked as if someone were waiting. He wondered if it were Fitch. "Now I am sure you have other things to do this evening than sit and talk to me."

"As a matter of fact . . ."

"The redhead?" Anderson asked with a knowing grin and Booth shook his head. "Wilkes, sometimes I think I envy you more for your way with the ladies than I do for this venture."

Booth smiled, pleased with the flattery. "I must be going, Alan," he said, offering his hand.

They shook hands and the actor left. A moment later there was a soft knock on the door. "Who is it?" Anderson asked.

"It's Fitch, Mr. Demming."

Anderson opened the door and Fitch came in. He was so wet and tired that Anderson decided to relax his strict rule about Fitch and spirits.

"Sit down and have a drink, Joseph. You look as if you could use one." He handed Fitch a glass and a bottle of Baker 1851.

Fitch removed the cork and filled the tumbler nearly full. He drained half the glass and wiped his mouth on the sleeve of his shabby coat.

"What have you found out?" Anderson asked, sitting opposite him.

Fitch shrugged. It was sometimes difficult to tell what was important to Anderson and what was not, so he reported everything in detail and let his employer sift through the facts.

"Herold does not see Booth often. He lives with his mother and sisters in their house on Eighth Street East, but is always at Booth's beck and call. He was employed at Thompson's Pharmacy on Fifteenth and The Avenue, but he doesn't work there any more. I went in and asked for him to find out why and McKim the pharmacist told me that Herold couldn't even mix a simple prescription without someone looking over his shoulder. The druggist thinks he's simple. I've watched him for weeks now and the only money he gets is what Booth gives him." Fitch paused to take a sip of whiskey, then continued.

"Arnold and O'Laughlin, the two you saw in Baltimore are living in a boarding house on 420 D Street. There are no meals offered there so they eat at another place on the corner of D and Eighth. They spend almost all their time drinking with a bunch of Irishmen at Pullman's Hotel. When I overheard them at the bar they told their drinking companions they were being paid twenty dollars a week, but they didn't say for what. The horse and carriage is kept at Naylor's Stable, which is around the corner from the boarding house.

"Surratt does nothing. He's a loud-mouth kid who lives at home and acts important. He ain't done nothin' since this whole thing started and I think if push came to shove, he'd leave town."

Anderson's expression didn't change, as he digested the information Fitch was giving him. Once again Fitch took a sip of the amber liquid in his glass. He could have easily drained the glass and had another, but he knew Anderson wouldn't approve.

"Atzerodt is a carriage painter from Port Tobacco. He's also a boatman who, no doubt, runs the blockade from time to time. He's staying at the Kirkwood. He doesn't go very far or do much except drink. Spends a lot of time in the bar buying drinks to make friends.

"Payne, the new man, is staying at the Surratt house and he's chummy with John Surratt. He's using the name Wood. Every once in while, they all meet at the Surratt house, but I don't know what for. I've also seen another man there, but I don't know if he's part of it. His name is Spangler. He works at Ford's Theatre and keeps horses for Booth in a small shed behind it." He stopped and there was a long silence. Anderson was thinking.

"Continue watching everyone," Anderson instructed. "It can't be too long now, and we'll have to be ready to act at any moment."

"What are we going to do?"

"I really don't know yet, Joseph. It all hinges on whether or not we can rely on Booth."

"I wouldn't bet on him to do anything right," Fitch retorted before drinking the last of his whiskey. "Except maybe act."

"As usual, Joseph, you are an excellent judge of frail humanity, so, this is what I want you to do. Find a small house or a barn to the south of Uniontown. It must be isolated enough so that a gunshot would not draw undue attention. Once you have found a likely place let me know. If it's appropriate then we shall have to make some improvements."

"Anything else, Mr. Anderson?"

"Yes. Find us a place in Swampoodle, too. We may need some place in Washington less public than the National. We're dealing with too many people to stay anonymous and if we have do deal with any of them face-to-face, I don't want it to be here."

"I understand," Fitch said with a brief grin.

"Now, go home, dry off, and get some rest," Anderson told his assistant. "I don't want you catching a chill right now. We are going to be very busy the next few weeks. Also I want you to clean up and look and act respectable."

Fitch nodded, stood up and left. Anderson locked the door behind him. He had a good idea of what he wanted to do, but he had to keep Booth safely away from the law if it was going to work. After that he would have to be disposed of, but in such a way that no one would suspect that Booth was merely a pawn. Anderson allowed himself a smile. He felt much better now that he had devised a course of action. Tomorrow he would begin putting his plan in a notebook in cipher. As soon as the plan was drawn up, he would drive the roads and visit the places that were crucial to it. Then he would do a rehearsal, checking distances and times, looking for any possible obstacles that could affect the plan. Following the rehearsal he would complete the plan and commit to memory and then burn the notebook.

Washington City
March 2, 1865

It was six-thirty in the morning and Hasselmyer's Restaurant was crowded. Hasselmyer's was a small working man's eatery with a whitewashed front, located a few doors from the corner of K Street on Eighteenth. The owner, waiter, and one of the cooks was Friedrich Hasselmyer, a fat, bald, jolly German with muttonchop whiskers and red cheeks. He had a heavy accent and a nice word for everyone. The other cook and waitress was Mrs. Hasselmyer, who was just as round as her husband, only shorter. She had a pretty face and wore her hair braided on top of her head. Their place was cramped with only a dozen tables so that people sat where they could, even if that meant with strangers. No one seemed to mind, since Fritz and Hilda, as they were known to regulars, served up some of the best meals in the city at reasonable prices. The walls were bare except for a U.S. flag, a portrait of Lincoln, and a daguerreotype of the Hasselmyers' son who was in the Army of the Potomac. The Hasselmyers were staunch Unionists.

Ingalls drew his watch from his pocket and wondered if something had happened to Everett, when his partner walked in. He looked worried as he made his way through the crowded maze of tables filled with working men having their breakfast. A couple of them raised an eyebrow, not because he was colored, but because he was well dressed.

"Sorry, I'm late, George. I stopped by the Surratt place just to make sure."

"What's up?"

Before he could answer, Hasselmyer in shirtsleeves and a stained white apron came to the table.

"What's good?" Everett asked.

"Same as mine, Fritz," Ingalls told Hasselmyer. "Hotcakes and eggs."

Hasselmyer nodded with a smile. "*Kaffee?*" he asked.

"Yes, please," Everett replied.

The fat man nodded again and left.

"Now what's going on?" Ingalls asked.

Everett leaned closer so he didn't have to talk above the din of the other patrons. "Someone's following Surratt."

It didn't take any time for the implications of Everett's report to sink in. The expression on Ingall's face was one of bafflement and concern.

"Are you sure?" was the first question.

Everett nodded, but said nothing as the waiter brought a steaming mug of hot coffee. The detective took two heaping spoons of sugar from the sugar bowl and stirred them into his cup.

"That's why I was late," he said. "On Tuesday I was tailing Surratt as usual. It was payday and he was in front of the National with Booth. I was going to try and get close enough to overhear them when I noticed a man on the corner taking a lot of interest in Surratt and being very circumspect about it. Before I got across the street, Surratt was heading up Sixth to the stable and this man was following him. He followed Surratt all day, then went to Pointer's in Swampoodle."

"Pointer's?" Ingalls was astounded and even more confused than before. "Pointer's is a hangout for pickpockets. I was damned familiar with the place when I was a Pinkerton."

"It didn't seem the right place for a clean-cut detective so I left." Everett blew into the coffee mug and sipped it carefully.

"That was very wise, Clarence. You're smarter than you look."

Everett ignored the jibe. "I followed him all day yesterday and he was waiting for Surratt this morning."

"What did he look like?"

"Slight build, dark wavy hair, excellent dresser."

"Flower in the lapel buttonhole?"

"Yes, do you know him?"

Mrs. Hasselmyer brought two large platters of eggs, hotcakes, sidemeat, and grits and put one in front of each of the detectives. "Somesing else?"

"No, thanks, Hilda," Ingalls said. Everett nodded.

Everett looked at the breakfast, obviously delighted.

"Not bad for thirty-five cents, eh?" Ingalls asked.

"George, this place must be the best kept secret in the district."

"Working man's place," Ingalls said, buttering his hotcakes.

"What?"

"Working men come here. Working men don't have the time for frills or the money for fancy food. If you want plain good food at a reasonable price, go to a working man's place."

Everett began eating heartily. "My mother would have loved you," he said. "Now why did you ask about the flower? Do you know this man?"

"I might. It sounds like a man named Eddy the Sneak. He's a pickpocket who steals mainly from women, and he's very good at it."

"Did you arrest him?"

Ingalls with a mouthful of hotcakes shook his head no. As soon as he swallowed he took a sip of coffee and wiped his mouth. "Eddy used to do jobs for Pinkerton. Being a resident of Swampoodle, he could easily go places forbidden to strangers like you and me. I'll bet he's working for someone else right now."

"But who?"

"Whoever is paying Booth's bills."

"Something doesn't wash," Everett said.

"What?"

"Let's finish breakfast and get out of here. I need some air and time to think."

"Good."

They finished the rest of the meal in silence. Everett was mulling over some very disturbing theories. Ingalls kept wondering how Eddy the Sneak could be involved. However, the case in hand was not all Ingalls had on his mind. He was taking Nora to one of the fancy balls that were being held on Saturday to celebrate Lincoln's second inauguration. She had asked if he were going to the inauguration and he told her he couldn't because he was working on Saturday.

"I thought that all government workers had the day off." She sounded disappointed.

"The Telegraph Office works twenty-four hours a day, seven days a week, just like the war," he asserted. He consoled himself by reasoning that it was not an outright lie. The telegraph did operate twenty-four hours a day and he would be working in the crowd keeping an eye on Booth and his followers. Ingalls could not imagine a more dangerous scenario than a large public gathering with a lunatic like Booth on the loose.

The detectives left the eatery and began walking up the street toward The Avenue. The weather was cold and overcast, and it had been raining, which made the streets muddy and dangerous.

"What are you thinking, Clarence?" Ingalls asked, raising his collar and putting on his gloves.

"This may sound crazy," Everett said. "But, here goes. The only facts we have are these:

"One—Booth hates Lincoln.

"Two—Booth has no assets to speak of. He only has a few hundred dollars in the bank and his Pennsylvania oil stock is worthless.

"Three—He went to Canada presumably to get support for whatever he intends to do. However, we know from our man in the Canadian Cabinet that they haven't given him any money. Yet he has enough money to support himself and half a dozen accomplices in comfortable surroundings." Everett paused.

"So the long and the short of it is, we won't really know what's going on until we find out who's giving Booth the money."

"In a nutshell."

"Any ideas?"

Everett looked at him. "Just speculations."

"Shoot."

"First of all, whoever is doing this has so much money that a few thousand dollars means little or nothing."

"That narrows it down to a few thousand men," Ingalls said, his humor tinged with sarcasm.

Everett laughed loudly with his mouth open, his gold tooth conspicuous.

"It wasn't that funny," Ingalls said.

"You're right," Everett said. "I guess I needed a good laugh."

"I know what you mean," Ingalls said, smiling with some of his partner's infectious good humor.

"We haven't even considered the motive," Everett said and Ingalls looked at him curiously.

"From the start we have assumed that the Confederates are the ones that want Lincoln dead."

"Who else would want him dead, except maybe the Democrats?" Ingalls said, mildly frustrated. He couldn't quite get on the same mental track as Everett.

"That's one of the possibilities," Everett said. "Let's look at who would want Lincoln dead—whatever the reason."

"All right."

"First, there are the lunatics. For every great man there are dozens of lunatics who think that killing the great man will solve the world's problems."

"Booth?"

"Possibly. Next come the Confederates. They hate Lincoln because he thwarted their bid for independence. No matter that his death will be deleterious to their situation after the war, they are motivated by hatred which precludes logic. Then there are the politicians. I would ignore the Democrats, but I wouldn't ignore the Radical Republicans."

"Why?"

"Lincoln wants to rebuild the South, the Radicals want to subjugate the South and punish it. The only person standing in their way is the one whose death will insure they get their way. For them it would be perfect."

Suddenly Ingalls turned to Everett. "Everything we're talking about is political," he said.

"Yes, of course."

"What if it's not political?"

"I don't follow you, George."

"What if it has to do with money?"

"You mean all of these scandals? I don't think so. Lincoln hasn't said too much about them. It's Baker who's following those cases. Suppose if Lincoln dies, the price of gold goes up. Someone could make quite a killing—no puns intended."

This time Everett didn't laugh. "That brings us back to where we started."

"I know. We still have to find out who's giving Booth the money. That's the only way we'll get an answer, and the inauguration is the day after tomorrow."

"Certainly they're not crazy enough to try anything at the inauguration."

"I don't know, Clarence, I guess we'll find out Saturday."

CHAPTER 7

Washington City
Inauguration Day
March 4, 1865

THE MORNING DAWNED gray and wet and the streets were quagmires after days of intermittent cold rain. It was an inauspicious setting for the inauguration of the leader of a nation at war with itself, but as the morning grew brighter, it was obvious that the citizens of Washington City were bound and determined to make this day a festive occasion. After four years of bloody war, coupled with defeatists and detractors, the end was in sight and they felt they deserved it. Washington was going to have a party and nothing, not even foul, damp weather, was going to stop it. The inauguration itself was scheduled for noon, but hours before, Lincoln arrived at the Senate to sign bills into law. Shortly before the president arrived at the Capitol, a parade started from the White House down The Avenue to the Capitol. Despite the drizzle, the cold air, and the muddy streets, cheering crowds lined the way. Ladies in crushed crinoline and mud-stained skirts stood beside men with mud-caked boots and cheered noisily. Along with the marching soldiers rolled horse-drawn displays built by numerous organizations. The most unique exhibit was a huge monitor with guns that fired salutes as its horses churned down The Avenue. Another wagon supplied by the printers' union had a press which printed handbills with the day's programs. As they went by, the printers tossed them out to the spectators. The parade was a joyful one and, as if to mark the change of eras, for the first time Negro troops marched as inaugural guards and with them marched the Negro Grand Lodge of Odd Fellows. It was a sight that Clarence Everett and the other colored citizens of Washington watched with no small degree of joy and satisfaction.

As the parade passed each point, thousands followed it toward the Capitol, daring the bad weather to ruin their happy mood. In the Capitol, the notables of the nation and visiting dignitaries entered the Senate chamber. Gen. Joseph Hooker represented the Army and Adm. David Farragut represented the Navy. Not even the decorum of the inauguration could dispel the lightheartedness of the moment. Sen. Solomon Foot of Vermont, the presiding officer, rapped his gavel to quiet the crowd, but no one could hear it over the din. The ambassador from one of the small German duchies tripped over his ceremonial sword and tumbled down a flight of steps. He sat up at the bottom slightly disheveled and indecorous, but none the worse for wear. Another member of the diplomatic corps showed up in a tunic so tight that he had to unbutton it in order to sit down.

Finally, the president came in and sat in the center chair of the front row. Around him were Salmon P. Chase, the former Secretary of the Treasury and now Chief Justice of the Supreme Court. Chase had tried hard to become president and with no little irony was about to give the oath to his chief rival for the highest office in the land. At noon every dignitary and official was in place except one. Vice President-elect Andrew Johnson entered the chamber two minutes late. He entered supported by outgoing Vice President Hannibal Hamlin and Sen. James R. Doolittle. When Hamlin asked if Johnson was ready to take the oath of office, Johnson approached the podium and said, "I am." He then commenced a long rambling, boring, and embarrassing speech that revealed to the world that the vice president-elect was drunk. He had been ill and was apprehensive about the ceremony and had tried to brace himself, but he had not eaten and the whiskey hit him hard. John W. Forney, the Clerk of the Senate and Johnson's drinking partner of the night before, tried to stop Johnson with loud whispers, but the new vice president didn't hear. Hannibal Hamlin, the outgoing vice president, even tried tugging at his coattails, but that didn't work either. Many senators covered their faces to hide their chagrin or squirmed agonizingly in their chairs. Finally, Vice President Andrew Johnson took the oath of office and sat down. It was not a good beginning.

When Lincoln rose, all the dignitaries, except Johnson, followed him out to the platform where his oath of office would be taken. As he emerged from the Capitol door the drizzle stopped and a tremendous roar went up from the throng that had come to see him regardless of the weather. Many noted that it was a far cry from four years before when the president-elect had to be smuggled into the city and sharpshooters lined the rooftops in case of trouble. The new Capitol dome at that time had lain in pieces on the ground as if reflecting the dissolution of the Union. Now it was complete with the statue of Freedom at the top. When the president began his speech, "Fellow countrymen . . .," the crowd fell respectfully silent.

What Ingalls saw mortified him. Booth was standing above the president and to his left. Just below the platform only a few feet from the president were Herold, Surratt, Atzerodt, and a large man he didn't recognize but who seemed to be with them. If anything happened, the president would be caught in a murderous cross fire. Ingalls motioned to Everett and the two of them forced their way through the crowd to try to get to Booth. Despite his hurry Ingalls still listened to Lincoln's address and was moved by it.

Watching from above, Booth, dressed in an overcoat and top hat, glared down at the president. For him the words meant nothing. In his eyes, Lincoln was no longer a man, but a cancer that was eating away the country that he loved—a cancer that needed to be excised. Next to him stood Anderson dressed in a tweed coat and wearing a flat-topped, broad-brimmed hat. As Alan Demming he sported chin whiskers and no mustache. He watched Booth closely. The actor was fuming and clenching his fists, but all he was doing was watching. Anderson was ready to keep him from trying anything foolish. This was neither the right time nor the right place because the president was too far away for an effective pistol shot. Anderson listened to the president's speech and thought it was a good one. Once during the address, the clouds parted and sunshine broke upon the president and the surrounding throng. The crowd cheered this as a good omen along with the fact that Venus could be seen in broad daylight when the sky was visible.

Lincoln mentioned briefly that the war was going well, but did not go into detail. He mentioned the past and said, "Both parties deprecated war; but one of them would make war rather than let the nation survive; and the other would accept war rather than let it perish." Later in the speech, Lincoln referred to the slaveholder as a peculiar interest which was somehow the cause of the war. Then the president referred to the war as punishment from the Almighty and concluded, "Fondly do we hope—fervently do we pray that this mighty scourge of war may speedily pass away. Yet, if God wills that it continue until all the wealth piled by the bondsman's two hundred and fifty years of unrequited toil shall be sunk, and until every drop of blood drawn with the lash shall be paid by another drawn with the sword, as was said three thousand years ago, so still it must be said, 'The judgments of the Lord are true and righteous altogether.'

"With malice toward none; with charity for all; with firmness in the right, as God gives us to see the right, let us strive on to finish the work we are in; to bind up the nation's wounds; to care for him who shall have borne the battle and for his widow and his orphan—to do all which may achieve and cherish a just and lasting peace among ourselves, and with all nations."

The crowd erupted into a great cheer even though they had cheered and applauded several times during the address. Anderson looked at Booth who was still seething. Lincoln's speech was superb and it helped to explain why the president had to die. If Lincoln had his way the country would turn in upon itself and spend years healing its wounds and bringing the former slaves into society slowly enough so that their inclusion would be painless both to themselves and their former masters. It was a very human thing and typical of Lincoln. Morgan, on the other hand, saw a nation ready to expand west. It was the concept of a boom town on a continental scale and damn the human cost. Anderson never took sides in political disputes, but he felt that Morgan's vision would suit the times far better than Lincoln's. He thought little more about it because he had a commission to fulfill, and that was that.

The parties on the platform slowly began moving back into the Capitol and Anderson watched them. Suddenly Booth headed for the door.

"I must speak with him," Booth said to no one in particular. "I must make him understand."

Anderson grabbed him by one arm trying to restrain him. "Wilkes, calm down," he said soothingly.

Booth, like a man possessed, declared, "I must speak with him," and wrenched himself free of Anderson's grasp.

Fortunately, Anderson impeded him just long enough for the president and the justices of the Supreme Court to pass through the door so that when Booth reached the entrance, Lincoln was no longer in sight. Lt. John Westfall, one of the guards at the door, restrained the actor from going any farther.

"I must speak with him," Booth repeated. "I must make him understand."

Anderson helped Westfall constrain Booth and suddenly the actor turned away dejected. Anderson put his arm around Booth's shoulders and led him away with a sigh of relief. The guards, thinking Booth was just another office seeker, forgot the incident.

"I only wanted to tell him he was wrong," Booth said. It was nearly a sob.

Anderson led the actor back to the National. He gave him a stiff brandy and put him to bed. Booth was drifting into melancholia again, but he would be all right in the morning. One of these days he would not be all right in the morning and Anderson hoped his commission would be complete before that day arrived. All Booth had to do was last a few more weeks.

Washington City
Inauguration Evening
March 4, 1865

The colored man bowed politely as he held the door for the couple to enter. Nora entered first and Ingalls stopped long enough to show the doorman his invitation. The doorkeeper bowed again and with a sweep of his arm gestured the way to the cloak room. The Kirkwood may not have been as luxurious as the other hotels, but this evening Ingalls could not have imagined anything more splendid. The entire hotel seemed to be covered with flags and bunting as well as fresh flowers and garlands. A servant took his coat and Nora's shawl and gave them a ticket. Then Nora took his arm and they proceeded into the ballroom. If the lobby had been splendid, the ballroom was breathtaking with more bunting flags, flowers, and garlands. Large portraits of George Washington and Lincoln adorned the wall opposite the door. Around the other walls were portraits of Grant and Sherman and lesser military notables such as Meade and Thomas. There were no pictures of Andrew Johnson, which Ingalls found amusing.

"Oh, George," Nora said. "This is sumptuous."

Ingalls looked in the direction of her gaze. The invitation had indicated that a buffet was provided but he had not expected anything like this. The long, linen-covered table with its silver chafing dishes seemed to go on forever. There were dishes of chicken, beef, pork, mutton, vegetables, breads, pies, cakes, and fruit.

"I don't see how the people in the White House could fare any better than this," Nora said.

"Nor do I, Nora," he replied. Then with boyish enthusiasm, "What are we waiting for?"

Nora gave a little giggle and they joined the line at the buffet table. After their first trip through the line they danced. Ingalls knew he would remember this night forever. The music was provided by a very good band from a Connecticut artillery regiment and he held Nora in his arms for the entire evening. Her hair, her mouth, her bare shoulders, and her slim waist made her the most beautiful woman he had ever known. Whenever they danced she looked directly into his eyes. On one hand he felt as if he could evaporate in her presence; on the other, his desire for her was limitless.

By the time they returned to the Surratt House it was after midnight. They were delightfully exhausted and feeling mellow with the wine they had drunk. Ingalls drew her to him and kissed her parted lips. Her arms went around his neck and when he forgot himself and caressed her she pressed closer to him. How long they stayed that way he didn't know, but they broke apart when the door of the Surratt house opened. Out came Atzerodt, and another man. Ingalls could see Surratt and a taller man in the doorway. Nora drew closer to Ingalls.

"It's them again," Nora said.

"Who?" Ingalls asked.

"They're friends of John's. I don't think they're very nice men. Especially Mr. Wood."

"Who's Wood?"

"He's tall and actually very handsome except that he doesn't speak. He's supposed to be a Baptist preacher," Nora's voice reflected the disapproval of her Catholic upbringing. "But he doesn't act like any preacher I ever saw. I wish John would get a job. Ever since he met with Wilkes Booth, he does nothing. Booth seems to give him all the money he wants. It must be nice to be an actor and have money to give away."

"It must," Ingalls agreed. He was angry. The spell of the evening had been broken, as it was bound to be eventually, but it had been broken by the men he had come to regard as a menace to the president. Nora sensed it, too.

"I must go in, George."

"I know." They kissed again and he walked her up the steps to the door.

"George," she said softly. "This has been the most wonderful evening of my life." She kissed him lightly on the lips and disappeared inside.

The National Hotel
March 5, 1865

Booth stood at the window of Allen Demming's room and watched the rain pour down the window, puddle on the sill, and careen down three stories onto the mud-covered sidewalk.

"He didn't want to listen," he said vacantly.

Anderson, sitting on the bed, was slow to reply. Lincoln had been nowhere near the door when Booth approached, yet in the actor's mind the president had given him a personal snub and he was dwelling on it. This was further evidence that the actor was tottering on the brink of madness and it was only a matter of time before Booth plunged into the depths of uncontrollable melancholia or became a screaming lunatic who needed to be hauled away in a straitjacket, babbling incoherently. Anderson would have to be careful to soothe and cajole him to keep the actor pliable a little longer.

"Wilkes, you take too much on yourself," Anderson suggested comfortingly. "You must remember that you are dealing with the cruelest of tyrants. He will now probably remain president as long as he lives."

"What?" Booth said, turning from the window. He had the expression of a man who had just been slapped into consciousness. "What did you say, Alan?"

Anderson wondered if he had struck a nerve. "Why nothing, Wilkes."

"No, it was not nothing. Please, what did you say?"

"All I said was that he will now probably remain president as long as he lives."

"Yes, yes, now he will become emperor unless he is stopped."

"In that case, perhaps your own gentleness is standing in the way, Wilkes."

"What do you mean?"

"Perhaps he should be done away with all together."

Booth thought for a moment, then shook his head. "I appreciate your emotions in this matter, Alan, for I hate this fiend as much as you do, but he is more valuable to us alive. You will see. Once he is delivered into the hands of the authorities in Richmond, the fortunes of the Confederacy will change and she will be given a new chance at life. If it were not for that I would surely strike him down as the enemy of mankind that he is."

Anderson smiled warmly. This was the first time that Booth had even mentioned killing Lincoln. This was, indeed, progress.

"Wilkes, as usual you are far more perceptive than I. I cannot wait to see the expression on his face when we capture him and trundle him off to meet President Davis. Perhaps we should arrange to make a photograph of his capture. It will certainly be an historic event."

The idea of a photograph pleased Booth. "Yes, it would make a wonderful monument to posterity. The Devil and his captor. Let's have a drink on it." He poured two glasses half full of brandy and mixed them with water. Then he handed Anderson a glass and they both drank. Anderson sipped his, but the actor drained half his glass. Lately Booth was drinking more heavily, and this was another thing Anderson would have to watch closely.

"If it's not a secret, Wilkes, when do we strike?"

Booth grinned. "In a little less than two weeks actually. On Saturday, the eighteenth of March, he will be in our hands."

"Are we going to capture him at the theater?"

"Yes," Booth said. "On the Friday before, I will gather the band together and give them all their parts. I myself will be playing Pescara in *The Apostate*. You must come with us, Alan."

"You are the soul of kindness, Wilkes. I dearly wish I could, but I would only slow you down, and . . ." He paused and sighed deeply.

"And what?"

"What would your band think with a cripple man in their midst. It wouldn't do. And if anything went wrong they would blame it on me because I'm lame. They would probably be right, too."

Booth gazed sympathetically at Alan Demming. "You are right, of course, Alan. I wish there were something I could do or say . . ."

"There is nothing you need to say, my friend. I am playing the part I can. When you capture the tyrant, you will reveal my role in it, so that my name can blaze beneath yours in history. Until then, I am content. Do you need any money?"

Booth said nothing, so Anderson went to the wardrobe and produced another envelope with money in it. He handed it to Booth without ceremony. The actor opened it. This time there was only a thousand dollars in it, but Booth remained silent. He still had more than five hundred dollars from Demming's last contribution. "Thank you, Alan," he said, putting the envelope in his inside coat pocket. This time he mentioned nothing about paying the money back. Anderson was pleased. Booth was now used to taking the money. They made small talk for a few minutes and Booth left. Anderson resisted the temptation to follow him.

H Street
Washington City
March 8, 1865

The weather was terrible. Ingalls and Everett huddled in their coats in a rented phaeton. The top was raised and the side curtains were down, but it did little to ameliorate the damp cold that permeated everything. They were half a block from the Surratt house where they could easily see the house and the small landau containing Eddy the Sneak who was waiting for John Surratt to begin his day. Ingalls felt particularly bad because he had told Everett about Nora Fitzpatrick and him.

"I wouldn't want to be in your shoes, George," Everett said sympathetically. "There's no way you can tell her anything about yourself without compromising the case."

"Or my case with Nora," Ingalls added.

"Look, the girl is innocent," Everett said. "There's no reason for her to know anything about it or even get involved if Booth does something stupid. Don't worry, your romance is safe and I plan to have a good time at your wedding."

"Thanks, Clarence, that means a lot."

Even though Everett sympathized with his situation and offered to do everything he could to shield Nora from the conspirators, Ingalls felt that he had somehow betrayed his beloved. Like most men in love he wondered why life couldn't be simpler.

"As far as I can tell," Everett commented, changing the subject to the business at hand, "Surratt is Booth's messenger. Usually, Surratt either stays at home or goes out drinking. Lately, he's been pretty active going from place to place delivering messages to the various members of the gang." Everett pulled a pocket notebook from his vest." From the information we've gathered there appear to be eight of them. There's Booth, of course, a druggist named David Herold, John Surratt, and this man Wood who is staying with him.

"George Atzerodt is a carriage painter from Port Tobacco. From what I gather from the barflies he associates with, he's also a boatman and a blockade runner; when he's in town he stays at the Pennsylvania House—not exactly a member of high society.

"There are the two men over on D Street—I don't have their names yet; and the one you saw the other night. His name is Ned Spangler. He works at Ford's Theatre and keeps horses for Booth there. From what we have, that's all of them. The only things they all have in common are Booth and liquor. They are more like a gang of second-rate thieves than a conspiracy to assassinate a president."

"They're still dangerous," Ingalls told him, then added, "look, there's Surratt."

John Surratt, dressed in a heavy black overcoat and broad-brimmed hat, stepped out of the door. He walked down the steps and headed west on H Street.

"He's going to the stables around the corner," Everett whispered as if Surratt or the pickpocket could hear. "There's no need to follow directly. I'll circle the block and meet him as he comes out of the street. He'll go to see the two on D Street first, then he'll go to the Pennsylvania House. I usually get a little ahead of him so neither he nor Eddy suspect."

As soon as Surratt turned the corner, Eddy's carriage began to move slowly in the direction that Surratt had gone. Everett began moving also, but in the opposite direction. They were standing on the corner of F and Sixth when Surratt drove by in a hired curricle with Eddy's landau a safe distance behind.

"Surratt usually hires a horse," Everett said. "He's the manly type, but it's too cold even for him today."

John Surratt followed his usual route. Not once did he double back or use any of the tricks of a man who suspected he might be followed.

"You're right, Clarence," Ingalls told his partner. "He's either stupid or doesn't care."

The day was cold, dreary, and boring. When Surratt stopped for lunch they were each able to get a large sandwich wrapped in paper and some coffee, but they had to buy the mugs in order to take it with them. They ate their sandwiches huddled in the phaeton while Surratt and his tail ate in restaurants.

"The coffee is already cold. We need a tin pail," Ingalls remarked, munching his sandwich in the phaeton. "That way we could carry the coffee with us."

Everett nodded. "I'll split the price with you."

At the end of the day, Surratt returned the curricle to the stable and walked home. Eddy waited a short while then he stepped down from the driver's seat to light the headlamps. When he climbed back into the driver's seat, Ingalls and Everett left their headlamps dark and followed him closely. Eddy led them straight to Swampoodle. Two streets from Pointer's, Eddy made a right turn then headed up an alley.

"Do we follow?" Everett asked.

"Let me off here," Ingalls told him. "If I'm not back in twenty minutes, leave without me."

"Whatever you say."

Everett parked the phaeton and Ingalls descended to the muddy street. He could see the lights of Eddy's landau stopped in the alley. He carefully made his way along the wall, expecting to be attacked at any moment. At the end of the alley was a large parking area and a small building that had one time been a carriage painter's. He could see a light on in the window and he edged close to it. Eddy and a man he couldn't see clearly were at a table talking, but he couldn't hear a word they were saying. In plays and novels, every word in overheard conversations could be heard clearly and distinctly. Out here Ingalls could hardly hear a thing. He looked to see if he could find another entrance in the dark, but then he did hear a chair scrape back on the wooden floor. Ingalls stepped back into the shadows just as Eddy emerged from the door. The pickpocket strode to his landau and mounted it. The lights of the landau passed across Ingalls' hiding place, but Eddy didn't notice him. Ingalls waited briefly then returned to the end of the alley where Everett had parked the phaeton. Ingalls lit the headlamps and checked his watch. Everett had waited thirty-two minutes instead of just twenty.

"You should have left me there," Ingalls said.

"I know, but since I saved your life, you can buy me a nice hot supper," was his partner's reply.

"Somehow, I don't think you're taking this seriously," Ingalls said.

"After a nice hot supper, I'll take anything seriously. Did you learn anything?"

"Eddy met someone I couldn't see. Maybe it's the man who's paying Booth's bills."

"Should we pick Eddy up?"

"Not here unless we're in the mood for suicide. Let's pick him up tomorrow on the street. It should give us a better chance. Where do you want to go for supper?"

"Brown's Hotel has excellent roast beef on Wednesday night."

"Why do I get the impression that Eddy the Sneak is not the only pickpocket I'm dealing with?"

"George, you can't spend your entire life in workingmen's eateries."

Washington City
March 10, 1865

Cold rain and sleet struck Washington on Thursday and neither John Surratt nor Eddy emerged from their lairs. Ingalls and Everett gave up before noon and went home. Both men, exhausted from their constant vigil, slept the day away. Friday it was still cold, but it was clear and much drier. Surratt emerged from his house about 10:00 A.M. and went up the street to a local tavern.

"Nothing's going to happen today," Everett declared. "Eddy will go up the street to have lunch."

"That's where we'll nab him," Ingalls indicated. "This is a respectable neighborhood. There shouldn't be any trouble. Do we take him to the Blue Jug or the Old Capitol?"

"I think we ought to take him to the Blue Jug," Everett replied after thinking about it a moment. "The Old Capitol Prison might frighten him too much, plus the fact that once we put him in, there's no sure way of getting him out. If we take him to the Blue Jug and he tells us what we want to know we can let him go and follow him."

"I agree completely," Ingalls said. "Let's get him."

The restaurant was nearly empty this early in the day, so Eddy had chosen a table near the back where he was enjoying a plate of corned beef and cabbage.

Ingalls stepped in front of Eddy. "Good morning, Mr. Wooding," he said, using Eddy's real name. "May we sit down?"

Eddy was baffled at first. It had been a long time since he had been called anything but Eddy. Ingalls sat in front of him and Everett sat behind him. He glanced over his shoulder at Everett then looked at Ingalls. "You cops?"

"Something like that, Mr. Wooding, or would you prefer we call you Eddy? We'd like to talk to you."

"About what?"

"About the job you're doing right now. Isn't following Surratt a little out of your line?" Everett added over his shoulder.

Eddy looked at them without betraying any surprise. He was definitely a cool customer, Ingalls thought. "Since when do they have colored cops? Look, if you're cops then you know I pay every month, so get off my back."

Eddy's hand moved imperceptibly toward the knife by his plate. Ingalls detected the movement and clamped his hand on Eddy's wrist and squeezed.

"Jesus," Eddy gasped. "You're breaking it."

"I will if you don't tell me what I want to know."

"What the hell kind of cops are you? I pay you to stay off my back, so stay off."

Ingalls maintained his grip and leaned menacingly close to the pickpocket. "Number one, we're not Major Richards' apes. I'm Ingalls and he's Everett. Our boss is Lafayette Baker. Number two, if you don't come with us, I'll break your arm in so many pieces that you'll have trouble picking burlap sacks, never mind pockets."

"Baker? I don't have anything to do with Baker." For the first time Eddy's voice sounded less than confident. The Metropolitan Police were eminently corruptible, but Baker's men were not. As long as the Metropolitan Police were paid, there was nothing to worry about. Baker's men could not be bought. When you were arrested by the Metropolitan Police, there were judges, lawyers, and trials. When you were arrested by Baker's there was only the Old Capitol Prison.

"You do now," Everett said over his shoulder. "Are you coming peacefully?"

"Yeah, sure. I'll come. Can't I at least finish my lunch?"

"No."

Outside the restaurant they frisked Eddy thoroughly and found he wasn't armed. They took his wallet, a pocketknife, and his big watch and chain.

"Nice watch, Eddy," Ingalls said.

"Just you see I get it back," Eddy said.

Ingalls held it up by the chain. It was a large gold watch made by Howard & Company with Roman numerals on the face. "This is a railroad man's watch, Eddy. And it has initials on it, see? 'R.L.M. 1860.' I'll bet the railroad could check the initials and tell us who it belongs to."

Everett handcuffed Eddy to the front seat of the phaeton before the detectives got in. Ingalls drove while Everett sat behind Eddy.

The pickpocket looked relieved when the phaeton pulled up in front of the Blue Jug.

"We could have taken you to the Old Capitol, Eddy," Everett said. "But once you go in there, you can't get out very easily. If you're nice to us here, we can let you go."

They took him to one of the interrogation rooms that Eddy found all too familiar. The walls of the room were solid stone with no windows so it was difficult to hear a scream unless you were standing outside the door. The only furniture in the room was a small table with two chairs facing a single chair. The single chair was large and sturdy enough so that a man could be bound to it and hit hard without the chair falling over. Ingalls and Everett took off Eddy's handcuffs and sat him in the chair. They didn't bind him and they left the door open. There was even a pitcher of water on the table. Then they offered him a cigar and gave him a match to light it. Ingalls politely explained the situation to him.

"Eddy, we're not sure you really know what you're involved in, so we'd like to enlighten you. John Surratt is a spy, a known blockade runner, and a Confederate courier, and for those reasons he is currently under investigation. You have been seen following him day and night and you are not employed by the government. Therefore, your activities have been viewed as suspicious and that is why you are dealing with us and not the Metropolitan Police. Have I made myself clear?"

Eddy nodded that he understood.

"All right, then, why were you following Surratt?"

Eddy looked from Ingalls to Everett and back again. He squirmed uncomfortably in his chair, but he said nothing. Ingalls pulled a chair up in front of him and sat in it back to front, so the back of the chair would protect him if Eddy tried anything.

"Eddy, I'm not going to tie you up and I'm not going to beat you. I don't believe that sort of thing does any good. What I can promise you is this: If you tell us what we want to know, you can go free, and that means with your watch. If you don't, the watch is only part of your troubles. First, you'll be taken to the Old Capitol Prison and held there until someone sees fit to review your case. The war could be over by that time. It might be possible that you'll be hanged as a spy." Ingalls paused to let the words sink in.

"Even if you're not hanged, you could go to the penitentiary for at least ten years and you know what a disagreeable place that is. Once you get out of prison, you will be tried for stealing the watch. I'll bet the man who owns that watch takes a dim view of people stealing his property. There might be another twenty years on top of the first ten. That's thirty years total. You'll be an old man when you get out, if you don't die of something while you're in there."

Eddy looked away. Then he looked first over his shoulder at Everett then back at Ingalls. "This is damned difficult, you know."

"No, it isn't," Ingalls told him. "All you have to do is tell us who you're working for and why, and you'll walk out—with the watch. It's not difficult at all."

"Can I have a glass of water?" Eddy asked.

"Sure." Everett poured him a glass of water and handed it to him. Eddy drained half the glass then looked at it as he rolled it nervously between his palms.

"Fitch paid me to watch Surratt and hire men to watch a bunch of other people."

"Who is Fitch?" Ingalls asked.

"Joseph Fitch. He used to be my partner until about two and a half years ago, then he started working for Anderson."

"Who is Anderson?"

"That's something a lot of people would like to know."

"What do you mean?"

"Anderson is a killer," Eddy said nervously. "That is, he kills for money. People pay him to get rid of wives and business partners they don't want. Always makes them look like accidents or suicide. That sort of thing. He's very good and charges lots of money."

"Where can we find this Anderson?" Everett asked.

"I don't know that either. The only person anyone ever sees is Fitch. He comes and tells you what he wants done. If you refuse, you're dead. If you do it, you get paid well. I get five hundred dollars for watching Surratt every day for a month. The others get two-fifty."

Ingalls whistled. "You get paid five hundred dollars just for watching someone?"

Eddy shook his head. "Anderson always has money, lots of it. If anyone suspected I even mentioned his name I could be killed."

"Whatever you tell us won't go beyond this room," Ingalls told him reassuringly. Eddy wasn't convinced.

"Just a minute," Everett said and motioned Ingalls over to the other side of the room.

"Do you believe this man?" he asked softly.

"I don't know what to believe. I've had a lot of experience in Swampoodle and I've never heard of a wealthy specter named Anderson. The only thing is that Eddy's frightened and he's not frightened of us."

Everett looked over at the pickpocket. "I'm not sure I'm ready to believe him."

"He's our only lead. Let's get what else we can and let him go. Following him will probably give us more clues than following Booth or Surratt."

Everett nodded his head and they walked back over to Eddy.

"If you don't know where this Anderson is, where does this Fitch live?"

"I don't know much about him any more except that he hangs out at the Chain and Anchor. It's off Fourth Street East, near the Navy Yard. Don't go there dressed as cops. They'd as soon kill a cop as look at him."

"What does he look like?"

"Short. A little shorter than me. Slim, brown hair, kind of pointed jaw. Sometimes he wears a beard, sometimes he doesn't. Bad teeth."

"Who were the others you were supposed to watch?"

Eddy didn't know the names of the men the others had to watch, but he accurately listed the addresses of all of Booth's band. Ingalls said nothing, but looked at Everett, who raised an eyebrow.

"Okay, Eddy, we believe you. Let's go to the desk sergeant and get your things."

Eddy was up from the chair, heading for the door when he realized that he still had the glass in his hand. He returned it to the table and walked to the desk sergeant between Ingalls and Everett. Eddy quickly gathered up his belongings and left the Blue Jug. Ingalls and Everett watched him go.

"What do you think?" Everett asked his partner.

"I don't know what to think, especially about this Anderson business. We'll have to wait and see."

"Let's get a bite to eat," Everett said. "I'm hungry."

Mentioning Anderson's name in the confines of the Blue Jug was a mistake. One of the policemen standing near the desk with a drunk overheard. He had seen Eddy with the two detectives and knew the information would be worth plenty of money, and he intended to collect.

Washington City
March 13, 1865

Monday was an exceptional day. The temperature had risen and the sun was out. Abruptly, it was beginning to seem like spring. Eddy was back on the job and so was Everett. The detective found tracking the pickpocket very difficult now. Eddy was more concerned about being seen than observing Surratt. Everett had also decided that Surratt was not worth watching. Instead his daily quarry became Eddy. The pickpocket was frightened, but he was skillful in avoiding detection. It was, no doubt, due to his years of practice in avoiding the Metropolitan Police. Eddy could have shaken any tail who wasn't a professional. He doubled back to check his own trail and randomly entered crowded bars, sometimes leaving through the back door. Unfortunately for Eddy, Everett was no amateur. Twice the detective thought he had lost the pickpocket, but he picked up his trail by asking questions. Colored vendors and shoeshine boys were amazed he was a detective and helped him regain the trail. Soon it was obvious that Eddy was making his way back to Swampoodle. The trail ended at Pointer's. This time Everett did not leave. He stayed in the shadows, avoiding passersby, and keeping an eye on the door.

By 10:00 P.M., Everett was convinced that Eddy had retired for the night and he was about to go home, when he saw the small man in the dark overcoat enter Pointer's. He didn't look like one of Pointer's usual clientele and Everett wondered if this might be Fitch. He tried to gain a better vantage point so he could see something of the man's face when he came out, but it was nearly impossible. The light was bad and he dared not get too close. A few minutes later the small man emerged with Eddy and began walking along Tiber Creek. Everett would have preferred a dark alley. Along the creek was too open to follow closely even at night.

When Fitch had been instructed to go get Eddy, he assumed he would be followed and he was determined to shake any tail who didn't have eyes like a cat and know Swampoodle like the back of his hand. Even though he never saw Everett personally, he had lost the detective in twenty minutes. He doubled back to see if anyone was following, but Everett had decided to limit his vulnerability and leave Swampoodle.

"See anybody you know, Eddy?"

"No, no one. Now, where are you taking me?"

"Didn't I tell you? Mr. Anderson wants to see you—in person."

"Anderson?" Eddy didn't even try to hide the fear in his voice. "Wha . . . what does he want to see me for?"

"It's about the two cops who picked you up the other day."

"Honest, Fitch, it wasn't my fault . . . I . . ."

"Relax, Eddy. Mr. Anderson is very happy."

"He is?"

"Definitely. You flushed out the opposition. As a matter of fact, I wouldn't be surprised if there wasn't a little something extra in it for you—and I mean gold."

"Oh," Eddy sighed in relief. He felt a lot better.

"Come on," Fitch said. "We have to hurry. We can't keep Mr. Anderson waiting."

Fitch led Eddy to a narrow back alley near Tiber Creek above the bridge at H Street. There, in a rundown house that catered to many tastes, Anderson waited in an upstairs room. Eddy was surprised to find Anderson a man of medium height and build. In the dim light his hair and mustache looked brown. This killer of killers looked very ordinary.

"Ah, Eddy," Anderson said congenially, "I'm very happy to meet you."

"Likewise, Mr. Anderson."

"No need for the 'mister,' Eddy. Can I get you something? A beer, perhaps?"

"Sure, fine."

"Why don't you get us two beers, Joseph, and one for yourself?" Anderson asked Fitch amiably.

"Glad to," Fitch said with unusual civility.

"Have a seat, Eddy. We need to talk. You've been very helpful and I want you to know that I appreciate it. But first, I need to know more details."

"Like what?"

"Who were the men who picked you up? Were they Pinkertons?"

"They were Baker's men. National Detectives. One was a big white man named Ingalls. The other was a nigger named Everett. He's about my height only stockier. Has a gold tooth on the left side."

Fitch returned with the beer. He offered Eddy a mug first, then gave one to Anderson. All three sipped the beer and Anderson smiled.

"You really have done well, Eddy. What else did you learn?"

Eddy told Anderson everything he could remember and the killer's face took on a worried look, but he soon smiled.

"Eddy, this is serious. If it hadn't been for you, our plans might have been foiled. Don't you agree, Joseph?"

"Yes, sir. I told you that Eddy was the right man for the job."

Anderson reached into his pocket and pulled out a leather pouch. "I hope that you'll accept this as a token of my thanks, Eddy."

Eddy took the pouch. It was heavy.

"Don't be shy, Eddy. Go ahead and open it."

Eddy dumped the contents of the pouch in his hand. It was full of double eagles.

"I don't know what to say, Mr. Anderson."

"When someone does a good job he deserves a reward and I can't tell you how much you've helped," Anderson said, extending his hand. "Now, if you wouldn't mind going with Joseph, he has another assignment for you."

"Certainly."

Eddy followed Joseph out of the house and down the alley to a deserted part of the creek bank. Eddy never understood until Fitch turned, smiled, and plunged the long blade of his knife into the pickpocket's belly again and again until Eddy slumped to the ground with hardly a whimper. Fitch cut Eddy's throat just to be thorough and wiped the blade on Eddy's coat. Then he cleared everything out of Eddy's pockets, stuffing it all into his own before dumping the body into the creek. There was a muffled splash as Eddy's corpse began drifting downstream. The body would be found in the morning, but no one in Swampoodle would ask how a pickpocket had got his throat cut and his body dumped in the canal. They would all know that it was a message from Anderson. Fitch strode away from the area to put some distance between himself and the body. Finally, he stopped by a lamppost and looked at Eddy's belongings. He pocketed the pouch of gold (Anderson would want that back) and the money from Eddy's wallet. He also kept Eddy's watch and ring. The wallet, a handkerchief, some papers, and two keys, he tossed into the mud. Fitch thought of using Eddy's money to visit Jasmine. Suddenly the idea seemed very funny and he began to laugh.

Metropolitan Police Headquarters
Tenth Street
March 15, 1865

Ingalls was awakened early in the morning by a messenger with a note from Major Richards. It simply read:

March 15, 1865

Dear Mr. Ingalls:
   I have some information that may be of importance to you. Please come earliest.

Yours &c.
A. C. Richards

Ingalls washed and shaved then dressed quickly and drove to Everett's rooms. He found his partner ready to go to breakfast.

"What do you think it is, George?"

"I don't know, Clarence. Let's go and find out."

Almarin Cooley Richards was a spare man with a full beard who was dapper in his manner of dress, He sat at his paper-covered desk, smoking a cigar and looking very unhappy. He had known Ingalls when the detective was a Pinkerton and they had kept on good terms even though Richards felt that Baker trespassed on his territory from time to time. There was little that went on in the city that escaped him.

"Oh, Ingalls, good morning." He rose and shook hands with Ingalls. "This your new partner?"

"Oh, yes. Major Richards—Clarence Everett."

"Good to meet you, Mr. Everett."

"An honor, sir."

"Well, I'm a busy man so I won't beat around the bush. Don't ask me how I know, but you were seen in the Blue Jug, Friday, with one Charles Wooding alias Eddy the Sneak. I know he used to do work for Pinkerton. Is he one of your stool pigeons?"

"Not exactly, sir," Ingalls replied. "We have been following him, hoping he would lead us to someone else, but we lost him Monday night and haven't been able to pick up his trail."

"The trail has just come to an abrupt end. They found him in Tiber Creek yesterday morning. I didn't find out about it until late last night—damned paper work." This last was muttered as he looked for a piece of paper on his desk. "Ah, here it is. It's the report by the men who found the body."

"Thank you, Major."

"You can have that copy. By the way, whom did you want Eddy to lead you to?"

Ingalls glanced at the report, then looked at Richards. "Eddy said he was working for a man named Anderson, a hired killer."

Richards gave him half a smile and shook his head. "I don't know what to tell you about that one. Everyone who spends enough time around Swampoodle or Murder Bay knows the name Anderson. Sometimes I wonder if he really exists. Whatever you find out, let me know. I'd appreciate it."

"Consider it as good as done, sir. By the way, would you happen to know which funeral parlor the body was sent to?"

"Some place in Swampoodle or not far from it. I think it's on the report."

Ingalls looked at the report. "Ah, yes. Trantor's. I think I know it."

They left the office and Ingalls grinned. "Up to a trip to the undertaker before breakfast?"

"It has been such a thoroughly enjoyable day so far why do anything to spoil it? Lead on."

Trantor's Funeral Parlor was on the southern edge of Swampoodle near the corner of F and East Fourth Street. It was a plain store front which had at one time been painted white, but it had faded to a streaked and dingy light brown. There was a sign over the door that said in large old English letters "Trantor's Funeral

Parlor" and beneath it in smaller letters "Neville Trantor, Mortician." On either side of the door was a window displaying coffins.
The selection ranged in style from a plain pine box to a carved oak
casket with a quilted inside and silver handles. When they walked
into the parlor, Ingalls and Everett removed their hats and were
greeted by Neville Trantor in person. He was typical of his profession, tall, gaunt, and bearded, dressed in a black suit with a white
shirt and black cravat. The place was decorated in draping of dark
red and black. Seats lined either side of a single aisle at the end of
which was a black bier for holding a coffin. There was a cross on
the wall above the bier. Mr. Trantor bowed respectfully.

"May I assist you, gentlemen?" he said in his quiet funereal
manner.

"We're looking for the body of Charles Wooding, alias Eddy the
Sneak," Ingalls said.

"Are you relatives of the deceased?" Mr. Trantor asked.

"I doubt it," Everett said with a smile.

"We are all God's children here, sir," Trantor replied somberly.

Everett didn't know whether the man was serious or not so he
let it drop.

Ingalls flashed his badge. "We are detectives. We understand
that Mr. Wooding met with a violent end and we would like to see
the body."

Mr. Trantor, unperturbed, gave them his funeral-parlor smile
and said, "We always assist the forces of law and order when we
can. Mr. Wooding's earthly remains are being prepared now. This
way, please."

Trantor led the two detectives to the morgue, which was in the
back of the establishment. It was a plain whitewashed room with a
dirt floor. Along one side on stretchers were bodies covered with
white sheets. On the opposite side under a window that was
painted over was a work bench upon which rested various kinds of
knives and saws. Above the bench were bottles of chemicals, along
with blocks of wax and cosmetics to make the dead more presentable to the living. In the center of the room was a long marble-
topped table. Eddy the Sneak's naked body lay on the table while
one of Mr. Trantor's assistants pumped embalming fluid into its
veins. The face looked sunken, but recognizable. Ingalls speculated that a cold night had prevented its decomposition. The

gaping wound in the throat had been sewn up as had been the wounds in the stomach. Everett swallowed hard and lost his appetite.

"What can you tell us about the wounds?" Ingalls asked.

Trantor looked as if he were considering the answer, then he shrugged. "Not much. There were four stab wounds in the stomach. All were from below which probably means the person who killed him was several inches shorter than he. The killer then cut his throat. I would speculate that he was in no particular hurry."

"Why?"

"Even after being in the water, there were blood stains on the clothes that indicated the killer took the time to wipe his blade on the victim's clothes. Someone in a hurry would have stabbed the man once or twice and fled."

"Thank you, Mr. Trantor." Ingalls and Everett bowed politely.

The mortician bowed. "May I show you out?"

"We know the way."

Both men took a deep breath when they emerged from the funeral parlor. Even the foul air of Swampoodle was preferable to the miasma of death and formaldehyde in Trantor's embalming room.

"Breakfast?" Ingalls asked.

"Let's get out of here," Everett said, loosening his collar, "before I get sick."

They got into their phaeton and headed south on First, then took a right onto The Avenue. By the time they had gone half a mile they both felt better.

"What do you think, Clarence?"

"About what?"

"Anderson."

"He's real."

"Just like that?" Ingalls asked.

"No, there are a number of reasons," Everett said considering his words carefully. "First of all, Eddy was killed shortly after we spoke with him."

"Merely coincidence. It could have happened to anyone in Swampoodle."

"True, but he was also killed by a shorter man. Trantor said the killer was a few inches shorter. Fitch is about four or five inches shorter than Eddy was."

"Even if he were killed by a midget, it doesn't prove anything," Ingalls added, slipping into the role of devil's advocate.

"That is also true except for one thing that ties all this together."

"And that is?"

"Victims in Swampoodle and other such parts of our fair city are usually taken from behind. They are customarily clubbed or stabbed and their belongings swiftly taken. Eddy lived in Swampoodle and, no doubt, knew its ways thoroughly. He would not have allowed himself to be taken from behind, but that really isn't the point. Eddy was not just stabbed and robbed. The man who stabbed Eddy must have been close, therefore, Eddy must have known and trusted him or at least not been afraid of him. It was also not a robbery because the killer took the time to rifle his pockets and then wipe his knife on Eddy's clothes before dumping his body in the creek. Then there's the question of why the creek? That's no place to hide a body. It was obviously meant to be discovered. Why?"

"Anderson was sending a message to his cronies."

"Exactly!" Everett thumped his hand with his fist in triumph.

"Well," Ingalls quipped. "At least the two of us agree. Now how do we convince other people? And there's one question we haven't addressed."

"What's that?"

"Where do Anderson and Fitch fit in with Booth and his gang?"

"I don't know. Why don't we discuss this over breakfast?"

"Feeling better?"

"Now that I'm away from that embalming room and the wonderful vista of Swampoodle, yes."

"Me, too. Where do you want to go?"

"I don't know. Someplace we can talk."

They returned to Hasselmyer's. It was after nine and the place was nearly empty, so they picked a table in the corner and sat down. Both men ordered a large breakfast with coffee. Everett looked down and made a circle in the sawdust on the floor with the toe of his boot.

"What are you thinking?" Ingalls asked, sipping the hot black liquid in the heavy white mug.

Everett moved his head back and forth. "There's something here that doesn't make sense, and I don't even know how to ask what it is. Do you know what I mean?"

"I think I do. It's the money. If Booth were paying Anderson to kill the president, then it would be cut and dried, but that brings up more questions, like where does Booth get the money and why hasn't Anderson acted?"

"I'm drawing a blank," Everett said in obvious frustration. "Anderson costs a lot of money, which Booth doesn't have. Booth has enough money to live on, but isn't working. I keep coming up with Booth is getting the money from Anderson, but that's so stupid."

"As in why would a wealthy hired killer pay an out of work actor to gather a gang to do stupid things, like try and kidnap the president from a crowded theater?" Ingalls asked.

Before Ingalls' partner could reply, Fritz brought their breakfasts and, in their hunger, they momentarily forgot Anderson and Booth. They resumed the conversation when the food was half gone.

"To cover up what really is going to happen," Everett remarked, picking up the conversation as if it had never ceased.

"I beg your pardon," Ingalls was confused.

"You asked why would a wealthy hired killer pay an out of work actor to gather a gang and kidnap the president from a crowded theater and other stupid things like that," Everett said pouring more syrup on his hotcakes.

"I guess I did, but I can't think of any reason why it should be unless . . . no, it's too . . ."

"What?"

"No, you would think I'm really crazy."

"Tell me. At least that way I really know if you're a lunatic or not."

Ingalls took a deep breath. "Okay. Suppose Booth isn't the one behind all this. Suppose he's just a dupe."

"You're so crazy, you're inspired, George. Go on."

"Suppose the man (or men) who wants the president dead (the reason isn't important right now) hired Anderson to do the job. Anderson accepts but realizes that he can't make the president's death look like suicide or an accident, which is what Eddy said he did."

Everett, a sausage impaled on his fork, leaned forward, hanging on Ingalls' every word. "It's good, go on."

"In order not to draw attention to himself, he finances Booth to do all these stupid things, so that no one will catch on to the actual plan."

"Which is?"

"To kill the president. But when and how? Why hasn't he acted already?"

"Maybe he's waiting for the end of the war?"

"Why would he do that?"

"Everybody's guard will be down once the war is over."

"Clarence, we need more men on this."

"Last time I was in the office, Judge Lawrence said that Colonel Baker was due back tomorrow. Why don't we go see him and tell him what we've found. He's got to give us some men with a man like Anderson after the president."

"You're right."

Lafayette Baker's Headquarters
March 16, 1865

Ingalls and Everett strode purposefully into the house at 217 Pennsylvania Avenue and Judge Lawrence ushered them into Baker's office. The head of the National Detectives was smiling, but there was more gray in his hair than the last time Ingalls had seen him and his face was even more deeply lined from worry and lack of sleep. Nevertheless, he greeted the two detectives warmly and gave each a hearty handshake.

"Sit down, please," Baker said, motioning to two chairs. "I got your report on Booth's attempt to waylay the president at Ford's Theatre in January. I must admit it gave us all a good laugh in New York. Now what can I do for you?"

"We need more men," Ingalls told him.

Lafayette Baker rubbed his eyes. "More men, more men. Everybody needs more men. Why? What have you found out?"

"Anderson," was the only word Ingalls uttered.

"Anderson," Baker snorted. "Whenever you go into Swampoodle and Murder Bay, you hear the name Anderson spoken in frightened little whispers. He's supposed to be a man who kills silently and always makes it look like something else. Bah! Anderson is a myth invented by the superstitious morons who constitute the criminal element of this city. We have been in every corner of this city and I have never been able to find any trace of this so-called Anderson."

"What about the money he pays people to do things for him?" Everett asked.

Baker, ignoring the question, sighed wearily and picked a long cigar from the box on his desk. He clipped off the ends with a pen knife, put it between his teeth, and lit it with a match, rolling it until it was lighted evenly, then he looked back at Ingalls and Everett.

"Look, I have every confidence in both of you so don't think I'm brushing you off because I'm not. If we forget this business about Anderson and the fact that Booth is a clod, we still have a possibility that the president's life is in danger. We do agree with that, don't we?"

Both detectives shook their heads in agreement.

"Unfortunately, between the Treasury scandal here and the recruiting scandal in New York we are stretched to the limit. As much as I would like to, I cannot give you any more men. In fact, if this wasn't a question of the president's safety, I'd put you both on the other cases. Report back when you uncover anything significant."

The interview was obviously over and the two detectives got up and left. Outside the sun was shining.

"You know, Clarence," Ingalls said looking up at a clear blue sky. "I don't think I've ever been called a liar more politely."

Clarence Everett started to laugh. It was so stupid that if you didn't see the humor in it, you could go crazy.

CHAPTER 8

The Surratt House
March 16, 1865

GEORGE INGALLS KNOCKED at the door of the Surratt house, cradling a large bunch of fresh chrysanthemums and azaleas in his arm. He only had to knock once and Nora answered the door. There was a lovely smile on her face. She looked over her shoulder and down the street to make sure no one was looking and gave him a light kiss on the lips.

"I missed you," she said, leading him into the house.

"I missed you, too," he said, handing her the flowers. "These are for you."

"George, they're lovely. You shouldn't have." She stepped aside so he could enter. On the way in he surreptitiously squeezed her hand and she smiled.

"I'll go put these in water and I'll meet you in the parlor."

It was right after supper and the house was busy. Several people were going up or down stairs and before Nora could make her way to the kitchen, Wood passed right by them so that Ingalls could get a good look at him. Wood was taller than Ingalls, but not as broad in the shoulders. He was good looking with dark hair, a straight nose, and a strong chin. His eyes were devoid of any emotion and when Ingalls politely said, "Good evening," Wood just looked at him with that neutral gaze and continued on his way to the stairs.

"Friendly sort," he said to Nora.

She made a face and took his arm. "I don't like him, he scares me."

"I can see why."

Nora disappeared in the direction of the kitchen and Ingalls went into the parlor. As usual it was crowded after supper. Mr. Holohan was sitting on the settee with his wife Eliza and their daughter, a rather plain girl of fourteen. Ingalls had a nodding acquaintance with the Holohans and he said hello to them and to the daughter who smiled and blushed shyly. Occupying another chair was Mary Surratt who was wearing a plain brown dress with a white collar and a plaid shawl over her shoulders. She smiled pleasantly and said hello to Ingalls, and they passed the time for a minute or two talking about the weather. Then she returned to her needle work. She was having a difficult time with it and finally put it down. Ingalls wondered if she needed spectacles. Probably vanity prevented her from obtaining them.

There were three others in the parlor. One was the ubiquitous Mr. Weichmann. Ingalls exchanged pleasantries with him and left it at that. The others were Anna Surratt and her brother John. Anna greeted Ingalls pleasantly and introduced him to her brother. The two men shook hands and the detective developed an instant dislike to the man. He was smug, self-centered, and vain, and his attitude was nothing short of insolent when he found that Ingalls worked in the War Department. Ingalls then understood why the man was so easy to follow. John Surratt obviously felt that he could do no wrong. Surratt ignored Ingalls as soon as their introductory pleasantries were over and began talking at some length with Weichmann. The two had been friends at school and shared a room in the boarding house. They were a well-matched pair, Ingalls thought uncharitably. Surratt was the leader and Weichmann was the follower. Ingalls had a silent hope that one day Surratt would get into a situation that would fix his arrogance once and for all.

"Why don't we go for a walk?" he suggested to Nora as soon as she joined him in the parlor.

"All right," she said. "I'll get my shawl."

Walking west on H Street was a double pleasure. He was away from the people in the boarding house and he had Nora to himself for a while. She took his arm and they strolled easily down the sidewalk. There were puddles here and there but it was not muddy. The evening air was cool, but not unpleasant.

Nora talked about the new dress she had bought and he listened, not because he was interested in the dress particularly, but because he liked to listen to her voice just as he liked everything about her. Away from her he thought about her constantly, and when he was near her, he was nearly consumed by his desire for her. When the war was over he would tell her everything about himself and ask her to marry him. Mrs. George Ingalls. It had a nice sound.

"George?" she asked, then repeated, "George?" stirring him from his reverie.

"What, Nora?"

"Are you listening to me?"

"Yes, of course. You were talking about the dress."

She eyed him suspiciously. "Sometimes I wonder about you, George Ingalls. You looked like you were a thousand miles away."

He smiled. "I'll never be a thousand miles away from you."

"George, you're sweet."

"Will you have supper with me on Saturday, Nora?" he asked casually.

"Oh, George, I can't."

"But why?" he asked dismayed. They had seen each other every Saturday when his work permitted and he had come to depend on seeing her.

"Wilkes Booth, the actor, is taking us to Ford's Theatre to a play."

"Booth? John Wilkes Booth?" he asked anxiously. He didn't know what Booth was up to but he definitely didn't want him near her.

"Yes," she said. "John Wilkes Booth."

"You can't," he stammered, looking for a logical reason that wouldn't reveal his knowledge of the actor.

"Well, I certainly can and I will. Mr. Wood, Appolonia Dean, and I are going."

"Nora, you mustn't."

Nora began to giggle. "Why George Ingalls," she said teasingly. "I do believe you're jealous."

"I am not jealous," he insisted, raising his voice in frustration.

"There is no need for anger, sir," she said prettily. "You may escort me home."

Nora was delighted with what she felt was Ingalls' jealousy. The detective was beside himself. He had no idea what to say so they walked back to the boarding house in silence. He left her at the door and despite it all was delighted when she kissed him goodnight.

Brown's Hotel
March 17, 1865

Even before they sat down to breakfast, Everett noticed that Ingalls was not himself. He was concerned when his partner did not have his usual hearty breakfast and only ordered coffee. Ingalls was restless and distracted and there could be only one reason for this type of behavior. Everett smiled.

"You and Nora have a fight, George?"

"What?" Ingalls asked absentmindedly.

"I asked if you and Nora had quarreled."

"No, of course not," Ingalls said defensively. Then, "Well, not really."

"What do you mean, not really?" Everett asked playfully. "Either you had an argument or you didn't have one. Which is it?"

"How did you know we quarreled?" Ingalls asked suddenly curious.

"Oh, just a wild guess. You wander in here half distracted and only order coffee instead of your usual enormous breakfast. Nothing unusual."

Ingalls looked at him and actually blushed. "I don't know what to do. She's going to the theater with Booth on Friday."

"Alone?"

"No. Booth is taking Nora, Appolonia Dean, an eleven-year-old, and Wood to Ford's Theatre to a play."

"I wouldn't worry about it."

"Wouldn't worry about it?" Ingalls asked so loudly that other people in the restaurant looked at him.

"Keep your voice down, George," Everett cautioned him.

Ingalls looked around and felt embarrassed. "I'm sorry."

"You don't have to apologize, but I don't understand what the problem is."

"The problem is, the woman I love is going to the theater with a lunatic, that's the problem."

"You're repeating yourself, George," Everett said teasing him.

"Clarence, you're making fun of me," Ingalls said in frustration.

"Of course, but its only because you deserve it."

"Damn you, Clarence," Ingalls said, raising his voice again.

"George, if you'd calm down you would see that you have nothing to be concerned about."

"Nothing to be concerned about? Would you say that if it were your beloved?"

"George, nothing is going to happen."

"How do you know that?"

"Booth is taking a girl and a woman to the theater. He wouldn't do that if he were planning to try anything. They would only be in the way. Nora is going because he's a famous actor. Every woman in the country would fall over herself to go to the theater with someone famous like Booth. He's a celebrity."

"What if he wants them as hostages?" Ingalls demanded, not quite willing to give up.

"You are grasping at straws, my friend. If the president is there, they'll have the most important hostage in the country. They won't need Nora or Miss Dean."

Intellectually, Ingalls had to admit that Everett was right. Emotionally he wasn't quite ready to accept it, but he did calm down. "How is it you know so much about women?" he asked.

"Ah," Everett said leaning back in his chair. "It would take days for me detail my conquests of the fair sex."

"Clarence Everett, if you don't stop this," Ingalls threatened, "I'm going to take you outside and punch you right in the nose."

"All right, George," Everett said with a soft laugh. "I apologize. Do you want breakfast now?"

"No."

The two detectives left the restaurant and automatically looked at the National Hotel across the street. If they only knew what Booth was thinking, or was it Anderson who was doing the thinking? They got into the phaeton and Everett took the reins. Ingalls looked at him, since he usually drove.

"As distracted as you are you might drive us right into a train," Everett said.

"You're probably right."

"Where to?"

"I don't know. Just drive around. I need to think." Ingalls needed time to sort everything out and that was the one thing he didn't have. The carriage was pointed west so that was the direction they went. "What are we going to do—just the two of us?" Ingalls asked.

"I don't know. We have to find Anderson. I'm betting he's the key to this whole thing," Everett said.

"I agree. It seems that the only way we're going to get to Anderson is through Fitch."

"Then let's see if we can find Fitch. What was the name of the place Eddy mentioned?"

"The Chain and Anchor. He said it was near the Navy Yard. Why don't we go check it out?"

"Good idea." Everett turned into a side street and headed south.

The National Hotel

Anderson was looking out his window when there was a knock on the door.

"Who is it?" he asked.

"It's Fitch."

When Anderson opened the door he smiled. If he had not known Fitch well, he wouldn't have recognized him. The man before him was clean shaven except for a trimmed and waxed mustache and his hair was combed with tonic. He wore a gray jacket with a clean white shirt and new collar. The cravat was not new, but it was clean, as were the trousers. Fitch's habitual scuffed boots were replaced by shoes covered with spatterdashes. Over this ensemble, he wore a black topcoat with brimmed hat. In addition, he carried a silver-tipped walking stick and a worn, but good-quality valise. It was obvious that he had also bathed.

"Very good, Joseph," Anderson said as he motioned Fitch inside. "You look exactly like what you are supposed to be, a well-to-do business man. Now tell me what you are to do."

"My name is Jared Hopkins. I am a shoe merchant from Pittsburgh, Pennsylvania, who has come here to start a business. I have chosen Union Town to live in because it is quiet and not as expensive as Washington City. I am looking for land on which to build a house, but until then I need to store some furniture so I would like to rent a barn or old house for that purpose. I am willing to fix the roof if that is necessary."

"Excellent. Do you have the necessary papers?"

"They are in the valise," he said, opening it. Fitch had calling cards and a few miscellaneous papers including a letter from his "wife" that their son was ill. All of them confirmed that he was Jared Hopkins of Pittsburgh.

"Good," Anderson told him. "I am sure you will do your usual excellent job. Now, be off. I don't know exactly when we will need this place but it may be soon."

"Yes, sir."

Anderson went back to the window and looked down at the street. People walked in both directions. Most walked purposefully, others strolled. Some were in a big hurry. One drunk reeled aimlessly from one side of the walkway to the other. Anderson speculated that he took at least three paces to the side for every one he took forward. He felt uncomfortable. He was used to commissions in which he was able to control every aspect of the unfolding events himself. For a while he was sure that he had everything well in hand, but the incident with Eddy showed that his control was tenuous at best. It would have been easy to label his hirelings incompetent weaklings, but Anderson knew better. He was the one who planned and executed his commissions. Most people lacked his skills and patience which was why his services were in such high demand. This was why he preferred working alone except for the services of someone like Fitch. If Anderson had been less confident he might have regretted taking on a task as complicated as the one he currently faced, but that was not in his nature. In fact, the difficulty made it all the more exciting.

Now there were more difficulties. There were the detectives with whom Eddy had spoken. The Metropolitan Police were bad enough, but these were Baker's men. Ordinarily, Anderson was content to leave well enough alone when it came to the authorities. They usually accepted the facts as Anderson arranged them at the scene of the crime and did precisely what Anderson wanted. Killing an officer of the law, even a corruptible one, led to too many complications, because police were very clannish. They might be more than willing to look the other way when it came to other people, but were vengeful and self-righteous when it came to one of their own. Bearing these facts in mind, Anderson now had to decide whether or not to do anything about these two men. Extraneous bodies made a commission more visible and Anderson disliked visibility most of all. This commission already required two deaths—those of Lincoln and Booth. Eddy's demise was an unfortunate, but necessary, occurrence. With his limited resources, Anderson decided he would now have to find out how much Ingalls and Everett knew. They must both be exceptional men, he thought, to be given such a case to handle. Everett must be particularly exceptional. For someone to have overcome all of the ingrained prejudice against colored people to become a detective, the man must be dangerous, indeed.

The Chain and Anchor

Everett stood in the dark shadows of a doorway watching the comings and goings of the clientele of the Chain and Anchor. They were easily the dregs of Washington society, and that was being highly complimentary. A few doors down Ingalls stood in a similar doorway watching the same things. This was the most unglamorous yet one of the most important parts of detective work. It required patience, powers of observation, and the ability to correctly interpret what one saw.

During the hours the two detectives stood there, they observed humanity at its basest. Drunks staggered through the alley, relieving themselves or vomiting, a prostitute past her prime took her customer standing in a doorway, and two men beat another for what amounted to pocket change. Throughout it all, Ingalls and Everett remained out of sight. When dawn began to lighten the sky, the Chain and Anchor emptied as if the patrons were afraid to gaze on each other in the light of day. Even the man who had been beaten managed to stir himself and stagger off. Everett wondered which were worse, this or Trantor's embalming room.

Ford's Theatre
March 17, 1865

John Wilkes Booth walked into Ford's Theatre with Alan Demming in tow. The theater was empty save for the ticketseller and three stagehands, Ned Spangler, Jacob Ritterspaugh, and James Maddox. They greeted him cheerfully. Booth was popular with the backstage crew, because he was friendly and showed an appreciation for their work. Occasionally, he even bought them a bottle of whiskey.

"This is my good friend, Mr. Demming," Booth told them. "He's never been backstage before. I'm going to give him a tour."

"Sure thing, Mr. Booth," Maddox said. "Are you on the bill tonight?"

"Tomorrow," Booth said, and then only to Demming, "for the world's greatest performance."

He took Anderson backstage to see how the scenery was shifted and how the curtains work. Anderson acted suitably impressed. Anderson had been to Ford's Theatre many times and had even been backstage, but his time he paid close attention to every detail.

Ford's Opera House, its official name, was a moderate-size theater which could seat approximately seventeen hundred patrons. The cane-backed seats were arranged in curving parallel rows cut by two aisles. There were also aisles along each wall. In the lobby was a double staircase leading to the dress circle and the boxes which overlooked the stage. The president's box, or State Box, was at stage left. It was actually a combination of Boxes 7 and 8 with the partition removed.

The stage was not particularly impressive. It was so shallow that a patron sitting in the boxes could see the back of some sets. To the rear of the stage on stage right was the door to the alley which could lead to either E or F Street. Beneath the stage was a passageway that connected both sides of the stage and the alley. This was the path everyone took to Taltavul's Tavern. The passageway was also used by the orchestra, since there was no orchestra pit. The musicians played in a space between the footlights and the front row. The entire theater was gas lighted and all of the lights could be controlled from a single valve beneath the stage.

Booth showed Anderson the subterranean passage that led to the south alley. Then the actor led his friend to the edge of the stage and helped him down. Anderson made sure his pantleg rode up so Booth could see his "wooden" leg. They walked through the orchestra to the back of the theater and took the stairs to the dress circle. Anderson followed the actor south along the aisle until they came to the president's box. The doors to the boxes were light pine and the locks on both doors had been broken for some time, so they just walked in.

"Here is where it will happen," Booth said, dramatically spreading his arms wide.

He quickly outlined his plan. It was another iteration of the plan Anderson had heard before. Spangler was to turn off the gas and shut down the house lights. Booth and company would then rush in and manacle the president and lower him to the stage, where they would take him to the alley and into the waiting barouche. Anderson feigned interest while he studied the surroundings. There were no chairs in the box so Anderson asked where they were.

"Oh, they don't put the chairs in until they're sure he'll be here," Booth said. "Usually, he sits over there." The actor pointed to the place at the front of the box where Lincoln habitually sat.

Anderson took note of the position. Lincoln's back would be to the door. A right-handed man could walk right through the open door, place a pistol against the president's head, and kill him before the others could get out of their seats. But how could he escape? That was the question. He walked to the edge of the box and looked over the railing. It was not a high jump, but a man could break a leg if he didn't land just right. Another problem was the bunting on the box. A jumper could get his leg caught in it and break his neck, never mind his leg, and Booth wanted to lower a bound six-foot man that distance by hand. The actor was, indeed, mad.

"I find your courage and determination admirable, Wilkes," Anderson said in a tone that bordered on worship.

"You have made it all possible, Alan. That's why you are invited to dinner tonight. I am going to the theater with friends and then after I drop the ladies off we are all going to Gautier's for a late supper. I want you to join us."

"I'd be honored to meet the rest of your compatriots, Wilkes. Truly honored."

Anderson had no intention of being seen at such a gathering. He would arrange a reason to be absent later. He still had to find a way to thwart Booth's plan for Saturday. Booth and his band were so unreliable that he dared only do it on the day of the event.

When they returned to the hotel, Booth offered to buy Anderson a drink at the bar, but he declined saying that his artificial leg was irritating the stump of his amputated leg.

"Is there anything I can do?" Booth asked with genuine concern.

"No, thank you, Wilkes, I just need to rest." With that, Anderson limped painfully upstairs.

"I'll call on you after I return from the theater, Alan," he called.

"I'll be waiting, Wilkes."

As soon as Anderson got to his room, he penned a note to Booth.

March 17, 1865

Dear Wilkes,

    My leg pains me deeply and I have gone to see a physician. I will meet you at Gautier's about 10:30 P.M. or as soon as the performance is over.

Yours &c,
ALAN

Anderson gave the note to Bunker the desk clerk and asked him to be sure to give it to Booth before he left for the theater, then he told Bunker he was going to see a doctor about his leg and asked the clerk to have a boy get him a cab. A few minutes later he was on his way. He had the cab stop in front of a likely looking doctor's office then paid the cabbie and tipped him. As soon as the cab departed, Anderson removed his beard and artificial leg and went to get another cab. He decided to spend the night at the carriage painter's shop in Swampoodle. The assassin needed to be alone so he could think.

The weather was at least bearable for Ingalls and Everett as they spent another night watching the Chain and Anchor for a sign of Fitch without success.

Gautier's Restaurant
Washington City

Gautier's, one of the most expensive restaurants in the city, was located on The Avenue between Sixth and Four and a Half

Streets. The outside was unprepossessing, but inside it was fabulous. If the restaurant of Willard's Hotel with its hardwood paneling, thick carpet, and crystal chandeliers was elegant, then the interior of Gautier's could only be deemed lavish. The paneling was polished to a high luster, the carpets were deep-blue crushed velvet, and the gas chandeliers were huge and bright. The table settings were china and silver, and the napkins were the finest linen. A member of royalty could hardly ask for a finer table. If the visual presentation was excellent, then the food was superb. Gautier's catered all of the most important functions both government and private. Since Booth was dealing with Alan Demming's money he spared no expense. He engaged a private dining room. Because this was a late supper, the table was laid with sliced beef and mutton. In addition there were cold cuts from Italy and Germany and cheeses from England and Holland. Loaves of bread lay already sliced and there were several types of pickles and relishes. Mustard and butter were available in small silver tubs. Drink was provided with the food. Several bottles of the best Baker and Overholtz whiskies were on the table with water. Off to one side were sliced lemons and powdered sugar for those who preferred a sweeter drink. To complete the amenities, in the center of the table was a silver holder with two dozen of the finest Cuban cigars wrapped in Connecticut Broadleaf. At Booth's request there was also a fine French champagne. Booth insisted that his fellow conspirators received only the best.

Booth's arrangement with Mr. Lichau, the owner of Gautier's, insured that they would not be disturbed even by waiters. It was close to 11:00 P.M. by the time they all assembled. Arnold and O'Laughlin sat together and suspiciously eyed Herold, Surratt, Atzerodt, and Payne. Booth was ebullient. He smiled broadly as he viewed this table occupied by his minions. The only one missing was poor old Alan Demming, but the actor was in too good a mood to worry about his crippled benefactor. He would fill Demming in on the proceedings tomorrow. Booth greeted them as a group and proceeded to fill a large crystal flute with champagne.

"Ah, we few, we band of brothers . . ." he said expansively. "Let me introduce you all around." He pointed at each man in turn and said his real name, which included Payne who was still using the name of Wood.

"We all know why we are here," he said. "And that is to save the Confederacy by capturing the tyrant Lincoln and taking him to Richmond. There we will hold him ransom for all the Confederate troops in captivity. Gentlemen," he said raising his glass, "I salute you."

As Booth drained his glass, the conspirators looked at one another. First Arnold and O'Laughlin looked at each other then across the table at the other conspirators who looked at each other then back. Each was searching for a sign of approval from the others. John Surratt glanced briefly at everyone with an expression of doubt then looked into his glass of whisky and water. Atzerodt, looking like a trapped ferret, chewed on a Cuban cigar and darted glances at each of the others. He was ready to go with the majority, but he was hoping the majority would not agree with Booth's plan. After looking he drained a glass full of whiskey and wiped his mouth with his sleeve. Herold sat in worshipful silence, sipping his whiskey, lemon, and sugar, looking at Booth and hanging on every word. Payne looked around the table with an expression of utter contempt for what he regarded as the unaccountable fear of the others. Arnold looked scared and totally opposed to the whole thing as he took healthy swallows of his whisky. Michael O'Laughlin stroked his moustache and twirled the ends. He was drinking neat whiskey with an expression of total disapproval.

Booth, draining his glass, was oblivious to the interplay among his followers. He refilled his glass and continued to address "his men."

"I realize that this will be a difficult operation," he said, "but it is well within our ability to accomplish." Taking another sip of champagne he continued.

"Payne and I will enter the theater and proceed upstairs to the presidential box. We will be armed and once we have everyone at gunpoint we will close the curtains and bind and gag everyone. Sam," he said nodding in Arnold's direction, "you will be waiting in the wings opposite the presidential box.

"Once I open the curtains you will walk out on stage with a six-shooter, call for quiet, and wait for us to lower Lincoln to the stage. As soon as his feet touch the stage, Mike (he indicated O'Laughlin) will turn the valve and cut the gas to the house lights.

"Davey," he indicated Herold with his champagne glass, "will drive the barouche.

"John and George," he said, gesturing to Surratt and Atzerodt, "know the route we must take intimately, so they will be waiting on the opposite side of the Navy Yard Bridge. Once we are across, they will be our guides south to the boat."

Booth refilled his glass again. "Sam, you will hop into the barouche with Davey. Mike, Wood, and I will all ride single mounts." Booth finished and stood there, glass in hand. He was smiling and waiting for comments on the plan. As the air grew heavy with silence, his smile faded. The corners of his mouth drew back and it was obvious he was becoming angry.

Finally Arnold cleared his throat and Booth gave him a dirty look. Arnold ignored the look and spoke. "Wilkes, first I want to tell you that I am and always will be your friend and that what I'm about to say is not meant as a reflection on you. But, I don't know if I can go along with this plan, and I'd like to enumerate the reasons."

Booth, dumb with shock that anyone would have the audacity to criticize his plan, stood stock still and Arnold, taking this as the actor's tacit approval, continued.

"First, there is no guarantee that Lincoln will attend the theater. Remember, we've tried this before and it failed for that very reason.

"Second, what makes you sure that Lincoln isn't going to put up a fight? Just because he talks nicely doesn't mean he's a sissy. He's big enough to whip any two of us except for Payne over there.

"Third, there are going to be over a thousand people in that audience. They are all going to see who we are and, I would venture to say that a few of them will be carrying pistols."

"Fourth, this city and the entire Union will be under arms before we get halfway to the Navy Yard Bridge. We'll be lucky if we aren't taken within an hour." Arnold would like to have added that the Confederacy was so near death that it was all pointless anyway, but Wilkes was his friend and he didn't want to cause him additional distress.

Booth walked forward and leaned over Arnold. The self-appointed savior of the Confederacy was furious. Arnold was not intimidated. He looked up at Booth and sipped his drink. "You, know, Wilkes, there's an easier way to do this. I read in the newspaper that on Monday the president is going to a matinee at the Soldier's Home way out on Seventh Street. It's my opinion that it would be easier to take a man away from a couple of guards on an empty country road than from a theater full of people. This way it would be quite some time before anyone could give the alarm and we could be halfway to Virginia before they knew what happened."

By now Booth was livid.

Arnold paused. "There's another thing," he said. "If this thing isn't finished in a week, I am withdrawing from this company and going back to Baltimore."

Booth was furious. Not only had someone criticized his plan and had the audacity to suggest another one, but he had also given Booth a deadline. What made it all the worse was that this person was a boyhood friend. He spoke slowly and distinctly. "I ought to shoot any man who talks of backing out." He was looking directly at Sam Arnold.

Arnold calmly looked at Booth and smiled. "Wilkes, two can play that game."

The actor, still pale with rage, backed away. He drank another glass of champagne and the anger subsided.

"I'm sorry, Sam," he said, repentantly. "I should never have spoken to you that way."

"No offense taken, Wilkes," he said.

"How many of you favor Sam's plan?" he asked.

Surratt, freed from the responsibility of being the first, spoke up. "I agree with Sam, here," he said. "We'd have a hell of a better chance with a lone carriage on a deserted country road than in a theater."

"Yes, he's right," Atzerodt said, taking another drink of whiskey."

"I'm with Sam," O'Laughlin said. "We'd have a much better chance."

Everyone else looked at Herold and Payne.

"Whatever you say, Wilkes," Herold said.

Payne said nothing.

"All right," Booth said suddenly. "We'll do it Sam's way on Monday. I'm playing at Ford's tomorrow night so I will get whatever information I can. John, I'd like you and George to take some things to your mother's tavern in Surrattsville. Take Davey with you so he can learn the route."

Herold smiled at Booth and the other two nodded. There was little more discussion on the plan. Most didn't like the idea anyway, but felt more comfortable with Arnold's version than with Booth's. Only Herold and Payne were willing to follow Booth without question. For the rest of the evening, they spoke of trivialities. The sky was growing lighter when they left Gautier's.

The National Hotel
March 18, 1865

Booth rode his horse around the deserted streets of Washington before going back to the National Hotel. He was a man who saw his duty clearly and had set an example for the others to follow, but it seemed that only Herold and Payne were the ones who were willing to do all for the salvation of the Confederacy. He had created a foolproof plan to capture Lincoln, but the others were unable to see the genius behind it. He felt Arnold's betrayal most strongly. He sighed, still hopeful that they would succeed. After all, without his perseverance they would not have gotten this far. The plan didn't matter actually. It was he, John Wilkes Booth, whom history would applaud as the man who brought down the tyrant Lincoln. When he noticed shops opening up and people beginning to fill the streets he headed back to the National. He would have to see how Alan Demming was doing. Without Alan there would be no money.

Booth knocked on the door of Demming's room.

"Who is it?" Demming's voice asked.

"It's Wilkes, Alan, how are you?"

Booth listened to the uneven tread of the man with the wooden leg. When the door opened, he was appalled at how bad his friend looked.

Anderson was pleased when he saw the look on Booth's face. The light make-up he wore was effective. It consisted of a very light powder on the face, a little darkening under the eyes, and just a bit more gray in his hair to make him look ill.

"How are you, Alan?" Booth repeated, not sure how to proceed.

"I'm fine," Anderson said wearily. "I just need some rest. I am sorry I wasn't able to attend your meeting. Come in and tell me about it."

"It went very well," Booth said, following Anderson into the room. Anderson sat on the bed, lifted his "wooden" leg up onto the mattress, then lay back with a soft moan.   ˇ

"Is there anything I can get for you, Alan?" Booth asked solicitously.

"No, I'm fine, really. The stump has become fevered. It happens from time to time. I shall be incommoded for a day or two, that's all. Now tell me what is going to happen."

"I have devised a new plan," Booth said. "We are going to capture Lincoln Monday."

"Not tonight?"

"No, he will be riding unescorted in a carriage to visit the Soldiers' Home up on Seventh Street on Monday. It will be a lot easier to take him on a lonely country road than in a theater."

"Yes, of course." Anderson wondered which member of Booth's band had come up with this idea. It clearly wasn't the actor. Anderson wondered how he was going to thwart this plan without revealing himself to the authorities. Booth was becoming tiresome.

"Well, I have to get some rest, Alan. I'm doing Pescara in *The Apostate*, you know. Would you like a ticket?"

"Yes I would, maybe I'll feel well enough to go this evening. Just drop it off at the desk."

"Get well soon, Alan. After Monday we will have a lot of celebrating to do."

"I'm sure of that, Wilkes."

"I hope we can get together after the performance."

"I do, too."

Booth hesitated and there was a period of silence. Anderson knew what it was and he let Booth stew. The actor needed money, but wouldn't bring the subject up. Anderson now knew that he was the actor's only source of income and *that*, if nothing else, would tie Booth to him. Booth realized he was just standing there and left.

Anderson waited until he could no longer hear Booth's footsteps in the hall before he got up and locked the door. He had two days to come up with a surreptitious way to foil the actor's scheme and he'd better get at it. Another anonymous note was out of the question. No doubt the good Major Richards learned that the last anonymous warning was genuine. Another would make him overly suspicious. This had to be done without raising any suspicion whatsoever. But how?

Anderson was still mulling over the problem when there was another knock on the door. "Who is it?" he called in a soft sickly voice.

"It's Fitch. Are you all right?"

Anderson opened the door and Fitch's jaw dropped. "You look like hell," he said.

"It's only make-up, Joseph. Come in and tell me what you've found."

Fitch walked into the room and eyed the bottle of whiskey on the table. "Go ahead, have a drink." Anderson said.

"You want one?" Fitch asked, pouring a glass tumbler full of the liquor.

"No," Anderson replied as he eyed Fitch. He didn't mind Fitch drinking as long as he didn't get drunk during a commission, but he was beginning to wonder if Fitch were succumbing too much to the temptation of drink.

Fitch took a swallow and sighed. "I've been riding since before dawn," he said. "What I found was an old barn south of Uniontown about half a mile from the road. There was a house near it, but it burned down a couple of years back. Nearest house is about a mile and a half away. The man who owns it soaked me ten dollars a month for rent. I gave him thirty dollars."

"Good, you can take me down there Tuesday. I have work to do until then. Get some rest and meet me back here about 8:00 A.M. Tuesday. Before you leave, get me a *National Intelligencer*."

"Yes, sir."

Fitch disappeared for a few minutes then returned. "We are in important company," he said, handing Anderson the paper.

"How so?"

"The governor of Indiana just checked in with a mob of people."

Fitch took his leave and Anderson began reading the paper. There was the usual war news, but on page four was the notice that the 140th Indiana had captured a Rebel flag and were bringing it with them when they visited the city on Monday. Anderson put the paper down and began to pace. How was he to . . . Then it came to him. It was simple and brilliant, but the timing would have to be just right.

Headquarters, Cavalry Corps
Military Division of the Mississippi
Gravelly Springs, Alabama
March 18, 1865

Maj. Gen. James H. Wilson emerged from his tent with a grim, determined look on his face. He was a man of medium height with a handsome face decorated with an imperial. Today he had on a plain blue fatigue blouse worn by most Union soldiers and dark blue trousers with a yellow stripe on the seam. His thinning brown hair was covered by a kepi. He did not look like the man in command of the finest mounted force that the American Continent would ever see, but that is precisely what he was. He was also a man with something to prove. A few months before, he had been relieved of his command by Phil Sheridan for his performance near New Market and sent west to get him out of the way. Under Gen. George Thomas, the "Rock of Chickamauga," Wilson completely revamped the Union cavalry in the West and turned it into an irresistible strike force. Now he was going to show the world what he could do with it.

Wilson mounted his horse and looked at his command. There were three cavalry divisions totaling 12,500 veteran Union cavalry. They were superbly armed and equipped and their horses were in splendid condition. They were accompanied by three batteries of horse artillery that could move as fast as the cavalry, a bridge train of light canvas pontoons, and a supply train of 250 wagons. It was a force, truly, to be reckoned with. Wilson was about to prove that Sheridan's opinion of his leadership ability was wrong and, as so often happens in war, it was the enemy who were going to pay for a personal slight. Wilson nodded and his subordinate commanders put the long columns in motion. It was the start of what would be the most destructive campaign of the war save for that of Sherman. In a few short weeks, Wilson's troops would rip through Alabama and North Georgia, sweeping all before them. They would destroy rolling mills and factories and anything else of use to the dying Confederacy. What the inhabitants of South Georgia, the Carolinas, and the Shenandoah Valley had suffered was now experienced by the heartland of the South. To them it was Armageddon, to the grimly happy Union troopers it was just punishment for the double sins of secession and slavery. By April 2, Wilson's troops would have Selma. By April 10 they would be across the Alabama River. By the cessation of hostilities, they would have Montgomery. After that, they would go on to capture Jefferson Davis. The tragic end of Booth's world was drawing near.

The National Hotel
March 20, 1865

Both the city newspapers and the actors at Ford's Theatre confirmed the fact that Lincoln would be visiting the Soldiers' Home on Monday afternoon. Booth left at 10:00 A.M. to rouse his followers. He gathered Payne and Surratt first then picked up Herold, who was waiting in front of his mother's house. Atzerodt was picked up next, and O'Laughlin and Arnold last. The seven men then rode slowly up Seventh Street. They looked for a grove of trees in which to hide, but it wasn't easy. The trees were still bare except for a hint of buds. Just north of Boundary Street near a bend in the road they found a suitable grove of trees that would hide them all. The sky was overcast and the air was cold with the kind of bite that was typical for March. The breath of the men and horses was quite visible. As they rode their horses into the trees, they lost sight of the road. Booth gave his last-minute instructions.

"When we sight the carriage coming down the road, John and I will ride out to meet it. We will take position a little ahead of it and allow it to catch up with us. The rest of you will wait a minute or two and then ride in behind it. Don't do anything until you see John or me grab the reins and stop the coach. Then you must come to our assistance at once.

"Wood," Booth said, addressing Payne by his alias, "you will leap into the coach and subdue the president. John and I will take care of the driver, then John will put on his livery. John will drive the coach and Wood and I will keep him covered inside the coach."

"Are there any questions?"

"What are the rest of us supposed to do?" Arnold asked.

"You and Mike will take care of any mounted guards, George will remain a few yards behind to assist anyone in trouble.

"Now, just take it easy."

Everything fell silent except for the snorting of the horses and the sound of their bridles when they tossed their heads.

Arnold checked his watch. It was 2:05 P.M. He looked around, then leaned over to O'Laughlin and whispered. "Mounted guards, my foot. If there's an escort of Yankee cavalry, I'm leaving."

"You and me both, Sam," O'Laughlin agreed.

By this time the others were whispering to each other.

Suddenly, Booth called, "Quiet!" in a loud whisper.

Everyone stopped talking. Above the sound of the wind in the trees, they could hear carriage wheels and hoofbeats.

"How many are there?" Booth asked.

There was no answer because none of them could see the road. Booth then spurred his horse to the road and around the bend. He almost shouted for joy. Coming toward them was a black coach being driven by a driver with a top hat. It was the president's coach and there was no escort! He returned quickly to the woods. The others in unrestrained curiosity had edged closer to the edge of the road.

"This is it!" he announced.

John Surratt spurred his horse forward. They rode ahead of the coach and let it catch up. They parted as the coach drove between them. Booth reined in his horse and looked inside. The only occupant was a young, clean-shaven man he had never seen before. The man looked startled. In a fury, Booth signaled Surratt to break away. When they returned to the group, Booth announced that the president was not in the coach.

"What?" Arnold said, his temper getting the best of him. "Not in the coach? That's it, Wilkes, I've had it. I'm going home."

"You can't leave," the actor said. He tried to make it a command but it sounded more like a plea.

"I'm going with Sam," O'Laughlin announced.

"Damned traitors!" Booth screamed.

"Traitors?" Surratt exploded. "I've risked my life for the Confederacy, Wilkes. I threw in with you because I thought your idea was good, but I can see that none of this *opéra bouffe* will ever amount to a hill of beans."

"Damn you!" was all the actor could manage.

Surratt spurred his horse south. Atzerodt was already heading south. Booth turned. Only Herold and Payne were still there. They stood silently, waiting for orders. The place of the conspirators who had fled was marked by piles of warm horse manure steaming in the cold air.

The National Hotel

As soon as he was sure Booth was gone, Anderson donned a dark blue suit, put on a false mustache, and went downstairs with the newspaper article about the 140th Indiana Regiment. He waited patiently until Gov. Oliver P. Morton and his party came down to breakfast at 9:30 A.M. The governor was a large stout man with thinning light-brown hair that was turning gray. Bushy eyebrows and a full beard completed the image of an imposing man. He sat down to breakfast with four other men that Anderson could only assume were his staff or bodyguards. He waited until they were served, then walked over.

"Governor Morton," he called as he strode over to the table waving the newspaper.

One of the other men stood up and positioned himself between Anderson and the governor. "Who are you, sir?" he asked threateningly.

"Out of my way, sir," Anderson said indignantly. "I am a constituent and a good Republican."

Morton waved his hand and the man stepped aside. The governor removed his napkin from his collar and smiled wearily at Anderson. "What may I do for you, sir?" he asked, expecting a petition from another office seeker.

"It is what you can do for the State of Indiana, Governor," he said and stuck out his hand. "Slater's the name, Howard Slater — from South Bend. Have you seen this paper?"

Governor Morton shook Anderson's hand and leaned over to see the article in the paper. He read it and looked puzzled.

"I can see you and I are thinking alike, Governor," Anderson said. "What an honor it would be if our own 140th Indiana could present this captured Rebel banner to the president personally."

No one has to mention a good idea to an astute politician twice.

Morton's eyes widened and his face broke into a broad grin. The others at the table were also smiling.

"Joe," he said to one of the men at the table ". . . Oh, never mind. I'm going to see the president personally.

"Mr. Slater," he said turning to Anderson and pumping his hand again. "It is always a pleasure to meet constituents who are concerned for the welfare and honor of our great state. Have a cigar, sir, and when you visit the state house next, come and see me. You don't need an appointment, just give the clerk your name."

Anderson acted appropriately awed as the governor and his staff hurried out of the hotel to the White House. Anderson looked at the cigar. It was a very good one. He put it in his pocket and left the hotel. He went to the nearest stable, rented a horse, and rode up Seventh Street. Booth's men were easy to spot and he waited down the road in a smaller copse. When the president's coach drove by, he rode out and waved. A cursory glance showed that the president was not in the coach. The driver waved back and Anderson continued to ride south to the city. It was not until later that Anderson learned that while Booth and his men were waiting in the grove of trees to kidnap Lincoln, the president was addressing the 140th Indiana on the steps of the National Hotel itself. He had to laugh. It was very funny.

That evening, Booth left for New York, Surratt left for Richmond, and Payne left for Baltimore. The only one of the conspirators remaining in Washington was David Herold who had gone back home. That did not disturb Anderson. He now knew Booth well enough to know the actor would return as soon as he needed money. Anderson pushed Booth to the back of his mind. Right now there were other things to do.

Uniontown, Maryland
March 21, 1865

It was a pleasant day, though somewhat overcast, as Anderson and Fitch rode across the Navy Yard Bridge to Uniontown. Uniontown was a prosperous little farming community, just south of the nation's capital. At the start of the war it had been staunchly secessionist in its views, but with the waning fortunes of the Confederacy and the utter collapse of Confederate currency, there was less talk about joining the Southern Cause or going to fight for it and more commerce with the Yankee authorities in Washington for their greenbacks. The two men rode past the neat white and brick houses that made up the village. Soon the houses grew sparser as the scenery changed from town to field. Farmers were already plowing their fields and planting. By the time Fitch turned off the road, the farms had been left behind and the scene was one of pastures and trees. Anderson made note of every foot of the route. Once he had memorized it by day, he would travel it two or three times by night so he could literally follow it blindfolded.

The barn was old and had not seen a paintbrush in some time, but it was still sturdy. To the casual observer, it was not the kind of place where someone was likely to store anything of value, and that made it perfect for Anderson.

"Is it dry on the inside?" he asked Fitch.

"As near as I can tell," Fitch replied.

They stopped in front of the door and dismounted. Fitch lifted the wooden latch and opened the door. Light flooded into the dank interior. Anderson looked for a lantern and found one hanging from a nail on one of the main supports. Checking to see that it was full, he lifted it off the nail, struck a match, and lighted it. He held it above his head as he walked through the structure. The barn had stalls on the left side and an open bay on the right. The hayloft ran the length of the barn and it was empty. At the far end of the barn on the right was what looked like a room.

"Is that a tack room?" Anderson asked.

"Yes, sir," Fitch said.

"Excellent." Anderson was pleased.

He went directly to the tack room and observed that the room was dry and it had a stove. After the tack room Anderson looked at the outside of the barn. There were some bad spots on the roof, but they were inconsequential for his purposes.

"Joseph, when we get back to Washington City, I want you to buy some used furniture. Buy a sofa, three chairs, a china cabinet, a dining room table and chairs, a bedroom suite, and a single bed. In addition get two padlocks, one for the front and one for the back. Hire some men to bring them down and unload them in the barn for you. Everything goes in the barn except for the single bed and two chairs. They go in the tack room. I want everything in place before the first of April. Any questions?"

"No, Mr. Anderson."

"Good, let's return. We still have to lure Booth back to Washington. Hopefully this time we can keep him here until we need him."

Fitch said nothing. He learned long ago not to ask questions and not to say anything. Anderson knew what he was doing.

Swampoodle

On M Street, four doors from the corner of First Street, was the office of Hiram Merriweather, one of several men known to the residents of Swampoodle as "Doc." It was an accurate title, because Merriweather was, or at least had been, a doctor. His practice in Philadelphia before the war was closed down by the authorities when they discovered that his specialty was terminating pregnancies at a premium price. One of his patients, the wife of a prominent businessman, wanted to make sure there was no evidence of her infidelity. Unfortunately, there were complications and the wife died. The grief-stricken businessman was influential enough to demand and get an investigation. Merriweather got wind of it in time to leave town in a hurry. After trying Lancaster and Baltimore, Merriweather settled in Swampoodle where he established a thriving practice treating bullet wounds that were usually inflicted by the police, terminating unwanted pregnancies (there were no penalties for mistakes in Swampoodle), and dealing in stolen quinine and morphine, a substance which was finding increased popularity as a painkiller among soldiers who had been wounded.

Anderson had a little difficulty finding Merriweather's office since it was dark and there were no signs or other advertising. Finally he found the right place and knocked on the door. The doctor, wearing a dressing gown and trousers, answered the knock as he was more accustomed to late-night visitors than most physicians. The door opened partially and was stopped by a chain. The doctor's hand was in his pocket and it was obvious he had a pistol.

"Yes?" he asked.

"I am in need of some medical advice," Anderson said.

"I'm not in habit of giving advice," Merriweather said.

"I would be willing to pay handsomely for it, say a hundred dollars for a few minutes of your time."

"Let's see the color of your money," the doctor said.

Anderson reached into his wallet and pulled out five twenty-dollar greenbacks, whereupon Dr. Merriweather smiled and opened the door. The two men did not shake hands since the doctor's right hand remained on the pistol. Anderson was not offended. He respected a man who took no chances. The doctor took the money and stuffed it into the left pocket of his dressing gown and led Anderson to his consulting room. It was no different from any other one Anderson had ever seen. The wallpaper was a tasteful striped pattern and there were Oriental carpets on the floor. For his patients there was a settee and two upholstered chairs. In the middle of the room was an Italian leather-topped table. Merriweather lit a lamp on the wall, gestured to a chair, and offered his visitor a drink. Anderson sat in the chair proffered, but declined the drink.

"Now, sir," the doctor said, avoiding the use of names. "What type of advice are you seeking?"

"How do I convince someone that he has done something?" Anderson said.

The doctor smiled mirthfully. "I beg your pardon."

"I am perfectly serious, Doctor. It is essential that I convince a man that he has done something."

"Then may I respectfully suggest that you try a mesmerist." Merriweather was not taking this very seriously.

"I don't want him to cluck like a chicken or bark like a dog," Anderson stressed. "I want to convince him that he committed a specific act."

"What kind of act?"

"I am not at liberty to say."

"H-m-m." The doctor looked at Anderson and furrowed his brows. The man in his consulting room was serious. "You could try getting him drunk."

"I have already considered that. It would debilitate the man too much. Is there no drug that would render him tractable, so that when he recovered he would be able to function?"

The doctor smiled. "An interesting problem. Come back in two days. I'll see if I can find you an answer."

Anderson looked at him skeptically.

"I will give it my full attention, sir, I promise."

Swampoodle
Washington City
March 23, 1865

Anderson returned to Dr. Merriweather's office on Thursday evening. This time the physician was more congenial. He stood in his vest and shirtsleeves with a broad smile.

"Come in, sir. I may have an answer to your problem, although it remains to be proved."

"And that is?"

"There is a doctor from a Pennsylvania regiment. I think his name is Cade or Cady, who claims that a person who is rendered half-unconscious with chloroform is somehow compelled to tell the truth. He claims to have extracted information from Rebel prisoners in this way."

Anderson was puzzled and the look on his face showed it. Before he could say a word, the doctor raised his hand.

"Hear me out before you react, sir. I know that the truth is not what you are seeking. What I am suggesting is that if a man's will is weakened to the point that he must tell the truth, must it not follow that his will must be weakened so that he can be made to believe certain things, especially if he is predisposed to them?"

"I can't deal in suppositions," Anderson said flatly.

"Precisely," the doctor said. "So why not bring the man in here and try it?"

"That's not possible. Could we try it on someone else?"

"Certainly. I suggest you supply the subject. That way you will be certain there is no chicanery."

Anderson thought for a moment. "Saturday?"

The doctor shook his head. "Saturday is always busy. How about Sunday, say, at 6:00 P.M.?"

"Sunday, it is, but on Saturday I will inform you of the circumstances since the object of the experiment must not know that he is a part of it."

Dr. Merriweather nodded. "Discretion is the word."

The Barroom
Willard's Hotel
Washington City
March 24, 1865

Ingalls decided it was time to act. It was time to give Nora some token to show that his affections were genuine. He decided that a piece of jewelry would be appropriate, but what kind of jewelry?

"Clarence?" he asked as they stood at the bar of Brown's Hotel.

"Yes?"

"What kind of jewelry would you buy a woman to show you cared?"

"You're asking me?" Everett said, sipping his beer.

"Haven't you ever bought a gift for a woman to show her you loved her?"

Everett thought for a minute. "Flowers maybe. Jewelry no."

"Some ladies' man you are," Ingalls said in frustration. "You're no help at all."

Everett shrugged. "In that case buy her a brooch or a bracelet."

"Why a brooch or a bracelet?"

"Because it's not a ring. It's a nice gift, but you're not making a commitment."

"But I want to make a commitment, Clarence."

"George," said Everett, putting his hand to his heart, "believe me. If you want a commitment, a bracelet can lead to it, honest."

"You're not just kidding?"

"You don't believe me? Then ask this gentleman here," he said, gesturing to the man next to them at the bar. He turned to the man. "Sir, may I have your opinion on a delicate matter?"

The man turned. He was in his mid-forties. He had blond, thinning hair and a curly mustache and beard, all of which were turning gray. He was well dressed and he had a slight paunch. And, most important of all, he was wearing a wedding ring. "Look," he said, regarding Everett with a little suspicion. "I don't want to seem unfriendly, but I never discuss politics at the bar."

"No sir, this isn't politics. This is about an affair of the heart."

"Huh?"

"My friend here is in love with a woman and wants to buy her a present. We have narrowed our choice to a brooch or a bracelet. You appear to be a married man. What is your opinion?"

"Get her a brooch."

"Why?" Ingalls asked.

"I got my girlfriend a bracelet twenty years ago and now I have a wife and four daughters—only one of which is married off. Take my advice, get her a brooch and save yourself the trouble."

Everett laughed along with the man who gave them the advice. Ingalls knew he had been had.

Fort Stedman
The Siege of Petersburg
March 25, 1865

The Confederate defensive line at Petersburg was over thirty-seven miles long. To hold this, Lee had little more than thirty-five thousand men. Realizing that his line was stretched to the breaking point, Lee decided that it was time to abandon Petersburg and Richmond and head south to join Joseph Johnston's forces in North Carolina. He reasoned that the two Confederate armies could unite swiftly, defeat Sherman's army in North Carolina, then return north to fight Grant in the open field. It was a concept worthy of a great general, but how to accomplish it with limited resources? The solution was typically Lee. He decided to launch an attack to force Grant to shorten his lines. By rupturing the Union lines and capturing the railroads beyond them, he would force Grant to take troops from the western end of line to restore the situation and leave the way open to North Carolina. The initial target for the attack was Fort Stedman, a Union-held position on the eastern part of the line. It was the closest enemy work to the Confederate lines, no more than 150 yards away. In addition, the Union Military Railroad was less than a mile behind Fort Stedman.

The attack began at 4:00 A.M. and initially was very successful. Fort Stedman was taken with hardly a shot fired, but from there everything went awry. The plan called for the attacking troops to seize three works beyond Stedman, but these did not exist. The attacking columns lost their way and the attack bogged down as hungry Confederate soldiers stopped to loot food from captured

Yankee positions. The delay gave the Union forces time to react and they counterattacked in overwhelming strength, recapturing positions on either side of Stedman. Then they subjected it to a deadly cross fire. At 7:30 A.M. Lee gave the signal to withdraw, but the occupiers of Stedman preferred surrender rather than face withdrawing across the shell-swept ground. Union losses were fifteen hundred. Lee's losses were four thousand, a staggering 12 percent of his total force. Although no one yet realized it, the attack on Fort Stedman was the last offensive of the Army of Northern Virginia.

The National Hotel
Washington City

Booth checked back into the National on Saturday morning while Anderson, disguised as Alan Demming, was sitting in the lobby reading a newspaper. Booth is back sooner than I expected, Anderson thought, he must be totally broke. He rose from his chair, went up to the actor, and greeted him warmly.

"Wilkes, it's good to have you back."

Booth looked dazed as if he were a man who was at the end of his tether, then he smiled. "Alan, you look so much better," he said.

Anderson shrugged. "The doctor gave me some pills and the fever broke a few days after you left. Come up to my room. I have something for you."

The actor gave him a look of hopeful interest. "I'll be there as soon as I have my things sent up."

"Wonderful, Wilkes." As soon as Booth walked away Anderson went to the desk and had the clerk send up some brandy and water.

Booth knocked on Anderson's door a few minutes later and they talked about the course of the war. The actor drank a lot of brandy and rambled, which made Anderson wonder if he was well. He gave Booth an envelope and the actor took it with great glee. Suddenly the actor was crestfallen. There were only two hundred dollars in greenbacks in the envelope. Anderson smiled to himself. There were to be no more envelopes in the thousands. He planned to keep a tighter rein on Booth from now on.

Booth made one more attempt to organize a kidnapping when he read in the March 27 Washington *Star* that the president would be attending the opera *Ernani* on Wednesday, the twenty-ninth. Booth wired Arnold to bring O'Laughlin. Surratt could not be contacted and neither could Atzerodt. Herold and Payne were the only ones who responded. Booth returned to Room 231 at the National Hotel and fell into melancholia so deep that he contemplated suicide.

Swampoodle
Washington City

Anderson thought about Dr. Merriweather's proposal and wondered if he were wasting his time. Booth was already drinking heavily and it would not be difficult to get the actor into a stupor. The trouble was that right after the act, he would have to be well enough to ride a horse. He decided to try the doctor's experiment and if it didn't work, he would get Booth drunk and gamble on the actor's ability to sober up quickly. The next question was who would be appropriate for the test. The doctor mentioned someone who was predisposed to do something. Booth was certainly predisposed to kill Lincoln though he obviously wasn't capable of doing it. If he was, he would have tried to kill the president on Inauguration Day. Who would be predisposed to do something? Anderson smiled. A pickpocket. For a moment he regretted having Eddy killed so quickly, but he knew a suitable replacement. It was a young man named Frank Morris, another habitué of Pointer's.

Anderson decided to go to Pointer's himself. Since Eddy's demise, Fitch was considered a pariah even though he paid well for Jasmine's company. He went to Pointer's as a businessman requiring someone with a particular talent. He entered the tavern nervously and attracted the attention of everyone in the place. He didn't belong and he obviously wasn't a policeman. Anderson went to the bar and ordered a beer.

Looking anxiously over his shoulder, he spoke to Clem, the bartender, "Can you tell me where I might find Mr. Frank Morris."

"Are you a friend of his?"

"I was given his name and was told he might retrieve an object for me—for a suitable fee, of course." Anderson sipped the beer with a shaky hand and spilled some.

Clem smiled wryly. This man was scared of his own shadow. He turned to an old colored man who was sweeping the floor. "Hiram, go upstairs and get Frank. Someone wants to see him."

The old man put down his broom and shuffled upstairs. In a minute a young man in his mid-twenties wearing shirt and trousers came down the stairs. Morris was tall, thin, and good looking with a long straight nose and curly blond hair. He was a talented pickpocket who liked to work in crowds. The bartender pointed to Anderson and Morris gestured to a table.

"May I get you something?" Anderson asked apprehensively.

"Clem, a beer," Morris called. Then, "What can I do for you?"

"I need a man's watch taken," Anderson whispered conspiratorially. "The reason why is not important. It's worth two hundred dollars."

"Pretty important watch," Morris said, taking the beer from Clem. "When do you want this done?"

"I will pick you up here at a quarter 'til six on Sunday. We will go to this man's house. He is a doctor. I will introduce you as my nephew. You are having pains. When he examines you, you can get the watch."

Morris looked at him. "If it's that important, it should be worth three hundred dollars," Morris said, raising the price.

"I'm not a wealthy man," Anderson whined.

"Three hundred or no deal."

"All right," Anderson said, caving in. "But no money until after it's done."

"See you Sunday, Mr.—ah. "

"Smith," Anderson supplied.

"Smith," Morris said with a self-satisfied smirk.

Swampoodle
March 26, 1865

Anderson picked Morris up at the appointed time and drove him to Dr. Merriweather's.

"Ah, Mr. Smith," the doctor said cordially. "Come in. And this is your nephew, Mr. Morris. Come in, please."

"Well, Mr. Morris, you uncle tells me that you have a pain in your left side."

"Uh, yeah," Morris said.

"Well, if you would be so kind as to remove your coat and step into the examining room, we shall see if we can discover the source of your distress."

Merriweather's clean, modern examining room surprised Anderson. The walls were white and the floor was stone. On one wall was a desk and a bookcase full of medical books. Against the opposite wall were cases filled with instruments and chemicals which he assumed were medicines. In the center of the room was a table with hand wheels for elevating various parts of the body. Morris climbed onto the table and lay down. Then the doctor prodded his left side, asking if it hurt. All the while Morris winced when the doctor pressed too hard, but kept his eye on the doctor's watch chain.

"Now, Mr. Morris," the doctor said, stepping back. "I am going to check your breathing to see that your lungs are not affected. I have a gauze and I am going to put it over your nose. Breathe deeply. If your lungs are clear of infection you will not cough. Understood?"

Morris looked confused and looked over at Anderson who nodded yes. The doctor placed the gauze over Morris' nose and mouth and the pickpocket took a couple of deep breaths before his eyes fluttered closed.

"Is he . . ." Anderson was silenced when the doctor signaled him to be quiet.

"Frank," the doctor said quietly to Morris.

"Yes," Morris said dully. His eyes fluttered partially open then closed again.

"Are you Frank Morris?"

"Yes." It was almost a hiss.

"Do you live at Pointer's?"

"I . . . Yes."

"Did you come here to get a watch?"

"I—no," was the mumbled reply.

Anderson frowned but Merriweather wasn't paying attention.

"Yes you did," the doctor insisted soothingly. "You came here to steal a watch."

"Yes." There was a pause. "Steal."

"It does indeed seem to work as a truth serum," the doctor whispered to Anderson. His delight was evident. "Now let us see if my supposition is true.

"Frank?" the doctor began.

"Yes."

"You are taking the watch."

"No." It was barely audible.

Anderson moved forward, but the doctor held up his hand.

"Yes, you are, you are slipping it out of his pocket and you are so quick and so smooth that he doesn't know."

"Quick . . . Doesn't know."

"It was easy, very easy."

". . . Easy."

"It was child's play."

". . . Play."

"This is the easiest three hundred dollars you have ever made."

"Easiest three hundred dollars . . . ever . . . made."

The doctor repeated the statements three times and then waited for Morris to start stirring, then he gave Anderson his watch.

"Quickly," the doctor instructed. "Get him out into the air and don't forget the watch."

Anderson and the doctor got Morris to his feet, got his coat on, thrust the watch into his pocket, and got him outside in the cool night air.

"Are you all right, my boy?" Anderson asked solicitously.

"I—I think so," he said groggily. "What happened?"

"The medicine must have made you drowsy, but you got it and that's what counts."

"I did?" Morris was trying to remember.

"May I have it?"

"What?"

"The watch. It's in your pocket."

Groggily, Morris reached into his pocket and withdrew the watch.

Anderson took the watch from Morris' hand. "You've earned your money," he said, thrusting three hundred dollars into the pickpocket's coat.

"Easiest three hundred dollars I ever made," Morris said trying to find his balance. "Child's play."

Anderson smiled with satisfaction.

"Nice doing business with you, Mr. Smith." The pickpocket called as he began walking unsteadily back to Pointer's.

Anderson went back inside. The doctor held out his hand for his watch. "It went rather well, don't you think?" he asked.

Anderson gave him a genuine smile. He reached into his coat pocket and pulled out a pouch containing a thousand dollars in gold coin. He handed it to the doctor with the watch. "Now show me how to do it."

The doctor showed him just how much chloroform to put on the gauze.

"What if the person is going to be out for a long time?" he asked.

"How long?"

"About five or six hours at most."

The doctor frowned. "That is a long time. Give him a heavy dose and when he starts to come around put another three or four drops on the gauze, no more. Too much can kill a man. Start by asking him his name, what he does, and where he lives before you tell him what you're doing. Be firm, but gentle, and repeat it if you have the chance. It will help if the subject is weak-willed. I believe you will need this." The doctor produced two brown pint bottles of chloroform and a paper package of gauze.

"Thank you, Doctor, goodnight."

"Best of luck in your endeavors, Mr. Smith."

CHAPTER 9

**Washington City
March 31, 1865**

INGALLS TOOK NORA to Willard's for supper since they couldn't get tickets for the theater. He wanted the surroundings to be pleasant when he presented her with the bracelet he had purchased for her. It was a small gold lady's bracelet with garnets mounted across the top and it fastened to the wrist with a light golden chain and clasp. It had cost twenty-nine dollars at Hood's on The Avenue and he was hoping she would like it. "If she likes you, she'll like it," Everett told him but he couldn't be sure about anything Clarence said about women, because Clarence teased him unmercifully about his feelings for Nora. Despite his hopes for a pleasant evening Nora looked somber and downcast and showed no appetite for the excellent shad.

"Nora," he said, carefully choosing his words. "If you'll forgive my saying so, you seem very out of sorts this evening."

"I'm sorry," she said, not looking at him.

"Is it something I've said or done, dearest?"

"No," she said starting to cry. "It's not you, George. I couldn't bear it if it weren't for you." She reached into her bag for a handkerchief.

"What is it then?"

"Everything," she sobbed. "It's terrible."

207

Ingalls sat there not really knowing what to do. Until now, he had known Nora as a happy young woman. Seeing her like this was unbearable. He felt clumsy and awkward, so he reached his hand out to hers. When his hand touched hers she grasped it.

"It was such a happy house until John began associating with Booth."

"John? You mean John Surratt?"

"Yes, he's nearly broken his mother's heart."

"What happened?"

"I—I don't know. Last Monday a week, Booth came by about ten o'clock in the morning. He picked up John and Mr. Wood. They were all on horseback. It had something to do with the president, I think. John is very Sesesh, you know. He used to run the blockade and worry his ma. That's one of the reasons she moved to the city from Surrattsville. He seemed to have settled down and got a good job at the Adams Express Company and then he met Booth. After that John quit his job, because he got all the money he wanted from him. Booth's an actor and very rich. At first I thought he was very nice. He's handsome and has nice manners, but now I don't know." She wiped her eyes.

"Where did they go?" Ingalls asked as tenderly as possible. He had heard most of this before, but the fact that Booth had gone out with his entire gang was very interesting.

"I don't know. They came back around half past six. First John came back, he was carrying a pistol saying that his prospects had been ruined, then he asked Lewis to get him a clerkship. Before Lewis could say anything he went upstairs. Then Booth and Wood came in. Wood was carrying a pistol and Booth came in and paced around cursing his luck. I don't even think he saw poor Lewis who was stunned. Then they all left.

"As a result of this, John left for Richmond with a Mrs. Slater who was visiting last Saturday. John, Mrs. Slater, and Mrs. Surratt left last Saturday 'to go to the country,' which means to Surrattsville. That evening, Mrs. Surratt returned on the Port Tobacco Stage. Later, I found out that Lewis had seen guns laid out on Mr. Wood's bed a few days before. When she found this out, Mrs. Surratt was so upset that she asked Mr. Wood to find another boarding house when he returned. Since John left she cries herself to sleep every night. The poor woman." By this time she was sobbing. "I didn't mean to ruin your evening, George."

Ingalls was at a loss. The fact that Booth and company had tried something else without his or Everett's knowledge was, to say the least, upsetting. So was the fact that the woman he loved was being made miserable by the same events he was trying to interpret and understand. He wanted to give her the bracelet tonight and he decided to do that, if nothing else. "You haven't ruined my evening, Nora," he said solicitously. "I just wish I could cheer you up. Here, perhaps this will help a little."

He took the little velvet-covered pasteboard box from his pocket and handed it across the table to her. She looked at him a little confused, then noticed the box.

"For me?" she asked.

He nodded.

She wiped her eyes and her nose, then she took the box and opened it. Her eyes went wide when she saw the contents. "Oh, George, it's beautiful. Help me put it on."

Nora stretched out her arm and pulled her sleeve back to expose her wrist. Ingalls took the bracelet from the box and looked at it. It took him a moment to figure out the tiny clasp, then manipulate it with his large fingers. He put in on her wrist and fastened it. She held it up to the light and looked at it on her wrist.

"I'm so happy," she said and began to cry again.

Ingalls sat there, feeling clumsy and awkward. What was he to do?

Uniontown, Maryland

Anderson looked carefully at the road as the two men that Fitch hired unloaded the used furniture and put it inside the barn. People whom he assumed to be curious neighbors rode by from time to time and Anderson waved to them and they waved back. To the good citizens of Uniontown it looked as if Mr. Jared Hopkins of Pittsburgh were, in fact, storing his household goods in the barn. The only important things were the bed and chairs in the tack room. Fitch paid the men when they were finished and they left. Anderson waited until they were well on their way before he spoke.

"Joseph, I want you to familiarize yourself with the route to this place so that you can drive it day or night in any kind of weather in a wagon or a carriage. I don't know if we are going to have to use this place at all, but if we do, it's going to have to be at a moment's notice."

"Yes, Mr. Anderson. Is there anything else?"

Anderson thought for a moment. "Yes, there is. Rent a carriage—a small landau would be fine—and have it available twenty-four hours a day. Then I want you to get a wagon and have it painted as a freight wagon."

"A freight wagon?"

"Yes, and make sure the sides are tall enough to hide a crate containing a man. And, you might as well get a crate large enough for that purpose, as well as a couple of empty crates to make it look believable. I also want the freight wagon available night and day. Buy the horses if you have to."

Fitch nodded. He didn't have to write anything down. His memory was one thing Anderson knew he could rely on.

"Finally, I want you to get a man with the same build as Booth. He is going to have a few minutes of work and he must be believable. I will pay him a hundred dollars for those few minutes."

"I think I know the man. His name is Charlie. He's a trickster and he hangs out at Pointer's."

"As usual, I will rely on your judgment, and Joseph . . ."

"Yes, Mr. Anderson?"

"From now until the end of this commission, no more spirits."

"Yes, Mr. Anderson.

"Now, let's get back to the city. I have many preparations to make and I have need of a tailor."

Richmond, Virginia
April 3, 1865

The fall of empires has never been noble or poetic. Richmond, long the proud symbol of the Confederacy, now lay abandoned by those who had sought to make it the capital of a new nation. President Jefferson Davis had abandoned it at 11:00 P.M. the night before, and all night, army units either evacuated the city or melted away as soldiers, who had been through four years of hell, decided it was time to go home. All through the night explosions echoed through the streets as stores, warehouses, and weapons were destroyed to prevent them from falling into enemy hands. Citizens familiar with the city listened with dread as the explosions and fires progressed. Finally, at dawn, a huge explosion downriver signaled the end of the remaining pathetic craft of a once hopeful navy.

At the commissary depot, a hungry mob broke into the now unguarded complex. It was stocked with flour, ham, bacon, sugar, coffee, and, of course, whiskey. The fact that these provisions were never sent to Lee's starving army a mere twenty miles away was a condemnation of the inept Confederate Quartermaster Department and the government itself. Crying, yelling, and screaming, the mob burst through the door. Men and women fought each other over the stores. Many were injured and some were killed. In a few short minutes the streets were littered with everything from flour to beans. Later that morning, perhaps thinking of the fate of Columbia, the government ordered the destruction of all the stocks of liquor in the city. Kegs of whiskey, gin, and brandy poured into the streets. Capt. Clement Sulivane, the engineer officer in charge of the destruction of military supplies, looked on in horror as men and women knelt in the gutter trying to catch the rivers of liquor in pitchers and buckets. Some didn't bother with containers. They just drank what they could as it flowed by.

As Sulivane prepared the last bridge for destruction, Gen. Martin W. Gary and his band of South Carolina cavalry crossed the bridge at a gallop. The general reined in and saluted.

"It's all over," he told the captain. "Good-bye—blow her to hell."

The captain nodded and began setting fire to his charges. As he walked across the bridge, it burst into flames. At the other end he could see blue-coated cavalry. They fired in his direction but didn't hit him. Before he rode away he heard cheers as the United States flag was raised over the capital.

Gen. Godfrey Weitzel received the surrender of the city that morning. Thousands of Union soldiers then began working tirelessly to save the city. By mid-afternoon, they had stopped the rioting and restored order. They blasted buildings and created fire brakes, which with thousands of blue-coated firefighters, brought the blazes under control. Finally, they established order, prevented private property from being looted, and began issuing rations to the needy. "For these things," one Richmonder wryly remarked, "the citizens of Richmond never forgave the Yankees."

The War Department Telegraph Office
Washington City

Earlier in the day messages had been received that Petersburg had been captured and that Grant was now in pursuit of Lee's army. This was wonderful news, but around 9:00 A.M. one of the cipher operators in the telegraph office sat stunned as the message began "From Richmond." He listened to the news, then leaving an assistant to copy the message, he ran to the window and threw up the sash. "Richmond has fallen!" he screamed at the top of his lungs, "Richmond has fallen!" The news spread like wildfire. Government offices emptied and the streets were packed with crowds of people who grew progressively less sober with each passing moment. Banners were unfurled, church bells were rung, and cannons boomed. Secretary of War Stanton came out to address the crowd that had gathered around the War Department. He read a dispatch from Grant stating that Richmond was on fire. What should he do? Stanton asked the crowd. "Let it burn!" was the reply.

For some in Washington City, it was a day of mourning. Hopes, dreams, and hard work had all gone for naught. John Surratt came back home. He saw his mother and sister and had dinner with his friend Lewis Weichmann. Later, he exchanged forty dollars in gold for sixty dollars in greenbacks with John Holohan. Early the following morning, he left for Canada with secret messages for the Confederacy's Canadian Cabinet. In a few days they would be fugitives instead of representatives of a belligerent power. Mary Surratt, herself a secessionist at heart, remained in Washington, but took no part in the celebration.

Rockett's Wharf
Richmond, Virginia
April 4, 1865

Early in the morning the steamer *Malvern* ran aground as it approached Richmond. Adm. David D. Porter, the senior officer on board, ordered a barge lowered for the passengers who wished to go to Richmond. A few minutes later, President Abraham Lincoln, his son Tad, and the guard, Crook, were rowed ashore to Rockett's Landing. It was the most understated triumphal entry in history. Initially, Lincoln was surrounded by Negroes who hailed him as their deliverer. Then they began a two-mile walk to General Weitzel's headquarters, which were in the former Confederate Executive Mansion. The citizens of Richmond lined the streets and windows to see their conqueror. There were no cheers and no catcalls. Whether the silence was due to shock or good manners none could tell. Crook found it eerie. Lincoln was greeted cordially by Weitzel and his staff. The president sat in Davis' chair, had lunch, and went for a tour of the city—this time in a carriage with a cavalry escort. The city that was supposed to hold Lincoln as a captive lay prostrate at his feet.

Washington City

Ingalls and Everett made their way through the crowd. It was almost impossible to find, much less track, anyone with this many people around. It was all the more frustrating because they could hardly hear each other talk. They finally got off The Avenue where the streets were not as crowded. They were both disturbed that they had missed one of Booth's attempts at the president.

"We can't be everywhere at once, George," Everett said. It was not an excuse. It was a statement of fact.

"I know," Ingalls said with a sigh. "If only we could find this Anderson. We don't even know what he looks like."

"We do know what Fitch looks like but he seems to have disappeared off the face of the earth," Everett remarked dryly. "Maybe we should split up again."

"How so?"

"One of us could continue to watch the Chain and Anchor and the other could nose around Swampoodle," he suggested.

"It's bad enough with two of us, but I guess we'll have to risk it—only no heroics. If you see anything, just observe it. It's too easy for one man to get caught in a trap."

"Which one do you want, George?"

"Swampoodle."

"Me too. I'll toss you for it," Everett said.

"I could pull rank."

"You could."

"We'll use my coin," Ingalls said.

"I get the feeling you don't trust me, George."

"Clarence, with your powers of deduction, you should be a detective," Ingalls said, taking a coin from his pocket.

"That was very unkind, George."

"Call it," Ingalls said as he tossed the coin in the air.

"Tails."

Ingalls caught the coin and slapped it onto the back of his wrist. When he moved his hand away, he muttered, "Damn!"

Everett smiled. "I'll check with you at headquarters tomorrow morning."

Everett changed from his normal business attire to workingmen's clothes. These consisted of a dusty, black, broad-brimmed, high-crowned hat; a blue-and-brown-striped flannel shirt; heavy gray, stained linen overalls; and serviceable, but well-worn, black Army shoes. Over this was a brown wool jacket with pockets big enough for a small revolver. He also carried a leather tool bag that contained hammer, saw, square, brace, and bits. The disguise was one Everett had worn many times before. In fact, if there was ever a question, he could use the tools rather skillfully. As any grocer's son will tell you, there's always something in the store that has to be fixed.

Everett doubted that he would see Fitch during the day, but he wanted to get to know Swampoodle better, and there was no better way than this. Every day, all over the city, colored people went to and from their work like their white counterparts. In a free society they were invisible. Everett first walked his way along the stinking cesspool that was Tiber Creek. He began at the outskirts of Swampoodle on the corner of Massachusetts Avenue and North Capitol Street and walked north. Along every other side street he turned east, walking one or two blocks one way and then one or two the other. It was tiresome and boring, but he knew that someday it might save his life.

Swampoodle, during the day, was relatively quiet. It was not until night that the delights of Swampoodle offered themselves to sensation hungry customers. Cockfights, dogfights, prizefights, and shows that would make those at the Varieties Theater seem tame provided entertainment, along with other pleasures. At night the streets were crowded with soldiers looking for a good time. Nightly, the naive and unsuspecting were cheated and there were those who, from time-to-time, wound up face down in the creek or in some alley. Eddy the Sneak had been just one of many. Everett walked along as if he had someplace to go but was not in any hurry to get there. No one bothered him, but he was always on his guard. The overwhelming part of Swampoodle's inhabitants were Irish, and the Irish, the most downtrodden whites, were violently anti-Negro, something Everett found astonishing. He wondered if the attitude were officially fostered. By keeping the Irish and the Negroes at each other's throats, neither one could go anywhere. It made him think of the New York Draft Riots in 1863 when Irish mobs ran rampant in the city indiscriminately lynching Negroes and burning buildings which included churches and orphanages. It was only stopped when battle-hardened troops arrived to put down the riot by the most violent means possible.

Everett was walking up a side street when he noticed a sign that said "Jake's Gen'l Merchandise" in an alley. Curious, he decided to visit the shop, so he walked up the garbage-strewn alley and entered. The utter chaos of the place amused him. Tools, harness, lanterns, clothes, and shoes were spread out on tables and hung on the walls. Glass cases containing every imaginable variety of watches, rings, and jewelry were in front of the counter. Even if Everett hadn't been on a case, Jake's would have been fascinating. He figured the fat man behind the counter must be Jake and gave him a cheerful hello. Jake looked up, grunted, and eyed him suspiciously. It was a reaction any outsider could expect in Swampoodle. Everett walked around the shop looking at shirts and picking up a pair of worn workman's boots to see if they fit. Gradually, he wandered over to the glass cases.

It caught his eye right away. It was a large gold railroad watch with a heavy gold chain. Seeing a watch like that in a place like this was one chance in a thousand. He knew it must be Eddy's watch and if it were, in fact, Eddy's then it must have been stolen by his killer, who, Everett would bet at this point was Fitch.

"Could I see dis here watch, suh?" he asked Jake.

Jake looked up. He had sized up the colored man as just another tradesman and paid no attention. If you asked Jake he would tell you that niggers never bought anything. He half believed it himself, but a sale was a sale.

"Which one did you say?" Jake bent down behind the case to see which watch Everett was pointing to.

"Dis here big gold one," Everett said pointing to the watch again. The moment he saw the expression on Jake's face through the glass, he knew he should have been more circumspect. It was too late. He had to go through with this.

"Yeah," Jake said. "It is a nice one, but it's a hundred dollars."

Everett scratched his head. "Hunnerd dolluhs a lot of money fo' a watch, but what da hell. Less see it."

Jake hesitated, then said. "I've got to get the key. It's in the back. It'll only take a minute." With that Jake disappeared into the back.

The O'Malley brothers were sitting in back playing cards and sharing a bottle of whiskey.

"There's a nigger out front," he said. "I think it's that detective we've heard about."

"A nigger 'tective?" Slim said. "Don't seem anybody could get so low as that—a nigger and a detective." He laughed at what he thought was a funny joke.

"Go out the back and circle round the front," Jake told him. "If he doesn't resist, we'll take him to Fitch for a tidy sum. If he puts up a fight, do what you have to."

"Sure thing, Jake."

Jake returned to the shop with an artificial smile. It was a dead giveaway. "Must be getting old," he said. "Can't remember where I put things anymore."

"Know how ya feel," Everett said with a disarming grin. He squatted down in front of the case and looked at the reflection of the front door in it. Someone opened the door, but Jake didn't bother to look up. Whoever they were, they were expected.

"This the one?" Jake asked, pointing deliberately to the wrong watch.

"Thas it, sho'," said Everett standing up. For a moment Jake was confused. Everett turned just before the O'Malley brothers were on him.

Slim pulled a large knife. "Hold it right there, nigger. We wanna talk to you."

Everett stood still and sized up the situation rapidly. The younger O'Malley was behind the older one in a bad position. Neither of them seemed to have a gun. In one swift move, Everett's arm swept along the counter and picked up a glass jar full of rusty screws and propelled it at Slim. He threw it low so the man couldn't duck. It hit Slim in the chest, but it didn't break. Nevertheless, it did what it needed to. Slim stepped back knocking both himself and his brother off balance. Everett deflected Slim's arm and hit the older O'Malley as hard as he could. Slim drooped the knife and went down but he was just too big and tough to stay down after a punch from a runt like Everett. The detective caught Jake's movement out of the corner of his eye. The fat man was raising a shotgun and Everett instinctively struck it to one side. It went off close to Everett's head, deafening him for a moment. Choking on the thick smoke he blinked and saw John O'Malley standing there with half his head blown away. Jake just froze with his mouth open as John O'Malley fell over backward, upsetting a table and knocking goods everywhere. The detective wrenched the shotgun away from Jake and turned. Slim was on all fours shaking his head. The blast of the shotgun brought him to his senses. Seeing the shotgun in Everett's hands and his brother's body, he put two and two together and picked up his knife.

"You black bastard," he screamed maniacally as he rose and lunged for Everett with the huge knife.

Everett stood spread-legged and hung onto the hand guard with his left hand while he pushed the steel plated butt in a horizontal arc with his right. The butt connected with the side of Slim's head with a sickening crunch and the man stopped in midair and fell to the dirt floor without even a groan. Everett, enraged by the attack turned to Jake and moved menacingly toward him, shotgun in hand. The fat man's face was a mask of fear as the detective approached.

"Look, it was a mistake, mister," Jake was babbling. "Look, take the watch and no hard feelings, okay?"

Jake continued to back up until he was in the corner and could no longer move. Everett motioned with the shotgun. "Get the watch," he said, coldly.

Jake edged along the wall to the case. He opened it without a key and reached in for the watch. "Slowly," Everett said. Jake did as he was told. He reached into the case and withdrew the watch. He handed it to the detective. Everett glanced at it. It was a Howard watch with Roman numerals on the dial. Engraved on the back was "R. L. M. 1860."

In the moment Everett was looking at the watch, Jake tried to run past him, but the fat man was too slow and clumsy. Everett tripped him and he sprawled on the floor.

"Get up," Everett told him, but Jake was so crazed with fear that he just sat up with his back against the wall. Everett didn't insist he get up. The detective held up the watch. "Where'd you get this?"

Jake just shook his head. He chewed one dirty hand while the other rested on the floor. Even in this condition he was more afraid of Anderson than he was of the detective with the shotgun. Everett, still consumed with rage, raised the shotgun and brought the butt down on the hand on the floor as hard as he could. Jake emitted the cry of a wounded, frightened animal and rolled on the floor cradling his injured hand.

"Please, please, don't hurt me anymore." Tears were running down his cheeks.

"Just tell me where you got this and I'll go away," Everett said. There was nothing in his voice to suggest charity or mercy.

"I can't, I can't."

Everett's anger was subsiding. He didn't want to hit Jake again, but he had gone this far and he wanted answers.

"Did you get this from Fitch?" he asked.

Jake looked at him as if he had been hit again. "How did you . . ." Suddenly he realized that he had said too much.

"Look," Everett said, "tell me what you know and I'll leave and not bother you again. Lie to me and I'll spread it all over the Blue Jug that you told me where to find Anderson."

"He'd kill me," the terror-stricken fat man whimpered.

"Do I appear overly concerned with your fate?" the detective asked coolly.

"You promise you won't tell anyone?" Jake whined.

"You can even keep the watch," Everett said.

Jake thought for a moment then said, "The day after they found Eddy's body in the creek, Fitch came by with his things and pawned the watch. I knew it was Eddy's, but what could I do? I gave him fifteen dollars for everything and he said he was going to use it on Jasmine."

"Who's Jasmine?"

"She's a mulatto whore Eddy liked," Jake sniveled. "Treated her like a queen. She was real shook up when he died."

"Where is she?"

"She works out of Pointer's."

"Anything else?" Everett asked.

"No, I swear."

"I believe you. Now, you've never seen me. If anyone asks about the mess, someone tried to rob you. Understand?"

Jake shook his head.

"Now remember our deal. If you don't tell Anderson, I won't either. Now, is there a back door?"

"That way," Jake pointed with his chin.

Everett grabbed his tool case and the shotgun and went out the back door to avoid the crowd that was gathering. On his way out of the alley he stuck the shotgun in a rain barrel.

Fitch did not show up at Pointer's that night. The following morning, Everett would learn from Ingalls why.

The Chain and Anchor

Ingalls stood in a doorway dressed in seaman's clothes and wondered how Everett was faring. He consoled himself with the idea he was having an equally dull and unproductive day. For a moment he regretted telling his partner the truth about the coin toss. There was only one way in or out of the Chain and Anchor and that was the alley leading to it. Unfortunately, there were no windows that overlooked the alley, so he couldn't find a room and observe the place with field glasses as he wanted to. That way he could at least be unobtrusive. On nights with bad weather not too many people would be out and he could stand in the doorway nearly all evening with few passersby. Tonight the weather was warm as if it were already spring, and people, especially the prostitutes, were out and about. One of them saw him in the shadows.

"Hello, sailor," she said, her voice husky with invitation. "Want to buy me a drink?"

When she came closer, he could see that she was typical of the women that haunted this area.

"Beat it!" he said gruffly.

She came closer and lowered her bodice. "I can be lots of fun," she said. "And very reasonable."

"Beat it," he repeated

"What's the matter, too long on a ship and don't like women?" she said nastily.

"Yeah, I like women," Ingalls sneered. "That's why I don't like you."

"Son of a bitch," she said as she walked away.

Ingalls watched her leave and felt exposed. The last thing he expected to see was Fitch walking into the alley on his way to the tavern. His clothes were better than either Eddy's description or Everett's but it was Fitch. Ingalls knew he was in for a long, boring, and dangerous wait. Fortunately, his only other visitor for the evening was a drunk who needed a light. Ingalls gave it to him and the man staggered on his way. Joseph Fitch left the Chain and Anchor a little after 10:00 P.M.

Fitch had a lot on his mind as he left the sleazy tavern. For the first time in many years, he had a feeling of foreboding and he didn't like it. He liked working for Anderson, even if his boss was a bit too rigid about drinking, but this time he wasn't sure that Anderson hadn't bitten off more than he could chew. The fact that the law had caught up with Eddy was evidence that they were getting too close. It was only a matter of time before they found someone else to spill his guts. Even Anderson couldn't last forever. Maybe it was time to move on. Fitch wouldn't like leaving Washington City, but that mattered little compared to survival, and above all, Fitch was a survivor. Many thieves had excuses for being the way they were. These ranged from no mother to a broken home or childhood in an orphanage. Fitch grew up in a comfortable home with his parents, brothers, and sisters. He was the third of seven children, three boys and four girls. His father owned a prosperous cooperage in Delaware, and all the children seemed to be destined to become solid, upright citizens—and they all did except for Joseph who learned at the age of fourteen that he liked women and stealing. He started out stealing small things, then money. First he stole from his parents, then neighbors. When he was sixteen, he raped a young girl who lived down the street. He was discovered

and escaped. He never looked back. His career, while unnotewor-
thy, was long, because he was never more than a petty thief. While
he could not always be considered smart, he always survived,
which to Joseph Fitch was the same thing. The reason he could
survive where others could not was that Joseph Fitch was a jackal
and the streets of Washington were his jungle. He had a sixth
sense about both prey and predators, which was why on that pleasant April night, Joseph Fitch knew he was being followed and that
he was being followed by the law. He could easily guess that whoever was tailing him was one or both of the detectives who made
Eddy talk. He didn't change his pace as he considered his next
course of action. His first reaction was to duck into a doorway to
see who came walking by. He knew that the detectives were a big
white man and a medium-size colored man.

Ingalls watched Fitch duck into the doorway and he stopped.
Fitch knew what he was doing, which meant that this was going to
be a long evening. Ingalls waited until a wagon rolled by. He ran
out to the street and ran along the side of the wagon, keeping it
between him and Fitch. He then ducked into a doorway half a
block down and across the street from the one his quarry was in.
When Fitch tentatively looked out he spotted no one, but his instinct said he was still being followed and he always trusted his instincts. Fitch headed for the wharves along Georgia on Anacostia
Creek. If anyone were following him he would find out there. Ingalls watched as Fitch quickened his pace. There was no caution as
the little man headed south on Fourth. Ingalls now knew that Fitch
wasn't leading him anywhere, except the wharves. The detective
reasoned that Fitch was probably leading him into a trap, but
nothing ventured, nothing gained.

The wharves were Fitch's briar patch. He knew this area of
Washington better than any other. He had been involved in everything here from hijacking cargo to white slavery. As soon as he
reached the waterfront, the open street turned into a maze of
warehouses, wharves, dark alleys, and forests of crates and barrels. Fitch fled quickly into the dark labyrinth, knowing he could
ambush the detective following him. One glimpse over his shoulder told him it was the big white man, Ingalls. He led him out onto

the wharves and into a storage yard full of crates and barrels piled twenty to thirty feet high. In between the rows of cargo were narrow paths for accessing different shipments. In this narrow maze a big man was at a distinct disadvantage. Ingalls began following cautiously, but as he got deeper into the complex he began to feel closed in, so he stopped. The smells of the various cargoes assailed his senses and confused him. He was now playing Fitch's game and that was stupid. Carefully, he backed out of the narrow passages of stacked cargo and when he was clear, Ingalls began running to the other end of the storage yard, hoping to catch the slippery little man by surprise. He nearly succeeded, but he wasn't fast enough.

Fitch heard Ingalls coming just in time and fled. Angered by his failure to catch his foe and nearly getting caught himself, Fitch led Ingalls to the water's edge and made sure the big man followed. The detective caught sight of Fitch and tried to outfox him, by running ahead of him as before, but it didn't work. Fitch headed for a dismasted ship tied to a wharf. Ingalls followed him onto it. The ship had been damaged in a storm and was in litigation so it had lain a long time without repairs. It stank of rot and the deck creaked under the big man's weight and seemed to give. Ingalls retreated and walked close to the railings because the deck was more solid there. He was on the outboard side when he saw the movement out of the corner of his eye, but it was already too late. Fitch waited until Ingalls was silhouetted against the dark sky, then stood up and threw the knife. With a target as big as Ingalls he couldn't miss. Ingalls tried to move out of the way and he lurched against the rotten railing which gave way beneath his bulk. The knife flew by him as he hurtled overboard with an involuntary yell and plunged into the dark water below. For a moment, Ingalls was stunned by the cold water. He tried to grab at the side of the ship but the barnacles cut his hand. He heard Fitch run across the deck to look over the side so he stayed as still as he could.

"Well, you won't bother anybody anymore, Ingalls, you big bastard," Fitch said, breaking into a laugh.

Don't bet on it, Ingalls thought as Fitch's footsteps retreated across the deck. Then he wondered how Fitch knew his name. It had to have been Eddy. It took Ingalls some time to find a ladder and climb out of the water. By that time he was nearly numb and it was a long, cold way home.

Washington City
April 5, 1865

Ingalls, in the grip of a high fever, was chilled to the bone and felt absolutely miserable. Everett looked at him with some concern.

"Christ, George, you could have been killed," he said.

"What about you?" Ingalls replied shivering. "Let's face it. We're both lucky to be alive. Anderson and his pet monkey know who we are. They were probably very nice to Eddy so he told them everything, and then when he wasn't expecting it, they killed him. Probably Fitch did the deed and relieved him of his valuables before dumping the body in the creek knowing it would be found, so it could be a lesson to all the good citizens of Swampoodle."

"This leaves us in a hell of a mess," Everett said, pacing back and forth beside Ingalls' bed. "Colonel Baker doesn't really believe us. I think he's leaving us on this case just to cover himself. Booth is an incompetent, but dangerous, ass being used by an assassin who knows who we are and what we look like. The only advantage is that he thinks you're dead."

"That could help," Ingalls suggested. "I could adopt a disguise—maybe a beard and spectacles with a dark wig."

"Do you think that would fool Anderson and Fitch?"

Ingalls shrugged and then sneezed loudly. "It would for a little while and that might just give us the edge we need."

"But only if you played it all the way. You couldn't see Nora until it was all over."

That gave Ingalls pause. Could he really do that? "M-m-m," he said noncommittally. He would have to think about that.

"What are we going to do now?" Everett asked, not pushing the subject of Nora.

"We have to find Anderson. It's that simple, but it isn't simple. I have a theory, but it's crazy. Want to hear it?" Ingalls asked.

Everett threw up his hands in frustration as he moved back and forth the length of the room. "Why not? Nothing logical works in this case. We've tried good police work, being nice to a suspect, and following leads, but they all lead nowhere. Crazy might just help."

"First, you can stop pacing back and forth and sit down," Ingalls said. "You're making me dizzy."

"Oh, sorry." Everett pulled a chair next to the bed.

"I think there is no Anderson . . ."

"You do have a fever, George."

"Hear me out, Clarence. I think there is an Anderson, but he's not known as Anderson except to Fitch and a few other people at most. Right now he could be Joe Smith or Fred O'Reilly, complete with a disguise. We can be pretty sure it's not one of Booth's men. I don't think he's that public. It's undoubtedly someone close to Booth. He may even be in the hotel. We have to get inside."

"That's easy," Everett said.

"It's dangerous. They know who you are now."

"They may know who we are, but they haven't seen our faces. If I shorten my hair, put a little gray in it, and wear spectacles, they'll think I'm one of the hotel house niggers."

"Be damned careful, Clarence," Ingalls said.

Everett reached over and took his friend's hand. "Don't worry, George, I will. Now you just get some rest."

Everett picked up his hat and coat as Ingalls was dozing off. He didn't like the idea of going into the lion's den, but if George was right then this would flush Anderson out.

Ingalls was half asleep when he heard the door close. He fell asleep, thinking of Nora in bed beside him.

Washington City
April 6, 1865

Secretary of State William Seward was thrown from his carriage and severely injured. He was placed in a heavy neck brace and ordered to bed. For weeks, the secretary would find any movement excruciatingly painful, but the heavy neck brace would save his life.

The McLean House
Appomattox Court House, Virginia
April 9, 1865

The Union officers stood on the porch and saluted as Gen. Robert E. Lee put on his hat and walked down the steps. He returned the salute and then stood absentmindedly slapping his gloves together. Suddenly, remembering where he was, he called for his horse and mounted. Just before Lee rode away, Gen. Ulysses S. Grant came out on the porch and raised his hat. Lee did likewise, then spurred his horse in the direction of the Army of Northern Virginia's final camp. By surrendering his army, Lee had shown incredible courage and vision. It would have been easy to agree to a suggestion to continue the war as guerrillas, but Lee knew better. The war that he did not want had cost the nation untold suffering. Lee himself had been hurt both personally and monetarily, but he knew that continued fighting would accomplish nothing. By stopping the bloodshed, he had made a final sacrifice for the new United States, a country of which he was unaware. Now came the painful duty of telling his comrades that they were no longer an army or a nation.

After the surrender, Grant left the McLean house. He, too, was preoccupied. He had tried very hard to make Lee's surrender as painless as possible, but no matter what he did the end result was that the Army of Northern Virginia and, for all intents and purposes, the Confederate States of America, were no more. His only hope was that the country would get back together as quickly and with as little distress as possible. He little understood that he was presiding over the birth of the new United States. While riding back to his headquarters, he was reminded that he forgot to notify the War Department. Always a dutiful subordinate, Grant dismounted and wrote.

> Head-Quarters, Appomattox C.H. Va
> Apl, 9th 1865, 4.30 o'clock P.M.
>
> Hon Edwin Stanton, Sec of War Washington
> Gen'l Lee surrendered the Army of Northern Va this afternoon on terms proposed by myself. The accompanying additional correspondence will show the conditions fully.
>
> > U.S. GRANT
> > Lt. Gen

Washington City

The message was not received by the War Department until 9:00 P.M. Lafayette Baker, just returned to Washington City from New York, was one of the first to receive the wonderful news that he had worked so hard for. He still would not believe that Booth was anything more than a harmless crank. Nevertheless, the bloodshed was not over.

Washington City
April 10, 1865

The citizens of Washington awoke to the sound of booming cannon, and the news of Lee's surrender caused another celebration in the capital. While not as raucous and unrestrained as the celebration of the fall of Richmond, it was nonetheless an astounding event. John Wilkes Booth sat in his hotel room in deep melancholia. Until the last he had refused to accept that there could be an end to the Confederacy. It had, for the last four years, been his Camelot or Avalon. It is perhaps true that dreams die hard, but for the actor this was worse. His dreams had not died. They had been intruded upon by a reality he could no longer keep from himself. The cheers, music, and cannon fire outside his window were taunts that kept reminding him that reality, cold and cruel, had won the battle over his enchanted Confederacy. He could no longer be the man to save his nation with one heroic act that would carry his name wreathed in glory through the centuries.

Alan Demming placed a gentle hand on the actor's shoulder. Inwardly, Anderson felt a degree of satisfaction. Booth had returned to Washington on the eighth of April. Although the fall of Richmond had depressed him, he still held out hope. This evening's news had plunged the actor into the depths of despair and Anderson wondered if Booth's mind were not already unhinged. All he had to do was last a few days more and it would be time for Anderson to complete his commission. Then he and John Wilkes Booth would play the most incredible scene in the history of the theater.

"Wilkes," he said, his voice cracking with emotion. "I—I don't know what to say."

"It's over, Alan," Booth said. His hand went to his eyes to stem the flow of tears. "That wicked tyrant has won. He has crushed the noblest race on this continent and freed the niggers so they can hold the white people of the South in bondage. It is as if the children of Israel were again under the heel of the pharaoh, only this pharaoh is worse because he has all the modern tools of destruction at his beck and call. I can't believe that God let me live to see this."

"I think, perhaps, He has spared you for a higher purpose, Wilkes."

"What higher purpose?" Booth said in anguish. "It is all finished, Alan."

"No, Wilkes, it is not finished. It is not finished as long as that gorilla and his henchman carry on their plans of subjugation and enslavement of the South. They must all be killed, Wilkes. Every last one of them must be killed else the nigger will hold the lash over white civilization for the next thousand years. Only a man who can see clearly can lead the way. We must strike!"

"You mean kill Lincoln?" The actor looked confused.

"I mean kill all of them—Lincoln, Johnson, and Seward. Now that Lincoln has the South prostrate at his feet, he will ask for the imperial crown and the mob will place it on his head. Wipe out the dictator and his top two toadies and this so-called government will collapse like a house of cards. It would give right-thinking men the chance to right the wrongs of the last four years. The man who would do that would be hailed as a hero to the end of time."

Booth turned and looked at him. His eyes opened as if he were seeing the light for the first time. "Yes, Alan, yes, you're absolutely right, but killing . . ."

"You must harden your heart, Wilkes. These are not soldiers, they are tyrants. I know you have a gentle nature and violence does not become you, but these are not men of honor with whom you can treat chivalrously. These are schemers who manipulate innocent people from backstage, tricking them into doing their will. They must be stopped."

"Yes," the actor agreed. "They must be stopped, but how?"

Anderson sat next to Booth and put his arm around him. "You have already answered that question. Where else to kill the tyrant but in the theater where all can see the hero and his deed? In the meantime your faithful followers can eliminate the rest of the tyrant's band. Your own plan to capture the beast can be used to destroy him. Once the deed is done you will not even have to flee. The crowd will acclaim you."

"Yes," Booth said with determination. "I must destroy him."

"Now, Wilkes, you must get some rest. You have much work to do."

"Yes, I'm very tired."

Booth leaned back on the bed and was soon sound asleep. Anderson put his feet up, removed his shoes, and covered him with a blanket. Sleep well, sweet prince, Anderson thought. Just a few more days and everything will be fine.

The National Hotel

Everett, using the name James Sylvester, showed up for work early in the morning as a waiter in the restaurant of the National. Since Booth was a late riser, Everett had plenty of opportunity to get a few stains on his jacket and shoes. When Booth came down to breakfast with Alan Demming, people in the dining salon began to greet them. He turned to Matthew Freeman, the head waiter.

"Who are they?" he asked innocently.

"Come on," Freeman said. "You mean to tell me you ain't never seen John Wilkes Booth?"

"The actor?"

"Yeah, the actor. Ain't you never seen him befo'?"

"Yeah, I seen him on stage," Everett said. "But there he looked a foot taller. Wow. Who's the man with him?"

"That is Mr. Demming and if he ever asks you to run an errand. Just say 'yes, sir' and fly."

"Is he bad?"

"No, he's anything but. He's a rich tanner and if he likes the service, he tips. You know, Jed, the little colored boy who works the second floor?"

"Yeah."

"The other day Demming asked him to get him some shaving soap and when he came back in half an hour, he gave him a fifty-cent shin plaster."

"No."

"Yes."

"How come he walks funny?"

"He's a cripple. Got a wooden leg."

"He and Booth together a lot?"

"He's the only one in this hotel that Booth associates with other than Miss Bessie Hale, if you catch my drift?"

"I do, if I think I know what you mean."

"Say, you're sure asking a lot of questions," Freeman observed.

"Got to if you want to get ahead."

"What do you mean?"

"You said Demming was rich, right?"

"So?"

"Rich men need servants, don't they?"

"You're not as dumb as you look, Sylvester."

"Thanks, let me wait on him then I can tell everybody I waited on Booth the actor."

"Everybody in his turn," Freeman said, nodding in the direction of the other waiters.

"It's worth a greenback," Everett said.

"You're funnin'."

Everett reached into his jacket and pulled out a dollar bill.

"You're crazy," Freeman said, taking the greenback with a smile. "The table is yours."

Everett took his order pad and walked over to the table. "Mawnin', gennelmen," he said. "Fine day. What can I get for you?"

Both the actor and Demming ordered ham and eggs with grits and biscuits and coffee to drink. Booth also ordered a brandy and water and Demming gave him a surprised and disapproving look. Everett watched both men but paid particular attention to Demming. There was little remarkable about the man. He was of medium height and build and he was wearing a good-quality brown business suit. He had good-looking features and a straight nose. His eyes were gray and he had a square jaw covered with chin whiskers. His hands were smooth like a clerk's. Those weren't the hands of a man who had spent a long time in the leather business. Everett wrote the order down and took it back to the kitchen. He wondered if Demming were Anderson. At first he rejected the idea. Eddy didn't indicate that Anderson had an artificial leg, but if Ingalls were right and Anderson was a master of disguise, then acting like a cripple wouldn't be a problem. Everett had an idea.

He returned to the table with a pot full of fresh, hot coffee and Booth's brandy and water in a tumbler.

"Boy," Booth asked as Everett was pouring the coffee.

"Yes, suh," Everett replied pleasantly.

"Would you get us a paper?"

"House paper or one for yourself, sir?" Everett asked.

"House paper would be fine." Booth said. "Washington *Star*."

Everett bowed and hurried to the front desk where he picked up a paper reserved for guests. When he delivered the paper, Booth gave him a ten-cent tip. Everett fumbled the money and dropped it on the carpet. He went onto his hands and knees to retrieve it and it gave him a good look at Demming's shoes. They were bent and creased as if worn on a normal foot. Artificial feet only creased a shoe in one place. This was more than enough to go on. Everett rose and apologized, then continued with his duties. He worked a long ten-hour day and, when it was through, he caught a street car for Ingalls' boarding house.

When Everett arrived, he found Ingalls awake and feeling much better. He was cleaning his pocket pistol after its unceremonious dunking in Anacostia Creek. The pistol caught Everett's attention. It was a breech-loading revolver with a brass frame and handle. The barrel and cylinder, which were blued, swung to the right for loading.

"That's quite a pistol, George," he said.

Ingalls looked at him and smiled. "It's a .32-caliber, seven-shot belt revolver made by Moore's in New York," he said. "Much better than a one-or two-shot muzzle-loader."

"I'll agree with you on that, George. I'm going to buy one myself. By the way, you look much better."

"I feel better. Have you eaten yet?"

"Is your appetite back?" Everett asked.

"I could eat a horse—a live one."

They left the boarding house and went to Hasselmyer's where Ingalls ordered a large meal of steak, potatoes, onions, and steamed turnips. Everett had pork chops with fried potatoes. They shared a pitcher of beer.

"What did you find out?" Ingalls asked, buttering a thick slice of bread.

"I think I found Anderson," Everett said. He began eating with gusto. A day of hard work had made him very hungry.

"What? Where?"

"I'm not completely sure, yet, but I don't know who else it might be. What raised my suspicion was the fact that Freeman, the head waiter, said that they were together a lot. We've followed Booth and seen all of his acquaintances and henchmen except Demming and he's been at the National for months."

"What else?"

Everett explained about Demming's hands and shoes.

"We may finally be getting lucky, Clarence."

"Maybe. I'm going back to work tomorrow. Maybe I can get into his room if he goes away."

"Be careful."

"I will. In the meantime see if you can trace an Alan Demming of Salem, Illinois. I managed to get a look at one of his calling cards. It says his leather business is on Main Street." Everett then gave him a complete physical description of Alan Demming.

"Good idea."

CHAPTER 10

The White House
April 11, 1865

PRESIDENT ABRAHAM LINCOLN woke with a start. He had been waiting up for dispatches and had fallen asleep. The room was eerily silent except for the faint sound of someone softly sobbing. Getting out of bed, he reached for his robe and began looking for the source of the sound. All the rooms were open and the lights were on but there was no one there. As he went from room to room, he found no one and first became puzzled and then, alarmed. Finally, he arrived at the East Room. There he saw a corpse with its face covered and dressed in funeral vestments on a catafalque. Around the catafalque were soldiers standing guard. Before it were crowds of people crying pitifully and wailing.

"Who is dead in the White House?" Lincoln demanded of one of the guards.

"The president has been killed by an assassin," the guard answered, and an unearthly wail arose from the crowd.

Lincoln woke up in a sweat. It was the worst nightmare he'd had since coming to Washington. The room was so quiet that he couldn't get back to sleep.

The National Hotel

Wednesday, April 11, 1865, was designated as the day of the official victory celebration, which made it a busy day in the restaurant. Still, Everett managed to keep an eye out for Demming. The leather merchant had breakfast with Booth around 9:30 A.M., then the two of them went out. The dining salon was empty about ten-fifteen, so Everett slipped out and found a bellboy's jacket. It was not difficult to find one that fit since many of the bellboys at the National were men who were older and stouter than he. Everett went upstairs, prepared to pick Demming's lock, but found the maids busy making up the beds. Demming's room was open and one of the maids was cleaning it.

"Mr. Demming asked me to clean his boots," he said, entering the room.

The maid looked at him. She was a large colored woman who knew hotel procedures. "You new here?" she asked.

"Yes'm," he replied.

"Figures. Shoes supposed to be done at night," she told him.

"I know," he said. "But this is special, and seein's how he's a big tipper an' all . . ."

"Come on in," she said, busy fluffing the pillows.

When she left Everett made a quick, cursory inspection of the room. There were leather samples, business cards, a notebook, and a sheaf of order forms and invoices on the desk. The notebook was new and unused, but some of the invoices and order forms were filled in. Demming's clothes and shoes were in the wardrobe along with his shaving articles. Everett was about to close the door and leave when he noticed a small jar in among the shaving materials. Without touching anything he peered closer. It was theatrical gum for attaching false beards and moustaches. He had seen enough. Everett left the room, debating whether or not to arrest Demming on the spot. But on what charge, wearing a false beard and a false artificial leg? If they pulled him in, Baker would probably laugh at them and let Anderson or Demming go. He had to get word to Ingalls. He grabbed one of the younger bellboys.

"I need you to run an errand for me," he said.

"You're a bellboy just like me," the boy said, offended that one of his own should expect him to run an errand.

Everett took out his pocket notebook, scribbled a note, then tore off the page. Then he pulled three bills out of his wallet. "This is a

dollar," he said, getting the boy's attention. "Take this note to this
address and bring this man back. Then you get the other two dollars."

"Three dollars?" The boy looked at him amazed.

"If you don't want it, I'll get someone else."

The boy grabbed the note, looked at the address, and ran for
the stairs. On the way out he passed Anderson entering the lobby.
The counterfeit leather merchant picked up his key and returned
to his room. He made a quick check of the room to insure that no
one had been snooping around, not that they would have found
anything. When he checked the wardrobe he became concerned.
The maids changed linen and picked up laundry, but didn't dust
in the wardrobe while a guest occupied the room. Anderson habitually put a light dusting of powder on the shelf in the wardrobe
every morning, then blew on the powder until it was very faint. In
the white powder, he drew a line. If anyone so much as breathed
on the powder, it obscured the line. This afternoon the line was
blurred. There were three questions: When had it been done?
Who had done it? Why had it been done?

The answer to the first question was obvious. It had been done
today. Next he concentrated on the who. Once he knew that he
would know why. Anderson focused on the events of the day, recalling everyone he had encountered. There was Booth, the desk
clerk, the bellboy, the waiter . . . the new colored waiter. How
could he have been so stupid? The new waiter had taken an unusual interest in him. He had even gotten under the table. Why?
To check his shoes. Anderson debated for a moment. He was
guilty of nothing, but even a short stay in jail would ruin his plans.
That left two courses of action. He could leave everything in the
room, pay for it, and not come back, or he could clear out and
make them believe he had fled for parts unknown. Anderson
quickly decided on the latter course. If he chose the former there
would undoubtedly be someone stationed at the National to wait
for him. Since he had to come back and see Booth that would be
self-defeating. Anderson packed a valise and went to Booth's
room. Fortunately, the actor was in.

"Wilkes, something has happened and I must leave."

"Alan, what's wrong?"

"Some of my work for the cause has come to the attention of the authorities, so I must disappear for a time. I will be in contact with you. Do not fear. Tell your men to be ready and don't believe the note I leave for you downstairs."

"Alan, I . . ." Booth paused and the silence was embarrassing.

Anderson nodded and reached into his coat for his wallet. He gave Booth two hundred dollars in greenbacks. He knew the actor could spend that in a night without trying, but he probably wouldn't need much more.

"Thank you, Alan." Anderson left him holding the cash as he hurried down the hall.

Anderson walked into the lobby and up to the desk.

"I'm afraid I've received some bad news from home, Mr. Bunker," he told the clerk. "I have to check out."

"I'm sorry to hear that, Mr. Demming, I'll get your bill."

"May I have a pencil and a piece of paper, I'd like to leave Mr. Booth a note."

"Certainly, sir."

Bunker handed him a pencil and a piece of hotel stationary and Anderson wrote that he was returning to Salem, Illinois. Anderson folded the piece of paper and Bunker put it in Booth's box. The clerk smiled as he accepted Demming's cash payment and gave him a receipt.

"Have a good trip, Mr. Demming, and I hope things are all right at home."

"Thank you, Mr. Bunker. Your hotel has excellent service. I shall recommend it to my friends."

"We're looking forward to your next visit, sir."

Everett watched Anderson leave the hotel and catch a cab. He was tempted to stop him, but decided that patience was the best course at this point.

Anderson told the cabbie to go to the B&O Railroad Station. At his destination, he paid the cabbie, gave him a good tip, and disappeared into the station. While purchasing a one-way ticket to Chicago he asked the ticket agent a bunch of inane questions until the agent got irritated. That way the man would remember him. Anderson left the passenger area and went into the freight area.

He was crossing the tracks heading for Swampoodle when he found some empty passenger cars. He went into one and used the facilities to remove the beard and wig and change into the working men's clothes he carried for just such an emergency. Dressed in canvas overalls, a checkered cotton shirt, and a cap, he walked along the track. He tossed his valise into the first open freight car he saw. That ought to make some vagabond very happy, he thought. With an easy gait he walked back to the house in Swampoodle. Detectives would expect him to be mounted and in a hurry. He wasn't.

Ingalls arrived at the hotel within half an hour and Everett gave the boy the two dollars.

"What did you find?" Ingalls asked.

"I'm sure Demming is Anderson," Everett said. "There was nothing suspicious in the room, but he uses theatrical gum for a false beard. He must have had someone watching the room, because as soon as he arrived he checked out unexpectedly. He took a cab driven by a man named Harris, who regularly makes the run from the National to the train depot. He remembers Demming because he gave him a good tip."

Ingalls thought for a moment. "I'll bet he went to the B&O station to throw us off his trail. I'll warrant he even bought a ticket, but he didn't leave town."

"How can you be so sure?"

"I wired Salem, Illinois. There's no Demming Leather Company there. Secondly, I believe more than ever that he's the one that's going to kill Lincoln and he's going to try it in the next few days. Therefore, I don't think he wants to leave town right now."

"And how does Booth fit in?"

"He's the cover. I don't know how yet, but he's the cover. Let's go."

"Where?"

"First, we have to check the train station to be sure. Then we're going to Swampoodle. After that, we're going to start watching Booth. He's the key. Anderson or Fitch must try and contact him eventually. When they do, we'll have them."

Alan Demming or Anderson had disappeared. Certainly the cabbie and the ticket agent remembered him. He was a medium-size man in a blue business suit. He had on a wide-brimmed hat and he sported chin whiskers. No one had seen him get on the train. Ingalls and Everett got into their rented buggy and drove to Swampoodle. After two hours of riding around, Ingalls decided to call it quits.

"They've gone to ground," he said. "We'll never find them this way. Let's go find Booth."

The White House

Surprisingly, the crowded streets of the capital were quiet during the daylight hours of this Wednesday, the official day of the Victory Celebration, and some were wondering if Washington were so hung-over from the celebration of the capture of Richmond that it didn't have the energy to do justice to the day. At 6:00 P.M. the sun set and it became evident that there was no need to worry. The party goers had husbanded their strength to make it a night that the city and the nation would not soon forget. The city was illuminated from one end to the other. Fireworks and alcohol were used freely. Freed slaves danced in the streets singing "The Year of Jubilo" and there was free entertainment wherever one went. The crowds were tightly packed but were in a good mood. Several ladies fainted and, since the crowd was too closely pressed to allow them to be carried through, they were gently passed overhead by the milling throng until they were clear of the crowd.

Shortly after dark, the crowd around the White House began to thicken and gather closer. The attitude of this group was different from the others. The Marine Band on the lawn played marches and airs to entertain them, but they had not come to be entertained. They had come to hear the man who had led them through four years of uncertainty and trial to total victory. They had come to hear him utter words that would tell them that the enemy had been crushed and that the Confederacy's leaders would hang. They had come to hear words of vengeance. In the crowd were three who did not belong, they were John Wilkes Booth, David Herold, and Lewis Payne.

In a short time the crowd became restless and began to chant, "Lincoln, Lincoln, Lincoln!"

French doors opened and the curtains were pulled back. The president could be seen in silhouette waving both arms. The cheer that broke forth from the crowd was frenzied and unearthly. This gorilla, this tyrant, this homely man with his ridiculous stories had suddenly become their hero and idol. No one was more aware of their fickleness than the man on the balcony. The president produced a cylindrical sheaf of papers and rolled them in the opposite direction until they lay flat. The milling throng grew quiet and an arm holding an oil lamp appeared. Lincoln adjusted his spectacles and began to read his speech. His voice was so soft that cries of "quiet" and "shh" were heard in the masses.

They waited for words of exuberance and rejoicing; they waited for eloquent cries of victory; and they waited for words that would tell them that the men who had caused all this would pay. In their frenzy they had forgotten that this was a man of vision and of courage. This was not a man of the mob, but a man opposed to it. In the last four years Lincoln had sometimes been the only one strong enough to carry on while others despaired. He would not change now. The speech was slow and measured. It spoke of reconstruction and the future and it spoke of amnesty and Negro suffrage. When it came to this part, John Wilkes Booth moved away from the crowd and Herold and Payne followed.

"That's the last speech he'll ever make," the actor muttered, theatrically.

It was a sober speech and the crowd was quiet and respectful. However, when Sen. James Harlan of Iowa stepped up to speak after the president and asked with arms outstretched what they should do with their wayward brethren, the mob answered with one voice, "Hang 'em!" On the question of pardon, "Never!" Chagrined at this reaction, Harlan suggested that the majority of the people in the South were not guilty, and got stony silence. Realizing he had lost the moment, Harlan proclaimed that he would follow the president's leadership in this matter and ended his speech. The people gave him an enthusiastic hand as he left the balcony and the Marine Band struck up "The Battle Cry of Freedom." It began to drizzle and the crowd broke up, little realizing that now only one hand was capable of protecting the prostrate South from unrestrained retribution.

Washington City
April 13, 1865

Thursday, the thirteenth of April, was a glorious day. Spring had arrived at last. The sun was shining and the trees were in bud. The tulips along the mall were displaying the first hint of their kaleidoscopic glory. The deep mud of the streets was beginning to congeal even though that process would take days. Booth was not hard to follow. The day before, he wandered around the city, sometimes speaking to people he knew and sometimes in the company of Herold and Payne who followed worshipfully. He spent much of his time in Deery's Saloon on E Street. The saloon was close to Grover's National Theatre and, for that reason, it was a popular place for theater devotees. It was also a mecca for billiard aficionados because John Deery, the proprietor, was the national billiards champion. Deery knew Booth well and he was worried because he had never seen the actor so low. He also noticed that the thespian was drinking heavily. When Deery tried to inquire what was wrong Booth became even more morose.

The actor was a very troubled man. He was walking an emotional and mental tightrope that was beginning to sway uncontrollably. If reality had intruded on his perception of the Confederacy, it had also intruded on his perception of himself. He wanted only three things in life and those were to be a better-known actor than his brother Edwin, to save his beloved Confederacy, and to be remembered as a hero through the ages. He had failed at the first two, but the third was still within reach. The problem was that in order to become that hero, he would have to kill someone, and no matter how much he hated the man he didn't know if he could do it. Capturing Lincoln was the best of all possible worlds because that way he could be a hero without hurting anyone. He had always boasted about doing the president harm, but that was just braggadocio. Alan had been right, he would have to harden his heart, but could he? At the same time, could he tell the one true friend he had that he couldn't do what was necessary to rid the world of this tyrant? Alan had stood by him through all the attempts to capture the ogre. His financial aid made them all possible and now Alan was pursued by detectives for his help to the cause. How could Booth let a man like that down? Booth took another drink of brandy and stared at the blank wall of his room looking for an answer.

Dressed as a priest, Anderson walked by the National Hotel twice scouting for the detectives that he knew were watching for him. Occasionally, there had been adversaries, but Anderson had usually been able to catch them unaware. Now he had two adversaries who were not only intelligent, quick, and determined, but who seemed to read the very thoughts in his head. But why hadn't they gotten any more men? The obvious answer was that the authorities didn't believe them, and that made Anderson smile. One could always count on the authorities, especially the Metropolitan Police, to do precisely the wrong thing at precisely the right time. Anderson could almost depend on it. But these two detectives were far above the rest and what made them all the more dangerous was they were willing to track him down on their own. Fitch claimed the big one, Ingalls, was dead. Fitch had not seen the body so if Fitch believed it he was a fool.

On the second walk past, Anderson spotted the big detective standing across the street wearing a suit and reading a paper. The false beard and wig he sported were very good. Anderson had missed him the first time but the detective's surreptitious interest in the National gave him away. The colored detective was not in sight. Anderson could only surmise that he was inside the hotel. He had to get in to see Booth and had very little time to play cat and mouse. Anderson went into the telegraph office and passed through it to the lobby of the hotel. Everett was standing where he could see both the stairs and the desk. Anderson decided to be bold. He walked up to the desk and asked for a room for a week. The clerk, obviously not a Catholic, asked him to pay in advance, which he did. While signing the ledger as Father Dunnehey he told the clerk his bags would be arriving later by express. Everett looked carefully at the stout, balding Irish priest in the cassock and decided that it couldn't be possibly be Anderson.

Anderson could not allow himself the time to gloat over his success. Those two might discover him any minute. He went to his room and took off the cassock. In the false stomach was another change of clothes, make-up, and a few things he needed. He rapidly became Alan Demming, went to Booth's room, and knocked on the door.

"Who is it?" Booth called.

"Open up, Wilkes, it's Alan."

"Alan," the actor said, throwing the door open. "It's good to see you."

Anderson rushed into the room and closed the door. "They're all around the hotel," he said dramatically. "I don't know if they saw me."

Booth went to the window to draw the curtain back, but Anderson pulled him back into the center of the room. "If they see you looking out they might guess that I'm here."

"What is going on, Alan?"

Anderson had decided to take a chance. The Lincolns would be celebrating with everyone else on Friday night. Since Congress complained about the lavish way the first lady entertained at the taxpayers' expense, Mrs. Lincoln had begun giving theater parties, which were popular and considerably less expensive. Another reason the theater was fashionable was it allowed people to see Lincoln who was now the most popular man in the nation. If the Lincolns went to the theater, which Anderson was sure they would, there was a choice of Ford's or Grover's. Either would do. It was time to set his plan in motion.

"We are going to do it tomorrow night, Wilkes, but there are some things you must do." Anderson was looking Booth square in the eyes and the actor avoided his gaze.

"What do you want?" Booth asked.

"Tonight, notify everyone that tomorrow is the day. Atzerodt is to kill Johnson, and Payne is to kill Seward. Send Herold with Payne to guide him through the streets. Tell them you will meet them at 9:00 P.M. where Ohio crosses C. Everyone must be mounted. Surely, I don't have to tell you, Wilkes. It's your plan."

"Will you be there, Alan?"

"I will be there, but don't tell any of the others. You know how men feel about cripples doing anything like this. They might think I'd be putting them in jeopardy. I can't say as I blame them. I will meet you in this room at 5:00 P.M. tomorrow so we can go over any last-minute arrangements. Don't be late."

"Alan, I . . ."

"Yes, Wilkes?"

"Nothing. I won't be late."

"Good, tomorrow morning there are also a few things you must do. They may seem trivial, but they are extremely important and only you can do them."

"Of course, Alan. What are they?"

"You must get a good night's rest. That is most important. Tomorrow will be a long, but eventful day. When you get up, have a good breakfast, then go to the barber here in the hotel and get a shave. You must look and feel your best. As for the errands:

"First, go to Ford's Theatre, pick up your mail, and find out if Lincoln will be there tomorrow evening. Then go to Howard's stable over on G Street and have them deliver your one-eyed roan to the shed Spangler keeps for you.

"Second, go to Mrs. Surratt and give her these field glasses and a bottle of whiskey. Ask her to take them to the Surrattsville tavern and tell Lloyd to have the guns that John Surratt hid there ready for us to pick up tonight. We will need to pick them up quickly as we will be moving fast."

"Third, go to the Kirkwood and see the vice president. If he is not there, leave your *carte de visite* with the vice president's secretary and be sure you sign it. You can also visit Atzerodt to make sure he knows his part.

"Next, get a good fast horse. I think the one you've been renting from Pumphrey's is fine." Anderson picked up a sealed letter. "Then, deliver this note to Hess at Grover's Theatre. It is for the *National Intelligencer*. Tell him not to open it until tomorrow morning. If Hess is not there, give it to someone you trust. Then come back here.

"Don't worry about remembering any of it, Wilkes. I have a list for you." He put a hand on Booth's shoulder. "And Wilkes, don't worry. You won't have to do anything you don't want to, but the fame and glory will all be yours. You'll be the most famous actor in the world."

Booth said nothing. He felt much better. Perhaps he would become a hero, after all. If so, he would reward Alan.

"I have to go," Anderson said. "I'll see you tomorrow. Don't forget. Tell the others."

"I will, Alan. I promise."

Anderson looked carefully out of the door and limped away.

Booth left the hotel after dark, and, not knowing he was followed, went to each of his men and told them what the morrow would bring. Herold was excited he was to follow his hero in a great undertaking. Payne showed no emotion. He just nodded and said he would be ready. Booth found Atzerodt at the Pennsylvania House on C Street. The boatman was shocked and suddenly not so sure of his place in the scheme of things.

"I only signed on for a capture," he said. "Not to kill anyone."

"You're a damned coward, Atzerodt!" Booth snapped, irritated that anyone else would mirror his own reluctance. "Are you going to let all of us down at this late date?"

Atzerodt said nothing. These men were his friends, the only friends he had.

Booth handed him twenty dollars. "Get a room at the Kirkwood House. Johnson has a suite there. You'll be in a better position to kill him."

Atzerodt took the money. "Yes, Wilkes."

On the way back to the National, Booth was elated. Tomorrow he would be famous and would not have to do anything he didn't want to. That appealed to him. When he returned to his room he penned a short letter to his mother. It was a light letter telling her he was well. John Wilkes Booth was in a good mood.

Anderson was pleased at Booth's reaction but didn't smile. As he had long suspected, Booth was a man of little character and what there was happened to be vain and weak. Once Anderson began giving orders, Booth, never a leader, followed willingly. The errands that he gave the actor were not trivial. They would serve to highlight Booth as the villain of the piece and throw suspicion on everyone he came in contact with from the vice president to Mary Surratt. The letter, an artistic forgery that looked like it had been written by Booth, would hang the lot of them when it fell into the right hands. Once his commission was complete, people would be so busy pointing fingers at one another and trying to distance themselves from Booth that no one would ever suspect the real killer, his employers, or their motives. When he left Booth's room, Anderson returned to his own and put on the priest's garb.

He waited until Booth left and was followed by the detectives. Anderson cursed Ingalls and Everett silently. They knew that Booth was the lynch pin of the entire scheme and were making sure the actor didn't leave their sight. Well, gentlemen, he thought, we shall see what tomorrow brings. Once Booth and his shadows were out of sight, Anderson headed for the shop in Swampoodle. Fitch was waiting for him in the office, none too patiently.

"Did you get the wagon and the crates, Joseph?"

"Yeah, they're in the shop."

"Let me see them."

Fitch led him to the warehouse where a wagon was covered by a tarpaulin. He pulled it back. It was an Adam's Express Company wagon painted bright red with black letters outlined in yellow. It was wagon #28.

"Did you steal this?"

"Yes, but they won't know it until morning. I took it from their yard just as it was closing. The horses are out back."

Anderson was upset with Fitch, but didn't show it. He had asked Fitch to paint a wagon resembling an express wagon so nothing would be traceable. Now it was too late to do anything about it. He climbed up on the wagon. In the back were several crates, one of them large enough to hold a man. He looked inside; it was empty.

"Put some padding in this. I don't want Booth injured on the way out of the hotel. Did you get Charlie?"

"Yes, sir."

"Good. You and Charlie will arrive at the National at 5:00 P.M. It is all right to be a little late, but do not arrive earlier."

"Yes, Mr. Anderson."

That afternoon, Lafayette Baker returned to New York.

Fort Sumter
Charleston Harbor
April 14, 1865

At 10:00 A.M. the citizens of the defunct Confederate States of America were reminded that their attempt for independence had come to naught. Fort Sumter was a symbol to both sides. To the South it was the first Federal installation taken by force of arms and, though battered to ruins by Union gunboats, it never fell while in Confederate hands. To the North it was the symbol of a calculated insult, and that insult was about to be repaid. Four years after they were lowered in surrender by Maj. Robert Anderson, the same Stars and Stripes were raised in victory over the ruins of Fort Sumter by Gen. Robert Anderson. Four years ago, the citizens of Charleston had cheered as Confederate artillery shattered the night with the first bombardment of the war. Now they listened sullenly as Federal cannon occupying those same positions fired a thunderous salute. But it was not this that made the citizens of Charleston wince as much as the attitude of Southerners in other states who had no sympathy for their brethren in South Carolina.

"They led us to this," the other Southerners said bitterly. "Serves 'em right."

The country was getting back to normal.

Washington City

Good Friday dawned slightly overcast and with some ground fog. As the sun rose higher in the sky, the fog burned off, and the sky was clear. Except for occasional periods of overcast it promised to be a fine, cool day. The city was quieting down after three days of celebration. In addition, this was a sacred day for Christians regardless of their denomination. Mrs. Lincoln informed her husband they were going to the theater to see *Our American Cousin* at Ford's Opera House. It was a lackluster comedy except when Laura Keene herself starred in it, as she would tonight. The president was tired and didn't want to go, but as a married politician he was unable to resist the double pressures of a wife who wanted to go to the theater and an electorate who wanted to see him. He invited General Grant, but in the afternoon the general declined. Grant was going to New Jersey to visit relations. This was true, but the general could have gone to New Jersey the following morning and spent less time on the train. The reason he and Mrs. Grant were leaving early was that the warm, modest Julia Dent Grant could not stand the imperious Mary Todd Lincoln. Lincoln would as soon go to the theater unattended, but Stanton insisted he take someone along. The president asked Stanton if he could borrow Maj. Thomas Eckert, head of the War Department Telegraph Office. Eckert was a physically powerful man and the president joked that if anyone could protect him it was Eckert. Eckert also declined, because his workload was still extremely heavy. The officer who agreed to accompany the president and the first lady was Maj. Henry Rathbone along with his fiancée, Miss Clara Harris, one of the beauties of Washington society. They were a handsome couple. The tall, slender, and good-looking officer was twenty-eight and a trusted attaché at the War Department. The dark-haired, full-figured Miss Harris was the daughter of Sen. Ira Harris of New York. The major was his stepson.

The National Hotel

John Wilkes Booth arose feeling better than he had for weeks. Today he would gain fame without having to do that which he did not want to do. Alan Demming had told him that, and he believed it. Demming had been the truest friend and patriot to the Southern cause (beside himself, of course) that Booth had ever known. The thought there might be a catch to those conditions didn't cross his mind. All John Wilkes Booth knew was, after tonight, he would be famous. The first thing on the agenda was a good breakfast, which the actor ate heartily. Next he went to the hotel barber for a shave before he went back upstairs to dress and pick up Alan Demming's list. Shortly after 11:00 A.M., the actor left the National, followed discreetly by Ingalls and Everett. On the way out he asked the clerk at the desk to have a boy post the letter he had written to his mother. Booth followed Demming's list meticulously except for some minor deviations.

His first stop, as instructed, was Ford's Theatre. There, the actor picked up his mail and discovered that the president and Mrs. Lincoln were coming that evening. Booth smiled at the news and went out on the steps to read his mail. A few minutes later, he left. A little before noon he stopped to talk with James Ford who was returning to his theater with flags borrowed from the Treasury Department. Ford was disappointed that the huge thirty-six-foot flag was still on loan and had not been returned. Around 2:00 P.M. Booth stopped off at the Herndon House to see Payne and remind him what he was supposed to do. Johnson was not at the Kirkwood, so Booth left his card as instructed. Atzerodt was also not in, so Booth left a note. By this time he was running late. Hess was not in at Grover's, so Booth left the letter Anderson had given him with John Matthews, a fellow actor who refused to become involved in any of Booth's plots. Matthews agreed to deliver the letter to the newspaper if he didn't hear from Booth the following morning. After the assassination, Matthews would open the letter and read it. Fearful he might be implicated, he would burn it, after looking at the names listed on the bottom in Booth's handwriting. Hurrying back to the National, Booth ran into Atzerodt and reminded him again of what he was to do. When the dirty man complained, Booth called him a coward and Atzerodt whined, but agreed to go through with it. On his way back to the National, Booth saw hawkers passing out handbills announcing that the president would be at Ford's Theatre that evening.

At 4:45 P.M. Anderson, dressed as Father Dunnehey, parked the carriage in front of the National and went to his room to become Alan Demming. At 5:07 P.M. Booth returned to the National. Three minutes later, Fitch, disguised as a portly bearded teamster, and Charlie, a young man with a pock-marked face and a nose that had been broken and set badly, backed the wagon into the alley behind the National. John Wilkes Booth picked up the key and went upstairs to his room. Ingalls followed as far as the lobby. Everett, whose turn it was to wait outside, watched as the big red Adam's Express wagon backed into the alley that opened on Sixth Street. When the wagon could not be seen from the street, Fitch and Charlie went into the back door and up the stairs to the hallway outside Booth's room.

Almost as soon as the actor closed his door someone knocked on it.

"Wilkes, it's Alan," came the whisper.

Booth opened the door and smiled as his friend Alan Demming slipped into the room.

"How did it go?" Anderson asked.

"I did everything you told me to," the actor said. This wasn't a lie. Booth's perception of precision in executing a task was far different from the deadly, efficient Anderson. The assassin knew this and had taken it into account. "What do we do now?" Booth asked.

"We have to wait a few hours until the nine o'clock meeting. I suggest we rest, then go downstairs and have a good supper. We are going to have a busy night."

"Good idea," Booth said. He lay down diagonally across the bed so his spurs would not cut the covers and began to doze.

Anderson could not help smiling. The actor was making this too easy. Anderson pulled a gauze already soaked with chloroform from his pocket and placed it gently over Booth's mouth and nose. The actor inhaled deeply and was soon sound asleep. Anderson covered Booth's face then opened the door. Fitch and Charlie were waiting outside.

"You know what to do?" Anderson asked Charlie.

The young man nodded and began removing his overalls. He put on a wig, a false mustache, one of the actor's suits, and Booth's cloak. Anderson sat him in front of a mirror and combed the wig with some of the actor's hair tonic.

"There," Anderson said. "You won't pass close examination, but you'll do. Go!"

Charlie left the room and started downstairs.

Clarence Everett, growing increasingly suspicious of the wagon, left his post in front of Brown's hotel and walked to the alley. The wagon, Adam's Express #28, was unattended.

Charlie walked quickly across the lobby, and, as instructed, looked over his shoulder at Ingalls. The detective waited until the man he thought was Booth went through the door before he followed. He knew Everett was outside to see which way Booth went. He emerged from the hotel entrance in time to see Booth climb into a parked landau and drive off, heading east. Everett was nowhere to be seen. Ingalls ran to the corner and looked for his partner. When he saw Everett near the alley, he shouted. Clarence Everett was about to go into the alley when he heard Ingalls call. He turned and ran to the corner.

"What's wrong?" he asked.

"Booth's taken a carriage," Ingalls shouted.

The two detectives ran for their horses and spurred them after the landau.

"Help me," Anderson told Fitch as he pulled the unconscious actor from the bed. Booth groaned softly when they tried to get him to stand. He wouldn't stand and his body slid back on the bed. "I guess I gave him too much. I'll have to carry him."

Fitch moved Booth to a sitting position, then Anderson knelt down and put the actor over his shoulder. He lifted him up with a grunt. "Get the door."

Fitch opened the door for Anderson and, following, paused to close and lock it. He gave Booth's room key to Anderson and they went down the back steps to the wagon. While Anderson held the unconscious actor Fitch opened the long crate, which was now padded inside like a coffin. The two of them lifted Booth into the wagon then into the crate. As Fitch closed the lid, Anderson noticed the air holes drilled in the sides and top. He handed Fitch the bottles of chloroform, the pack of gauze, and a bottle of whiskey. Fitch gazed on it longingly.

Anderson grinned. "Take a drink of that and you'll be dead within the hour," he said.

Fitch's jaw dropped, "Poison?"

Anderson smiled. Fitch didn't like poison or anything else he couldn't see. "Remember, let him get about half awake then only give him four or five drops on the gauze. About 10:00 P.M. do what I instructed."

Fitch climbed into the driver's seat and nodded.

"Now, get going," Anderson said.

Fitch headed the wagon southeast on The Avenue toward the Navy Yard Bridge.

Anderson returned to Father Dunnehey's room and sat in front of the mirror. He opened a theatrical make-up kit and began to darken his eyebrows. He was about to play the greatest role of John Wilkes Booth's career.

Ingalls and Everett, used to following Booth at his normally leisurely pace, nearly lost him as Charlie drove rapidly down The Avenue, then turned north on First Street East. They hurried to catch up.

Everett looked over at Ingalls as they followed Booth's landau which was heading straight for Swampoodle. He didn't like it. The expression on his face must have shown it.

"What's wrong?" Ingalls called.

Instead of shouting a reply, Everett spurred his horse forward, and overtook the landau. The driver with dark curly hair and moustache was not Booth.

"Stop," Everett commanded.

Charlie flicked the reins on the horses' backs to move faster, but Ingalls caught up, grabbed the horses' bridle, and pulled them to a halt. Charlie started to get out of the carriage, but Everett pulled his pistol. "One more move and I shoot." Charlie raised his hands.

Ingalls stared at the man with bad complexion. "We followed the wrong carriage," he said. "I missed Booth."

"No you didn't," Everett said, dismounting. Still holding the pistol he commanded Charlie to get down. Then he walked over and pulled off Charlie's wig and false mustache.

"Take off the cloak," Everett told him. Charlie complied and Everett looked inside. The name "J. W. Booth" was embroidered on the inside. "Where did you get these?" Everett demanded.

"I ain't sayin' nothin'," Charlie said defiantly.

"He's more afraid of Anderson than he is of the Blue Jug," Ingalls said.

At the sound of Anderson's name, Charlie looked directly at Ingalls. Everett noticed it, too.

"Where'd Anderson and Booth go?" Ingalls asked.

"I told you, I ain't sayin' nothin'."

Everett smiled. "All right, be that way," he said. "But we're going to Swampoodle and tell everyone there that you told us what you know about Anderson. Then he'll fix the problem."

The expression of defiance fell away and stark terror replaced it. Charlie swallowed. "I was paid to come in the freight wagon and go upstairs. Then Fitch and this man with a beard give me the wig and the mustache and the cloak and told me to get in the carriage and drive like hell for home. That's all, honest."

"The freight wagon?" Everett exclaimed. "Let him go. We have to get back to the hotel."

"What?"

"Hurry!"

They mounted their horses and hurried back to the National. Ingalls walked up to the desk and showed the desk clerk his badge. "National Detectives," he said. "I want the key to Mr. Booth's room."

George Bunker stared at the large man and then at the badge. As any good employee of the hotel, his first duty was to protect the hotel and avoid scandal. Since he had not seen Charlie go across the lobby, he looked at the key rack.

"Mr. Booth's key is not here so he must be in his room," he said.

"The key," was Ingalls only reply.

Bunker hastily looked around and took the spare key from its hook. "You will be discreet," he whispered as he handed the key to Ingalls.

"Of course."

Ingalls and Everett went upstairs to Room 231. When they opened the door, Ingalls stopped and sniffed.

"What's that?" he asked.

"It sure isn't hair tonic," Everett replied, sniffing along with him. "Chloroform," he said.

They looked around the room. Booth's trunk and clothes were still in the room. There was nothing to indicate that he had gone. They left and relocked the door.

"Chloroform?" Ingalls said more to himself than Everett. "Why chloroform?"

They returned the key to Bunker after a quick check of the bar and dining salon. Booth was nowhere to be found. When they left the clerk decided the entire incident was best forgotten. Outside, the two detectives stood looking at the traffic going by. It was ten minutes of six.

"He could be in one of the other rooms," Everett said.

"No, I don't think so," Ingalls said absentmindedly. Then, "Why chloroform? It's used for putting people to sleep during operations, right?"

"Right."

"Oh, no!" Ingalls said.

"What's wrong?" Everett asked.

"The wagon you saw. What was it?"

"Adams Express Company, number twenty-eight."

"Let's go."

"You've lost me, George."

"I'll explain on the way," he said as they mounted their horses.

The Washington office of the Adams Express Company was located near the B&O station. It consisted of a white, one-story wooden office and a repair shop. The agent for the company was Charles Dunn, a short man with a spare frame. He was bald with a full beard and a helpful, pleasant manner that made him a success with clients. He was in his shirtsleeves going over ledgers when Ingalls and Everett knocked on the door. Politely he came to the door to tell them they were closed.

"We're not here to ship anything, sir," Ingalls said, showing Dunn his badge. "We're National Detectives and we were hoping you could help us with an investigation."

"Whatever I can do to help," Dunn said. "Come in, please."

"One of your wagons, number twenty-eight, made a stop at the National Hotel in the last hour. Could you tell us why?"

"Certainly," Dunn said, going to his desk. He opened a ledger and began looking down the page. "That's odd," he said.

"What?" Ingalls asked.

"It doesn't show twenty-eight being dispatched today. Just a minute." He went to the door connecting the office with the repair shop.

"MacDougall, Fredericks," he called. "Would you come in here for a minute?"

In a moment two men, one white and one colored, appeared at the door. Their clothes were stained with axle grease and covered with sawdust. Dunn did not introduce them. "Where is twenty-eight?" he asked.

"It's in the lot," the white man said with a brogue. This was obviously MacDougall.

"I fixed the singletree last week," the colored man said. "It was dispatched the other day."

"Check on it, will you please?"

Both men nodded and left. In two minutes, they were back with puzzled looks. "It's not there."

Dunn turned to the detectives. "It appears, gentlemen, that wagon number twenty-eight has been stolen."

"You had best report this to the Metropolitan Police," Ingalls said. "And thank you so much for your cooperation."

"My pleasure, gentlemen."

Ingalls stood outside the office with a puzzled look on his face. "I'm stumped, Clarence. I was sure that Anderson was using Booth as a dupe. If that's the case, why has Booth disappeared?"

Everett shrugged. "There's something we're not seeing. Look, I do my thinking better on a full stomach. Why don't we have supper and see if we can figure it out."

Anderson stood in front of the mirror. The reflection that looked back was that of the famous actor, John Wilkes Booth. The disguise Anderson practiced in the carriage shop in Swampoodle was nearly flawless. He might not pass inspection in broad daylight or by any of Booth's intimates, but it wasn't daytime and he wouldn't be seeing Ella Turner or Bessie Hale, he hoped. Anderson left his room and went downstairs. He strode across the lobby and left Booth's key at the desk.

"Good evening, Mr. Booth," George Bunker said. Anderson had passed the first test. He walked out of the hotel and mounted the horse Booth had rented. It was not the one he had before, but it was spirited and would do. He looked up and saw that the sky was once again overcast. He smiled. That meant that it would be dark that much earlier and darkness was his friend. Anderson then rode to F Street where he dismounted and opened the billboard gate leading to the alley behind Ford's Theatre. He rode down the alley past shanties and boarding houses occupied by some of the poorer colored citizens of Washington. He avoided the knots of children playing and waved back at those who waved at the lone horseman. When he reached the back of the theater, he dismounted.

"Ned," he shouted in Booth fashion, and Spangler and Maddox came out.

"Stable this mare, would you please? And make sure it's a strong halter. I don't want her to run away."

"Sure, Mr. Booth. Jake," he called to Ritterspaugh. "Get that good halter out of the property room, will you?"

Ritterspaugh brought the halter out and Spangler took it and the horse to the small shed. He removed the bridle, replaced it with the halter, and gave the horse water and feed.

"How about having a drink with me?" Anderson asked. "Can you spare the time?"

"Sure, Mr. Booth," they chorused.

He led them backstage and down to the underground passage to the south alley to Taltavul's where they sat at a table.

"Drinks for my friends," Anderson told the waiter.

Peter Taltavul came over from behind the bar and said hello. "There was a boy looking for you earlier, Mr. Booth," he said. Anderson thought it was probably Herold. He thanked Taltavul.

"Well, don't any of you have any work to do tonight?" Anderson asked, bantering with his companions as the waiter set down the glasses.

"You know stagehands don't do no work," Maddox joked. Booth was one of the few actors who appreciated their work and showed it. They liked him.

"In that case I should retire and become a stagehand," Anderson quipped back. The three men laughed.

"Everything's set up for tonight," Ritterspaugh said. "Not much to do until curtain time."

Anderson smiled. He had passed another test. After a little more light conversation, he excused himself.

"I have to go," he said. "But there's no need for you to. Waiter!" he called. "A bottle of Overholtz for my friends." He handed the waiter three dollars. Two dollars for the whiskey and one dollar for the tip. He left to calls of "Thank you, Mr. Booth."

Anderson returned to the theater and went back up on the stage. It was dark except for a few gaslights dimly glowing. He looked up to his left at the flag-draped box then went across the stage. He picked up a piece of pine he thought would suffice and jumped off the stage into the orchestra. He followed the route to the back of the theater and up to the dress circle that he had walked with Booth. He went to the door leading to the state box and stood still. The theater was deathly quiet. He walked in, closed the door behind him, and struck a match. He took the piece of wood and fit it between the door and the wall. Laying a handkerchief on the floor beneath the spot where the board hit the wall, he proceeded to gouge a niche for the board in the plaster. He tried it twice before it fit to his satisfaction. Anyone coming after him would have to break down the door to get into the box area. Anderson struck another match. He picked up the handkerchief full of plaster and pieces of wallpaper and put it in his pocket. Then he blew away any loose plaster on the wall. He removed the board and secreted it behind the door.

The box was already set up for the presidential party. The partition had been removed and the chairs had been arranged. Both doors opened since the locks were broken. He walked to the edge of the box, stood between the president's rocker and Mrs. Lincoln's chair, and looked down. He would have to be very careful of the flags, or else he and Booth would have the same accident, and that wouldn't do. Anderson drew his pen knife, opened it, and made a cut in the edge of the flag in front of the box. This would enhance the drama.

Next, Anderson used a small gimlet and a penknife to drill a small hole in the door directly behind the president. He caught the shavings in another handkerchief and checked his work. He would be able to see the president's head and shoulders clearly. If the president was in the box tonight, Anderson would kill him. If not, he would wait for another chance. Satisfied, he returned to the F Street alley and retrieved the mare. He rode back to the National to have supper and get some rest. He told the night clerk if anyone called for him to tell them he was out. He then went to the room he had rented as Father Dunnehey. It was 7:06 P.M.

Ingalls and Everett went to Ferguson's for supper. Everett was hungry. He ordered pork chops with potatoes, onions, and gravy, which was accompanied with a schooner of beer. When the meal arrived he pitched into it with gusto. Ingalls ordered stew with a glass of cider but hardly touched it.

"What's the matter, George?" Clarence asked. "Booth?"

Ingalls nodded.

"Shouldn't let it spoil your appetite. A growing boy like you needs nourishment."

The big detective smiled faintly in appreciation of his friend's effort to cheer him up.

"There's something and I can't put my finger on it."

"We're concentrating on Booth. Maybe he isn't important anymore. Maybe Anderson killed him and took him away in that wagon," Everett said between forkfuls of potatoes and gravy.

"What did you say, Clarence?"

Everett repeated what he said.

"That's it!" Ingalls said so loudly that the other diners turned to look at him. He lowered his voice. "That's it! Clarence, you are brilliant."

"I am? What is it?"

"Booth is no longer important, but he's not dead. They knocked him out with chloroform to take him God knows where, probably the warehouse in Swampoodle. What is important is that he is out of the way. Don't you see? That's why Anderson kept him around. Anderson is going to kill Lincoln tonight, and when he does it, he's going to look like John Wilkes Booth."

Everett shook his head. He wasn't sure. "That's stretching it, George."

"Is it? You've seen Anderson. What does he look like?"

Everett thought for a minute. "Medium height, chin whiskers, gray in the hair. Not a thing like Booth . . ." He stopped. "That was a disguise, without it he would be . . ." The thought was left unfinished.

"Let's go," Ingalls said. "Ford's Theatre."

Everett looked at his watch. It was 7:45 P.M.

Anderson got off the bed and stretched. He hadn't been able to sleep. He was thinking about the two detectives who were dogging his heels. He had a grudging admiration for them. They were worthy adversaries, but he had managed to stay one step ahead of them so far. As soon as this commission was finished he planned to kill them both. Anderson removed a false beard and a make-up pencil from his make-up kit. When he did the deed he would look like Booth in a very bad disguise. He loaded the derringer he had taken from the actor, slipped it into his pocket, and stuck a large knife in its sheath in the waistband of his trousers. In his other coat pocket he put his Uhlinger .32-caliber breech-loading revolver and some extra cartridges. After the Stonewall Jackson commission he no longer relied on a single-shot pocket pistol. He left the room and locked the door. Fitch would have to retrieve the good Father's things tomorrow. Anderson went downstairs and dropped off Booth's room key.

"Are you going to Ford's Theatre, tonight?" he asked the clerk.

"I hadn't thought of it, Mr. Booth," the night clerk said.

"You should. There will be some exceptional acting there tonight."

As he left, Anderson glanced at the clock in the lobby. It was 8:10 P.M. The Lincolns were just leaving the White House gate in a barouche. They stopped by the home of Senator Harris and picked up Major Rathbone and the senator's daughter. Both the major and his lovely Clara were excited as they joined their host and hostess for this singular honor. At the last minute, the major decided to go in civilian clothes and not wear a side arm. The ladies began talking about the latest Washington gossip as soon as Miss Harris sat down.

Everett and Ingalls arrived at Ford's Theatre shortly after eight. The performance had not yet begun. They flashed their badges at Buckingham, the ticket taker, and went directly upstairs. The theater was filling with patrons. Ingalls and Everett went straight to the State Box. The president had not yet arrived. From the shadows of the box, they looked across the portion of the audience they could see. Neither Booth nor anyone who looked like him was visible from their vantage point. They returned to the lobby just as John Parker, the president's night bodyguard from the Metropolitan Police, was going up to check the box.

"Not him," Everett whispered to his partner.

"You know him, too, I see," Ingalls said.

"Every policeman and detective in Washington has heard of John Parker. He's been up on charges more times than I can count. How he's allowed to keep his badge is beyond me."

Ingalls was about to reply when the presidential barouche pulled up in front of the theater. The president and Mrs. Lincoln came in, followed by Major Rathbone and Miss Harris. The ticket taker bowed. The overture had already started. Parker, returned from checking the box, led the presidential party up the stairs. The two detectives could hear the audience cheer and applaud when the president arrived. It was 8:41 P.M.

"What now?" Everett asked.

"Let's check around the theater and the tavern."

Anderson rode to the corner of Ohio and C and waited as Herold, Payne, and finally Atzerodt showed up.

"You all know your assignments," he told them. "Payne, you will kill Seward, which shouldn't be too difficult since he's flat on his back in bed."

Payne's mouth stretched. For an expressionless man Anderson guessed it was a smile.

"Davey," Anderson said to Herold, "you will be Payne's guide."

"Yes, Wilkes."

"Atzerodt, tonight you kill Johnson."

Atzerodt said nothing.

"George?" Anderson asked.

"I will kill Johnson," Atzerodt repeated mechanically.

"Men, tonight we avenge the South. God bless you in your noble work," Anderson told them.

They slowly went their separate ways. Atzerodt plodded back to the Kirkwood. Anderson guessed he would get drunk and do nothing. Payne, he figured, just might kill Seward, but it didn't matter. What did matter was the confusion they would create. He headed for Ford's Theatre. It was 9:05 P.M.

Ingalls and Everett checked the alleys around the theater which took them over half an hour. There was no sign of Booth. They went to Taltavul's saloon and although it was crowded, they saw no sign of Booth or anyone who looked like him. They went back to the lobby and asked Buckingham if he had seen Booth this evening. The ticket taker shook his head. He had not. Ingalls was beginning to feel uneasy. They needed at least a dozen men for this operation.

"Why don't we check around the theater once more?" Ingalls said. "With Parker on the door that should delay Anderson a few minutes, anyway. I'd like to get him before he gets into the theater."

"Me, too."

They left the lobby and right behind them came John Parker. Bored with guarding the president, Parker walked downstairs and left the theater. He saw Francis Burns, the president's driver, dozing in the driver's seat of the barouche.

"Hey, Francis," he said. "How about a glass of ale?"

Burns, only half asleep, stretched. "Sounds good." The two men went into Taltavul's.

Anderson rode into the F Street alley and called for Spangler. Spangler was busy changing a scene and could not come so he sent another stagehand, whom everyone called Johnny Peanut, because he also sold peanuts at the theater. Anderson went inside and was told to use the underground passageway, so he would not be seen on stage. Anderson complied gladly. As he walked beneath the stage he heard the creaking of the boards and the laughter of the audience. For a passé comedy, it seemed to be doing very well. It was 9:36 when he reached the end of the passage. The moon would rise at 10:02 to aid his escape. Booth had time for one more public appearance, so Anderson went to Taltavul's. He was beginning to wonder where Ingalls and Everett were. By now they probably knew what was going on so Anderson expected to see them in or near the theater. He was very careful going into Taltavul's. The detectives were not there, but John Parker, the president's bodyguard, was. He was sitting at a table with the president's driver and another man. Anderson smiled. This might go better than he planned. He sat at the bar and Peter Taltavul came up.

"What'll it be, Mr. Booth?"

"A bottle of whiskey and water," Anderson said.

"Whiskey?" Taltavul said. "I thought you were a brandy man."

For a moment, Anderson froze. He had committed an error and he should have been more aware. Recovering quickly, he said with a smile, "Everyone needs a change now and again."

"You're right, sir," Taltavul said and went to get the whiskey.

When he returned, Anderson paid for the whiskey and gave him two more dollars. "Send some drinks over to those three men at that table," he said pointing to Parker. "A little something for our city's policemen."

"Sure thing, Mr. Booth."

Anderson sipped the whiskey and waited. At 9:45 he got up to leave.

A drunk at the bar shouted, "You'll never be the actor your father was."

Anderson, out-Boothing Booth, raised his hat. "After tonight, I will be the most famous actor in the world."

On leaving the saloon, Anderson was accosted by two Booth admirers, one of whom offered to buy him a drink. He smiled graciously and told them he had promised Laura Keene that he would watch her performance. He bowed as they went into Taltavul's and turned to go to the theater. He froze. Emerging from the theater, and coming his way, were Ingalls and Everett, probably to check Taltavul's. This was neither the time nor the place to deal with these two. Anderson ran into the street and hid in one of the unattended parked carriages that lined the curb and breathed a sigh of relief as Ingalls and Everett walked by. Time was getting short. As soon as the detectives had passed, he headed for the front door of the theater, keeping the parked carriages between the detectives and himself. When he walked in, Buckingham asked for a ticket before he realized who Booth was.

"Do you want a ticket from me?" Anderson asked with a warm smile. Actors were allowed into Ford's free at any time.

"Compliments of the house, sir," Buckingham said with an exaggerated bow.

Anderson saw that Buckingham was chewing and asked for a small bite of tobacco. Later, Buckingham would swear he was Booth.

Buckingham handed him a plug. "I have some friends that want to meet you, Mr. Booth," the ticket taker said.

"Of course, John, but later," Anderson said, going up the stairs to the dress circle. He went directly into the unguarded door, closed it, and lifted the bar into place. He put on the false beard, but had no time for anything else.

Ingalls walked into Taltavul's first and Everett came in right behind him. When the two men saw Parker sitting with his two drinking companions, they both headed for the door and bolted for the theater.

Anderson crouched at the door and looked through the spy hole he had cut earlier in the day. He could see Lincoln clearly. He stood up, cocked the derringer, and made sure the cap was in place. Then he opened the door and walked in.

Harry Hawk, alone on stage as Trenchard, was saying "Well, I guess I know enough to turn you inside out, old gal—you sockdologizing ole man-trap!"

The audience was laughing as Anderson walked up, put the derringer behind Lincoln's ear and pulled the trigger.

Ingalls and Everett ran past Buckingham and up the stairs. They pushed on the door. It was locked.

Lincoln's head bobbed forward on his chest. Seeing the smoke from the derringer, Mrs. Lincoln turned around in the middle of a laugh. Anderson dropped Booth's derringer and pulled the knife as Major Rathbone grabbed for him.

"Revenge for the South," Anderson screamed and plunged the knife into the young major's arm. Rathbone reeled back. Anderson leaped to the edge of the box and jumped, making sure he cleared the flag. On the way down he grabbed the flag, tearing it. Once he was on the stage, he went down on all fours and began hobbling off. Harry Hawk, baffled at what was happening, looked at him as he passed and muttered, "Booth."

"Stop that man," Rathbone shouted.

Maj. Joseph B. Stewart, sitting in the front row in civilian clothes, repeated the cry to stop the man and climbed up on the stage and followed the man who had just hobbled into the wings. Once he was in the wings, Anderson stopped his fake hobbling and began to run. At the back door, Johnny Peanut was sleeping on the steps with the reins of Anderson's horse in his hand. Anderson kicked him, took the reins, and hobbled to the horse. He jumped into the saddle as Major Stewart behind emerged from the stage door. Anderson rode up the alley and went out through Ninth Street, then out onto The Avenue. He galloped for the Navy Yard Bridge.

Inside the theater the patrons gradually began to learn what had happen and pandemonium erupted. Hundreds of people were shouting at once.

"What has happened?"

"The president's been shot."

"Who did it?"

"I don't know."

"It was Wilkes Booth, I'll swear to it."

"Burn this theater to the ground!"

"I think he broke his leg when he jumped."

Ingalls and Everett rushed out into the street. The big man was nearly in tears. He had failed. Everett cursed the Metropolitan Police and Lafayette Baker.

"Well," Everett quipped cynically. "Maybe now they'll believe us."

CHAPTER 11

The Navy Yard Bridge
10:45 P.M., April 14, 1865

AFTER A FAST RUN through the streets of Washington, Anderson, disguised as Booth, but with the false beard removed, trotted up to the Navy Yard Bridge and stopped. One of the sentries grabbed the mare's bridle as Silas Cobb, the sergeant of the guard, stepped forward.

"Who are you, sir?" he asked.

"My name is Booth," Anderson replied.

"Where are you from?" the sergeant asked.

"From the city."

"Where are you going?"

"I am going home," Anderson told him.

"Where is your home?"

"Charles," Anderson said, being deliberately vague.

Sergeant Cobb assumed this meant Charles County and asked, "What town?"

"I don't live in a town."

"You must live in some town," the sergeant insisted.

This sergeant is a stickler for detail, Anderson thought. "I live near Beantown, but not in the town itself."

"Why are you out so late?" the sergeant asked. "Don't you know that persons are not allowed to pass after nine o'clock?"

Anderson did know. He also knew that the enforcement of such rules at this bridge had been lax even at the height of the war.

"That's news to me," Anderson swore sincerely. "I had some business in the city and thought I would have the moon to ride home by."

The sergeant thought for a moment. "All right, you may pass."

Anderson was relieved that he wouldn't have to kill the guards. Unnecessary killings left a trail. The soldier released his bridle and Anderson spurred the horse forward across the bridge. There were still things to do.

Uniontown, Maryland
April 14, 1865

It was getting dark when Joseph Fitch parked the wagon in front of the barn. He liked it dark, because it insured that there would be no nosy neighbors. He opened the door to the barn, and drove the wagon inside. He closed the door, lit a lantern, then opened the crate. Booth was sleeping like a baby. Fitch rolled the actor out of the crate, by tipping it on its side, and pulled him to a sitting position on the tailgate of the wagon. With a yank, Fitch put him over his shoulder and carried him to the bed in the tack room. He placed some gauze over the actor's nose and put four drops of chloroform on the gauze. Fitch caught his breath, then started a fire in the stove to lessen the chill in the air. A bottle of whiskey would be nice, he thought, as he coveted the bottle on the table, but Fitch lived in dread of things he could neither see nor touch, so there was no chance he would sample its contents. He glanced over at Booth as the room began to get warm, then he dozed off.

Fitch was awakened by the sound of Booth groaning. Waking up quickly his first reaction was to pour more chloroform on the gauze, but he thought about the instructions Anderson had written for him and decided against it. The little man fumbled in his pockets and found the folded piece of paper, unfolded it, and read:

> At about 9:30 P.M., let Booth come awake to the point you can talk to him, then only give him three drops chloroform per hour. Once you can talk to him say these things, but say them softly. Insist, but don't raise your voice. Do this once an hour.

Fitch checked his watch. It was 9:20. Close enough. He pulled a chair up to the bed and began.

"Are you John Wilkes Booth?"

"Yes," came a mumbled answer.

"Are you an actor?"

"Yes." This time it was barely a whisper.

"Do you live in the National Hotel?"

"Yes."

"Do you hate President Lincoln?"

"Yes."

"You are going to kill President Lincoln."

"No. Don't want to kill anybody . . ."

"You are walking up behind him."

"Behind him . . ."

"You are pointing the gun at the back of his head."

"Gun . . . head."

Fitch read the next instruction twice, before he picked up his pistol and fired into the floor. Booth twitched on the bed and muttered "No, no."

"You jump out of the box and break your leg."

"Break . . . leg."

"You have escaped."

"Yes . . . escape."

Fitch watched Booth and then gave him another three drops of chloroform. Fitch repeated his instructions again at 10:30. Anderson arrived at 11:10.

"How is Booth?" he asked.

"I did what you told me. He answers the questions."

Anderson sat next to the bed.

"Wilkes, can you hear me?"

"Yes, who . . ."

"It's Alan, Wilkes."

"Alan . . ."

"You are going to kill Lincoln."

"Yes, kill Lincoln."

"You are going to be famous."

"Famous . . . yes."

"You are raising the gun to his head." Anderson put a revolver in Booth's hand.

"Gun . . ."

Anderson put his hand over Booth's so that the gun fired. This time the actor jumped and started to sit up. Anderson pushed him back. He got up and leaned close to the actor's ear.

"You are jumping off the stage."

"Jumping . . ."

"You break your leg."

"No . . ."

Anderson picked up a Spencer carbine and raised it above his head. He brought it down with all his might so that the steel butt plate struck Booth's shin right above the foot. The actor screamed as his leg broke. He was now sitting up, confused and in pain. Anderson uncorked the poisoned whiskey and put it to the actor's lips. Booth took only two swallows before he moved his head away and spat some out. Anderson knew Booth was a brandy drinker, but brandy doesn't cover the taste of arsenic as well as whiskey. Anderson reached inside Booth's coat and pulled out the actor's pocket diary. He had wanted to put a forged one in its place, but the detail had been overlooked in the complexity of the commission. The assassin opened the book, tore out a handful of pages, and returned it to Booth's coat. That should make everyone wonder, Anderson thought. He pulled Booth to his feet and the actor groaned pathetically as he put weight on his broken leg. Anderson pulled the actor's arm around his shoulder and got him to the horse.

"Wilkes, it's Alan. You must get away."

"Yes," Booth mumbled groggily as Anderson helped him to his horse, " . . . get away." Anderson led the horse and its rider to the main road, headed it south, and hit it on the rump. The horse headed down the road and Anderson wondered how long Booth would be able to stay on. He returned to the barn.

"As soon as we get the horses saddled," Anderson said, "I'm going to follow Booth to insure he's not captured alive. You are going to burn this barn and everything in it. Then you are going to the National, tell the clerk that Father Dunnehey is ill and you've come to get his things. Then I want you to wait for me."

"Yes, sir."

Anderson began removing his make-up to become someone else.

Washington City
11:00 P.M. April 14, 1865

Ingalls watched the crowd in the street gathering around the Peterson House.

"I'm going after him," he said.

"Are you sure it's a good idea?"

"We know what happened. Capturing Booth alive is our only chance of telling the whole story. If we don't capture him alive, then no one will ever know what happened here. I'm going home to get some things and go after him."

"God knows why, George, but I'm going with you."

"Good, I'll meet you at the Navy Yard Bridge in an hour."

They split up and went to pick up their gear.

The capital was in chaos. Lincoln lay dying in the Peterson House across from Ford's Theatre. Seward was injured but not in peril of his life. Payne had killed a State Department employee, beaten Seward's son badly, and slashed the Secretary's cheek, but was unable to stab Seward due to the heavy brace he wore. At the first screams Herold lost his nerve and rode away. Payne, alone, lost his way after the attack. Atzerodt got drunk, went up to Johnson's door, and turned away. News of the tragedy was beginning to spread. As official Washington came awake and began to move, one thought prevailed. The assassination was the result of a Confederate plot and had a broad base. Hysteria and total lack of coordination gripped the authorities. Although Booth had been identified by several witnesses, his name did not go out with the notice that Lincoln had been shot. Telegraph service was interrupted until 1:00 A.M. by a technical difficulty which caused a short circuit. Initially, this was seen as proof positive of a major Confederate conspiracy.

In the midst of the chaos, Ingalls and Everett were turned back at the Navy Yard Bridge. Sergeant Cobb's relief was a stickler for orders. No one was allowed to pass after 9:00 P.M., and that included National Detectives.

Upon hearing what her beloved Wilkes had done, Ella Turner put Booth's picture under her pillow, soaked a lace handkerchief in chloroform, and pressed her face into it. Her attempt at suicide miscarried and she was awakened the following morning.

The Peterson House
Tenth Street, Washington City
April 15, 1865, 7:22 A.M.

President Abraham Lincoln breathed his last, lying diagonally across a bed that was too short for his long frame. The people of the North were in shock. They felt angry and betrayed that the man who had led them through the nation's worst crisis had been felled after it was over. The millions of recently freed slaves were dumbfounded. What was to become of them now that their deliverer was gone? Most in the South were also appalled by the act. When shown the news during surrender negotiations, Joseph Johnston, commander of the last Confederate army, broke into a sweat. He could not imagine a greater calamity for the South.

Nevertheless, other Southerners shared the opinion of President Jefferson Davis as he fled with the remnants of his cabinet to nowhere. "If it is to be done, then it is best done well," Davis said. It was typical of the arrogant men who had brought the South to ruin. Now they gloated, little realizing that the only obstacle between a prostrate South and the Radical Republicans had been removed.

The first instinct was for vengeance and, for a short time, Secretary of War Edwin Stanton became the de facto dictator of the nation. His every order was carried out. In a fit of mindless vengeance, the Fords and their employees were arrested and the theater seized. Washington was placed under what amounted to martial law and the sale of all spirits was suspended. Gen. Christopher Augur, the commander of all the troops in Washington, was ordered to apprehend the murderers. Like all military men given police duties, Augur tried to treat it as a military campaign and sent out patrols willy-nilly. Major Richards of the Metropolitan Police sent out detectives who clashed, though not violently, with Augur's men. Lafayette Baker was in New York and the Army and the Metropolitan Police preferred that he stay there. Anderson had done his work well.

Washington City
April 16, 1865

Col. Lafayette Baker returned to Washington City on the morning train. What he found was chaos. No one had secured photographs or descriptions of the suspects, no handbills or wanted posters had been issued, and no organized searches had been conducted. Baker's first call was on his boss, the Secretary of War. Stanton was at his wit's end. After revealing to Baker the extent of the disorder, his only direction was, "Go to work, Baker, go to work!"

Baker's next call was on Major General Augur, who didn't want a civilian meddling in what he felt was the Army's business.

"There is no need for you, Baker," Augur said imperiously. "We can handle the pursuit."

The only problem was that there was no pursuit. Major Richards of the Metropolitan Police was equally curt, so Baker decided to do what he did best and that was to carry on alone with his detectives. His first act was to circulate a handbill that offered a reward of thirty thousand dollars for Booth as the assassin of the president, and his physical description. It also contained a description of Payne without his name, since it was not known at the time. Suddenly, Baker's detectives were everywhere. Their tactics were little different from those of vigilantes. They arrested suspects and tossed them into the Old Capitol Prison, not bothering to sort out the legal niceties until later. But, a method began to emerge. A systematic search of Booth's hotel room was conducted and links were gradually forged to Herold, Atzerodt, Payne, Surratt, Arnold, O'Laughlin, and Spangler. Eventually, Mary Surratt would also be gathered into the net along with everyone in her household, including Nora Fitzpatrick. By April 18, only Booth and Herold remained at large.

Despite all the activity, Ingalls and Everett found themselves on the periphery and went to see their chief. As they walked up to headquarters, Alexander Gardner and his assistant were removing their equipment from the premises.

"A bit soon for victory portraits, isn't it?" Ingalls commented nastily to his partner.

"We want to see Colonel Baker," Ingalls announced to Judge Lawrence as soon as they were inside.

"He's busy right now," the receptionist told them curtly. "You'll have to wait."

Everett wondered why they were suddenly denied free access to Baker and guessed it was because no powerful man wants to be reminded that he was wrong. He was prepared to sit it out, but Ingalls lost his temper, brushed by Lawrence, and stormed into Baker's office, uninvited. Everett followed, offering Lawrence a smile and a shrug. Baker was sitting at his desk with Everton Conger, one of Baker's oldest associates, and Luther Baker, the colonel's cousin, who was known by his middle name of Byron. There was a map in front of them. Ingalls didn't have to see it to know that it was a map of Prince Georges and Charles Counties, Maryland.

"What do you want?" Baker snapped when he saw it was Ingalls. "I'm busy."

"Too busy to take a report from two of your own detectives?" Ingalls shot back.

Byron Baker shot Ingalls a dirty look. Conger straightened up as if to say something, but Baker put his hand up to silence them. However high-handed Baker might be, he was always loyal to his men. He leaned back in his chair, removed his spectacles, and rubbed the bridge of his nose. "I deserved that," he said. "Sit down, please." He motioned to two chairs. He looked exhausted.

Ingalls and Everett sat down. "I should have called you earlier," he said. "Undoubtedly you both have much to tell. Would you like some coffee?"

Both detectives nodded. This was an olive branch and they accepted it. Baker called out to Lawrence to bring two cups of coffee, then leaned forward in his chair with his elbows on the desk. "Tell me what happened," he said.

Ingalls began relating their experiences and Everett filled in as they went along. The only interruption was Lawrence with the coffee. Baker was not humoring them. He listened carefully to every word. When they were through he sighed.

"You're still convinced this Anderson is real?"

Ingalls was silent for a moment. He decided to play his last card. "Colonel Baker, it is unimportant whether either of us believes in Anderson or the apparition. We are after the same thing. What I recommend in the strongest terms is that we take Booth alive. That is the only way that either of us can ever be sure." He looked over at Everett who nodded and smiled.

Baker looked at Conger. "I agree with Ingalls," he said. "We need Booth alive. After that we can find out if he was paid by Jeff

Davis or the man in the moon. See that it's done," he ordered Conger.

"We'd like to go," Ingalls announced.

Baker looked at Conger who said, "We can always use a couple more good men."

Byron Baker nodded in agreement.

"It's settled then," Baker declared. "You'll leave tomorrow morning. Anything else?"

"I'd like to see you on a personal matter, if I may, sir," Ingalls said deferentially.

Baker looked puzzled. "All right."

Everett and Conger stepped outside.

"There's a woman, I've been seeing," he began. "Her name is Honora Fitzpatrick. She lives in Mrs. Surratt's boarding house. She isn't a party to any conspiracy. I'm sure of that. If I may, I'd like to get a pass to see her, and I'd like to get her released."

Baker actually smiled. "George, I didn't think you had it in you. Of course. Tell Judge to make out a pass and I'll sign it. I promise I'll see about the release."

"Thank you, sir."

The Old Capitol Prison

The Old Capitol Prison was originally built to house Congress after the British burned the Capitol and President's Mansion during the War of 1812. It was originally a three-story brick building to which had been added walls and internal wooden buildings. It was painted white on the ground floor and left dirty gray brick on the top story. From the temporary home of a budding democracy which sheltered the likes of Webster and Calhoun, it had passed from offices and dwellings to a derelict of a building housing a poor cobbler and his family. The outbreak of the war gave it new life. At first the dilapidated building with its broken windows was used to house runaway slaves. Whose idea it was to turn it into a prison no one knows, but Lafayette Baker saw its potential and, by late 1862, had turned it into his Bastille. An annex known as Carroll Prison was used for female prisoners.

It had a definite Baker style. Each "room" was a large bay with three tiered bunks. The rooms were numbered and each housed a particular type of criminal. Room 16 was reserved for

Copperheads and spies; Room 17 for Union officers suspected of treason or corruption. Rooms 14, 15, and 18 were for couriers, blockade runners, saboteurs, and partisans. In the prison compound there was a hospital and drugstore. Certain prisoners were allowed to buy their own food and luxury items from peddlers who charged exorbitant prices. A mess hall provided meals to those who were destitute. William Wood, the superintendent of the prison, saw to it that the food was decent and palatable. By the standards of the day it treated its prisoners much better than many other prisons, North and South. Until Rose Greenhow was imprisoned in the Old Capitol, most prisoners were allowed to see friends and relatives. When Baker took over, visitors were limited. Even those who waved to friends in prison from the street were sometimes pulled in and questioned. The suspects in the Lincoln assassination were not allowed visitors unless they had a special pass.

Ingalls shuddered as the guard checked his pass and allowed him through the large iron door which was the entrance. He walked into a spacious ante room filled with soldiers who sat at tables and benches. Along the wall in racks were rifles with their bayonets fixed. An officer checked Ingalls' pass and looked at him with no little awe. This large man in the brown tweed suit must be someone important, indeed, to get a pass to see a prisoner.

"Follow me, Mr. Ingalls," the officer said as he led the detective to a huge room with several heavy wooden tables and benches in its center. The solid brick walls were whitewashed.

"Have a seat, sir," the officer said. "I'll have the prisoner brought here."

Ingalls waited an eternity until they brought Nora to him. He was shocked at the way she looked. Her hair was unkempt and her face was drawn. Her dark brown dress was rumpled and dirty. A guard stood at the door in full view. She was still wearing the bracelet. The expression on her face when she saw him made it all worth it.

"George," she cried, as she rushed into his arms, sobbing "Oh, dearest, I thought I'd never see you again."

Ingalls held her closely, loving the way she felt in his arms.

"Are you all right?" he finally asked, touching her tear-streaked face. He kissed her lips even though the guard was looking.

"As well as to be expected. They arrested all of us, even little Olivia."

"I'm trying to get you out of here as soon as possible."

Nora stepped back and looked at him. "How?" Suddenly the expression on her face changed to disbelief and then suspicion. A few days in prison had made her very wary. "How did you get to see me? We were told that no one would be allowed to see us."

"I managed to get a pass," he said, showing it to her.

"This is signed by that devil Baker," she said. "How did you manage to . . . George you're not just a clerk, are you?" It was an accusation.

"No, dearest, I'm not," he said holding both her hands. "I didn't tell you what I do because I was afraid you wouldn't approve. I wanted to wait until the war was over, then this happened."

"What do you do, George?" she asked, drawing away from him, but not removing her hands from his.

"Please try to understand, Nora . . ."

"Tell me!" she demanded shrilly.

"I'm a National Detective."

"One of Baker's men?"

He nodded. She jerked her hands from his.

"You vile beast," she said. The eyes in which he had always sought warmth were cold with hatred.

"What?"

"You used me!"

"No!"

"You courted me to spy on Mrs. Surratt, you heartless brute!"

"No, he said. "It's not true."

She tore the bracelet from her wrist and threw it at him. It hit him in the chest and he caught it in two hands. "And I thought you loved me!" she screamed and slapped him twice. Then she began to cry harder.

"Nora, please, listen to me," he said, reaching for her.

"Get away from me!" Her voice was shrill and hysterical. She pulled away and ran over to the guard. "Take me back. I'd rather be here than with him!"

The guard and Nora disappeared and Ingalls left the prison in a daze. Had it really happened or was it a bad dream? He walked out into the street and looked back at the Old Capitol. He thought he had everything, and now it was gone. A tear cascaded down his cheek.

Charles County, Maryland
April 15, 1865, to April 24, 1865

John Wilkes Booth's head did not begin to clear until he was well away from Uniontown, but he was still confused. He knew he was on the route he was going to use when he captured Lincoln. Instead, he had killed the president. His broken leg ached. How had he broken it? Jumping from the president's box? His memory of killing Lincoln was dreamlike and lacking in details, yet here he was. On top of everything he had an upset stomach. He should not have drunk so much today—or was that yesterday? On his way up Good Hope Hill, Booth encountered Polk Gardiner, a businessman, on his way to Washington and asked the direction to Marlboro to throw off any patrols that might question Gardiner. If he couldn't clearly remember what happened, it was best to be safe. The businessman told him to stay on the straight road. Herold was just a short distance behind.

When Booth realized he was being followed, he stopped in a grove of trees and came out as the rider passed. He called for him to halt, and Herold, recognizing his idol's voice, turned around. They rode on together, but with Booth's leg broken, they couldn't travel the eighteen miles to Port Tobacco in one night. They traded stories about the events of the evening. Herold thought that Payne had killed Seward. He didn't tell Booth he had abandoned his co-conspirator. Booth, the pain in his leg getting worse, didn't ask. A little after midnight they stopped at the tavern in Surrattsville. Lloyd, the tavern keeper, wasn't glad to see them. When Herold told Lloyd what they had done, he was anxious to get rid of them. Booth didn't dismount. Herold took one of the carbines and Booth took the field glasses but didn't want to carry the other carbine. They both drank some whiskey and it made Booth feel queasy again. When Booth asked Lloyd if there were a doctor in the area, Lloyd said the only doctor around didn't practice, so they rode on shadowed by Anderson.

At 4:30 A.M., they stopped at Dr. Mudd's. The doctor set Booth's leg and let him stay to rest and clean up. Later in the morning, Herold tried to obtain a carriage for his injured leader, but there were none to be had unless he bought one, and neither he nor the actor could do so because Anderson had left them with almost no money. A friend of Mudd's made Booth a crutch and the actor shaved his mustache. They left the doctor's house in the afternoon.

At midnight they reached the home of Samuel Cox near Pope's Creek. Cox, a Confederate sympathizer, put them under the protection of his stepbrother Thomas Jones who had a house across from Mathias Point. From that evening until April 22, 1865, Booth and Herold hid in the woods near Jones' house. Jones kept them supplied with food, water, and newspapers. Booth found that the reward for him was up to $175,000. Ordinarily, he would have been elated and flattered but he was feeling very ill. On the twenty-second they shot the horses and attempted to get across the Potomac in a small boat, but failed. The following morning they tried again and succeeded.

On April 23, 1865, the two fugitives were taken in by Mrs. Quesenberry who lived at Machadoc Creek and they only stayed the night. By now even die-hard Confederates were beginning to have second thoughts about Booth and Herold. Word of Baker's relentless pursuit and imprisonment of anyone to do with the plot had some bearing on it, but many Southerners were beginning to realize that Booth had brought them an even greater calamity than losing the war. The next stopping place was Dr. Richard Stewart's home in Cleydale, Virginia. Stewart, a staunch Confederate, was not happy to see the two men, and reluctantly let them stay in the barn. Booth was indignant. In the morning Stewart hustled them into a wagon driven by a colored man named Lucas and sent them to the Port Conway ferry. Once they were at the ferry, Lucas refused to take them any farther. His employer wanted his wagon back.

The Port Conway Ferry
Port Conway, Virginia
April 24, 1865

At the ferry, Booth and Herold encountered three Confederate officers, Ruggles, Bainbridge, and Jett. Still in uniform, they were on their way home. Herold spoke to the three, asking for assistance, but the actor having little regard for his companion's abilities, stepped down from the wagon and hobbled over to Herold and the three men.

"I am John Wilkes Booth, the slayer of Abraham Lincoln," he announced, drawing a revolver. "And I am worth $175,000 to the man who captures me."

Major Ruggles looked at him defiantly. "We do not approve of who you are or what you did, sir, but since we promised Mr. Herold, here, that we would help you across the river, we will. We are not the kind of men who would take blood money, so put up your gun."

"I know Caroline County on the other side of the river," Captain Jett said. "I will find you a place to stay."

"God bless you, sir," Booth said, putting away the gun.

When the ferry arrived, Booth was helped on to Ruggles' horse and they walked onto the scow. Booth was now regaling them with the epic of his adventure. The three Confederates listened politely, wishing they were rid of their new companion. Rollins, the colored boatman, listened closely and said nothing.

Anderson watched the ferry leave the shore. The timing could not have been worse. This was the last ferry of the day and he could have made it, but he could not risk the chance of being recognized by Booth, however small it might be. He was disappointed that the arsenic had not killed the actor, although when he looked at him through his field glasses, Booth looked pale and ill. Anderson, himself, was no prize. After a week of sleeping on the ground and not washing, he looked and smelled like a vagrant, which was an excellent cover, since the people he encountered on the road avoided him. It was time to end Booth's life. Anderson wanted to catch the two men alone, but now they always had companions. Even having to kill a Negro servant would arouse too much suspicion. He had missed his chance in the woods at Pope's Creek, but at that time it looked as if the poison were doing its work. What concerned Anderson was that if he found them this easy to follow, then Baker's men would surely pick up the trail soon. As soon as it was dark, he would have to find a boat and swim his horse across.

The Sixth Street Wharf
Washington City

At approximately 3:00 P.M. Ingalls and Everett stepped aboard the steam tug *John S. Ide*, with the others who were going in search of Booth. The party consisted of thirty-one men. There were four detectives and twenty-five cavalry, commanded by a lieutenant and a sergeant. The detectives were Conger, who was in command since he ranked as a colonel, and Lt. Byron Baker, who was second in command. Ingalls and Everett had no place in the command structure because they held no military rank. The cavalry detachment was commanded by First Lt. E. P. Doherty, a tall, arrogant young man with muttonchop whiskers and a moustache. With his gauntlets and black hat with gold cords he looked every inch the cavalry officer. He had been told by General Auger personally that he, and no one else, was to be in command and he had believed it until he encountered Conger. Doherty's second in command was a short, thin sergeant named Boston Corbett. The sergeant had a long nose, big ears, and a wispy blond imperial beard. Ingalls made the mistake of speaking to the sergeant and was immediately subjected to the story of Corbett's conversion to Methodism, much to the amusement of Corbett's men who had heard the story many times before. The sergeant's given name was Thomas but changed his name to Boston because that was where he was when he was "reborn" at a revival. Ingalls could not get away from the man fast enough, after he told Ingalls that when he had been aroused by prostitutes after preaching a sermon he had gone home and castrated himself. He boasted that he prayed for the soul of every Confederate he had killed and had once been saved from execution by Lincoln himself. Ingalls, normally polite, turned his back and walked away while Corbett was still talking. Everett was standing a short way down the rail trying not to laugh.

"Did you hear what he said, Clarence?"

"What, that he gelded himself because a couple of whores excited him?"

"Yes. He offered to show me proof."

"According to his men, it's true."

"How did we ever win the war with lunatics like that?"

"I guess in war it probably helps to be a little crazy. Seeing one man dead after a street fight is bad enough. I can't imagine what it would be like to see thousands. When do we get to Belle Plain?"

"It's supposed to take about seven or eight hours depending on the tides."

"I forgot to ask. Did you get to see Nora?"

"Oh, yes," he said, laughing bitterly.

Everett was suddenly concerned. "What happened?"

Ingalls told him, his voice controlled and superficially emotionless.

"I'm sorry, George," Everett said putting his hand on Ingalls' shoulder. "I really am. Maybe it was just the tension of being in that place. After it's all done, you could . . ."

"Thanks, Clarence, I appreciate that, but if you had seen the look in her eyes . . ."

"Sure, I know," his partner said, but Everett didn't know, because he had never loved a woman that much. He wondered what it must be like and, in a way, envied Ingalls for it. For a long time they stood there at the rail staring at the black water, Everett reaching up to comfort his tall friend. The soldiers, like all soldiers, were now asleep, even Sergeant Corbett. The only sounds were the rush of the water and the throb of the engines.

Port Conway, Virginia
April 25, 1865

They landed at Belle Plain just before 10:00 P.M. but, there was no time for rest. They mounted and began searching down the river toward Port Conway. They knocked at plantation doors looking for a lame man. No one had seen him. They kept on. At dawn, they stopped for food and rest. A few days before, they would have commandeered the food. Today they paid for it in greenbacks. A few days before, the countryside would have been alive with Rebel agents and partisans. Tonight, the roads and woods and small towns were quiet. Around 5:15 P.M. they stopped a mile from Port Conway to rest and feed the horses. Lieutenant Doherty rode with his bugler to Port Conway. Conger was exhausted. He was so pained from recently healed wounds that he had to be helped off his horse. Everett, who had enough riding for the day, stayed with him. Ingalls and Byron Baker took Joe Zigsen, one of the soldiers, with them to act as messenger and they rode along the river until they came to the colored ferryman's house. Rollins and his wife were sitting on the front porch enjoying the evening air after supper.

"Are you the ferryman?" Baker asked.

"I am, sir, but the ferry is closed until morning."

Baker and Ingalls dismounted. Ingalls, not used to riding for such long periods, found he needed a moment to find his land legs.

"Did a lame man, and perhaps a companion, use your ferry, recently?"

"As a matter of fact, they did," Rollins said. "I believe it was the last ferry yesterday. He was with three Rebel officers who were not pleased with his society, it appeared to me."

Byron Baker pulled a number of photographs from his saddlebag. They were pictures of Jefferson Davis, Judah P. Benjamin, and other members of the official Confederate cabinet believed to be part of the plot, as well as Booth and Herold. Rollins looked at the photographs and stopped at the one of Booth.

"That's the lame man," he said. "Except he shaved his moustache and it ain't growed back yet. He also don't look this good. Very pale. Even for a white man," the ferryman said with a smile.

Ingalls laughed a little and so did Baker. They were getting close.

"This is his friend," Rollins said, holding up the picture of Herold.

"He's the one with the carbine."

"Who were these Rebels?" Ingalls asked.

"The only one I really know is Cap'n Jett. He has a lady in Bowling Green about fifteen miles from here. Her name is Goldman and her father owns a hotel."

"You must take us to Bowling Green, then," Baker said.

Rollins leaned forward in his chair and whispered conspiratorially, "you know there ain't too many Yankee lovers about and I have to live here, but if you was to arrest me, I wouldn't have no choice, would I?"

"Mr. Rollins," his wife said worriedly, "I don't like this."

"Hush, woman," the ferryman said, patting his wife's hand. "Nothin' to fret about."

"I promise nothing will happen to your husband," Baker said. "This way when he goes with us you won't have to tell your neighbors a lie." Baker pulled his huge pistol from his holster and pointed it above Rollins' head. "Mr. Rollins," he said solemnly. "I arrest you on suspicion of aiding the assassin John Wilkes Booth. Now can you ferry us across tonight?"

"Best get started," he said. "Ferry's on the other side."

Baker's face split into a wide grin and he nearly jumped for joy.

"Zigsen," he called to the cavalryman. "Go get the lieutenant and tell him to come here immediately."

Zigsen spurred his horse back the way they came. In a few minutes Doherty arrived with the entire command.

It took three trips to ferry everyone across the Rappahannock. On the other side, the detective saw two men watching the operation from a hill. He waved to them to come to him, but they rode away. The men were Herold and Ruggles. The cavalry had gone about a mile and a half when one of the men riding ahead as lookout came back to Conger and Doherty with a man on horseback. He was an average-size man with a mustache and a scraggly beard who was dirty and disheveled.

"I found this man on the road ahead," the scout said eagerly. "I think he fits the description of one of the men."

"Don't count the reward just yet," Conger told him. He stopped his horse as the man came closer. The detective struck a match and raised it. The man looked like a beggar. It definitely wasn't Booth or Herold. "What's your name?" Conger asked.

"Willard Sluss," the man said as Lieutenant Doherty and Sergeant Corbett rode up.

"What are you doing here?"

"I'm just trying to get back home, sir."

"Where's that?"

"Warwick Court House," he said.

"Got any papers?"

The man reached into his coat and pulled out two letters addressed to Willard Sluss at an address in Marlboro. They were several weeks old.

"What are you doing this far from home?" Conger asked.

"Three months ago, a man from Marlboro said he had work for me tending horses, because he bought them and sold them to the government. I went and it paid fifteen dollars a month, but now that the war's over he don't need me."

"Did you see any riders go this way? One of them lame?"

"No sir, just y'all."

"Okay," Conger said. "You're not under arrest, but you must ride with us."

"Yes, sir. Excuse me for askin', Cap'n, but who are you after?"

"The men who assassinated President Lincoln, sir."

"That a fact? My Lord. I read about that in the Bryantown newspaper. Terrible."

"Ride at the rear of the column."

"Uh, Cap'n . . ."

"Yes?"

"Could you spare a body a bite to eat?"

"Ask one of the men."

"I'd be happy to share what I have with a man in need," Corbett offered.

"All right," Conger said. "Let's keep it moving."

No one paid attention to Sluss. It was dark and they were all tired. Sluss fell into line and rode along with Corbett who produced some hardtack and jerky.

"Thank you, friend," Sluss said.

"Do not thank me," Corbett said. "Thank the Lord."

"Amen," Sluss said. "But 'God loveth a cheerful giver.'"

"That pleases me, sir," Corbett said. "Amen."

They spoke for a while and Corbett told Sluss of his conversion. Sluss was silent for a moment then continued the conversation.

"That reminds me," Sluss said. "Do you think you're going to catch this Booth fella?"

"So far the Lord has guided us and on the morrow we will apprehend him."

"What happens then?"

"He shall be removed to Washington to stand trail for his crimes."

"That's asking for trouble if you ask me."

"Why?"

"Is it not written that 'he that committeth sin is of the devil,' and by this they are 'children of the devil'?"

"Yes," Corbett agreed. "That is true."

"That man you're after is really an antichrist, ain't he?"

"I . . ." Corbett looked at Sluss in the dark. "You are right," he said. "It was really he who cut down our noble president."

"'For this purpose the Son of God was manifested, that he might destroy the works of the devil,'" Sluss quoted. "It appears to me if he's not killed, he'll get stronger and spread sin the length and breadth of this land. That is, if he hasn't done it already."

Sgt. Boston Corbett thought for a moment and turned to Sluss. "Your words are indeed food for thought, sir. I must consider them and pray."

"God bless you, brother," Sluss said as he began eating and dropped behind Corbett. Anderson chewed on the stringy jerky and smiled. Perhaps he was on to something. Maybe the army would finish the business for him. He thought of another quotation, "The devil oft quotes scripture to serve his own purpose," and was genuinely amused.

They did not find Booth in Bowling Green but they did find Jett. He denied knowing Booth until Conger put a gun to his head. Jett agreed to lead them to Booth if they wouldn't charge him with complicity in Booth's crime. Conger consented.

CHAPTER 12

Garrett's Farm
Caroline County, Virginia
April 26, 1865

WILLIAM GARRETT WAS HAVING a restless night because his visitors made him uneasy. They had been brought to Garrett's place on Monday by Willie Jett, who was a friend of the family, but the farmer was becoming suspicious. One of them, a Mr. Boyd, who had a broken leg, said he was trying to return to his family in Petersburg. The other guest was a young man named Harris. Tonight they were both sleeping in the barn so as not to disturb the family when they left at an early hour. Last night only Boyd had slept in the house while Harris stayed at Mrs. Clark's Boarding House in Bowling Green. Along with the two strangers came word of Lincoln's assassination. Garrett's suspicions began when Boyd asked to see a map which the farmer had tacked on the wall. When Garrett took it down, Boyd traced a line not to Petersburg, but to Norfolk, then Charleston, then Galveston. The farmer asked politely where he wanted to go, Boyd answered, seriously, "Mexico." The two men asked to rent a horse from Garrett, but he refused, because he felt that once they left, he'd never see the animal again. By asking around, Boyd and Harris managed to strike a bargain with Jim, the colored farmer down the road. Jim agreed to pick them up shortly before dawn and take them to the nearest railroad station. It would be dawn shortly and Garrett would be relieved to see them go. Around 4:00 A.M. fatigue took its toll and Garrett began to doze off.

Conger followed Jett to the road near the farm. Doherty's troops dismounted and surrounded the house and barn. Ingalls and Everett stayed with Conger. When everyone was in position Conger struck a match and looked at his watch. It was almost 4:00 A.M. He nodded at Byron Baker and the detective drew his pistol. With Ingalls and a few men at his back, he rushed through the gate and in true Baker style he pounded on the door to the house.

Garrett, thinking the knock came from one of his guests, opened the window near the door and asked, "What's the matter?"

Baker grabbed him by the arm and put a gun to his face. "Unfasten the door and strike a light," the detective ordered.

Garrett, confused and frightened, did as he was told as Conger came up.

"Where are the two men who stopped here at your house?" Conger asked.

"They have gone," claimed the terrified farmer.

"Gone where?" The detective's tone was menacing.

"Gone to the woods," Garrett told him, but the farmer's voice had so little conviction that Conger knew he was lying.

"Well, sir, whereabouts in the woods have they gone?"

Garrett shaking with fear and close to tears said, "I was forced to take them in against my will . . ."

"I don't want a long story," Conger said exasperated. "All I want to know is where these men have gone."

Garrett said nothing.

"Get a rope," Conger said to one of the soldiers.

"Don't hurt the old man," someone said. It was Garrett's oldest son, Jack, a young man in his early twenties, recently returned home from the Confederate Army. He had come downstairs from his bedroom to see what the ruckus was about. "He is scared. I will tell you where they are."

"That's what I wanted to know. Where are they?"

"In the barn. They wanted us to take them to Louisa Courthouse, but we couldn't take them, so they arranged to go with Old

Jim who has the next farm over. They asked to stay in the barn. We told them they could, but we were afraid they'd steal our horses so we locked the barn. They can't get away."

Baker grabbed the hand of sixteen-year-old Tom Garrett, who had also come downstairs, and a candle and told him to take him to the barn.

"My brother is in the corn crib with the key," Tom Garrett said. "I'll go get it."

"No you don't," Baker said. "I'll go with you."

It didn't matter. Some soldiers had already found eleven-year-old William in the corn crib and were bringing him and the key.

Conger, Baker, still with Tom in hand, Ingalls and Everett, and the soldiers they had with them, walked down to the barn. Their conversation had awakened someone in the barn and they could hear him moving around. Did they finally have Booth cornered?

Baker set candles in a semi-circle in front of the barn door and they all drew their pistols. Baker went up to the door and unlocked it. He turned to Tom.

"Go in there and tell them to come out and surrender."

"They're armed. They'll kill me," the boy protested.

Ingalls thought sending the boy into the barn was cruel and volunteered to go himself. "Let me go, Byron," he said stepping forward. "It's too dangerous for the boy."

"Back away, George," Baker said. "We're doing this my way."

Everything around the barn was silent as Baker pushed the boy through the open door.

"Damn you, sir," Booth hollered as Tom stepped into the light of the candles. "You have betrayed me. Get out or I will shoot you."

"Give this man your arms and surrender," Baker called, holding a candle above his head. "If you don't, we'll burn the barn."

Tom Garrett stuck his head out the door. "Mister, let me out. I'll do anything you want but I'm risking my life in here. And put down the candle or he'll shoot you by the light."

Baker put down the candle but he didn't move for fear that Booth and Herold might break for it. He motioned to Tom to come out and the boy ran for the safety of the house as Baker slammed the door shut.

"Throw down your arms and surrender," Baker called again.

"There is a man in here who wants to surrender," Booth called, then obviously to Herold, "Leave me, will you? Get out! I don't want you to stay."

A moment later Herold was at the door begging to be let out.

"Bring out your arms and you can come," Baker demanded.

"I have none," Herold whimpered.

"You have a pistol and a carbine," Baker insisted.

"He has no arms," Booth called. "They are mine and I am going to keep them."

"Oh, God," Herold begged. "Please let me come out, please."

Baker opened the door a little. "Put out your hands," he said.

Herold put his arms out of the door, Baker seized them and pulled him out. Two soldiers took him away and tied him to a tree.

"You had better come out, too," Baker told Booth.

"Tell me who you are and what you want of me," Booth said. "It may be that I am being taken by friends."

"It makes no difference who we are," Baker told him. "We know you and we want you. The place is surrounded. You cannot escape. We do not wish to kill you."

Booth melodramatically asked Baker to withdraw his men and give him a fighting chance. Baker reminded the actor they were not there to fight, but to take him. Booth then asked time to consider, saying he already had had half a dozen chances to kill Baker but he didn't want to.

"Withdraw your men and I'll come out," Booth said. "Give me this chance for my life. I will not be taken alive." The words sounded more like part of a script than they did from real life.

"Your time is up," Baker stated emphatically. "Come out or we'll fire the barn."

"Well, my brave boys," Booth said dramatically, "prepare a stretcher for me. One more stain on your glorious banner."

Conger came around the barn with a handful of dried corn blades. He shoved them into a crack in the barn wall, struck a match, and lit them. In a few short seconds, the interior of the barn started to burn. Baker opened the door. He could see the silhouette of the actor turning this way and that trying to make up his mind. Baker didn't fire. Everyone was so intent on the front of the barn that no one saw the man they knew as Sluss move forward to where Sergeant Corbett was crouched behind a rail fence.

"Now is your chance to do the Lord's work," Anderson whispered to him. "Slay the antichrist."

Corbett never even looked at Anderson. "Yes," the sergeant said in a frenzied whisper. A look of ecstasy spread over his face as he rose and moved toward the rear of the burning barn. He found a wide crack in the wall and discovered he could see Booth clearly against the fire even with the barrel of the pistol in the crack. He took careful aim.

Baker watched Booth as the actor threw away his carbine and crutch. He raised his revolver and began hobbling to the door when a pistol shot rang out. The actor pitched forward on his face and Baker ran in to drag him out of the burning barn.

"Who fired that shot?" Conger demanded.

"I did," Corbett said, coming from behind the barn. "It was either you or Booth. I saved your life," he said, obviously confusing Conger with Baker.

"You stupid son of a bitch!" Conger roared. His face was purple with rage. "You shot Booth without orders. I ought to string you up."

Corbett stood to attention and saluted. "Colonel, God Almighty directed me to shoot Booth."

"He must have," Conger snapped, "for you to make that shot."

Booth was hit in the back of the neck, and it was a mortal wound. The four detectives carried him to an apple tree, while the soldiers tried to help the Garretts save what they could. The Garretts managed to save their horses, but not the barn.

They tried to give Booth some water and he muttered, "Tell mother, tell mother . . ." A little later they moved him to a mattress laid on the ground in front of the house. He passed out but they revived him with a brandy-soaked cloth. He begged them to kill him.

"No, Booth, we don't want to kill you. You were shot against orders." Booth then lapsed into unconsciousness. Conger thought he was dead so he took all of Booth's personal effects and weapons to carry the breathtaking news to a waiting world. As he prepared to mount his horse, the man he knew as Sluss approached him.

"You still need me, Cap'n?" he asked.

"No," Conger replied absentmindedly. "We never did. Go home."

"Thankee, sir."

Anderson looked at the knot of people around the man on the mattress and mounted his horse. All in all, things had not worked out too badly. Now he needed to get back to Washington City to prepare a homecoming for Ingalls and Everett.

However, Booth was still alive. Twenty minutes later, his eyes fluttered open. Ingalls and Everett were the first to notice.

"Booth," Ingalls asked directly. "Did you really kill Lincoln?"

"Dream . . . Alan," he said softly, looking at Ingalls. A brief smile crossed his lips.

One of the soldiers, seeing Ingalls talking to Booth, shouted, "He's still alive," and everyone rushed over. Baker pushed Ingalls aside and bent over him.

"My hands," Booth said and Baker picked up Booth's hand so he could see it.

"Useless, useless," the actor sighed. "Is there blood in my mouth?" he asked licking his lips.

"No," Baker said gently. "There's no blood."

"Tell mother I died for my country," he said deliriously. "I did what I thought best."

A short time later his eyes and mouth closed and he expelled a last breath. Baker was still holding his hand.

"Let's go," Ingalls said to Everett.

"Where?"

"Back to Washington," Ingalls said. "By train."

"What about Baker and the cavalry?"

"They didn't need us when we started and they don't need us now. I have to see Baker. Did you hear what Booth said?"

"Yes, he said 'dream . . . Alan.' The man was dying. It could mean anything. George, I know you think it means it was a dream and Alan Demming who was Anderson put it there, but nobody is going to believe it."

"I hope you're wrong. Because, if you're not then we're bigger dupes than Booth was."

Washington City
April 28, 1865

Everett, as usual, was right. He and Ingalls had gone to Baker's headquarters to see him and were not surprised to find he had been made a brigadier general. The general was smiling and expansive and he politely told them that now that Booth was dead all that remained was to round up the Confederate officials who had planned Lincoln's assassination and financed Booth, and the case would be closed. He recognized their hard work and told them to take two weeks off with pay for a well-deserved rest. They were then whisked out of his office with a pat on the back.

Even in death John Wilkes Booth exerted some influence over events. His body was secretly buried in an unmarked grave in the Old Arsenal Penitentiary on Greenleaf Point. Officially sanctioned rumors stated his body was weighted down and dumped in the Potomac. All this was done to prevent his remains from becoming a rallying point for a Confederate plot that didn't exist. Baker's plan backfired and rumors persisted that Booth was still alive, even after his remains were returned to his family in 1867. One woman would even go so far as to claim she was Booth's granddaughter.

Ingalls and Everett walked out into the sunlight.

"Shall we get a cab, George?"

"Let's walk."

"What are you thinking now?"

"For one thing, our 'vacation' is a less than clever way to maneuver us out of sharing in the reward."

"Baker wouldn't do that," Everett said but he didn't sound convinced of it himself.

"If you'll notice, we weren't put on any official orders, therefore we weren't there."

Everett looked at him. "Have you always been this cynical or has this business with Nora got you down?"

"Let's just say, the events of the past few weeks have torn away some of my naivete." Ingalls had a smile on his face.

Everett looked at his partner and didn't like what he saw. Ingalls' smile was cold and grim. "Well, things would be different if we found Anderson. Then the real story would come out and we'd be rich men."

"We won't have to find him, Clarence," Ingalls said flatly.

"What do you mean?"

"He is going to find us. We know he exists and he can't afford that. I suspect he'll try to lead us into some sort of trap."

"You sure?"

"Positive."

"When?" Everett asked.

"Next day or two," Ingalls told him.

"And we're standing out in the open?" Everett said, looking around.

"No danger. It's too public."

Suddenly Everett shivered involuntarily.

"Are you all right, Clarence?"

"I believe the expression is 'someone just walked over my grave,'" he said.

"You don't have to go," Ingalls said. He meant it.

"Oh sure, you go get yourself killed and I have to face Anderson alone. No thanks."

Swampoodle

Anderson finished the note, and looked at it.

> Washington City
> April 28, 1865
>
> Dear Mr. Ingalls,
>
> I have a proposal to discuss that would be of mutual benefit. If you are agreeable, come to the Keyser Warehouse on K Street. Meet me there at 7:00 P.M. o'clock on the evening of April 30. Please come alone and unarmed. I will do the same.
>
> Respectfully yours,
> ANDERSON

Anderson blotted it and put it in an envelope. He handed it to Fitch. "Send this to Ingalls' rooms by messenger," he said. "Don't go yourself. I have another errand for you."

"Do you think he'll fall for it?" Fitch asked.

Anderson actually laughed. "Of course he won't fall for it, Joseph. He will come with his partner and they will be armed to the teeth."

"Then why the note?"

"In case you haven't noticed, Mr. Ingalls and his colored friend are very astute. Not only that, they are honest, tireless, and considering that General Baker, Major Richards, and General Augur don't believe them, most relentless. They are the only ones in this entire city who figured out what was going on, and that makes them very dangerous. I cannot afford to have men like that running around.

"Once you give this to the messenger, I want you to hire two men who are handy with guns and have no compunction about killing. The pay is two hundred dollars per man."

"I could get you an army for that," Fitch said.

"Ingalls and Everett wouldn't come for an army," Anderson said. "We are using these two men as bait."

"Bait?"

"I'll explain it later. We have much to do."

When Ingalls returned home that evening, he found the note sipped under his door. He picked it up and read it. In the morning he would tell Everett. They had much to do.

Washington City
April 29, 1865

Anderson was up at 3:00 A.M. For the first time in years, he could not sleep so he went over to the unused warehouse, which he rented from its owner. He knew Ingalls and Everett would be there to reconnoiter the building in daylight and he had to plan accordingly. The kinds of traps most men would consider elegant were of no use. For the first time in his career, Anderson was facing adversaries that were alert to his presence and aware of his capabilities. He would have to set traps within traps and they would have to be simple and invisible, because he felt that in the search for complex traps they would overlook the simple.

Anderson lit a lamp and walked through the building. It was a structure more than a hundred yards long and perhaps fifty yards wide. The interior was barren except for a second story containing offices that extended out to about one-quarter the length of the building from the back. The tin-covered roof was supported by wooden posts and beams. Leading to the second story on each side of the warehouse was an open staircase with a crude railing. The roof was approximately two and a half stories tall. The floor was dirt. Barred windows lined the first story the length of the building on either side. Along the base of the wall every fifty feet or so were two-foot-square wrought-iron grates used for drainage. On each end were large swinging doors wide enough to pass two wagons side by side. On both ends of the building there was a small access door in one of the large doors. The two detectives would have to come in either end of the building. He would make it easy for them to come in the front. That's where he would begin springing the trap.

When Ingalls and Everett visited the warehouse later that day, it was open and empty, just as it had been when Anderson was there.

"Son of a bitch," Ingalls cursed as they walked the building inside and out.

"What is it?" Everett asked, drawing his pistol.

"He wanted us to see this place, because it's not going to be like this tomorrow night. He's trying to lull us into a false sense of security, making us think we know this place, but when we get inside, we won't know it at all. If that's the way he wants to play then we have a few tricks, too."

"Would you mind telling me what they are?"

"Certainly, if you'll buy lunch," Ingalls said with a smile.

Everett grinned. "You must be feeling better," he said. "You haven't conned me into buying lunch in ages."

They went to Hasselmyer's and both ordered the beefsteak with cooked vegetables. Everett had beer and Ingalls had cider. Everett was glad to see that his partner was back in appetite. Ingalls was getting over Nora and there was nothing like a suicidal encounter with an assassin to help, Everett thought cynically. (What was he saying?)

"As I see it," Ingalls said, gesticulating with a piece of beef impaled on a fork, "when we get there, there will be only one way to get in. Once we get in, we will find the place full of crates and barrels and Anderson will have a couple of toughs in there to try to kill us while we're trying to find our way around."

"How many toughs?"

"Two, I think, three at most. He knows we're not stupid and won't stay around if the odds are too great."

"Nice man. What if we get by the toughs?"

"Then he'll have something very devious, you can bet."

"Is there anything we need?"

"Yes, we'll need a two-horse freight wagon, two one-pound cans of blasting powder, about fifty feet of fuse, two hundred feet of rope, two grappling hooks, and a couple of lanterns. That should do it. Wear good boots and carry two good breech-loading pistols and a knife."

"Sounds like we're in for a thoroughly enjoyable evening," Everett said.

"Let's start getting our gear together."

Swampoodle
April 29, 1865

Anderson, who had adopted the name Miller for this evening, took one last look at the warehouse now full of goods. Then he went over to the two men Fitch had hired. They looked the part. Marty Hazer was a large burly man with a full reddish-brown beard that was stained with tobacco juice. He wore a dirty checked shirt along with army trousers and shoes. Anderson wondered if he were a deserter or had stolen them. Hazer carried two .44 Colts and a large knife. Isaiah Roberts was tall with long scraggly blond hair and moustache. He was lean and wiry. He wore a workman's canvas jacket and overalls. If possible, Roberts was dirtier than Hazer.

"They will be here around 7:00 P.M.," Anderson told them. "I don't know which way they will come in. Be careful of the back, and the north side steps. We've put a torpedo in both places. The torpedoes will go off if anyone disturbs them."

"Don't you worry none, Mr. Miller," Hazer said. "They'll be dead before they get two steps inside the door."

"That's what I'm trying to tell you," Anderson said. "they may not come in through the door."

"Ain't no other way in," Roberts added. "Windows are barred."

"I'll be upstairs," Anderson said. He turned and went to the office area which was barricaded with crates. Fitch was handling his gun nervously.

"You certainly picked a couple of intellectual giants," Anderson told him.

"They're big and mean. If you wanted college perfessers you should have said so." Fitch laughed and Anderson could smell alcohol on his breath. He was at the point he couldn't stay away from the stuff. That wouldn't do at all. Anderson looked at his watch. It was six-thirty. He wagered they would be early.

"Turn off the lamps," Anderson ordered.

Ingalls and Everett stopped the wagon a hundred yards from the warehouse and checked their equipment.

"Ready?" Ingalls asked.

"One more detail," Everett said. He hopped down and relieved himself against a fence. It was a natural reaction. He climbed back into the wagon and said, "Let's go."

They drove the wagon along the north side of the warehouse and knew they could be heard inside. First they went to the rear door and checked. The wire was too obvious.

"Torpedo," Everett said. "I guess they want us to come in the front."

Ingalls placed one can of powder at the base of the door. He had drilled a hole through a cork, put a ten-minute fuse through the cork, and set it in the can. He placed the can against the door and laid two pieces of scrap lumber against it. Then he slit the fuse with a knife and placed a match head in the slit. He struck another match and set it to the match in the fuse. The match flared and the fuse started to burn. They went around to the south side of the building and put a similar charge with a seven-minute fuse under one of the windows. Then they went back to the wagon. One end of the rope was already fastened to the wagon. They tied the other end to the bars of a window. Finally, they removed the grappling hooks with ropes attached from the wagon and went to the front corner of the building.

"Ready?" Ingalls asked.

Everett nodded. They swung the grappling hooks onto the roof and ran back to the wagon.

Hazer looked up as the grappling hooks hit the tin roof with a hollow metallic ring. "They're climbing the roof," he hollered.

Nothing is ever as obvious as it seems, Anderson thought to himself. He was waiting for the other boot to drop, but he forgot that two men meant four boots. The wagon pulled forward and the grate was pulled off the window. As everyone turned to look at the north side window, the charge at the rear door exploded. By itself it would not have done much damage, but by setting off Anderson's torpedo it blew the big double doors off their hinges, splintered them, and started a fire. The double blast threw Anderson to the floor and stunned him. Next, the south side window exploded. It twisted the iron bars of the grate and sent glass flying into the warehouse. The place was so filled with acrid smoke and noise that the crate crashing through the unbarred north side window followed by the two detectives was, at first, not noticed.

"There they are!" Roberts yelled and he fired his .44-caliber pistol at the shadows in the smoke.

Ingalls and Everett found themselves in an aisle on the north side of the building. The front of the warehouse was nearly open with a few crates in the center of the floor. If they had come in that way they would have been in the open with no chance at reaching cover. About a third of the way back, the building was packed with crates, barrels, and sacks that in some areas nearly reached the office level. The two detectives took cover near the front of the building behind some low crates they could see over.

"Well, Clarence, we're in. Now let's see if we can get around them. You stay here. I'll go through that opening." He nodded to a passageway between rows of crates.

"Okay," Everett agreed. He began firing at the flashes in the smoke.

Ingalls ducked between the rows of crates. It was dark and he made his way cautiously. He walked in for about fifteen feet then ran into a wall of crates. He felt around and discovered a turn to the right. After another ten feet there was another wall of crates and a turn to the left. He stopped and muttered, "That son of a bitch." Instead of putting the crates in rows, Anderson had arranged them as a labyrinth. Ingalls made his way back. Everett, thinking he had been outflanked, turned to face him.

"Clarence, it's me."

"What are you doing here? I thought you were going to outflank them."

"The rows between the boxes aren't straight. It's a maze in there."

"So what do we do?"

"I guess we go over."

"My turn," Everett said. As soon as he stood up bullets started flying from the second story. "Bad idea. What now?"

"Follow me," Ingalls said. He began crawling toward the back of the building where flames were beginning to lick at the crates. The north side stairs to the upper story lay unguarded. Ingalls looked carefully then realized why. He looked back at Everett who pointed up. Ingalls shook his head no. He waved his partner forward and pointed to the torpedo rigged to explode when someone treaded on one of the steps. There was barely enough room to make it between the steps and the crates, but they managed to squeeze by.

Once they were by the steps, they ran to the back of the building where the smoke was thick. What Ingalls suspected was true. Both the north and south side lanes were clear. The others were not. They circled the warehouse and could hear Roberts calling, "Where the hell are they?"

The two detectives reached the south side stairs. Ingalls ascended backward while his partner went in front. Fitch was surprised to see them and fired twice before barricading himself in one of the offices. Everett fired back but didn't hit him.

"They're on the steps!" Fitch called.

Hazer ran down the aisle toward the steps and realized his mistake too late as Ingalls fired twice at his midsection. The big man went down face first.

"Keep their heads down," Ingalls told Everett. He went to Hazer, picked up his gun and threw it on top of the crates. Then he rolled him over. Hazer was hit once in the stomach and once in the chest. Frothy blood was coming from between his lips. He wouldn't live.

"Help me, please," he said, coughing.

"Later." Ingalls left him and went down the aisle to the open front of the warehouse. Roberts was standing in the open space surrounded by smoke. "Throw down your gun," Ingalls shouted. Roberts whirled and fired and the same time Ingalls did. He was good. He fired twice. The first shot gouged splinters out of the crate in front of Ingalls and the second tore into the detective's left shoulder. Ingall's bullet caught Roberts in the left arm. Roberts ran for cover. Ingalls, ignoring his own pain, followed him as he ran down the north side aisle. In his panic, he forgot and ran up the steps.

Ingalls shouted "No!" but Roberts' foot was already on the fourth step. The explosion blew Roberts' mangled body minus his clothes and the legs from the knees down at Ingalls' feet. The detective turned away to keep from vomiting.

Meanwhile Everett was having his own difficulties. Although he had Fitch pinned down, the little man also had him trapped. He couldn't stay there and he couldn't go back. So, the only way was forward. He quickly reloaded his pistol and waited for Fitch to show himself to fire. Then came the explosion. Everett rushed up the stairs and crashed in on Fitch who was momentarily distracted by the explosion. Fitch swung his gun toward Everett, but the detective fired first. He hit Fitch three times and the little man sprawled on the floor with a moan. Everett tossed Fitch's gun away and crouched behind the crates wondering where Anderson was. He could see the flames through the cracks in the floor and it was getting decidedly warm.

Anderson was in the process of cursing the way the two detectives had wrecked his scheme and had gone to the north side of the second story to get a clear shot at Ingalls when the explosion caused by Roberts' panic knocked him down. When his head cleared he decided that things were going so badly that it was time to leave. He was about to get up when he saw a figure crawl out of Fitch's barricade. He was lying flat on the ground when he called, "Fitch!"

"I'm hit," the little man called. "Help me." The sound did not come from the crawler.

So the crawler was not Fitch. Anderson aimed his Spencer carbine and fired at the figure. He pulled the trigger and worked the lever four times. The first .56-caliber slug broke Everett's shoulder, the second put splinters in his face. The third shattered his left hand and as he tried to roll over to get out of the way the fourth hit him in the chest. He completed the roll and tumbled down the steps. Anderson could no longer lie down. The floor was becoming too hot. He went to Fitch.

"Please," the little man sighed. "Get me out of here."

"Joseph," Anderson said. "You have become a distinct liability, but I will not leave you here to burn."

A look of relief showed on Fitch's face until he felt the cold barrel of Anderson's revolver against his head. His mind shouted

"No!" but the bullet passed through his brain before a sound could leave his lips.

Ingalls saw Everett at the bottom of the steps and went to him. "Anderson . . . upstairs . . . get him."

Ingalls started carefully up the steps. The dry timbers of the warehouse itself were catching fire.

"Anderson," he called. "Throw down your gun and come down with your hands up."

"Mr. Ingalls, you of all people should know better than that."

Ingalls peeked over the top of the steps. He could see Anderson in the flames. The assassin fired twice then the hammer fell on an empty chamber. Ingalls took aim and fired. As he did the floor beneath Anderson's feet gave way and the killer screamed as he fell into a pit of flame. Ingalls didn't have time for satisfaction, grim or otherwise. He got to the bottom of the stairs and picked Everett up over his shoulder.

"Leave me. Save yourself," Everett moaned.

Ingalls told his partner to shut up and headed for the front door. He stepped over Hazer who was half sitting in the aisle.

"Don't leave me," Hazer begged.

"I'll be right back," Ingalls said sincerely. Just before Ingalls got to the door, the flames reached some barrels full of turpentine. Hazer shrieked for what seemed a long time before the flames engulfed him entirely. Ingalls ignored him and put Everett into the wagon as the fire brigade came galloping up the streets with a crowd of people. The metal roof was beginning to sag as he drove madly through the streets to the Washington Infirmary on E Street. He didn't know how long it took to get there, but he carried his partner inside. The staff looked at Ingalls in horror. He was covered with soot and blood from his own wound and Everett's. They put Everett on a stretcher and took him to a doctor. Another doctor, a young, friendly man, had him remove his coat and shirt. As the doctor began cleaning the wound in his shoulder, Ingalls winced in pain.

"You must have had a rough time," the doctor said soothingly. "How did you and your servant get so shot up?"

"Servant?"

"The colored man," the doctor said, innocently.

Ingalls, seized with rage, grabbed the doctor by the collar and held him against the wall. "That colored man is a National Detective and my friend," he said through clenched teeth.

"I am truly sorry," the doctor said contritely, but he was not terrified. "Please forgive me. In either case, shouldn't you let me finish dressing your shoulder before you break my neck."

Ingalls put the doctor down and did what he had not done since he was eight years old. He wept. When they told him that Clarence Everett was dead, he continued to weep. He wept for Clarence, for Lincoln, for Eddy, for Booth, and for himself. He wept until he could weep no more.

The Old Arsenal Prison
Washington City
July 7, 1865

It was an unbearably hot day and Ingalls didn't know why he had come. The gallows stood stark against the sky as soldiers lined the walls. Four nooses dangled from the great horizontal beam and beneath the gallows were four newly dug graves. Rumors circulated that only three would be used, because Mary Surratt would be reprieved. There was a lot of milling around and then at a signal, the soldiers who had been joking and drinking water, fell in, forming lines around three sides of the gallows. A hush fell over the crowd as the condemned were led out to the place of execution. First came Mary Surratt, dressed in a black dress and a black bonnet. Her arms were bound and she was flanked by two priests. Surely she would be freed, people whispered in the crowd. Ingalls thought not. Her boarder Weichmann had testified against her at her trial, and some whispered he only did it to save his pudgy little neck, but Weichmann's testimony was only part of it. Mrs. Surratt had been a thorn in Baker's side when she hid Rebel couriers in her tavern in Surrattsville. The bleeding hearts who wanted to save her because she was a woman did not understand that there were more debts than Lincoln's assassination being paid this day. Someone on the scaffold held an umbrella over her head to keep off the sun. Next came Payne, wearing a sailor suit and a straw hat, emotionless to the last. Perhaps, Ingalls thought, he wasn't emotionless, just a poor stupid man who really didn't understand or care. The third in line was Herold. Since Garrett's Farm, reality had intruded into the make-believe world of brave men he wanted to belong to and he was terrified. The last in line was Atzerodt. He was a pathetic nobody who wanted to be friends with someone. He stood sobbing and trembling. The condemned spoke with the people on the scaffold as their feet were tied, their heads were covered, and the nooses were placed around their necks. Hancock and Hartranft, the generals in charge, waited for Mary Surratt's reprieve as long as they could. At 1:26 P.M. the soldiers detailed to do so knocked the pin from the trap and the four conspirators dropped to their deaths. Ingalls supposed he should somehow feel sorry for them, but he didn't.

The detective didn't wait to see the bodies cut down. He went directly to the bar at Willard's Hotel for a cold glass of beer. He drank the beer slowly, recalling images of the past few weeks. He had gone to the trial and watched Nora testify in behalf of Mary Surratt. He had tried to catch her eye, but she never looked his way. Just as well. The bar was now filling up with men who had come from the hanging and he didn't want to listen to what they had to say. He finished the beer, and reached into his coat pocket for the money to pay for it when he felt something odd. He pulled it out. It was the bracelet he had given Nora and she had thrown back at him. Standing at the bar surrounded by talk and cigar smoke, he finally understood why he had gone to the hanging. It closed a chapter in his life and from now on he would be able to point to July 7, 1865, as the day he put Anderson, Booth, Nora, and even Clarence Everett behind him.

The conversation all about him was of the trial and the hanging. Some were already calling it judicial murder and demanded the resignations of those responsible. The man standing next to him at the bar sounded terribly upset about the verdict and the hanging. He was about twenty-six. His ring showed he was married and his hands showed he did little physical labor. A lawyer, Ingalls thought. The detective decided to leave before he got involved in any of it and started for the door, but he was too late. The man caught his coat.

"Sir," he said to Ingalls. "Give us your opinion. What do you think about hanging those poor people?"

"What do I think?" Ingalls looked at the man and his companions waiting for him to agree with them. "I think they were nobodies." Without waiting for their reaction, he turned on his heel and walked out.